ONE LAST VERSE

The Encore Book Two

N.N. BRITT

Cover Design by Cat at TRC Designs

Edited by Shannan Saunders

Copyedited by R.C. Craig

Due to strong language and other adult content, this book is intended for mature audience only.

❋ Created with Vellum

Chapter One

Malibu was famous for its glimmering, breathtaking sunsets. Never for its sunrises. Especially not the kind that came with bloodshot eyes and three cups of espresso.

I sat on the terrace and stared at the sun bleeding into the dark spread of the Pacific below. My head was a pounding vortex of endless questions and scenarios. My phone lay on my lap. Screen down. Sound off. I knew sooner or later, I'd have to look at it, but I was putting that moment off as much as my sanity would allow.

The world was raging after last night's show. Hall Affinity's first reunion concert marked the shortest set in the history of sets. And the unhappy fans and internet trolls were having a field day on social media.

Brooklyn was on the phone in the living room. The terrace door was cracked open and I could hear her throaty voice bouncing off the walls of the house like an unruly soccer ball. I caught bits and pieces of her conversation. Mostly agitated words that sounded serious but made little sense to me.

I had no doubt that being Frank's assistant right now wasn't the most wanted job.

The first rays of light licked the trembling water and danced along the curve of the tide. It was a beautiful sight—the one I loved the most. It reminded me of that first time Frank brought me to this house. The first time we were intimate and the first time we had breakfast together. That was the morning we jumped into a relationship that I could no longer separate from myself. Just like I could no longer separate myself from the man whose name half the planet was trashing online right now.

And it terrified me—the sudden bone-chilling dependency on another person.

After Frank fainted in the shower last night, the nurse set up an IV in his bedroom. The medication put him to sleep almost immediately while I tossed and turned next to him in the bed. My mind refused to shut up. I kept replaying the events of the entire evening in my head, trying to understand what had caused him to faint.

At first, I questioned if it had been his fear of not meeting the fans' expectations. But the nurse explained, *His blood pressure dropped again,* and that opened up additional questions.

As I lay there beside him, my gaze drifted to the IV drip and I wondered if Frank felt the tube. Or if he felt anything at all. I wondered what was going to happen when he woke up. There were two more shows to play and he was dead set on going through with them.

I watched him breathe for what seemed like the entire night, until my eyes couldn't remain open anymore. Then, at some point, exhaustion knocked me out and I fell into a strange state of temporary lethargy.

It was anxiety that roused me a few hours later.

"TMZ got a hold of it?" Brooklyn's voice moved toward the door, snapping me out of my thoughts. A pause. "Okay. Good." Another pause. "No. We'll wait for Corey. I'm not authorized to make that decision." Her heels clacked against the floor as she walked away. Did this woman ever sleep or wear sandals? People surrounding Frank seemed to favor official, well-put-together attire. Even Hannah. Since

she was in charge of managing the household, she was a bit more relaxed when it came to clothes, but she loved looking photoshoot-ready. Makeup and hair always on point.

I pulled my legs up on the couch and rested my chin on my knees, fighting the urge to check my phone. The air was still crisp and dewy, but the morning fog had already vanished and the day promised to be hot. Figuratively and literally.

My heart raced from coffee overload when I finally mustered the guts to open my Facebook app. The feed was full of Hall Affinity videos and links to articles that were cheap, sloppy attempts to get more clicks. I knew this trick. Levi had taught me all of them. In today's world of digital reign, traffic was everything. Traffic meant money and fame. The quality of the content was secondary.

Another set of footsteps, light and unsure, neared the door. It was Janet. She had a plate of freshly baked madeleines and a large mug of coffee.

"Good morning," I said, straightening up on the couch.

"Good morning, child."

"Did you get any sleep at all?" Janet put the food on the table and when she sat next to me, her flowery scent reached my nose.

"Yes, I did."

"You should get some more."

"In a bit." I inhaled deeply and dropped my legs to the floor.

We sat in silence for a few minutes. Janet sipped her coffee. I checked my Twitter.

"Last summer, when he confessed he wanted to tour again, I told him he wasn't fit for this lifestyle anymore," Janet said with a sigh.

I felt a lump pushing against my throat.

"It's in his blood. The showmanship and the need to entertain," she went on. The breeze whipped her silver strands against her thin shoulders. "He was born to perform. He didn't even know he had a voice to go with his charisma until he turned twelve, but he was always hungry for attention and to make people smile."

"He's got an amazing sense of humor," I agreed. "I've laughed with him more than I have my entire life."

"That's my boy." Janet nodded.

Just like Frank, she was full of light. Lots of it. Bright and warm.

"Will you tell me about him?" I asked. "What was he like when he was a kid?"

"Sweet. Radiant. Different." Her breath caught and she took another sip of coffee.

I waited.

Frank had a habit of dropping very personal things on me at the most random times, as if he didn't have any memories of those events and felt compelled to share them as soon as they resurfaced in his mind in case they disappeared again.

The picture of him in my head still missed a few pieces, and I wanted to find them. I wanted to see him whole. I wanted to see who he was beyond his years and scars.

"Billy and I couldn't have kids," Janet began. "We tried to conceive for so long, but the medicine wasn't as advanced in our day." A sad smile twisted her lips. "At some point, we gave up on the idea and decided to foster a child to see if it was something that could become a long-term arrangement. You're not always sure if it's going to work when you plan on taking a stranger in. I wasn't exactly young or fit to care for a baby anymore, so we thought it would be best to find someone a little older. Preschool age. The moment I saw Frankie, I knew he was the one. The way he looked at me made me want to hug him and never let go. *Please love me*, his eyes had said. We didn't look back after we brought him home with us. He was such a good, loving boy, and he made us extremely happy."

My chest expanded from the onslaught of emotions. The world was strange. How could this woman love someone else's child so self-lessly while a man like my father couldn't care to stick around to watch his own kids grow? A whimper gathered in my lungs and I had to bite my lip to prevent it from breaking through.

"Billy was still touring then." Janet lowered the mug to her lap and stared at the stretch of ocean in front of us. "Sometimes he brought Frank along to help out. They developed this strange bond that occasionally made me a little jealous." She laughed softly.

"When Frank was eighteen, he went with us to Los Angeles, where Billy's band played a show on Sunset Strip. That's where he met Dante, whose band was on the bill along with my husband's. They were all green and very bad. I don't think any of them ever made it in the music business except for Dante. That boy didn't fit in with those guys. Even back then, he was impressive. He played like he'd been possessed by the devil himself. It's the kind of talent that comes around once every few decades if we're lucky. A couple of months later, after we returned to Arizona, Frank approached me and said, *Mom, I want to move to Los Angeles and play music.*"

Janet stopped and her gaze swept over to me. "So I gave him five hundred dollars and I let him go. The rest is history." When she finished, there was a smile on her face. Covert but real. A smile of love and adoration that I could feel wrap around my thundering heart and whisper a soft lullaby.

"My son is very lucky," Janet said. "With everything that happened to him after the accident..." Her voice faltered. "Not everyone has the guts to do what he's done. Pick himself up and move on with his life. Not after the kind of pain and suffering he's been through."

I held the oxygen in my lungs because I was scared my breath would disturb the fine balance between us.

"The only things he never had luck with were women and dating." She shook her head. "My Frankie never knew how to choose them. I always told him to find a nice girl and he always went for the most scandalous and most unavailable. Imagine my shock when he told me he'd met someone who wasn't another celebrity."

A flutter filled my stomach.

"I'm aware of your arrangement with my son"—Janet moved closer—"and I appreciate you honoring his condition. He can't go through another round of public relationships after everything that happened between him and his ex-wife."

At that moment, I wondered if Janet knew about Dante, but my tongue remained idle. I didn't want to open Pandora's box by bringing it up.

"He looks so happy when he's with you," she whispered. "There's a calmness in you, child. You balance him out. That's exactly what he needs."

Blush hit my cheeks. "Thank you."

We chatted for a little while longer, until another wave of exhaustion finally swept me under. I returned to the bedroom and curled up next to Frank. With my eyes closed, I listened to him breathe. I listened to every inhale and exhale carefully. I waited for a sound that would tell me he wasn't okay, but it never came. The stress lines on his face were gone and pink colored his cheeks.

"I know you can't hear me right now," I mouthed as my gaze followed a stray ray of light dancing across his forehead. "But I love you."

I wasn't sure why I said it, but I was sure I felt it.

I'd loved him even before I knew him. I'd fallen in love with his voice and his music years ago. I hadn't stopped loving him since.

It was the soft rustle of the sheets and a hushed voice coming from the bathroom that woke me up. The voice belonged to Frank. I cracked my eyes open and scanned the room. The IV still loomed over the bed, but the bag was empty and it didn't look as if the nurse had visited while I was asleep.

My phone sat on the nightstand and force of habit made me grab it. It was almost noon. Twitter, Facebook, and Instagram raged. Buzz-Feed's front page had a photo of Frank from last night's performance at the Forum.

"Hall Affinity's First Post-Hiatus Show: Can Frankie Blade Pull It Off Or Should He Go Back To Being History?"

Resentment boiled in my chest. I knew there was no way around bad publicity. Not for a person like Frank, but emotions still swelled. Mad at the entire world, I tossed the phone aside and sat up.

"I suggest you don't go online today if you want to stay sane." Frank's distorted voice drifted at me from the bathroom.

My eyes shot up to where he stood in the doorway. Shirtless. His broad chest and defined abs on display. A toothbrush stuck out from the corner of his mouth. There was a small splotch of blue and purple on his right side from yesterday's fall.

"I know. It's a stupid habit," I confessed as he resumed brushing his teeth. "Were you talking to yourself?" I slid from the bed and walked over to the bathroom. There, on the counter, sat his phone.

"Yeah." He laughed a little. "I was giving myself a pep talk."

"I can give you one." I inched closer and positioned myself behind him. My fingers skimmed over his bruise as I wrapped my arms around his body.

"I'm listening." He pulled the toothbrush out and spit in the sink.

"You're going to do great tonight," I whispered against his back as he went on with rinsing. "You look good. Rested."

"We're making a few adjustments to the set. The guys are going to be here soon. I should get ready." He patted my hand locked on his stomach.

"Were you really giving yourself a pep talk?" I asked as we returned to the bedroom. My mind couldn't conjure an image of Frank standing in front of the mirror and talking himself up.

"No." He shook his head and moved to the closet. "It was my lawyer."

There was something ominous about that statement. I couldn't think of a reason for him to need a lawyer after last night, and I didn't press for more. He had a busy day ahead of him and I didn't want to be in the way.

Frank must have felt my anxiety. "Doll"—he turned to me and his features softened—"I'm not ignoring you. I just need to get through today and tomorrow."

"Of course. Pretend I'm not here for the next two days."

"That, I can't do." He marched over to me and dipped his head to grab a kiss. "I need you here. Things are going to be very messy for the next forty-eight hours, and if I do or say something out of left field, don't hold it against me, okay?"

His hands slid to my waist and he drew me closer. Chest to chest, our bodies connected and then his mouth was on mine again. An incredible rush of adrenaline washed over me, and my blood thickened from the blend of desire and other emotions.

We checked out for a long moment. It was a perfect kiss, an explosive mix of tender and wild. A volcano of sensations. And it wasn't enough. I wanted this—the feel of his lips against mine and the sound of his moans swallowing my breaths—to go on until the end of days. Until we both turned to dust and floated together in the cool California wind. Ashes to ashes.

Dante, Carter, and Johnny showed up right after breakfast. Or at least, it was breakfast for us. Rock stars and their girlfriends didn't follow the typical nine-to-five routine. Late nights always resulted in missed mornings.

Brooklyn and Corey were in the office on a conference call with Jay Brodie PR. Billy and Janet kept their distance while Frank took care of business. I was left in the kitchen alone. My phone sat next to me, and the itch to go online was too strong. I had to. I wanted to know what Shayne had written about last night's show. I couldn't define the feeling within me very well as I read through her review on *Rewired*. Not until I hit the middle of the article anyway. Jealousy. That's what it was. She was good at weaving her words. The recap was a compelling read, with a bit of a personal touch that wasn't overdone. In some instances, I was certain she'd mimicked my style and it actually pleased me that someone had found my writing worth imitating.

I skimmed through the text until the end, and that's when the article took a sharp turn. I reread the last paragraph a few times to make sure I didn't miss anything, and the tone was exactly what Shayne had intended it to be...speculative.

Then I called Levi.

Frank was in the studio and couldn't possibly hear me raging over the phone, which was precisely what I was about to do.

The line rang several times. Finally, I heard a groan. "What's up?"

I went straight in for the kill. "Did you even read Shayne's article before you posted it?"

"I did." No explanation. Had Levi been secretly taking lessons from Frank?

"Are you shitting me right now?"

"I'm not. I read it. She's fucking good. I don't understand why you don't like her."

"I never said I didn't like her."

"Oh yeah? Well, right now, you're doing that thing again, Cass."

"What thing? What, are we in sixth grade? Why is she even talking about the length of the set?"

"Because it was a short fucking set and you wouldn't tell me what the hell happened." Levi paused to catch his breath. His voice dropped to a whisper. "Something went wrong, didn't it?

I contemplated revealing the truth but decided against it. "You know I can't tell you that."

That's when it happened. The crack between us. I heard it loud and clear. We were on opposite sides of the barricade now. I was the person with secrets and Levi was the person who wanted those secrets. Only, they weren't my secrets to divulge. They were Frank's.

"I'm just asking you as your friend. You fuck the guy who let half the planet down last night and you can't even tell me if he's okay? I'm not some heartless douche. I worry about you."

A ragged sigh rushed out of my lungs. I was torn. I knew he cared about me, yet his statement rubbed me the wrong way, so I was having a hard time choosing which direction to take. A snappy comeback lingered on the tip of my tongue and I held it in only for the sake of my sanity. "It wasn't a very good night."

"I see," Levi grunted.

I slid from the chair and began to pace. My pulse thrummed hard in my temples. My heart thrashed. Anxiety, coffee, and shitty sleep weren't a good combo.

His use of the word *fuck* to describe the nature of my relationship with Frank felt offensive. It wouldn't have a month ago. We did fuck. A lot. But there was something else. There were real feelings, his and mine, entangled in a complex knot. And I didn't want an outsider to call what we had a *fuck*.

"You understand where I'm coming from, right?" I pressed.

"I won't ask you anymore."

"Can you revise the last paragraph?"

"Just because you don't agree with her thoughts doesn't mean it's a bad article."

"I didn't say it was bad, but we don't speculate about things like this, Levi. She wasn't backstage. She didn't see what happened. She can't simply write whatever she wants."

"Robbie had a copy of the setlist before the show. They cut the last third out, Cass. You don't need to be a mathematician to put two and two together. Your boyfriend can't handle a ninety-minute show. Why can't he just come out with it?"

"If the setlist wasn't sent to him via official channels, which I know for a fact that it wasn't, then you have no right to use that information to write a recap."

Things weren't as simple as Levi what trying to make them. A band of their caliber had to meet fans' expectations. Frank wouldn't do it differently. I'd witnessed both his stubbornness and his dedication firsthand last night. His decision to go back on stage was pushing the limits of sane and lingered somewhere on the edge of stupidity.

All great talents were crazy.

"The article is wonderful, but I'm asking you as your partner. Speculating is not what *Rewired* is about, Levi. We've never been that. I don't want us to turn into another TMZ and feed the public with unconfirmed ideas and rumors."

"It doesn't work like that, Cass. You didn't write it. You don't get to play with it."

"Why are you being so stubborn?"

I heard the second line beep. "I have to take this," Levi barked and ended the call.

I stood in front of the glass wall and absentmindedly stared at the ocean. My heart was beating against my ribs fiercely. Part of me was convinced Levi pushed back on the post revision only because I'd pulled out from reviewing the Hall Affinity shows. It was his way of saying *screw you*. If I wasn't on board, I had no say. It stung, but in a way, I understood. I hadn't exactly been a good partner lately. The documentary was the only project I was involved with and cared about.

The conversation with Levi made me feel shitty, made me think about my priorities. What were they? Where did my loyalties lie? I couldn't remember the last time I'd seen my mom, and my brother was living alone in my apartment.

Frank was the worst kind of drug. He came first. Before all else. And this feeling, the dark, all-consuming euphoria that was him, frightened me. *I was losing myself.*

My lungs struggled for air and my brain needed a break. I walked out onto the terrace and tried to breathe through my sudden panic attack. Eyes closed, I lifted my face to the sun and let it caress my skin. The breeze tousled my hair. The ocean beneath me rolled.

For a brief moment, all my worries fell away and it was nice. Until the faint smell of cigarette smoke crept up my nose.

Snapping my eyes open, I whirled around and scanned the stretch of terrace running along the western side of the house. There, on the other end, was Dante. Shoulder against the wall and facing me. A cigarette dangling from the corner of his mouth told me he'd given up his attempts to quit smoking... Or he was too wound up to resort to a lollipop to do the job of what nicotine usually did so well, take the edge off.

Conflicted, I stared at him.

"Like what you see, darlin'?" He chuckled. His voice, though horse and broken after last night, carried over the noise of the crashing waves. He wore a pair of loose jeans and a plain white T-shirt that was thin enough for me to see some of his ink beneath the fabric. Unlike Frank, he hadn't gotten carried away and still had plenty of blank skin left. Back in the day, Dante didn't shy away from flaunting his lean body on stage, but he'd stopped taking his shirt off after the *Hollow Heart Dream* release.

Thin-framed and elegant, Dante had a strange, dark appeal. Women loved his flashy personality. However, right now, he wasn't anywhere near flashy. He looked...stressed. Hair pulled back, earring and other accessories absent, he almost looked his age. On the edge of forty. Of course, forty for a rock star was like another round of seventeen. People with money had access to all kinds of procedures to keep them young. At least on the outside. Botox for starters. Although Dante didn't look as if he needed it or had ventured into that territory.

"A little birdie told me Frankie-boy took another dive last night," he said. He took a long drag and his chest rose and expanded as he held the smoke in his lungs.

I headed his way and stopped in front of him. Our gazes locked and his red-rimmed eyes roamed my face.

"Are you cutting the set again tonight?" I asked.

He shook his head and turned away to release the smoke. "No. We can't. The fans will destroy us. Do you know how many people asked for refunds already? We'll just rearrange everything. Yesterday was shit. We should have started with *Hollow Heart Dream* material."

"Why would people ask for refunds? You played for almost an hour."

"Yeah? Do you remember how long every single set lasted during Guns N' Roses' reunion show? Two hours at least."

"Well, people waited for their reunion double the time. Hence double the time on the sets," I joked.

Dante laughed and turned back to me. "People are assholes." His lips stretched and the smile lines near the corners of his eyes deepened. "You know better than me, darlin'. You're the fucking reporter."

"There's press and there's shitty press, Dante," I countered. "Shitty press like to pull their headlines out of their asses to get traffic. I deliver real news and facts. There's a big difference."

"Don't get your panties in a twist, little lady." He laughed. "I know you're one of the good ones. I actually fucking admire your drive. You roped Frankie-boy into this little charity project of yours. He hasn't been this excited about doing some good in years."

"Are you just going to hold out? No comments?" I didn't remember seeing any Jay Brodie PR emails come in today. The band seemed reluctant to debunk rumors floating around online about Frank's well-being.

"Corey thinks it's best we keep our mouths shut for now."

"So you're not even going to respond?"

"What do we say? I'm sorry the set was short. Our singer is a fucking cripple and can't pull through the entire show without passing out, and we're not sure if he can deliver tonight, but hey, we have paramedics on standby and we still want your money, come what may."

Dante's words were harsh, but they were an accurate representation of what was going on right now. Frank was a ticking time bomb.

"Well, when you put it like that..." I rolled my eyes nonetheless.

A veil of smoke swirled around Dante. He finished his cigarette in silence while I stared at the ocean.

"I'll keep an eye on him, Cass." I felt his hand on my shoulder. It wasn't inappropriate. It was more of a friendly pat. Same type he'd give Frank or any other guy in the band.

"Are we friends now?" I looked at him.

"We've always been friends."

"Are you going to apologize?"

"Are you still pissed about the demos?"

"I need you to apologize, Dante." I stood my ground.

He tossed his head back and covered his eyes with the heels of his hands. His T-shirt stretched across his lean torso.

"I'm serious. You were wrong and I deserve an apology. From both you and Corey."

"I'm not responsible for the dude. You can ask him for an apology yourself," Dante growled, dropping his face to look me in the eye. "Here's mine. I'm sorry, Cassy." His cigarette breath grazed my cheeks. "Are you happy now?"

"Apology accepted," I mumbled.

"Okay, good. Now make sure Frankie-boy is happy too. He needs it."

I didn't fully understand what he meant by that and he didn't expand on his statement before walking off. All I knew was that something dark had lingered in the air all morning and my gut told me this was the part where the rollercoaster reached the top and I needed to get ready for a massive, once-in-a-lifetime drop.

Chapter Two

Contrary to popular belief, the controversial reviews of the first Hall Affinity night at the Forum didn't deter the ticket holders from attending the second show. On the way to the venue, I carefully checked social media to get a better idea of what the fallout was like. The refund crisis Dante had referred to earlier wasn't as bad as he'd described it. The man was overdramatic.

Apparently, a lot of people simply wanted to see the band perform because they were scared the upcoming tour would get canceled due to Frankie's health. Even if there had been any refunds, they'd most likely turned into crazy-priced resales, because there wasn't an empty seat when we arrived. I had a chance to get a glimpse of the audience when Roman led us upstairs, and the floor was jam-packed. The security in the pit was doubled. Eager fans trampled over each other to get to the barricade.

Further proof bad publicity wasn't that bad after all.

Ashton had begged me to get him a pass for tonight, but I'd decided to be a mean sister and told him he had to skip tonight to prepare for the second round of SATs and look for a part-time job because helping Levi with the documentary wasn't going to pay any bills. Bottom line, my little brother needed a reality check since his eighteenth birthday was approaching fast, and he couldn't just occupy my apartment indefinitely.

I didn't plan on being a total bitch, though. I was going to get him a pass for tomorrow. I'd also asked my mother if she wanted a ticket, but she wasn't a fan of rock 'n' roll. She'd politely declined my offer in favor of a movie night with her co-worker.

The air backstage was static with anticipation. We sat in the dressing room and I watched the stylist work on Frank's hair. Everyone was fixed on some task. No small talk took place. At some point, Janet and Billy stepped out, and then it was only me, Corey, Brooklyn, and Frank's physician. The drone of the blow dryer mixed with a Muse tune pouring from the speakers. Occasionally a walkie-talkie crackled right outside the door.

I felt as if I'd been thrust into the eye of the tornado that was Frank's professional life, and to the casual observer, I might appear to be an unwilling participant.

However, what they wouldn't have observed was that until yesterday, Frank had kept me at arm's length when it came to his career. Sure, we'd discussed his music and his relationship with the band members. And he'd taken me to a rehearsal, but that was the extent of my involvement. I'd been inside his home studio just once and I'd never accompanied him to any of his business meetings. Today was different. We drove to the venue together. He held my hand possessively as we marched through the backstage area, and I couldn't help but wonder if he was no longer dead set on keeping our relationship a secret.

Something had changed.

He didn't ask me to leave during his meeting with Linda. I sat there and pretended to be on my phone while listening to their conversation. The look on her face told me she wasn't sure what shocked her the most—to find me in Frankie Blade's dressing room wearing a pretty daring dress with a sweetheart neckline or to find out Hall Affinity's front man didn't want his health issues to become public knowledge.

"This isn't the '80s, Frank," she countered. "Your injuries can be a big plus. It's all about how we spin it during the campaign. Fans love when artists are upfront with their conditions."

"I don't have a condition. I simply don't want people to feel like they're playing Russian roulette by buying a ticket to a Hall Affinity show. Is the singer going to come out today or is he taking a night off because he's a fucking vegetable? The answer is no."

There was some truth to Linda's words, but Frank was uncompromising. He wanted it his way.

Brooklyn's phone pinged. She checked the message and touched Frank's shoulder to get his attention.

"I'm going to grab your guest. Are you good?"

He nodded and returned his gaze to Linda. "You know where I stand. Make it work. That's what you're getting paid for."

Frank wasn't kind today. I hadn't seen this harsh side of him yet, and while I didn't like it, I knew where this animosity was coming from. The fear of failure had pushed him over the edge. He snapped at people for no apparent reason. Even Janet had been in the line of fire all afternoon.

The stylist shut off the blow dryer and stepped back to evaluate. Truth be told, I didn't know why Frank needed someone to mess with his hair. He looked great and he was going to turn into a sweaty mess after three songs anyway.

His stage outfit differed from last night's. He wore a pair of tight black pants and boots. His shirt had strategically-placed rips on his chest, abs, and back to give the audience a little peek of what was underneath.

Corey was tapping out an email. The intense thrum of his fingers against the MacBook's keyboard matched the light rattle coming from the makeup station as the stylist began to put away some of her items.

Face hard, Frank slid from the chair and rolled his shoulders. His chest rose with his inhale, stretching the fabric across his pecs. Phone clutched in my hand, I watched. My heart thundered. There was something extremely primal about him today. Something dark and dangerous. Just like the night he took me for a ride in the mountains and then fucked me on his dining table. I adored that filthy side of him. Adored it to the point of physical pain.

"I didn't tell you"—Frank spun to face me, his gunmetal blues capturing my gaze—"but I invited Isabella and her mother to tonight's show."

"Oh." His confession rendered me speechless for a second. I hadn't expected him to get *this* involved. "I bet they're over the moon."

"I hope so." He let out a nervous laugh and approached me. His hands reached for mine, and I stood. We were mere inches apart and his heat started to consume me. He took all the air from my lungs. Being calm next to him when he was like this, sexed up for the stage, was impossible.

Frank dropped his mouth to my ear and whispered, "Did I tell you how gorgeous you look in this dress?"

I shook my head, my voice lost in my throat.

His broad palms encircled my waist. "I can't wait to take it off after we're done."

A light burn spread between my thighs. While I knew Frank's words were only for me and no one else could hear him, he said them with everyone in the room, as if he needed to make a statement.

"I can't wait for you to take it off," I uttered quietly, head dizzy. A small part of me wasn't sure he'd be fit for anything after the set, but I wanted to give him what he craved—hope that last night wouldn't be repeating itself. Hope that today's show would be great.

A knock snapped us out of our delirium. Smiling, Frank took a step back, his heat still a kindled flame on my skin and a maddening blaze in my chest. His fingertips slid over my knuckles softly as our hands parted. The door swung open and Isabella's wheelchair rolled into the dressing room. Hair teased and rock concert-ready, she pushed through with a big grin on her face. Maria and Brooklyn strode in next, then handshakes and hugs took place. The room came alive with a blend of laughter—Isabella's throaty and confident and Frank's deep and rich. I stood aside and listened to their banter. My heart was full and happy and I felt the same way I'd felt that morning. *I felt love.* And it was terrifying.

My gaze swung over to Brooklyn. She seemed content with the outcome of this short meetup while, eyes wide, Maria watched her daughter talking to a man who was about to perform in front of twenty thousand people. I could only imagine what was going on in Maria's head right now. She looked both flustered and shocked.

Frank had that effect on people.

"Did Brooklyn show you your seats already?" he checked with Isabella.

"Yes. Thank you so much for inviting us."

"Of course. I hope you enjoy the show."

Brooklyn signaled for Frank to wrap it up. The woman ran a very tight schedule.

Another knock came. It was Dante. Hat on, shirt half-tucked in, jeans alluringly low on his hips, he was stage ready. The glint in his eyes told me the man might be buzzed.

He marched over to Isabella and dipped down in front of her. "*Hola, mija. ¿Cómo estás?*"

"*Muy bien.*" Isabella grinned. Unlike her mother, she wasn't easily intimidated by famous people. "*¿Y tu?*"

He curled his fingers into a fist and they bumped knuckles.

"I don't think we've met officially. I'm Dante. I heard some of your singing. You're pretty good." A cocky, 'cool uncle' smirk lingered on his lips.

"You're not bad yourself."

Dante shook his head and the smile lines around his eyes grew deeper. "*¿De dónde eres?*"

They carried on their conversation.

I'd never heard Dante speak Spanish before. He hardly had any accent. In the past, I'd sometimes wondered if he actually knew the language or was simply flaunting his Hispanic heritage to win over the huge Latin American fan base that Hall Affinity had amassed. But now I knew Dante wasn't cheating.

"Don't let this guy fool ya." Frank patted his back. It was a light, brotherly tap. "He's not as nice as he seems."

A smirk touched Isabella's lips. "Nice guys don't sell rock 'n' roll." She returned her gaze to Dante. "Am I right?"

"Damn right, kiddo." He stood and shot Frank a covert glance. "We'd love to keep chatting, but we've got a show to get ready for. How about we talk some other time? Maybe when Frankie comes over to see you play, I'll tag along."

Hands were shook. Goodbyes were said. Brooklyn left with Maria and Isabella to show them to their box. Corey ushered the stylist out and asked one of the security guards to let Bruce know they needed him for the final show rundown. Dante sat on the edge of the makeup station and played with his hat while the doctor checked Frank's vitals.

"Blood pressure is a little low. Did you take your medication?"

Face grim, Frank nodded.

"He's not going to pass out again, is he, doc?" Dante questioned.

"If he doesn't overdo it, he should be fine."

There was a frustrated groan. "We're about to play a goddamn rock show, doc. What about Adderall?"

I shot Dante a warning look. He was getting overly creative.

"Adderall will interact with his pain medication," the physician countered, taking the cuff off. "It's not advisable."

Frank stood and his gaze intercepted mine. His shoulders were tense, jaw set. Suddenly, I couldn't read him. Sometimes he had these moments when he checked out, when he was far away. When his body was present, but his mind wasn't. Right now, I was witnessing one of those moments.

I heard a knock. Next thing I knew, Bruce, Carter, and Johnny poured into the dressing room. Their voices meshed into one anxiety-ridden drawl.

"Hey, doll." Frank walked over to me and ran his palm along the curve of my spine. "Give us fifteen minutes." His whisper set my cheek ablaze.

"Sure." I nodded.

A childlike plea followed next. "But come back, okay?" Hand still around my waist, he led me to the door, which closed after I stepped outside. I gave a small smile to Roman, who was standing to my right.

"How are you today?"

"I'm great. How are you, Ms. Evans?"

"You really need to stop calling me that." I shook my head. Everyone who worked for Frank was so official, you'd think he was a senator, not a rock singer.

In the lounge, guests were pleasantly buzzed. Background music blasted. Conversations were in high gear, loud and passionate. A few notable faces were scattered throughout the crowd. Chin up, I walked over to the bar and ordered a margarita. While waiting for the drink, I checked Shayne's article. Levi hadn't touched it. Disappointment and annoyance crept up into my chest. No doubt they were going to reside there indefinitely.

"Cassy!" someone called the second I got my hands on my drink. I spun around and came face to face with Linda. "What a surprise seeing you here." She didn't sound surprised, though. She sounded alarmed.

I didn't know how to respond to that. Linda was my friend. We had developed both a professional and a personal relationship over the course of the past few years. Yet I couldn't tell her anything. Not a word. Instead, I smiled and checked my phone. Frank had said fifteen minutes. *Seven more to go.*

"I know it's not my business"—Linda lowered her voice—"but I have to ask you." Her gaze drilled into mine. "Is there something I need to know about you and Frank?"

Then I felt it. A rock in my throat. The woman had just put me on the damn spot.

"Cassy?" Her thin brows slid up her forehead. Professional, tight-lipped smile intact.

I swallowed. "What makes you think that?"

Her lips spread wider to show her teeth. "I've been doing this too long, dear. You don't think I can't tell the brunette on those photos TMZ posted is you?"

I drew a slow, deep breath through my nose and counted to three. My dress stretched against my strapless bra. I hadn't worn anything this girly and open in years. Tonight, I'd done it for Frank. He made me want to look sexy and cute, but right now, I felt naked under Linda's assessment.

"Besides, Taylor Rhinehart is seeing Charlie Conroy."

"Get out of here. Are you serious? Isn't he married?"

"Separated. This is all hush-hush because he's trying to get full custody of his kids." Linda broke eye contact to scan the lounge. Her lips kept moving. "But I didn't tell you any of that."

"Of course, but...really?" For a moment there, my own problems seemed dull compared to the pickle Frankie's alleged love interest had gotten herself into. My brain needed time to process the biggest Hollywood secret. Charlie Conroy was an A-list actor. I would have never thought he'd fancy someone like Taylor Rhinehart. She didn't seem to be his type. But what did I know about the workings of the movie industry? I only dated a rock star.

"You don't have to worry." Linda touched my shoulder and her eyes met mine. "Your secret's safe with me. Frank is a client. It's my job to keep his public affairs in order and to make him look good. I'm just concerned about you. If this comes out—and trust me, it will—you and your family will take a beating."

"Why don't I like the sound of that?" I brought my margarita to my mouth and took a swallow.

"It's what fame does, dear."

I dropped my gaze to my drink and stared at the colored liquid for a few seconds, frowning. A clamor arose from the arena, growing louder. It was a wall of noise, a force against my eardrums, the sound of my life as I knew it cracking.

My mind blanked.

"Cassy," Linda called me out of my daze. "I want to make sure you're ready for the fallout when things get tough. Your name will be under a lot of scrutiny. *Rewired* will be under a lot of scrutiny."

Was Frank worth it? "I understand. I'm ready." I plastered a smile on my face. It was too late to back out. I'd said something to him today I never thought I would.

He was asleep, Cassy, my voice laughed. *It didn't count.*

Sure, it did. It was practice.

"Okay. You have my number." Linda touched my shoulder again before taking off.

Confused and puzzled, I stood near the bar and sipped on my margarita until my eyes registered Carter's mop of blond hair moving among the guests. That was my cue to leave.

I returned to the dressing room, where Frank sat in his tall chair facing the mirror. Alone. Head tossed back, palms curled around the slim wooden chair arms, he stared at the ceiling. His knee jerked to the beat of the Iron Maiden song playing in the background.

As I approached him, I drank in his reflection. He was enthralling. A fine combination of what every woman here tonight wanted. Sexy. Confident. Charming. He was the ultimate guy next door who'd made it. Proof that ambition and desire to be the best could take you to the top. He was the American Dream.

I was hardly a social drinker, and the alcohol had already started to course through my blood. A pleasant daze tickled my brain.

"Is everything okay?" I asked, eyes never leaving Frank's reflection.

"Yes." He nodded and slid from the chair. His height against mine was an intimidating power. Our gazes collided and I was suddenly aware of his every breath and his every move. Electricity filled the air.

He dipped down and whispered in my ear, "Take off your panties, doll."

I swallowed hard and watched him walk over to the door to lock it. My head spun. The icy glass chilled my palm.

After making sure no one was going to accidentally walk in on us, Frank turned to face me. "Take them off." The corner of his lips tilted up.

I felt the burn. Beneath my skin and in my chest. My mind and my ovaries fought one another. I'd already established Frank was far from boring during sex. For a man who was limited with how much weight he could put on his right shoulder, he was creative enough to make me sweat every time. I knew what this was, a less reckless way to get his adrenaline fix. The chances of breaking bones while fucking were sufficiently lower than while riding a motorcycle.

"Are you sure it's safe to do this before the show?" I croaked, shuffling my feet. The delicate fabric of my Victoria Secret underwear between my thighs dampened. *Boy, was I a goner!*

He crossed the dressing room and nudged me in the direction of the makeup station. My drink tipped, but he steadied it right before the liquid reached the spilling point. "We're not going to fuck."

"We're not?" I rested my free palm on his pec and started walking backward. His body vibrated under my touch, chest tight like a snare, pulse raging.

"Not until after." Tossing me a self-serving grin, he took another step and pulled the glass from my grip.

"But you want me to take off my panties now?"

"Yes, because if I do it instead, you won't have any panties left to wear while you're watching the show."

He was playing one of his games. I played along.

"Okay, so this is only temporary? You actually don't want me to be butt naked all night?" My back hit the makeup station.

"Just for the next ten minutes, baby," he husked against my cheek and set the drink aside. I heard a faint ragged gasp rushing out of his throat as his fingers fumbled with the skirt of my dress.

My body reacted instantly and want pooled between my legs. I shimmied out of my panties and licked my lips expectantly. My heart drummed in my chest, summoning my body to action.

"That's my girl." Frank put his hands on my bare hips and instructed, "Up."

I propped myself against the makeup station to help him raise me. The doctor's orders were clear. No heavy lifting. We definitely didn't want Frank to accidentally pull a muscle or cause damage that would prevent him from performing. This had to be a safe round of preshow sex...or whatever it was that we were about to do.

"You should wear this dress more often," he said, dropping his face to my shoulder. His lips traced a wet trail across my skin. Hands grabby, he spread my thighs. My skirt slipped between them, covering my sex.

Frank palmed my ass and pulled me toward the edge, thrusting his erection into my center. The fabric of his pants and my dress were in the way, but I felt it nonetheless. The thrill the press of his cock gave me. My body buzzed from head to toe. I wanted to sink my hands into his sandy locks and ruin all thirty minutes of his stylist's work. Instead, I rolled up my skirt and rubbed my clit against his bulge to increase the pressure. He smiled, his firm lips stretching against my cheek. The air between us was heavy with need. Our breaths quickened to shallow gasps on the verge of cries.

"This is only a sample." Frank lowered in front of me, planting his head between my legs. Feverish shivers ran down my spine when his mouth reached my exposed sex. He'd seen me naked hundreds of times before but never in his dressing room with dozens of people milling around the door and wanting to be inside. The fear of being ambushed made it more interesting. Made it dangerous. Made it fun.

The tip of his tongue slid along my opening, halting near my clit. A wave of dark, searing bliss gathered in the wake of his touch. He did it again. A slow, deliberate lick. Just enough to get me even wetter. I was dripping immodestly. It was the best and the dirtiest kind of torture.

"Frank," I groaned. "We don't have all night." His name was a gentle raze on my lips. "You can't do that." My eyes were half-closed. The fluorescent overheads glimmered behind the flutter of my lashes.

"Sure I can, doll." His whisper tickled my sex. Nerves coming alive, I felt my stomach pull in response. Electricity zinged through my legs.

I leaned back, steadying myself against the mirror. My hand never left his shoulder. I grasped his shirt in my fingers and wanted to rip it off. I wanted to touch him everywhere. Every hot inch of his beautiful primed-for-the-stage body.

"Please," I whimpered, biting my lip. Anticipatory shudders ran through me. Even the tips of my ears burned with desire.

Warm palms on my hips, Frank slowly dove in. His mouth sucked at my throbbing sex. The flicks and swirls of his tongue were delicate one moment and rough the next. His thick hair brushed the inside of my thighs as he lapped at me. The pleasure was absolute. A hurricane of sensations, wrecking and marking me.

The strokes grew faster and I jerked. The back of my head slid against the mirror, up and down. Frank's hands squeezed my thighs and spread them wider. Insatiable, he slipped his tongue into me.

A desperate scream filled my lungs. The room spun. The makeup station spun. The arena spun. I was losing control of my own thoughts and feelings. I was giving them all to Frank. He drew all my dreams and all my desires out of me, one by one. Moan after moan.

My chest heaved uncontrollably. Heart tripping, I came on his tongue. My body convulsed. My hips rolled. I rubbed against his mouth to ride out the wave of pleasure a little bit longer. To savor each press and grind of our wet flesh. To prolong the wild beat of the orgasm pumping inside my veins.

Frank's lips remained on my sex. I heard a low grunt as he dug his fingers into the softness of my thigh. Eyes closed, I rested my head against the cold mirror and tried to imagine how insanely inappropriate and incredibly newsworthy I must have looked right now with Frankie Blade's head between my legs.

Then I pictured myself giving the middle finger to the entire world and all the gossip chasers.

The dressing room smelled like sex. The filthy type. The type of the rich and famous. Fast, reckless, and unapologetic.

"I could do this all night," Frank rasped out against my inner thigh. Traces of my satisfaction stained his lips. His fingers skimmed over my calf and brushed the leather of my narrow-heeled pump. He paid attention to the smallest details—what I wore, what I said, what I wanted.

I'd been spoiled rotten as he'd promised, worshipped and fucked like a queen by the man who was one of the finest members of rock 'n' roll royalty.

"Is it the shoes again?" I laughed and snapped my eyes open.

"You know..." He paused and pressed a small kiss to my leg. "I can't decide whether it's the shoes or the dress, but like I said"—he rose—"that was only a sample." A sly grin twisted his mouth.

I couldn't help but wonder where all this newly found self-confidence had come from and if he should have stayed put before the show. But then I reminded myself who he was and that all he'd done was a fantastic round of oral.

Oral wasn't a life-threatening activity...was it?

Frank's booted footsteps echoed the tiny clicks of my heels against the cement floor as we marched down the hallway toward the stage. Roman had taken the lead as always. His bald head floated through the sea of various rock 'n' roll styled and bandana-clad hair. Billy and Janet were a couple of feet ahead of us. Corey and Brooklyn closed up the procession. They were discussing the post-Forum shows' social media strategy, and their hushed voices bounced between the walls.

My mind was adrift. I wasn't sure whether the reason behind the rabid beats of my heart and the nervous thrum of my pulse was the best cunnilingus of my life that I'd just received in the dressing room or the fact that Frank was holding my hand out in the open.

Did he not care about keeping our relationship a secret anymore?

As if sensing my question, he snaked his arm around my waist to pull me closer and whispered, "Every single person who's working the shows, including security, signed a confidentiality agreement." The tips of his hair brushed my neck as we kept walking, shoulder to shoulder. His voice was a rough caress against my cheek. A reassurance my life wasn't going to be smashed to pieces after tonight. Or as Linda had said, my family wouldn't "take a beating."

The crowd was reciting the band's name. The muffled chant filled the hallway and the backstage area as we passed a long line of people. Their eyes followed us, *followed me*, like a predator following its prey.

Roman halted near the stairs. Bruce trotted around Frank, rattling off instructions while the technician hooked up his monitor. Gaze on the floor, Dante sucked his lollipop as if his life depended on it. He seemed on edge and overly fidgety. A deep frown pinched his face.

Billy gave him an encouraging pat on the back. A piss-poor attempt to break the ice. Dante responded with a crooked grin and started pacing. His guitars were lined up on a rack, his tech ready. He always brought the entire arsenal, but the Stratocaster had been his instrument of choice for a few years now. They made a nice duo.

Brooklyn kept me company as I moved aside and joined the anxious knot of VIP guests. On stage, the massive screen behind the drum kit showcased the album cover artwork—the flickering image of the burning butterfly. It went in and out along with the beat of the set intro tune. There was something extremely symbolic about it. I'd never dared to ask Frank about the real meaning behind the blazing wings, but I sensed the fragility of it all.

I sensed the transience.

I sensed his fear of burning out.

The crackling of the walkie-talkies interrupted my thoughts.

Bruce ascended the stairs and disappeared into the thick fog clouding the left wing of the stage, where I saw bodies moving against the orange glow.

I felt the low rumble beneath my feet as the audience roared and clapped. Waves of excitement rolled one after another until the lights dimmed, prompting the fans to concentrate on what was coming. The air was heavy and thick. Anticipation filled every corner and crevice of the arena.

Minutes passed. The band repeated the group hug ritual from last night. Everyone took their spots. Guests and crew members held their breaths, as did all twenty thousand people opposite the stage.

Tonight would almost feel normal if not for the blue uniforms of the paramedics lingering in the background, waiting and ready.

Carter went first. He marched over to the drum kit and climbed the riser. Johnny followed him with his bass. The arena lit up. A wall of shaking hands quivered behind the shimmering veil of colored smoke.

Heat filled my chest.

I watched Frank as he listened to the roar of the crowd with his eyes shut. He was soaking in their voices. Taking them all in until it was enough. Then his hand jerked, fingers tapping against his thigh. I could tell his mind was slipping into another dimension where only music existed. Jaw tight, he readjusted his in-ear monitor.

Dante took off with his guitar strap wrapped around his neck. The spotlight followed him as he stalked across the stage with his typical swagger, ripping through a couple of simple chords and tossing smiles at the front row. The black body of his Stratocaster sparkled under a bright stream of orange.

Johnny walked over to the edge and raised his hand in the air to get the crowd going. The level of noise was no longer bearable, even where I was standing. I had to cover my ears for a brief second. I felt the tremble again and a shiver of excitement zapped down my spine.

Then the intro tune began to subside. Stage left lights flickered and dipped. Stage right followed suit.

Frank drew a deep breath and headed straight for the microphone. His silhouette moved purposefully against the phone-studded net encircling the inside of the dark arena. Fog swirled around his boots while he drank in the endless stretch of what promised to be the real mayhem.

The heat in my chest spread to my stomach. Frank neared the edge of the stage, dragging the microphone stand with him. His gaze danced across the floor as the security line tightened beneath where he stood. The frame of his carved-to-perfection body lingered against the infinite sea of hands that were thrust in the air.

I reminded myself to breathe. This was a stunning view. A view of power. I'd seen this exact image last night, but with Frank, every day was the beginning of a new adventure. Be it a midnight ride in a Ferrari or a rock show at the Forum. Palms pressed together, I watched him talking to the audience. Dante pitched in a few words. There were no excuses or mentions of yesterday's set. The speech was a short thank you and the fans loved it. They ate up everything Frank said. They clapped. They professed their love and bathed in the love he professed to them. The energy was off the charts. It felt as if the entire city was gathered here tonight. Not just physically but spiritually. Those who still had reception and could handle the rage of the crowd without going nuts livestreamed.

Borders and social status were erased. Music united people. Music brought peace.

And Frank's job was to make sure every single person would take a handful of beautiful memories home with them.

The band kicked off the set with the *Hollow Heart Dream* material. The first two songs were fast and anthemic, festival-worthy crowd-pleasers. I knew the lyrics by heart. My lips moved along with Frank's. His energy level skyrocketed with each second. Face and shoulders lax, he rocked on his heels to the beat. After the four song mark, he gave the microphone to Dante and went for a quick checkup backstage, where a bottle of water and a towel were handed to him. The crew was on standby and people moved in.

Frank's physician had insisted on monitoring his vitals during the set to avoid complications after the show, so as soon as Frank chugged the water, he whipped out an oxygen mask and then measured his blood pressure.

I stayed in my spot and watched, my heart thundering. Frank looked sweaty and ruffled, exactly what a rock singer should look like, but the dark spark in his eyes and the rigid movements of his body said it all. He was ready to get back into action. *He was fine.*

When the physician finally pulled off the cuff and gave Frank a nod, my chest released a loud sigh of relief.

As the show progressed, Frank turned up the heat. A lick of aggression colored his voice. Even during the slow tracks. He was riding the adrenaline high along with the rest of the band, the audience, the guests, and the crew.

"Are you having fun yet, L.A.?" The words shot through the arena with some slight feedback. The crowd reciprocated.

He spun around, dashed over to the stairs, and climbed them up to the platform that occupied the right wing of the stage. Dante produced a few rapacious chords and grinned at the people on the floor fighting for room to breathe. He reveled in the chaos he'd created. It was obvious that madness fed his dark, tortured soul.

Including the encore, there were seven more songs to go, and every second that passed was another second I could scratch off my imaginary clock. In my head, this set was a race against the unknown, a race against time, a race against failure. Was Frank going to make it or was the same animal that had caught up with him yesterday going to take him down tonight before all the songs were sung and all the solos played?

"I can't hear you, L.A.!" he screamed into the microphone as he walked to the middle of the platform. Another roar. His eyes met Carter's and they exchanged subtle smiles.

Dante ripped through another sequence of ragged chords and whirled in his spot, which caused him to lose his hat, but he didn't care to look for it. He seemed preoccupied with his guitar and the sounds it made. Notes finally fell together and the intro riff of "Adrenaline Lane" launched the arena into a state of absolute anarchy. Dirty, sweaty, music-infused anarchy.

I had no idea what was expected of me as the lead singer's girlfriend. Was I supposed to stand still and smile? Was I supposed to clap politely? Or was I allowed to let loose? There were no rule books on how to behave around filthy rich people when you dated one of them. My gut told me to enjoy it. And I did. I moved to the beat and I shook my head. A stupid grin spread across my face and didn't want to come off. My cheeks hurt, but at that moment, I truly didn't care.

Music and memories took me over entirely. My pulse pounded in my throat. My blood rushed through my veins, hot and thick. Frank's voice was everywhere—oxygen in my lungs, sparkle on my skin, and strength in my bones. We were an invisible cloud of dust and eternal ashes traveling through the universe and existing together.

Stage fog blurred my eyes and all I could register was Frank's silhouette on top of the platform. The pyro went off and everyone began to stomp. I felt the heat crashing into my face. My hair rose from the blast, floated down, and slowly fell back into place, its soft brush warm on my shoulders.

Their feet trampling, the crowd chanted. I squeezed my eyes shut and sang along. Line after line until Frank's voice perished among the clamor of the instruments.

Then came the gasp. It was a low, chilling sound that made my skin crawl. The drums still rattled, but the tremble of Johnny's bass had melted away and Dante's guitar went off key. Like a mile-long drop into an abyss of nothing. Heart clenching, I snapped my eyes open and scanned the stretch of space between me and the platform. Frank wasn't there. The fog was thick and the lights spun uncontrollably, slicing through the darkness. I couldn't see well, but I could hear the distressed screams as they grew louder. Then the music stopped.

Dread seized my chest. People behind me started to push, their whispers deafening. Static noise and panic took over the backstage area as paramedics barreled through. Janet and Bruce ran in after them. The fog was settling and bright lights flooded the entire arena.

That's when I saw him. He was on the floor, face up. Dante sat next to him, cheeks abnormally pale. Carter stood behind Dante. Johnny, like the true gatekeeper, still held on to the microphone, but terror twisted his features.

A howl tightened my lungs. *Frank wasn't moving.* I palmed my mouth and began my approach. My heart had fallen out of my chest somewhere along the way. It was the strangest sensation. The immediate need to know he wasn't hurt overwhelmed me. My emotions were fragments of feelings, similar to a broken mosaic that clattered inside my head.

I didn't make it past the safety line. Roman intercepted me and grabbed my arm. His grasp wasn't rough, but it was firm enough to stop me from going any farther.

"I'm sorry, Ms. Evans. It's best you stay back." His voice boomed over the noise.

Then I saw Corey shaking his head furiously and waving his hands. He didn't want me anywhere near Frank right now.

I understood. I would have become another unnecessary complication if I were to show up on stage in front of twenty thousand people in a dress that was made of a piece of fabric that was smaller than a bandana.

"Okay." I gave Roman a nervous nod. "What happened?" I tried to sound calm, but I was having trouble holding it together.

"Not sure just yet, Ms. Evans." Shaking his head, he released my arm and marched into the chaos surrounding Frank.

A stretcher was rolled on stage. I heard another collective gasp, then waves of worried murmurs rippled through the arena. The crowd was restless.

My shoes suddenly felt small, tight, and very uncomfortable. My spine stiffened. I balled my hands into fists and waited to the side while the paramedics tried to get Frank off the floor. My manicured nails dug into my palms, stabbing the tender skin, but I didn't feel anything. Not a lick of pain. It was all in my chest, squeezing and tearing at my hammering heart.

On stage, technicians and crew members ran around with their walkie-talkies, and I could see the pattern of Janet's dress behind the wall of bodies as she hovered above her son. The paramedics finally managed to put Frank on a backboard and lifted him up after a brace was settled around his neck. Cries filled the arena—a fusion of sounds of anger, fear, and disappointment.

Low thuds and feedback came from the speakers as Dante tapped the microphone. He pushed the tangle of dark, wet locks off his forehead and held up his hands, asking for silence.

When the paramedics pushed the stretcher away from the audience's line of sight, blind panic clutched my brain and I barreled my way in and grabbed the side rail, needing to look at him, needing to know what exactly he was going through. His eyes were wide open, unblinking and full of horror as they looked past me.

"Ma'am!" One of the medics elbowed me, knocking my purse off my shoulder. "Please step aside!"

My gaze swept the length of Frank's body, checking for blood. One small cut carved the skin near his sweat-coated temple. I reached for his fingers and they were stiff and unresponsive.

"Ma'am! We need you to step aside!"

"Miss Evans, please!" Roman insisted, ripping me away from the cluster of paramedics trying to work on Frank.

Dante's voice reverberated in the back of my head. He was talking to the fans. I heard Carter resuming on the drums. The noise of the show began to fade away as we scrambled past the backstage crowd and into the hallway. A muddle of sobs, shouts, and radio static trailed the stretcher as it clattered against the floor.

"Where are you taking him?" I asked no one in particular. My lungs were out of air and the words that tore through my throat were dry spurs. "Where are you taking him?" I caught Janet's sleeve.

She glanced at me over her shoulder. "Cedars Sinai."

The strap of my dress fell and my purse dangled against my leg as I trailed behind in my four-inch heels.

Outside, the distressed blues and reds of the ambulance gleamed against the polished bodies of the eighteen-wheelers that lined the dock.

The muffled roar of the audience filled the parking lot as I watched the medics loading the stretcher into the back of the vehicle. Janet and Billy jumped in behind it. Roman went next.

Eyes trained on Frank, I slung my purse over my shoulder and pushed through the chain of security.

"Only family!" a voice barked at me as the ambulance doors slid closed.

"I'm his girlfriend!" I cried out, my fist thrust in the air in an attempt to hit the vehicle, but my coordination was off. Heck, my brain was off too. My entire life was crumbling like a sandcastle under the tide.

"I'm sorry. Only family!"

"Roman!" I called and waved my hand to get his attention, but he was turned with his back to me.

"Ma'am, please step aside." A security guard rested his heavy hands on my shoulders. A flashlight jerked across my face.

Delirious, I stomped my foot. "Don't fucking touch me and don't fucking *ma'am* me!" My blood boiled with rage.

"You need to calm down, ma'am!"

I spit out another string of expletives, but the piercing noise of the siren devoured my words. The ambulance moved. Without me. I wasn't sure what exactly I felt at that moment. Mad. Terrified. Erased?

Emotions clogged my throat. I dropped my gaze to my chest and realized my backstage pass was missing.

People around me yelled and ran in different directions. Inside the arena, the noise was subsiding. The drums had stopped. I spun on my heels and scanned the crowd, looking for a familiar face. My heart was a thrashing mess somewhere in the pit of my stomach. My pulse raced. Brooklyn stood near one of the trucks with a phone pressed to her ear. I couldn't make out a word she said, but for the first time since I'd met the woman, I saw her emitting emotions. Mostly shock.

Corey was nowhere to be seen. My hands shook when I pulled out my own phone to check the reception. With twenty thousand people Tweeting and Instagramming about another Hall Affinity fiasco, the chances of getting an Uber from anywhere within a half-mile radius of the Forum were less than zero.

"Fuck, fuck, fuck," I growled, staring at the single bar in the top left corner of my screen.

The app lagged.

I felt it then. The tears of despair pooling at the back of my eyes. I didn't know what triggered them, the incident itself or the fact that I hadn't made it into the ambulance, but the sudden shift terrified me. The unknown terrified me. The helplessness terrified me.

It had been my sixteenth birthday when my mother shared her wisdom with me, the motto I'd always followed.

Don't ever let a man in to the point where when he's gone, he's taken a part of you with him.

She called it the breaking point.

Tonight was exactly that. The moment I'd been avoiding at all costs. And it happened the moment the ambulance left, taking Frank, taking my sanity, and taking my heart along with him. The entire night felt like an episode of a badly scripted reality show with an unlikable, unstable female lead. Me.

Stop it, Cassy. You're an independent woman. You don't fucking cry in the middle of a crowded parking lot.

I sucked in a deep breath through my teeth and choked down the wave of defeat. My gaze darted from person to person until it reached the dark shock of Dante's hair near the back entrance. Cigarette dangling between his lips, shirt unbuttoned, he was surrounded by the screaming crowd. Something told me some of those people might have been overzealous fans who'd snuck in. Carter was right behind him, drenched. He pulled off his shirt and used it to wipe the sheen of sweat from his forehead.

"Dante!" I called, rushing over. The click of my heels rattled in my ears.

He spun around and the wind whipped the sides of his shirt against his thin torso. People swarmed between us as we caught sight of each other. His expression was withdrawn, his eyes dark, and as they wandered across my face, I had to ask myself whether he understood what had just happened or he was experiencing the same type of delay Frank had felt during the motorcycle crash.

"Are you going to Cedars Sinai?"

Dante nodded. "You have a ride?" He plucked the cigarette from his mouth and spit on the asphalt. Anxiety riddled his face.

I shook my head. "No."

"Okay, come on." He jerked his chin and headed toward the black car that was waiting.

I followed. "What about Carter?"

"He's riding with Johnny."

We climbed in the back. The doors thwacked shut, separating us from the mayhem. Dante rolled down the window and continued puffing on his cigarette.

Phone clutched in my palm, heart racing, I stared at the arena lights smeared behind the tinted glass as we maneuvered through the developing gridlock. The traffic on Manchester was just as bad, if not worse. Cars lined up one after another.

Dante finished smoking, tossed the butt outside, and closed the window. His hand rested on his thigh, long fingers tapping out a nervous dance against the expensive denim.

"What happened?" I turned to face him as endless questions swirled in my head. "He was fine before the set."

Dante dropped his gaze to the floor. "I don't know. He tripped."

I needed more than that. I needed an explanation my brain could work with. "What do you mean tripped? It makes no sense!"

"I don't fucking know, Cassy!"

Our voices clashed inside the car like two cymbals. Mine was a raging high-pitch and his was frostbite on my skin.

I shivered. "But he was fine!"

Dante palmed his face, and I heard the rumble of his labored breath. "Can you shut up for a second, please?"

My phone buzzed. Again and again. Messages and email notifications that couldn't make it through inside the arena. I hid the device in my purse and tried to breathe through the panic. My pulse thrummed in my temples and my body shook uncontrollably. I wasn't sure whether it was from the AC that blasted from everywhere or shock.

Dante lit up another cigarette, this time not bothering to roll down the window. He smoked fast. Deep, nervous puffs. Rigid movements. His chest trembled.

I watched him from the corner of my eye. The tense set of his jaw gave away his temporary animosity toward me. Smoke was everywhere. In my hair, in my eyes, in my lungs. Suffocating me and reminding me once again why I'd never dated anyone who was addicted to nicotine. It was a deadly habit.

Cracking my own window open, I plastered my cheek to the glass and breathed. Cool air crept up my arms and legs. Worry for Frank settled deep in my chest.

Dante finally lowered his window. I heard the rustle of his clothes and the rough scratch of his vocal cords as he cleared his throat and spoke, "You probably want to call your family and make sure they don't talk to reporters. Mom. Dad. Dog. Just in case."

Wind rippled the light skirt of my dress. "No dad." I shook my head, not sure why I'd said that. Dante knew very little about my life outside *Rewired*.

"How come?"

"He left us."

I heard a chuckle. A bitter one. "Shitty fathers are pretty common these days, huh?"

I tore my cheek from the glass and looked at him. "What about you?"

He held up his cigarette between his fingers. Thick, rancid clouds streamed from his nose. "My father is six feet under. Heart attack."

"I'm sorry." I didn't know about the nature of Dante's relationship with his father. I knew he had passed. The news had circulated in the tabloids for a day or two when it happened. Dante was arrested for a DUI two days later.

"It's been a few years. I'm over it." His words hung in the air, somber. There was a pause followed by a long, shaky drag. "Did Frankie-boy ever tell you about his birth mother?"

"Some. Yes."

"Did he tell you why social services took him away from her?"

"Yes."

"Did he tell you how he fell into a pool once while she was out partying? He almost drowned."

Heaviness filled my chest. Frank had mentioned a lot of horrible things, mostly neglect, but not this.

I shuddered at the thought.

"He doesn't really talk about it." Dante studied the burning tip of his cigarette for a few seconds. Hot ash sprinkled across his jeans and he brushed it off. "I only heard the story once. Years ago. We were on tour in Europe. Amsterdam. It was Johnny's birthday and we decided to take him to a strip club. The elite shit with high-end dancers, bottle service, and all that jazz. Frankie-boy had a few drinks and got all sentimental during the fucking lap dance. Can you imagine?" Dante faced me, a one-sided smile twisting his lips. "That was before your lover boy married that Playboy cunt. He's not a dog, just so you know. He's not going to fuck around if he has a nice piece of ass like you."

I didn't understand why he needed to reassure me Frank wasn't a cheater. I ignored the last reference too. Dante Martinez was a spoiled, self-centered jerk and a womanizer. Piece of ass might have been a compliment for all I knew. But we had more important matters to discuss. "Why are you telling me this?" I caught his gaze.

This was the first time Dante had brought up Frank's wife and I sensed there was a lot more history behind that infidelity.

"I don't want you to think just because a man has access to all the pussy in the world that he can't be faithful. It's the same as going to an all-you-can-eat seafood buffet when you fucking hate seafood. You go because it's convenient. Cheap, close to your house. The cook knows you. What you really like is fondue. Problem is, fondue is an acquired taste and your homeboys think it's disgusting."

"I'm not following."

"Of course you're not." Dante laughed and slipped the cigarette between his lips again to take a drag. "You're fondue, darlin', and Frankie-boy likes fondue."

Satisfied with his brilliant conclusion, Dante leaned back and pushed the smoke out. I noted a flash of a grin. The man was deranged.

"Are you seriously comparing me to melted cheese while your best friend is on the way to the hospital in an ambulance?"

Dante tilted his head and gave me the side-eye. "I'm trying to tell you a fucking story, short stuff. About your man, whose mother left him to fucking die. Good thing she's gone. She was a shitty mother anyway. At least my mother cared enough to hit me."

My stomach roiled. Everyone had a broken childhood. Not just Ashton and I. And in a sick way, it made me feel better.

"He's not the best judge of character," Dante went on. "Someone had to look out for him when he moved to L.A."

"Let me guess. You were that someone?" I sifted through my mental notes. Hall Affinity was no different than any other band who'd hit the jackpot. One day they were playing opening sets in the clubs, the next, their songs were all over Billboard. A lot of money. Booze. Women. Drugs. I wasn't sure these guys were in any condition to look after each other, but I knew Frank had always been the smart one. He stayed out of trouble.

"I did my best." Dante nodded. "I told him not to marry the Playboy Bunny. He did it anyway."

"Why?"

"Why'd he marry her?" Dante gave me a one-shoulder shrug, tossed the cigarette butt out and grabbed another. "The fuck I know."

"No." I shook my head. "Why didn't you want him to marry Heidi Fox?"

"Because she was fucking around behind his back. Sooner or later, he was going to find out."

My throat tightened. I swallowed hard and broke our eye contact. The flick of a lighter snapped in my ear. "You're a shitty friend, Dante."

In my peripheral, there was a cloud of smoke.

"I'd rather he found out his wife was a cunt the way he did than via the newspapers, darlin'. She wasn't exactly keeping her affairs under the radar."

"So you seduced her?"

Dante snorted out a laugh. His chest shook along with his cigarette. "Have you met me, Cassy Evans? I don't need to seduce anyone."

I wanted to kick him in the shins. "I always knew you were an asshole, but this is a new level of low." The wicked drum of my pulse against my temples was deafening. Acid rose up my throat and coated my tongue.

"It's only low when you do it for your own benefit. I did it for Frankie-boy. Quick extraction. The world doesn't need to know what really happened."

I had no words. My anger simmered beneath the surface, hot, deep, and acutely confounded.

The hospital was cold.

By the time Dante and I arrived there, Frank had been taken to surgery. The only thing I could pull out of Janet was that he had several fractures that needed immediate attention. There were no other updates. Not for hours.

Dante was on edge. Trying to get him to tell me exactly what happened during the set was like trying to make a toddler sit still for five minutes. My sweet-talking techniques didn't even work on him for some reason. Desperate for some information, I hid in the restroom to check YouTube for footage. *Frankie Blade Stage Accident* was trending. The entire feed was littered with uploads from the show.

Different angles. Different quality. Same headlines.

The world was thoroughly disappointed.

Back against the tiled wall, I drew a breath through my teeth and skimmed through the links. My fingers felt clammy and the phone shook in my palm. I hit play. On screen, an image of Frank came up. Hair wild, eyes sparkling, he rocked out in the middle of the platform, unaware he'd be on the floor moments later. I wanted to dive in badly. To tell him to get off the damn thing. A sea of hands clapped beneath him. He moved to the beat and traced the edges of the structure carefully. Stage fog was everywhere and the image became unfocused and shaky for a brief second but quickly returned to Frank. The first blast of pyro went off. He shifted over to the truss in the corner, reached out with his right hand, and grabbed it to leverage himself while leaning over the edge.

That was the moment his arm gave out. His legs slipped and he went down.

One hand clamped over my mouth, heart thundering, I set the phone on the counter and replayed the last five seconds of the recording.

Why would he do that?

The door cracked. I heard footsteps. My mind was still spinning and I knew I needed to turn off the recording or at least lower the sound because the chances were high that the person who'd just occupied one of the stalls was a reporter or an overly enthusiastic fan.

But shock hit me hard. My feet were rooted to the floor and I couldn't move a single muscle.

Frank knew he wasn't supposed to put any pressure on his right shoulder. Trying to hold up the weight of his entire body was stupid. And reckless.

I didn't understand why he'd done it.

Another set of footsteps dragged me out of my stupor. The light in my brain switched on. I exited YouTube, slipped the phone into my purse, and returned to the waiting area, where Brooklyn, Corey, Dante, and Carter had teamed up for a meeting. Johnny was slumped in a chair two rows over, face off-color, eyes on the floor. Security lined the hallway. I settled across from Billy and Janet and pulled at my skirt as much as the fabric would allow me to cover my shaking legs.

Messages from Levi and Ashton begged to be answered, but my mind wasn't ready to face the rest of the world yet.

Dante disengaged from the group and disappeared down the hall. His voice carried from around the corner as he spoke to someone. I wasn't sure if he was on a phone call or flirting with a nurse, but he returned two minutes later with a hospital blanket and tossed it to me.

"You're going to turn into a popsicle." He stood off to the side and watched me cocooning myself for a minute, then flicked his gaze to Frank's parents. "Anyone want coffee?"

Billy accepted the offer and thanked him. Janet was quiet, dread lining her thin face.

"What about you, short stuff?"

I shook my head. It was an instant reaction. I was hungry and needed caffeine, but my brain hadn't processed the words correctly. I was still rattled by the YouTube video and our conversation about Frank's ex-wife. Part of me wanted Dante to take it all back. Shove the confession into his mouth and keep it there.

"Gonna be a long night, darlin'." He spread his arms wide and took a step backward. A juicy, devilish grin lit up his face, which was sprinkled with light stubble. "Last chance."

I reevaluated. Coffee sounded good. Best way to stay up. Besides, Dante Martinez was acting nice and human for once. Fetching drinks for others unless they were shots at a party was so out of his character. It almost felt as if he was trying to redeem himself.

"Okay. Sure." I nodded.

He marched off and never returned. At least, not for a while. I had to go and look for him in the cafeteria half an hour later because poor Billy and Janet really needed that coffee after the doctor came out to tell us that Frank was out of surgery.

"Can we see him?" Janet asked. She was wringing her hands and trembling like crazy I wasn't positive the woman was mentally equipped to be here right now, but what did I know? I'd been in Frank's life only a few months. She'd been with him through three decades of highs and lows. Those numbers scared me. They were just another reminder of how fickle, short-lived, and possibly not very serious this affair actually was.

"Not yet," the doctor said as he continued to ignore my presence. "He's still unconscious and I want to run a few more tests, so sit tight."

Fear trickled down my spine as I maneuvered through the rows of plastic tables in the cafeteria. Dante was leaning against the register chatting with the cashier. He had his smug face on.

Unbelievable.

I walked over and tugged the side of his shirt.

"Oh, hey, short stuff." He spun around and his gaze darted between me and the girl in the bleak hospital visor. "This is Leticia. She's making us fresh coffee."

"Really? Since when does it take thirty minutes to brew a new pot?" I said in a low voice and pulled him away from the register. "Frank is out of surgery."

The cafeteria was empty, not counting the cashier and the security guard at the door who'd been following me all night. Probably because Brooklyn had told him to. He did keep his distance, which I appreciated.

"Any news?" Dante sniffed and palmed his head. His eyes, blood red and wide, stared me down for a long moment.

It hit me then. I almost didn't want to believe my discovery, but the signs were all there. Come to think of it, he'd been like a cat on a hot tin roof all night. Especially in the car with his diarrhea of secrets. "Are you high?"

Ignoring my question, Dante turned to the cashier and yelled, "Make it six, darlin'! And throw in a couple of breakfast sandwiches too."

Talk about acting weird. I'd never seen the man lift a finger to do anything except for playing his guitar.

"Hey!" I called. "Did you hear me?"

He returned his scattered attention to me. We shared a glance for only a second.

"Answer me," I gritted out. "Are you high?"

"Are you my therapist now?"

"Oh my fucking God." My voice was a hiss. Wrath pulled at my chest. "You are high, aren't you?"

The cashier was packing our breakfast. The rustle of Styrofoam filled the cafeteria.

Dante's lack of response angered me. I slapped his arm to get him to say something. "Was he high too? Did you give him something?"

"Keep your fucking hands off me." He jerked his shoulder in a particularly childish manner.

Rage blinded me. Horrified, I hit him in the chest with my purse. "Is that how you look out for him, you asshole?"

The corner of the blanket fell to the floor and my heel tangled in it as I tried to stumble my way out of the cafeteria. Tears pricked my eyes for the second time tonight. I held them in, but I hated all these emotions fighting for room within me. There was a reason why I'd never gotten so involved with a man. Men were trouble. Men ruined the balance. Frank was the worst. He'd destroyed my perfectly normal life.

I didn't know where to go to be alone except the restroom. While I understood why the floor was packed with security, the fact that someone was shadowing me at all times felt a lot like an invasion of privacy. I didn't want some stranger to watch me having a meltdown.

Hours went by. The doctor let Janet and Billy see Frank at around four in the morning. I waited patiently and watched more people trickle in. Some wore suits, some wore casual attire. Dressed sharply but looking tired, Linda showed up at dawn.

"Have you seen him yet?" she asked as we settled in the corner, away from the eyes and ears of others.

"They're not letting me. Only immediate family for now."

"Then you should go home and get some sleep, hon."

"I will. After I make sure he's okay." He wasn't okay, though. I knew it.

Linda reached to pat my knee. "It's best if you leave now, Cassy. Trust me."

"Are there a lot of people outside?"

She nodded.

"What's next?"

"I need to see what the doctors say before I can assess the damage."

Damage. It was a word I'd come to hate lately. I breathed in hard and stretched my stiff neck.

"If someone sees you here looking like this, you'll be all over the internet," Linda urged.

"What, you don't like my poncho?" I joked.

She gave me a small smile. "How about I call you if I hear something?"

"Thank you, but I'll be careful."

Truth was, I couldn't leave the hospital without seeing Frank. I just wanted a glimpse.

Linda patted my arm, then rose to her feet and walked off. Reclining my head against the wall, I closed my eyes and waited.

It was nearly nine and I was chugging my third cup of coffee, trying to stay awake and alert, when Roman finally came to grab me.

My anxiety rushed back in as I stepped into the room. The lights were bright and sterile, and the monitors were obnoxiously loud. It made me wonder how someone could even sleep through this noise. Then I remembered Valium.

At first, I couldn't tell if Frank was awake. His head, limp against the raised top of the bed, was turned away and his eyes weren't in my line of view. The door behind me swung shut and I stood in my spot, hugging the blanket and staring at his sandy hair splayed across the pillow, until his cheek pulled and a hint of a smile stretched his lips. He turned his head slightly to see me better.

I held his gaze and tried not to look at the cast and the tubes prodding his veins.

"Why are you still here, doll?" Frank's voice was soft around the edges from medications and anesthesia.

"I wanted to make sure you were okay." I walked over and grabbed a chair.

He didn't move, but his eyes ran over my body, curious. I heard the swallow followed by a loud, shallow attempt at taking a breath. "Love the new cape." The corners of his lips curled up slightly.

Not sure who he was trying to fool, me or himself, I returned the smile. Mine was just as weak. "It's been a little chilly here." I settled in a chair and stared at his hand for a while, hesitant to touch him. Suspicion was driving me mad. The confrontation with Dante was like a fungus, growing bigger with every second. I'd never seen Frank do drugs, but the more I thought about it, the more his sudden boost of confidence before the show made sense, and the words danced on the tip of my tongue.

"Cassy," Frank spoke. "You should go home."

I felt the fear creeping through. It was everywhere. In the dullness of his gaze, in the tremor of his voice, in the shortness of his breath, in the dark shadows beneath his eyes. His cheeks were the color of diluted white paint. He looked...shattered.

Emotions consumed me. Biting back all my questions, I slipped my fingers between his and brushed our hands together. "I don't want to go, Frank. I want to stay here. With you."

"The next couple of days are going to be difficult with the press. Why don't you and Ashton get out of town until all this blows over? Brooklyn will arrange your tickets." His speech slurred. "Pick a place. How about Hawaii?"

"You want to send me away?"

"It's safer."

"Frank. I'm not a little girl who needs saving. Ashton is getting ready to retake his SATs. He has school. We can't just leave. It doesn't work like that."

He got quiet.

"You're going to need some help anyway." I motioned at his arm. The knot in my stomach tightened. My brain was still processing the consequences of the accident. I didn't know any details yet, but I'd overheard Janet speaking to a doctor. There were multiple fractures in the clavicle area and the fragments of his broken plate in his shoulder. Frank was going to need another surgery, which meant there would be no shows. At least, not for a while.

Dozens of different machines squawking in unison surrounded the bed. The room reminded me of a scene from a futuristic science fiction movie.

"Brooklyn will get a nurse," he said, his fingers moving against mine subtly and carefully.

"I don't want some random woman to bathe you."

He smiled again, but his face twisted and I realized he couldn't laugh, because he was in pain.

"Remember what you said to me in Aspen, Frank?"

"A lot of dirty things, as you requested."

"That too," I agreed. "You said you've never been in a relationship with someone who wasn't a high profile person."

He nodded.

"This is what a relationship with a middle-class woman is like. She's not going to hide out from the press while her man is going through shit."

"Nicely put. Going through shit. And I like that. Well, not that going through shit part, but how vocal you are about your dibs on me."

We stared at each other for a few seconds. "You need to let me be there for you, Frank," I said, our fingers still entwined.

"And you need to let me protect you from the shit I'm in."

"Are we talking compromise here?"

"Yes. It appears we are." The corner of his mouth tugged, but his voice was barely there.

"How are we doing this then?"

"First of all, you need to go home and get some sleep. The hospital will be surrounded by reporters while I'm here. I don't want you to come back. It's too risky. Just lay low."

My heart drummed in my chest as I held his hand and listened. He sounded like an undercover agent who was trying to get us out of a life and death situation.

"When will you be released?"

"A couple of days...hopefully." His jaw slackened. He was slipping away.

"Okay, then I'll see you at home?" It was half-statement, half-question.

"Yes, I'll see you at home, doll."

Exhausted, I slid into the back of the car Corey had arranged for me. My entire body felt as if it were falling apart. Worry swelled in my chest as I rattled off my Burbank address to the driver. We pulled out from the rear parking lot and rounded the building. A large group of fans in Hall Affinity T-shirts and reporters with cameras crowded the entrance. I noticed a news van across the street.

Frankie Blade continued to make headlines. Even from the hospital.

I wanted to check on Ashton and grab a few things before returning to Malibu. My brother had been texting me all night, asking about Frank. There were a couple of messages from Levi and one from my mother. She'd read about the incident on Facebook.

And then there was everyone else. Thirty-five new emails in my personal inbox and another sixty-three in my *Rewired* folder. I drew a tired breath through my teeth and looked at the Twitter feed. It was becoming too much. The tabloids, the people, the messages waiting to be answered. My head was a raging volcano, ready to burst any second from the overload of information.

The car merged with the morning traffic and continued its drive through the streets of L.A.

Drained, I shut off my phone and closed my eyes. My body went lax against the crisp leather of the back seat. The engine's hum lulled me to sleep. I passed out almost instantly and didn't wake up until the car came to a stop outside my apartment complex in Burbank.

Chapter Three

Levi's shadowed eyes stalled on my face. "Come again?" His brows pulled together. The thrumming vein on his neck told me he was in panic mode.

"It's for the best." Anxiety coursed through me as I spoke.

"Tell me this is a fucking joke, Cass."

"It's not a joke."

We were in Levi's living room. He was sprawled out on the couch across from me, his laptop and a large box of pizza sitting in front of him.

I occupied the chair. My heart pounded like a hammer. Everything had been falling apart. I felt it. He felt it too. We simply didn't have the courage to begin this conversation.

Frank's accident was the final straw.

Gotta get your priorities straight, Cass, my gut kept whispering. *Now is the time.*

"I'm still going to cover all the events I've already committed to. Stewie can help you with the rest." I tried to soften the blow, but my argument seemed weak.

Levi looked like he'd been hit by a truck, and I, Cassy Evans, was the damn truck.

I'd just told him I wanted a break from *Rewired*.

"Are you still pissed at me for not censoring Shayne's review? Is that what this is?" He leaned forward, his Red Bull hitting the coffee table between us.

"No. It's just become too much. The magazine and the documentary..." *And Frank.*

The silence between Levi and me dragged on. His foot was bouncing. He rested his elbows on his knees and absently stared at the slices of pizza inside the box.

"You knew when we jumped into this how much work the film was going to be. I can't keep doing both," I said. "It's wearing me down."

"Don't lie to me, Cass. It's because of him, isn't it?"

"It's not only him." I shook my head. "But I can't be in three different places at once. I'm exhausted."

Levi was right. Frank was one of several reasons why I needed to give something up. He was still a hot mess after the surgery and *Rewired* ate up all my time.

"I need us to see it through, Cass," Levi argued, his gaze focused on a stray pepperoni. "For Isabella."

"We will. I promise. That's why I want to dedicate more time to the project."

"The odds aren't in our favor."

I knew exactly what he meant by that. Frank's involvement was now up in the air. *Frank's career was up in the air.*

He'd been released from the hospital two days ago into an immediate madness of countless meetings with the lawyers and a disaster in the press. Mind dulled by the physical pain and the pills fighting it, he hadn't been able to produce a single coherent sentence.

My thoughts spun. I didn't know how to explain to Levi what was going on in my life right now without jeopardizing Frank's privacy. I didn't know how to tell him I hadn't been able to sleep at all since the accident. Instead, I'd tossed and turned in the huge empty bed in my lover's Malibu mansion, hugging the sheets that still smelled of him, wearing his shirt, pretending he lay near, pretending he was still his charming, sexy self, pretending his name hadn't been dirty-laundered online, pretending he hadn't been severely medicated in the hospital.

"I know," I said softly. "And trust me, I hate this as much as you do. I've given everything I have to this magazine, but I can't split myself apart. I need to take a step back."

We sat in silence for a little longer. My chest was heavy and stiff, and I felt the pain of the entire world gathering within me.

"You think I'm a traitor and a coward, huh?" I swallowed past the lump in my throat.

"I don't think you're a coward," he corrected me. "I think you're stupid, Cass. We're on a fucking roll." They were mean words, but there was no cruelty in his voice. He sounded more disappointed.

"Okay. Maybe I am."

"Trust me, I know what's going on in your head." Levi sat back, his eyes on mine. "Too bad you don't give yourself enough credit, Cass. If the two of you are for real, why hide it?"

"You know why."

"Paparazzi is always a great excuse. You're throwing away all your hard work for a rich dick."

"Well." I drew in a deep breath. "Thank you for your honesty."

"Hey, if it looks like shit and smells like shit, it's definitely not daisies, baby."

"You're just jealous," I called him out.

"Of course I'm fucking jealous." Disdain and anger tweaked his face. "We spent seven years creating something meaningful, and we're this close to making it to the top"—he held up his hand and pinched his thumb and forefinger together—"and he swoops in and takes you away."

"I don't think you understand that what I'm trying to do here is going to benefit both of us."

"He can hire an army of nurses to tend to his needs. You don't need to be by his side at all times."

Frank already *had* an army of nurses. We, along with everything happening and about to happen, were more complicated than that. *I needed to be by his side and I needed to distance myself from* Rewired.

"I'm simply refocusing my energy and time on what's important. I'll be able to get a lot more done working from home."

"Right. Like Mr. Perfect hasn't monopolized all your time already."

"No, he hasn't."

"The last two months of your relationship have proved the opposite."

"What do you know about relationships?" I scoffed. "When was the last time you went out on a date?" It was low of me to throw Levi's lack of certain skills with women in his face, but he was starting to get on my nerves.

"Oh, so we're comparing our sex lives now?"

"No." I shook my head. "We're not." I needed to defuse this before it got out of control.

He let out a long exhale as if to regroup. "Look, just think about it again before you pull the plug."

"I told you, I'm still helping you with everything already locked in on the calendar, but I don't want to book more on-camera interviews or take on more editorials. My hands are full with all the end-of-the-year stuff. Shayne's always wanted my spot. Let her have it temporarily. And don't forget, you've got Ashton."

"Come on." Levi let out a bitter laugh. "You know your brother can't weave words the way you do."

"But he's very persistent. And he loves the gig."

"You're fucking killing me, Cass."

"Believe me, we'll get things done faster this way. With me concentrating on securing sponsors and looking for venues while you work on the footage, the film will be ready right in time for the summer festivals. If we keep spreading ourselves thin, it'll take us years to complete the project, and Isabella doesn't have years. We need to do it now while there's still interest on social media. You know better than anyone how to delegate. Let Stewie and Shayne take on more workload. Have Ashton do smaller bands."

"Stewie has horrible grammar." Levi scowled, and the tilt of his head gave away his unease.

"Tell him to install Grammarly."

"Why do I feel like I just got dumped?"

"It'll be fine. I promise," I said, scrambling for my phone to check my emails. The app indicated there were currently nine hundred and seventy-five unread messages in my inbox.

Wonderful.

I left Levi's place after we went over the revised *Rewired* calendar.

My anguish over an indefinite break from the magazine was like venom. It filled my veins and burned my cheeks as I drove back to Malibu, thinking about new business cards and all the social media and website changes I'd need to do. They seemed so trivial, almost meaningless compared to millions of disappointed fans all over the world who were awaiting news on the upcoming Hall Affinity tour that was now up in the air, just like Frank's career.

Lately, I'd been feeling as if I were two different people. One was a self-made woman who desperately wanted her simple life back. The other was a woman who was crazy and irrevocably in love with Frank Wallace, a woman who wanted to shed her skin and dive into his bloodstream to give him what he needed right now, a second heartbeat to last through this battle. Because his own pulse was a fading flicker buried under a blanket of pain.

And it was tiresome—trying to find the balance amidst all this madness that surrounded Frank.

I made a small detour and went to Santa Monica Beach to clear my head. The roar of the ocean here was different than in Malibu. It was noisier, filled with the sounds of conversations crashing against the waves and the rattle of skaters rolling along the coastline.

I parked in a lot near the cliffside and sat in my car with the music on and a paper bag from In-N-Out in my lap, staring at the afternoon sun as it slowly slid toward the horizon. My mind was adrift and my burger was getting cold. Finally, I grabbed my phone from the cupholder and dialed the number I'd been itching to call all day.

Linda's voice on the line was crisp and low. "I don't have any specifics," she spoke carefully, but I heard a lick of panic in her tone. "I'm doing you a favor so you can get your things in order before this goes public."

My chest stiffened. "Thank you." I had no idea what else to say.

The information Linda shared with me was still an unconfirmed rumor—the label blamed Frank for the album leak. Everything in me sensed trouble as a dark cloud of smoke loomed on the horizon with the bitter, pungent scent of defeat.

By the time I arrived in Malibu, the house had quieted. For the first time since Frank had returned from the hospital, we weren't surrounded by other people nor was he knocked out by the pain meds. It was just me and him and the rumble of the ocean, and after giving him some space to adjust the past couple of days, I decided it was time to try to get some answers.

He was on the couch on the terrace, his body situated in a pile of pillows, and if not for the cast and the sling, he would've looked almost peaceful from where I stood.

I walked over and positioned myself across from him, needing to see his face, needing to take in every detail, needing to make sure his spirit hadn't left him. The last rays of light glimmered across his disheveled hair and his sunken cheeks.

"Hi," I said, then flashed him a small smile.

Frank's gaze found mine. "Hi." His voice was weakened by the medication, its seductive edge buried deep under many layers of stress. "How was your day, doll?"

I set my purse on the table and kneeled in front of him. My palms slid over his thighs. I didn't know why I liked when he looked at me from above. He was the only man allowed to do so. Maybe it was his experience. Maybe it was my sick need to feel his paternal streak he hid so well. Maybe it was the best angle to watch the sun flares coloring his unshaven face. The golden glow made him look...happier. Alive. And I wanted to soak in his warmth.

Or maybe it was none of those things.

"My day wasn't productive," I confessed.

"How come?" Frank's left hand covered mine and we stared at each other for a long minute before I gave him an answer.

"I saw Levi. I'm going to take a break from the magazine."

"Did something happen between you two?"

"No." I shook my head, and the gentle breeze ruffled my hair. "It's temporary. Just until things with the film ease up a little. We need to start looking for a venue and I can hardly find any time. I think dedicating the next couple of months solely to the film is going to get it off the ground faster. "I paused to take a breath. "Besides, I don't want to leave you alone right now."

A meek smile spread to his cheeks. "Don't be ridiculous. This house is like a hotel. I've lost count of how many people I've seen here today."

"I know, but I'm not people..."

"No, you're definitely not," Frank agreed.

My throat caught. I wasn't sure how to explain my true fears to him without making him upset or causing a fight. "I have to ask you something, but promise me you'll tell the truth."

The low wheezing sound in his chest told me he was trying to take a breath. His hand moved to my face and cradled my cheek. "I'll do my best."

I tilted my head, and the press of his palm against my skin made me dizzy. "I know Dante took something before the show," I said quietly, keeping our eyes locked. "He didn't deny it when I asked. Did you take something too?"

There was a pause. Frank's eyes darkened. His hand dropped.

"I'm not judging you. I just want to know if you took drugs before the show."

Another pause. The subtle grind of his jaw gave away his anxiety.

"Do you know what it's like to be trapped in this body?" he asked.

"You're avoiding my question."

"I almost drowned when I was three."

There he was, doing his strange reminiscence dump.

My heart pitter-patted. I knew the story, but now that he'd brought it up, I wanted to hear him say it. Word by word. I wanted to hear him bare his secrets, because part of me was jealous of Dante. Jealous of their relationship, jealous of their friendship, no matter how fucked up. That was what made it fascinating, the test of time and the test of betrayal.

"My mother, my birth mother, went out and left me alone," Frank continued, the dull pain of the memories twisting his features. "I was a curious kid. I sneaked into the backyard, slipped, and fell into the pool. I was too young to really understand what was happening to me. I remember only bits and pieces of that day. I remember water forcing the air out of my lungs. I remember not being able to breathe. Ever since the crash, I've been experiencing the same thing. I've been drowning these past seven years. The things I want to do aren't possible anymore. It's like all this music is stuck in me and I can't get it out, because I need to take a fucking breath and I can't. I'm broken beyond repair."

Blood rushed to my temples. I heard it pounding in my ears, I heard the sound of waves crashing against the cliffs below and the sound of my heart beating against my ribcage. Words, questions, and thoughts in my head spiraled. "Frank, music doesn't care what you wear and how you look while you're making it or delivering it. People listen to your songs because those songs mean something to them, because they touch them, because they aren't simply a show with a bunch of fireworks. Those songs are memories. Moments. Smiles. Feelings. You don't need to be anything at all to keep writing music. You don't need to meet anyone's expectations except your own."

"You're an idealist." He laughed softly. "That's why I like you so much."

"And you're not broken, Frank."

"Oh, yes. I am, doll."

"You're just tired." Needing to be closer to him, I slid forward and rested my chin on his knee. "What can I do to make you feel better?"

His finger skimmed through my hair, the brush of his fingertips soft as a feather. "Don't ask me about the things I do to keep this body going, Cassy. It's the only way to make it work."

It was wrong, unhealthy, and dangerous in so many ways. Yet I didn't argue. I pushed all my concerns to the back of my mind. He was stubborn to a fault. He was faithful to his vision and the brand he'd created. I couldn't blame him for pushing his limits. I often pushed my own limits too.

We sat in silence for a long time, listening to the wild roar of the Pacific and watching the sun disappearing into the glazed surface of the water. The twisted calm was full of salty air that clung to my skin as the breeze whipped my clothes and hair.

Frank spoke first. "You don't have to do this."

"What are you talking about?" I lifted my head up and surveyed his fatigue-ridden face.

"Sacrifice your time."

"I'm not. I'm just reprioritizing some of the things in my life." Worry raced through my veins. "It's not like I'm giving up the magazine for good."

"I'm not much fun to be around right now."

"Are you trying to get rid of me?" I stood and slid my palm into his.

"No." He shook his head, and the corners of his lips curled up. "I would never." He squeezed my hand, then drew me closer to stand between his legs and released a breath against my chest. I felt it burn through my skin and bone, a flame to my aching heart. "You know I've been thinking...about us and all this hiding..."

My heart wobbled.

"I don't want to hide anymore," he whispered into my shirt.

I waited. I wanted to hear more, but he was quiet.

When he didn't say anything else after several seconds, I let him off the hook. "Why don't you lie down?" I brushed the strands of stray hair off his forehead. "The doctor said you need rest."

"Come here." He snaked his left arm around my waist and pulled me to him as hard as his fractures would allow. His face pressed against my breasts in a strange needy way that was sexual yet innocent. He slid his cheek across my chest, trying to breathe.

Our heartbeats mingled. Emotions began to jam my throat. I was conflicted, sad, and in love, and I didn't know how to tell him.

If you could just read my mind, Frank.

"I'm glad you're here," he murmured. "I really am. You're the only good thing left, baby." My clothes had muffled his words, but I still heard it—the crack in his voice, the panic, the weight of the entire world.

"Where else would I be?"

"Chasing your next story."

"Stories can wait." I lowered my face and kissed the top of his head. He smelled of medicine and hurt, and I wanted to wrap my arms around his body and melt into him.

The news broke the next morning. I woke up late and my head felt heavy. Frank wasn't in bed. His side was a tangle of sheets, with an IV pole next to it and a tray of medicine on the nightstand. The room reminded me of the hospital ward in Cedars Sinai.

I reached for my phone and skimmed through my emails and social media apps. Every single outlet from *Rolling Stone* to TMZ was going berserk over the label's accusations. They claimed Frankie Blade was responsible for the leak of the upcoming Hall Affinity album.

The air left my lungs as I read through the doubt-casting head-lines. I made the mistake of reading comments left by the *fans* on the band's Facebook page too. People were mean and heartless, and it saddened me.

In the kitchen, Hannah was working on Frank's lunch. I grabbed a cup of black coffee and retreated to the terrace to call Levi.

"This smells like a major lawsuit," he shared his theory. "Either your boy is going to drag their ass to court for libel if he had nothing to do with the leak, or they'll sue him for all the millions he owes them."

"I think you need to stop watching legal thrillers," I deadpanned.

"Cass, you don't have to be an expert to figure out why KBC is going public with this. They're tired of waiting for Frankie Blade to deliver another three records."

"Two," I corrected, but Levi did have a point.

I could understand why the label was pissed off. I'd also be pissed if I were the investor whose investment wasn't turning a profit. Hall Affinity signed a deal for five albums. Over ten years ago. Frankie Blade was part of the package. Their attempt to replace the singer was shut down by fans and I suspected by Frank's lawyers too, but my brain struggled to understand all the legal nuances of the music business right now. Artists sued labels. Labels dropped artists.

Isabella was a prime example of how the industry worked. Suits used and spat out people who weren't deemed worthy products, and Isabella was a new name on the block without a massive following and a disability that, for some reason, certain people saw as a drawback.

Only, Frank wasn't just any artist. He was my artist. My goddamn lifeline. Anyone trying to cause him any harm, emotionally or physically, became my enemy.

Besides, I needed more coffee to get my thinking cells going.

"Let me call you a little later. I have some ideas for the screening, but I need to get my head in order."

"Sure. Do you still want to do Bowl N' Roll?"

"Yes."

The annual charity event that took place every spring in Calabasas and I were in a *there's a thin line between love and hate* type of relationship. I loved the concept. Bowling with celebrities was always fun. But I hated the pretentiousness. I also hated the fact that a lot of the money stayed in the pockets of organizers while they claimed all the proceeds went to local schools to support music programs for youth.

"I can find someone else," Levi offered, sensing my hesitation.

"No. I'm going. By the way, don't forget about Ashton's birthday."

"How could I? Your brother asked for a Sony a7. Twice."

"How much is it?"

"It's two grand for mirrorless."

"Get out of here! Just give him a Best Buy gift card. Twenty bucks will suffice. My mother and I are already getting him a used car."

"All right."

"I'll talk to you later."

"Later, alligator." He hung up.

I stood on the terrace in my PJs, with a cup of coffee in one hand and my phone in the other, and stared at the raging ocean beneath my feet. It was beautifully dangerous, the breathtaking drop that made me dizzy each time I looked down, and I wondered if Frank had chosen to live here because of the adrenaline-evoking view.

I heard the slide of the door and his footsteps as he entered the terrace.

"What's going on, Frank?" I spun around.

Our eyes met. His face seemed tense, and a shiver zipped down my spine. "Nothing my lawyers can't handle." He attempted a smile.

"Is there anything I should know?" I pressed.

"No. Everything's fine, doll." He pulled me against the side of his chest.

His wild heartbeat told me he was lying, though. It just wasn't until two days later that I found out what was really going on.

———

Later that morning, I left for the Valley to check on my apartment and look at a used Toyota at the small dealership down the street from my gym. Or former gym since I hadn't been there in weeks.

A Navigator was parked in front of Frank's house when I returned. And after I got inside, I heard Dante and Johnny's voices battling for dominance in the office. The door was cracked and the unsettling words slipped out into the living room, ricocheting off the walls like invisible bullets.

The three of them weren't quite arguing yet, but I felt the growing tension in Dante's tone as he shot out a muffled string of sentences. The house was still, but the air was full of an electrical charge.

I set my bag on the couch and walked over to the office, stopping outside the door. Restless and full of worry, I couldn't calm my racing heart as I peeked inside. Frank sat in a chair. Johnny was leaning against the desk, gaze on the floor, arms folded across his chest.

"Why can't you be upfront with us for once, man?" Dante sounded distressed. He was pacing. I recognized the rapid thumping of his boots against the floor. His frame was out of my line of sight, but occasionally, I could see his hand as he rounded the room.

There was a pause and the distant hum of the ocean that seeped inside through the open terrace filled the void. Finally, Frank spoke, "The answer is no."

I didn't know what was going on, but my pulse raged in anticipation of the upcoming disaster. Then it happened. Dante threw out his ultimatum. It was like a trigger pull, deafening and attention-grabbing.

"It's not just you." His voice shook. "It's the four of us. We all depend on this tour. Our careers, our livelihood. You're so fucking selfish, you're ready to drag us all down."

"It's the best option considering your condition," Johnny chimed in. "Your royalties stay the same. Everything stays the same."

"How is it the same when someone else is going to sing my fucking songs?" Frank half-screamed, and his desperation broke my heart. I felt a tightness in my chest, as if invisible hands were pressing against it.

"It's that or you're out!" Dante took over the conversation again. "You're blind if you still don't see that this is for your own damn good!"

I swallowed hard to dislodge the rock forming in my throat.

The footsteps moved in my direction. It happened so fast that I didn't have enough time to react. The office door flung open and a cigarette pack flicked past my eyes as Dante marched out. I felt the accidental brush of his shoulder and the spike of temper consuming the oxygen around me. He clicked his lighter and whirled around. His dark gaze drilled right through me. "This is between me and your boy. Stop fucking eavesdropping, short stuff."

Blood rushed to my face. "Fuck you, Dante." My comeback was far from ladylike, but I was too wound up by what I'd just heard to stick to my manners.

He headed for the door to the terrace without a word, shoulders stiff, strides wide and obnoxiously loud. I stood in my spot, angry, left with the horrible aftertaste of loss in my mouth and staring at the empty space in front of me.

"Don't take it personally, Cassy," Johnny said from off to the side. "It's been a stressful week."

My head snapped up, and he was moving toward me, an apologetic smile touching his lips.

"Sure. Two against one. How fair." I scoffed.

In my peripheral, I saw Frank rise from his chair inside the office.

"Whoever said the music business was fair has never written a single song." Johnny shrugged and shoved both hands in the pockets of his jacket.

My blood ran hot, and my ears rang. I watched Johnny tread through the living room, waiting for Frank's final word, but none followed. The silence was both awkward and cruel. My sixth sense told me not to act on my rage, so I stayed mute. Frank was slipping away. He moved over to the window and glared at the mountains with his back turned to us.

Johnny circled the room again and started making his way to the front door. "It's nice to see you, Cassy." He yanked his hand out of his pocket and waved at me. The gesture was less than enthusiastic.

Outside on the terrace, Dante was finishing up his cigarette. He stepped back into the house for a short second and said, "Tell Frankie-boy to think about my offer. He still gets to keep his share and write songs if we look for a different singer to take with us on the road. If his dumb ass wants to fight us on this, he'll lose. This is me being fucking civil, being his friend for once and seeing this shit for what it is, a fucking train going off the rails next time he decides to take the stage. The best thing he can do right now for everyone, for his own health, his parents, and his fans, who pay for all his houses and cars, is to stop trying to do the impossible. Ask his fucking doctor if you don't believe me. He needs another surgery."

Dante's speech was like a punch to my gut. Everyone seemed to know about it, and the fact that Frank hadn't mentioned anything to me hurt. He had no idea that I'd overheard the doctor talking about it at the hospital.

"If you really care about him, you'll see that I'm right."

His words rattled inside my head long after the Navigator disappeared behind the gate. I walked across the living room to shut the front door Dante had left standing wide open, then returned to the office.

Frank still surveyed the mountain view outside the window, his frame a sharp work of art against the backdrop of the cloudless California sky.

"Why didn't you tell me about the surgery?" I asked carefully. A strange fizzy feeling settling in my stomach. "I heard the doctor discussing it with your mother at the hospital. Why are you shutting me out?"

He dismissed my question. "They're looking to get someone else to sing live."

"But you'll still have all the creative control?" I clarified as my brain struggled to stay calm.

"It's my fucking band, Cassy." Frank spun to face me. His arresting gaze was a black hole, a vortex of hurt, wrath, and misery. I felt his hopelessness clutch at my lungs. The air between us burned a destructive, invisible fire. "I created the idea. I created the music. I'm not going to sit and watch some imposter trying to butcher my songs and all that my art stands for."

He sounded greedy and irrational. He wasn't light anymore. He was dark. Dark I hadn't had a chance to face yet but was about to.

Part of me blamed his anger on bad timing and medication, but another part of me blamed everything on Dante. He'd never given me a straight answer, but he'd never denied anything, just like Frank. It was as if their demons had conspired against me and their minds to keep doing the things that would bring them more grief and pain.

"You don't have to make a decision right this moment," I said as I watched him cross the room. He stopped in front of the mahogany cabinet and pulled out a bottle of what looked to be expensive whiskey.

Oh no.

My spine stiffened. Alcohol wasn't his friend right now. Not while he was shattered and while a mean cocktail of painkillers and other pharmaceuticals filled his bloodstream.

"Frank?" I called, approaching him from behind.

Silent, jaw tight, he grabbed a clean glass and poured himself a shot. No ice.

"Frank?" I pressed, stepping closer. My hand reached for his forearm, and his vein pulsed hard under my palm. He stood motionless for a while, fingers wrapped around the glass.

"First, he fucked my wife. And now, he's fucking me." I heard him say.

The room felt small. The entire house felt small. The world suddenly wasn't big enough for the two of them.

My stomach quivered and my breath caught. I didn't know what to say or do, because this, the battle against all the vices that drove people to their graves early in life, was new territory for me. Sure, I'd seen what it did to my father, but I had no idea how to fight it, because I was scared of it.

Frank drew away from my touch and moved to the center of the office. He stared at the glass in his hand, his chest rising at each strained inhale.

"Some kind of friend he is, huh?" His voice was a chill against my bones. His clouded gaze flicked over to me.

Wave after wave of angst flowed through the room. I felt it wrapping around my neck like a rope, squeezing me, cutting off the air.

"Frank," I squealed, trying to breathe through yet another episode of brain freeze. "You don't have to do anything about it today."

"Sure, I don't." He scowled. "Then they can all get a head start on stealing what's mine."

I wasn't prepared for what came next. Frank hurled the glass and it shattered when it hit the window. My body shook with awareness. He hurried out of the office without looking at me, and I followed him on a whim. We didn't speak. It was a silent run through the house as he marched past the paintings lining the walls of the hallway, leading us to the east wing, where his studio was.

I didn't have the right words, but I was too scared to leave him alone. Hannah wasn't around and Janet and Billy had gone back to Arizona for a few days to give us space. If Frank planned on acting stupid, I needed to be near to at least try to stop him.

"I want to be alone for a while," he said when we reached the studio.

I halted. My heart unhinged at the sound of his words.

Tilting my chin up, I asked, "Should I pack?"

Frank looked at me and confusion came into his eyes. They roamed my face in search of something, but I had no idea what. "No." Then came a slight shake of his head. He pulled the studio door open and disappeared inside.

I was left standing there by myself. No explanations. No apologies.

A small fraction of me resented Frank Wallace at that moment because my gut told me that this was the beginning of the end. Our end. I just didn't want to believe my gut. For once, I wanted my instincts to be wrong.

Chapter Four

He crawled into bed at sunrise. The mattress dipped under the weight of his body as he settled against the pillow. Soft fingers reached for my hair.

"I'm sorry about yesterday, doll," his voice, low and flat, came from above.

My chest felt heavy and my stomach squeezed. I hated everything about Frank's tantrum, but at the same time, I worried for him like crazy. My emotions had been at war the entire night. My pride told me to leave and let him stew in his anger. My heart had a different opinion.

"You didn't deserve it," Frank whispered as if he'd just read my mind. His knuckles brushed my cheek.

I rolled over to my back and stared up at him. "Why didn't you tell me about the surgery?"

"I didn't want to freak you out."

"Really? That's your excuse?"

"You have your hands full."

"That doesn't mean you should hide things from me. That's not how it works."

Frank was silent. His gaze wandered around the bedroom aimlessly. I'd left the shades up when I went to sleep and daylight was slowly creeping inside through the massive window. The ocean rumbled softly as the clouds of morning fog floated lazily across the sky.

Sensing his tension, I sat up and studied his face. "You wanted me near, so here I am. Talk to me."

His features remained hard, his eyes dark and stormy. "The doctor said there's a risk the plate fragments could reach the artery."

Dread prickled my spine. I needed a moment to process. "What does that mean?"

He dismissed my question. "It'll be fine. It's only a temporary setback, doll. The surgery should take care of the problem."

"Frank." I turned to face him. "You need to take a break."

He looked at me strangely. "I am taking a break."

"No, you're not resting enough."

"What do you suggest? That I just let it all go? Twenty years of my life? I thought we had this conversation yesterday."

"I know you're going to hate me for saying this, and yes, Dante is an asshole, but he's right. You're not well enough to keep up with the touring schedule."

"Don't, Cassy." He shook his head in denial.

"Okay, fine. Have it your way." Annoyance coursed through me. I slid from the bed and grabbed my phone from the nightstand.

"Where are you going?"

"To do some work," I said as I headed out. "Please get some sleep."

The office was quiet. My laptop sat on the desk next to Frank's. The first rays of light that peeked shyly from behind the mountain range spilled over the walls and floor. I flopped into a chair and spun, trying to get my thoughts in order.

Levi was right. Frank monopolized all my time, even when he wasn't around, and I hated it because there were other things that required my attention. My brother, my mother, my prior commitments to *Rewired*. End of the year editorials. Lastly, Isabella's documentary.

We'd already conducted over twenty interviews and collected a great deal of new footage. It made sense to start cutting the rough draft, but Levi wanted to wait a few weeks in case Frank was willing to make another appearance at the upcoming rehearsal or a live show. Only, I wasn't sure he had the time or desire for philanthropy. At least, not right now.

I spent the entire morning researching potential venues for the screening and sending emails. It was nearly noon when a Jay Brodie PR press release hit my inbox.

An hour later, the news was all over social media.

KBC Universal confirmed they weren't sure Frankie Blade was fit to continue as the lead singer of Hall Affinity.

There were no further comments from the label's rep or the band's management, but the following morning, Jay Brodie issued another statement to the press.

Dante Martinez Doesn't Want to Tour with Frankie Blade, the tabloid headlines screamed.

Those weren't Dante's exact words, but he agreed with KBC nonetheless, and that was all the press needed to spin it the way they wanted for more shock value.

Something was coming. I felt it with every cell in my body. Something dark. Something disturbing.

It happened right after Thanksgiving.

The world was festive and happy in anticipation of the upcoming holidays. Brooklyn hired a designer to set up a huge Christmas tree in the front yard and another one in the living room. Billy and Janet flew back from Arizona because of the legal dealings with the rest of the Hall Affinity band members. Nothing was official yet, but it was going to happen sooner rather than later. Dante and Johnny were in talks with their attorneys as well.

The word *lawsuit* lingered in the cool air like a stray snowflake after a storm.

As opposed to Frank's family, mine was modest when it came to celebrations in general. My father had always managed to make our holidays miserable.

Thanksgiving at my mom's was quiet. On Black Friday, I took Ashton to the mall to buy him a video camera. Then we went to help our mother with her Christmas tree.

After six hours of unpacking, arranging, and hanging all the ornaments, we sat in the living room and stared at the results of our labor with cups of hot cocoa in our hands.

"When were you going to tell me about your boyfriend?" my mother questioned out of the blue.

I shot a sideways glance at Ashton. He slumped in his chair silently, eyes wide.

"When the time was right?" I squealed, slurping on my drink.

"What does he do? Isn't he in some kind of rock band?" Apparently, my mother knew very little, which was a relief.

"He is." I nodded.

"I hope he's not doing drugs, Cassy."

"No, Mom. He's not."

Liar! my voice screamed inside my head.

We left my mother's an hour later.

"Did you tell her?" I punched Ashton on the shoulder as soon as we climbed into my Honda. I didn't dare drive the Porsche in this part of town.

"Ouch." He winced.

"You know this is just between me and you."

"I know, but you're gone all the time. She keeps asking where you are when she calls."

"Tell her I'm in the shower." I flung my hands in the air and gave him a dead stare.

"She's going to find out sooner or later. It's online anyway."

My brother's words were an equivalent of a kick in the head. "*What's* online?"

"You and Frank." Ashton pulled out his phone, typed something in, and handed it over to me.

There on the screen was a collage of our TMZ photos, along with the information about my height, weight, hair color, and a list of all the places I'd allegedly either been seen with Frank or in his proximity. Not all the information was accurate, but the blogger made a pretty good argument.

My pulse tripped as I read through the post. "Shit." I heard myself mutter as I returned the phone to Ashton. "Can you send me the link?"

"Why can't you just come out with it?" he pondered.

"It's a little bit more complicated than that." I started the car.

"What's complicated about it?"

"Oh, Ashton." I shook my head with a sigh. "Trust me. You're about to find out. Adulting is hard."

I dropped off my brother in Burbank and headed to Malibu. It was nearly midnight when I finally pulled up to the house. The lights inside were off and the darkness worried me.

Frank didn't care about electricity. There was always something blazing either on the terrace or in the living room at this hour, especially with guests over and the Christmas decor extravaganza set up.

I marched through the house, looking for signs of life, but the silence was thick, almost impenetrable. Chills rolled down my spine.

"Frank?" I called, traveling over to the east wing. The door to the studio was wide open, and that's when I saw him. He was hunched over the mixing board, a drink sitting next to him.

I stopped on the threshold, unsure whether entering his private space where he created his songs was okay. It was one room inside the house I'd been to once briefly, the room that was off limits to anyone who wasn't somehow involved in making music.

Cold danced along my skin.

"Hi," I said, shuffling my feet.

Frank lifted his gunmetal gaze from the board and looked at me through the darkness. The studio didn't have any windows, so its only source of light was the glimmer of the control buttons and the streak of moonlight hitting the stretch of hallway behind me.

He continued to stare. No words were said. I took it as permission to enter the room.

My eyes slid to the drink. I took a deep breath and tried to calm the burst of panic and rage forming within me.

"How was your day?" Frank asked absently, leaning back in his chair. His voice was a soft slur, and his right arm, which was still set in a cast, hung limp. He was scheduled for a second surgery next week.

"I saw my mom and hung out with Ashton. How was yours?" I skipped the part about the fan site my brother had come across. I'd send the link to Linda instead.

"Oh, you know. Same shit. My best friend is trying to steal my band." The anger in his tone was disturbing.

I reached for his shoulder. "Let's go to bed."

He shifted and rested his left hand on my thigh. I felt the tremor of his grasp against my skin and smelled the liquor on his breath. Old memories of my father swept me under. He hadn't been a violent drunk, but his indifference had hurt me just as much. He hadn't been there for us when Ashton and I needed a ride to school, because our mother was working two jobs. He hadn't been there for us when everyone else's parents took their kids to Disneyland, because he didn't want to leave the comfort of our apartment. He didn't like the world and the world didn't like him, and in the end, his responsibilities had crushed him. We, his own family, had crushed him.

The darkness inside the studio began to choke me, but I stepped closer and gave in to the lingering warmth of Frank's sloppy embrace. I let him wrap his arms around me, let him rub his stubbly cheek over my shirt. He was like a child. Uncertain in his thoughts and his movements. Together, we were plummeting into an abyss of desolation. And I didn't like the emptiness this fall filled me with a single bit.

"Come on," I whispered, brushing my fingers through his hair. "You need to lie down."

"I hate this," he mumbled into my chest.

"Frank, you're drunk and it's late. Why don't we talk about this tomorrow when your head is in the right place."

"My head hasn't been in the right place for years, doll." He laughed bitterly.

"Don't say that."

"I counted all my surgeries today. Do you want to know how many times I've gone under the knife?"

I felt the hard press of his cast as he slid closer and molded his body to mine.

"Sixteen."

"Do you want me to call the doctor?" I asked the first thing that came to mind. I didn't know if he was in pain or just delusional from the mixture of pills and alcohol, but the shake in his voice worried me sick.

"No."

"Do you want me to get Janet?"

"They're gone."

"Back to Arizona?"

"Yes. I'm tired of people."

"Frank, you need rest. All this legal stuff is wearing you down. Can you stop worrying about it for a few days?"

"That's easy for you to say, doll. You don't own a fucking million-dollar enterprise."

His words cut me open. I pulled my hands out of his hair and took a step back, needing to create some sort of distance between us. He hadn't been the same since the accident, and each day that passed put us on completely different ends of our relationship spectrum.

"I'm sorry." I heard his whisper. "That's not what I meant."

"What *did* you mean?" I asked, balling my hands into fists.

The silence grew thick. The room felt hot and the air burned my lungs and throat. I couldn't breathe. This, the way we were now, was suffocating me. It was as if he was speaking an entirely different language, a language I didn't understand.

Ignoring my question, Frank posed his own. "Have you ever skydived?"

"No, Frank. What does that have to do with us?" Exhaustion clutched my voice.

"I did it a couple of times before the crash." He fell back into the chair, his gaze never leaving mine. "There's this moment, right after you jump out of the plane, when the wind hits you and all your bones vibrate... That's always the scariest part because you lose control of everything you are and your mind freezes. It's beautiful. That fraction of a second when you don't need to decide or do anything. Instead, you just let the world carry you. Then it hits you. All the responsibilities that are waiting for you below. You have two options. Keep flying or deploy the parachute."

Frank quieted.

My heart thump-thumped in my chest like crazy.

"You know what I always thought about when I was deciding whether I wanted to die flying or go back to Earth and continue being the puppet that I was?" He gave me a sad one-sided smile.

I shook my head.

"I wondered if people needed me. I wondered if I was making them happy. Because if I couldn't make my own mother happy, how would I make a stranger happy? I felt her repulsion toward me every single day of the first three years of my life."

"What are you talking about, Frank? You make your parents happy. You and your music make millions of others happy. You make *me* happy." Not at this particular moment, but he did nonetheless.

"I made you sad, Cassy."

"That's not true."

"That's what you said when we met. Remember? 'Ambivalent' reminded you of your father. The ones we love the most hurt us the most. That's the way it's always been and that's the way it will always be."

"You made me feel, Frank. That's what music is meant to do."

"Feelings are overrated."

That was the strangest thing that had ever come out of his mouth. "You're drunk."

"Look who's talking." He laughed softly. "If my memory serves me right, you were hammered when we met."

"It wasn't my best moment."

"Oh, it definitely was. I wouldn't have asked you out otherwise. Yoga is a big turn-on."

I bit back my smile as the memories of my first unofficial meeting with Frank during Dante's party flashed through my mind. The man could be a charmer when he wanted.

"You don't believe me?" He cocked an eyebrow.

"I believe you, but can we talk about it later?" I held out my hand, hoping he'd get the hint. "I have a really long day tomorrow. My mom and I are trying to find Ashton a decent car for his birthday, and I need to be up early to make it on time for Isabella's studio session."

"Give him one of mine."

"Don't be ridiculous." I stepped closer, gesturing for him to get up. "He's eighteen. A Ferrari will be out of his league probably for another ten or fifteen years."

"You underestimate him. I drove my first car when I was fifteen."

"You're an exception, Frank. My brother is not. He needs to learn what it means to actually earn things, not just get them at the snap of a finger from his sister's boyfriend."

"Say that again."

"Which part?"

"The boyfriend part." His lips stretched into a lazy, drunk smile. He was impossible to be mad at. "I like it."

"Will you please stop being a baby and let me help you?" I grabbed his hand, and when he wouldn't budge, I rolled my eyes and said, "Boyfriend." His smile turned into a huge grin and he stood.

His body swayed dangerously as we walked through the hallway. The house was still and quiet, and all the Christmas lights in the living room were off. I stopped for a second to turn them on, and Frank continued into the bedroom on autopilot. He slowed down when he was halfway there and leaned against the wall for support. Then his back brushed the frame of one of the paintings as I hurried to catch him. He was heavy against my shoulder and we were a messy tangle of clothes and limbs when we finally reached the bed. He sat on the edge, his head hanging while I rearranged the pillows to make sure they were high enough for him to be comfortable.

"Don't do this again," I said, my voice something between a shake and a gasp as I struggled to lay him down.

The smell of liquor hit my face when he began to ramble, "I'm putting you through hell, aren't I?" His palm slipped over the curve of my hip.

"You are," I agreed, sitting next to him. "But I'm willing to stick around." It was half joke, half the truth.

"You don't have to."

"That's what people do, Frank." I drew a deep breath through my teeth. My stomach was woozy with what I was about to say. "When they love someone. They stick around."

The elephant had entered the room.

Frank didn't react. His fingers were a fixed grip around my waist. I didn't know whether the lack of response was a case of melted brain from excessive liquor consumption or just an honest kind of reply because he didn't have anything to say to me in return, but the silence hurt.

I freed myself from his grasp. The floor beneath me shifted and the oxygen left my lungs.

"Cassy?" he rasped out in a weak, dying whisper.

I wanted to take my last sentence back. Badly. I'd messed up. I shouldn't have said it while he was drunk, but I'd been carrying these feelings around in me for so long, they were bound to run free one day.

"I think I'm going to work for a bit. Get some rest."

I walked out of the bedroom and shut the door. My chest went in and out, following the mad beats of my weeping heart. I hated how attached it was to Frank, how my every cell wanted to be glued to his forever. He was like the nucleus of an atom, binding all my neutrons and protons together within him and keeping me whole.

Stupid, stupid Cassy, my inner voice screamed as I rushed to the living room, toward the lights. The walls and the windows glittered as greens, golds, and reds slid across them.

My phone squawked in my purse on the couch. It was late, but I grabbed it anyway. The text was from Linda. She wanted to know how I'd come across the article about Frank and me.

My brother. Do we have a problem?

Linda Schwab: Not unless it gets on TMZ or BuzzFeed's radar, which is highly unlikely. I'll keep an eye on it.

Thank you.

Then I paced. This house was suddenly suffocating me with its luxury, but I was too scared to leave Frank alone. What kind of woman would desert her man when he was at his lowest? It didn't feel right. So I stayed. I returned to the bedroom and lay by his side, listening to the sound of his labored breathing until sleep finally swept me under.

Frank was still in bed when I left for Hollywood. A conversation about what had happened last night, specifically the drinking part, was in order, but I decided to postpone it until the evening because my mother was waiting for me.

We drove down Sunset and stopped by a few smaller dealerships. I wanted to look for a car online and pay for it in cash, but she insisted on getting a loan to help Ashton build his credit.

"Mom, you understand if you co-sign and he doesn't make a

payment on time, it'll screw your credit too?" I tried to reason with her as we were leaving the first lot. "And it'll happen."

"It's not like I'm going to buy a house anytime soon." She brushed me off.

"Funny, you never offered to co-sign when I was trying to get my first car," I noted, getting behind the wheel of my Honda.

"You never asked. You just did whatever you had your heart set on without checking with me or your father."

We shut the doors and were cocooned in the comfort of my modest vehicle. This was the first time in years she'd brought up dad and it struck a chord with me.

"Mom." I spun in my seat and looked at her. "Can I ask you something?"

She flipped the visor and fixed her lipstick. "Sure."

Years of working two jobs had worn my mother down, but she was still a beautiful woman. Today, she'd styled her hair into a French twist and had put on daring makeup. These past couple of months without Ashton around had been good for her mental health, but while I enjoyed seeing the spark in her eyes, the fears were still there, constant and obvious. She desperately clung to the fading traces of youth and it was difficult to watch. Oftentimes, I wondered if the loneliness she'd been living in ever since my father walked out wasn't only his fault but also my and my brother's.

"What is it?" My mother flicked her gaze at me, eyes curious.

The question was stuck in my throat, heavy like lead. I swallowed past it and muttered, "Do you remember when dad started drinking?"

She froze, lipstick still open between her fingers. "Why do you want to talk about him? He's a goddamn quitter." I could hear her anger.

"I just—" My voice broke. "I just want to know how it started. I don't remember seeing him sober. Ever."

My mother closed the lipstick and tossed it in her purse. "That's because he never was." She turned her head away from me and glanced at the stretch of parking lot ahead of us. "First it was a beer or two after work, then it was beer for breakfast and vodka for lunch until he lost his job and then his license."

"What about rehab or AA? Did he ever try?"

"I talked to him about it many times. He promised to get help, but it was always *tomorrow*. He kept feeding me those tomorrows for years." She turned to me, and her tired face went blank for a brief moment. "You can't help someone who doesn't want to be helped, sweetheart."

"Do you know where he is right now?"

"No, and I don't care." Her expression was full of worry. "What's gotten into you? Don't tell me you want to see him?"

"No, it's not that. We just never talk about him."

"There's nothing to talk about. He left."

The urge to scream and bang my head against the steering wheel was so sudden, my solar plexus convulsed. Drawing a deep breath, I slid the key in the ignition and started the car.

"Good riddance." My mother scoffed, fighting the seatbelt. "We're better off anyway."

She wasn't wrong. Between living without a father or living with a money-sucking body, the choice was obvious.

Next, we made a stop at another dealership. Our fifth for the day. I was fixing myself a coffee at the refreshment station when my phone began to buzz. The texter was persistent.

"How about that Mini Cooper, sweetheart?" my mother called from across the room, motioning at the bright red car that sat outside in the yard. "It's only eight thousand."

My phone continued to ping. "For Ashton? Are you out of your mind?"

"It's got low mileage." She rushed over, a brochure in her hand.

"Trust me, he will not get behind the wheel of this car, Mom. Even if it's free."

"You think?"

"I'm pretty sure." I pulled out my phone and checked the incoming messages.

Levi: Just got the word from Maria. Frankie's coming.

Levi: Get your ass here. Pronto.

Butterflies fluttered in my stomach. I didn't think Frank was still on board emotionally and mentally. Especially after last night. With everything going on, it seemed as if Isabella's album was the last thing he'd be interested in.

"Mom?" I tore my gaze from my phone. "I have to be somewhere. Can we resume tomorrow?"

"What's the rush?" my mother questioned as I ushered her outside. "Is it your boyfriend? Are you ever going to introduce him to me?"

"Probably. Eventually." I opened the Uber app. "I'm going to get you a car, okay?"

"Where are you going? Did something happen?"

"Everything's fine. It's just work."

Another string of messages attacked my phone.

Levi: You need to be here!

Levi: Right now!

Levi: You're going to miss it!

It sounded so end-of-the-world serious, I almost ran a red light on my way to the studio. Roman stood outside when I pulled up to the building. A couple of kids were hanging around the parking lot and my gut told me they were here for Frank. I cut the engine and grabbed my phone. Isabella's Instagram story featured my boyfriend. It was a two-second snippet of him and her band in the studio. For a man who had every intention of keeping all his affairs and charitable causes private, he wasn't very careful with this one.

I heard a tap. Roman's face swam into focus as I rolled down the window.

"Ms. Evans, it's best you go around and use the back entrance," he said, his sharp gaze dancing across the lot.

I tossed my phone aside and surveyed my surroundings. What do you know? In a car two rows over sat a guy with a telephoto lens.

Panic took over me. Squeezing out a meek smile, I gave Roman a nod and slid up my window.

The rear of the building was in a narrow, unkempt alley lined by dumpsters with chipped paint. A thick layer of grime covered the rough pavement. I parked next to a limo that took up three spots and looked around to make sure neither the pap nor the kids had followed me. The coast was clear. Only two security guards and a studio employee on a smoke break, all of whom I knew well at this point, were in the alley. Tossing a casual greeting at everyone, I made a beeline for the door. Then the moment I stepped into the hallway, I heard Frank's voice. The notes bled through the walls, pulsing through the stuffy air, filling the hollow parts of the space with bliss.

The music was unfamiliar. Isabella's vocals blended with his in the most exquisite way one person could complement the other. She was a rough wave against his elegant tenor and a trail of goosebumps rushed across my skin.

I felt my heartstrings come undone in my chest. *Snap. Snap.* One after the other. My pulse tripped. My knees were suddenly soft like Jell-O.

I had to stop for a second to catch my breath. The duet was stunning. The lyrics and the instruments were muffled, but I knew it there and then. This, the way their voices melded, was pure emotion. Raw. Powerful. Unstoppable.

I heard Brooklyn rattling off something before she entered the hallway, interrupting the music. Standing across the way with the phone pressed to her ear, she waved at me, her face tense as always.

I shot her an inaudible hello and carefully pulled the studio door open to sneak inside with as little disturbance as possible.

The room felt at least twenty degrees hotter than the hall. I didn't know if it was because of all the people gathered here or because of Frank. He sat in a chair in front of the drum kit, broken shoulder secured inside the sling, hair slightly disheveled, posture sharp, despite last night's drinking spree. A microphone stood nearby. A sheet of paper lay on his lap. Isabella was right next to him. Concentrating solely on the words, they weren't paying attention to their surroundings. This was an instrumental break and the music wrapped around me like a warm balm, each note a pleasant prick to my skin. Story grinned from ear to ear while strumming through the chords on his guitar. Andy and Kit looked completely frazzled.

The light on Levi's camera that was positioned on the opposite side of the room blinked red, which meant the session was being recorded. He and Ashton hung in the corner. I tiptoed to the couch and took a seat next to Maria. My heart thundered.

Frank hadn't said anything about being here today. He hadn't left the house since his release from the hospital. This change of heart was sudden and strange after yesterday's very depressing conversation. Part of me feared facing him now that those words had been said.

The instrumental break ended and Frank reached for the microphone and laid on more vocals.

The fusion of music and his voice sliced through me like a hot knife through butter. The drums pounded in my temples along with my own blood. My entire body was a mad surge of electricity, a crackling entity. A cloud of adrenaline, endorphins, and other hormones that were unknown to humanity.

My gaze darted between Isabella and Frank as I watched them trade off notes and lines. They were mesmerizingly beautiful in their brokenness. She was an invisible force and he was a kind mentor. His face looked thin and void of color under the harsh stream of overhead lights. Dark shadows beneath his eyes gave away the anxiety and the weight of his emotional turmoil, but there was a genuine smile on his lips. It brightened his features. It brightened the entire room and set my poor hammering heart on fire.

He didn't notice me until the song came to an end. The music stopped and a scattered but very enthusiastic round of applause filled the room.

"How about that, huh?" Frank grinned at Isabella, fumbling with the paper.

There was no doubt they were musically compatible. I still shivered from the abandon of feelings I'd experienced but had yet to decipher.

She grinned back. "I might have a spot for you in my band."

"I'll take it. I'm pretty good at back-up."

Everyone laughed. Frank was his normal charming self. His eyes landed on my face. "Nice of you to join us, Cassy." He smiled, his expression playful.

Our gazes danced an invisible dance, and I felt his remorse and his apology. I wasn't sure he remembered everything that had been said and done last night, but I forgave him there and then. Seeing how music transformed him and how much joy it brought into his life made me happy.

Nothing else mattered.

The rehearsal ran late. Frank was on a roll, so he sang a few more songs—one of Isabella's originals and three covers—before finally stepping aside.

Around nine, Brooklyn pulled me into the hallway and broke the news.

"There's a huge crowd outside."

"Shit. What do we do?" Cold panic twisted my gut. I wasn't prepared for the press.

She cleared her throat and said, "Ask Frank."

"What do you mean? Isn't it part of your job?" I hissed, gawking at her.

"It's whatever he wants to do."

With my heart in my throat, I returned to the studio, where the band had already started to pack. Everyone said their goodbyes, and although Frank was pale with exhaustion, his voice was the loudest in the buzz of excited chatter that went around the room.

Ashton and Levi were putting away their gear. Brooklyn paced. The entire building felt as if it had been turned upside down.

Finally, after all was said and done, the band poured into the hallway. Cases with equipment rattled while shrieks of laughter bounced between the paraphernalia-lined walls. Maria and Levi were the last ones to leave. Ashton stood outside the door, waiting.

"There are a bunch of reporters in the front," I told Frank nervously.

"I know." His gaze found mine. "It's okay."

"We'll be all over the tabloids."

He stared at me intensely, his blue irises sparkling. "That's fine."

"Are you serious?"

"I don't want to hide anymore." His voice was a frail whisper.

My head spun. This was unexpected. We'd hardly discussed going public. There was no doubt I wanted it more than anything—the secrecy drove me insane. But we had no plan. My mother and Ashton would get caught in the fallout. "Me neither, but what about my family?"

"I'm sorry. I didn't think about that," Frank said calmly, touching my cheek. "There's a car waiting in the back that you can use." His eyes were bright and incredibly alive, and he shone like a lucid dream.

"What about you?" I wanted to hug him, but the fear of being accidentally seen by someone who had no business seeing us together rendered me motionless.

Frank grinned. "I'm going to go outside for a bit and sign some autographs." He pulled his hand away from my cheek and laced our fingers together. My skin went ablaze. We stood close, just a couple of inches separating our bodies.

"What about my car?" I asked, squeezing his palm gently.

"Roman will get it."

I nodded and his grasp weakened. Our hands fell apart as we walked out of the room. Face riddled with panic, Ashton was still waiting for me in the hallway.

"Umm, there's a bunch of reporters," he said, rubbing the back of his neck. "And I've got all this stuff." He motioned at the camera bags.

"Where's Levi?" I asked.

"Went to move the car."

"Text him to go around and meet us in the alley."

"I'll see you in a bit," Frank told me, smiling, then gave Ashton a pat on the back. "Are you keeping it gangsta, bud?

"Always." My brother's chin went up and his shoulders straightened. I would've sworn he grew at least two inches taller right before my eyes.

"Good. Just stay out of trouble," Frank said and headed over to the reception area.

The front doors swung open and I heard the noise coming from outside as it slipped into the building and carried across the corridor. Anarchy took over the parking lot. People shouted. Cameras clicked.

Frank was like a magnet. For a second there, it felt as if the energy of the entire city was gathered around him.

A limo waited for us at the rear of the building. Levi's truck pulled up a few minutes later and when Ashton got in with him, I was left alone. The silence soothed my erratic heartbeat. On Twitter, videos and photos of Frank and Isabella signing autographs outside the privately owned rehearsal space in Hollywood began trending long before he joined me. Roman had parked the limo around the block, and after he helped Frank inside, he hopped in the front.

"Home, boss?" he asked.

"Yes." Frank relaxed against the seat and pressed the privacy screen button.

I scooted closer until our thighs brushed. He breathed hard and loud, and fatigue lined his face. I could tell this had been a very difficult day for him physically.

"How are you feeling?" I asked.

Frank readjusted his arm in the sling and rolled his neck. "Like I've been fucking run over." He brought my hand to his mouth and kissed my knuckles. "I'm sorry about last night, doll."

There were so many things that I needed to tell him pivoting inside my head, I didn't know where to even start. My tongue refused to move.

"I can't seem to get a fucking break." He paused to catch his breath, eyes closed, chest heaving.

I wanted to straddle him and perform mouth to mouth so he wouldn't have to struggle, but I was scared I'd do something wrong. We hadn't had sex since before the accident. He was too strung out and mostly in pain and I was a ball of anxiety. But today, when I saw him sing, I felt hot in all the wrong places. His confidence made him sexy. One flip of a switch and I was a puddle of dirty, raw want.

"Did you find a car?" He rested his head back.

"Not yet. Shopping with my mother isn't fun. She wanted to get Ashton a Mini Cooper."

"You haven't shopped with my mother." He laughed softly while his eyes remained closed. "Janet is very... How shall I put it? Specific."

"Well, then our mothers will probably get along just fine."

"Probably."

Our hands rested in his lap.

"Frank?" I spun in my seat to face him. My throat tightened with the words that were trying to make their way out all at once.

"Hmm?" He didn't move. Having his fingers entangled with mine felt warm and nice. And extremely distracting.

My thoughts spiraled inside my head. I dipped my other hand in his hair and combed my fingers through it.

"What's wrong?" he said quietly.

"Please don't get mad," I whimpered.

"Did you do something?" His laugh caressed my ears.

"No, but I've been thinking a lot..."

"About what?"

My mind roared. I loved how in sync we were right now, but the events of last night were still fresh in my head and I hated that they reminded me of my father's weakness so much. "I know this isn't what you want to hear, but I really think you should take a step back from the band."

Frank opened his eyes and looked at me. "I thought you were on my side, doll?"

"I am on your side. What if you need a third surgery?" My voice was a plea of despair.

"I won't need a third surgery."

"You don't know that."

"What's gotten into you? Why are you so riled up?"

"I'm worried."

"What are you worried about? I'm fine."

"No, you're not fine, Frank." Here goes. "You know you shouldn't drink, but you did anyway."

"Is this about yesterday?"

I averted my gaze. "My father was an alcoholic."

"It was just once. It won't happen again."

"You didn't hear me, Frank," I insisted, my lower lip shaking. "I can't deal with this again."

"I heard you."

"Promise me you won't touch alcohol again."

"I won't touch it again."

We fell into dreadful silence. Sweat began to coat our palms that were pressed together. Jaw stiff, eyes hooded, he withdrew his hand first.

"This band is going to kill you," I said after a long pause.

"You want me to sit at home and receive handouts in the form of royalty checks while a bunch of impostors tour the world performing my songs?" he snapped. His voice was cold and bitter.

"Sometimes you're so fucking conceited you can't see past the end of your nose," I countered. Anger pulled at me and settled in my chest.

"The fuck I am! I created this band from my fucking blood and sweat, and now they want me out."

"Because you're hurting yourself, Frank!" I wasn't sure how else to get through to him. I was ready to pound the words into his head with a hammer if needed.

"At least I'm hurting myself for something that's mine, for something I believe in."

"You're not in the army. You're a musician. You don't need to be in that band all your life to give people what they want—songs. How can you not understand that?"

"I happen to like *that band*, Cassy. I happen to have millions of fans because of *that band*, millions of people who care about me."

"What about your parents? What about me?"

He stared at me unblinkingly.

"I care about you too. I don't want you to drop dead on stage somewhere in Cambodia, Frank. I want you to keep making music in a way that doesn't hurt you more than it already has."

He remained silent, confusion and pain twisting his features.

"You were breathtaking today. You don't need to be part of a band to write or perform music. You belong to you, no one else. Not your band, not the label. You have what every other aspiring singer on this planet wants, an incredible talent and an incredible voice, and you don't need anyone to sign off on the new songs you're going to write. You're free to do as you please if you just let the possibilities in. If a nineteen-year-old girl with a disability can do it, why can't you?"

My lungs needed more oxygen and every bit of me was trembling under Frank's dark, arresting gaze.

"Ah, fuck. Why do you always have to do that?" he murmured under his breath and slipped his hand to the back of my head to cradle it. "Come here, Yoko Ono."

There was an instant fire. My cheeks burned, my stomach lurched. I dipped my head and pressed my face against the hard curve of his neck. The hum of the engine droned in my ears.

"You know Paul McCartney admitted she didn't break up the band," I mumbled into Frank's T-shirt.

"Too late. It's already an urban legend."

"I'm not trying to drive you apart."

"Dang it." I felt the smile. It colored him and everything around us. "And I was hoping to blame it all on you."

"You could give it a shot." I stifled a nervous giggle. "But I don't think they'll buy it."

"You're awfully smart, Cassy Evans."

"And you're awfully tempting."

"Call it a match made in heaven."

"You think?" I put my palm on his pec and felt the low rumble of his heart, wondering if he remembered what I'd said to him last night.

"I'm positive." His hand slid to my neck and he tangled his fingers in my hair, tugging and playing with it. Pleasant shivers zipped down my spine. My panties were shamelessly damp against my swollen center.

Famished for his flesh and heat, I pressed a kiss to his neck. My lips slithered across his skin, stroking the ink lightly. I hadn't considered myself an awfully sexual creature until I met Frank. Everything about him—his height, his scent, his voice, his laugh—made my pulse race.

He pulled at my hair slowly and carefully to bring my face to his. His lips ghosted over mine and my nipples stiffened inside my bra. The torture was deliciously dark, like a box of chocolate truffles. Our chests heaved. Our frayed moans clashed. I was tender and tight between my thighs and I felt a wave of painful need sweeping me under when his skillful tongue probed my lips. He tasted of sweet sensation and I responded with a hungry, wet lick.

"Come here," Frank rasped into my mouth, resting his left hand on my ass to guide me.

"Are you sure? I don't want to squash you." Panic rushed through my stomach, tying it into a throbbing knot.

"As long as you limit yourself by riding my cock and not my broken shoulder, doll, we should be fine."

Hesitant, I balanced myself on my hip.

"I just want to feel your body," he whispered in my ear raggedly, pulling me over to his lap. Urgency was in his every movement. "We don't have to do anything if you're not comfortable." His hand roamed and he touched me greedily. His fingertips traced strange shapes over my clothes. I couldn't tell if he was writing something or simply drawing random pictures that came into his tired mind, but every inch of me was tense with desire. Thirst scratched at my throat. I straddled him, resting both hands on the seat behind his head. The leather upholstery squeaked under the weight of our bodies as we situated ourselves to get comfortable.

"I don't want to hurt you," I confessed, brushing my lips over the stress line above his nose.

He laughed against my cheek and ran his palm up and down my back, wrinkling the fabric of my top.

Discussing sex safety with my lover was strange. I'd never had to think about where to grab him and how hard to ride him before the accident. But now he was a wall of fractured bones and broken plates wrapped in scars, and I wanted to cuddle him into the softest blanket and lull him to sleep.

"You were so good today, Frank. You really were." I had to compliment him over and over again.

"Did you like the song?" he asked.

"I did."

"She wrote it. It's called 'Afterburn.' A beautiful composition."

"I loved your voices together. You were magnificent. You should record it with her."

"You didn't even hear the beginning."

"Trust me, I don't need to hear the entire song to tell you whether it's good or bad. I've been doing this way too long."

"Have you now?" He tossed his head back and eyed me, his gaze rapt.

"Please stop flaunting your life experience in front of me, Mr. Blade."

"Are you saying I'm old?"

"No, silly. You're not old. You're perfect."

He stared at me with the intensity of a thousand suns. "I hate this." His left hand slipped under the hem of my top. "I'm rich and hot and I can't even rage fuck you in my own limo." A smirk tugged the side of his mouth. Though miserable, he still found time to be cute.

"I can fuck you," I purred, rubbing against his growing erection. "I've got two hands and enough rage for the both of us." I held up my palms and squeezed my thighs invitingly.

He cupped my cheek. "I'm not with you because of the convenient sex, Cassy." His tone was heated but serious.

My stomach flipped.

"I know sometimes you doubt me and what we have."

I shook my head. "I don't—"

Frank pressed his index finger to my lips before my sentence made it out. "Let me finish, baby."

I swallowed down the words.

"I'm not a saint," he continued. "I did a lot of shit back in the day. I've seen and tried a lot of things. I've dated some of the richest and most beautiful women in the world, but I've never felt as at ease with anyone as I feel with you. You're not just there to agree with everything I say like most people do. You listen to me and you're not scared to speak your mind, and that means something to me. I don't want to be with a woman who's there because of what I am with the backing of my money. I want to be with a woman who's there because of what I am without it. I know you had doubts about us because we were this big secret and I didn't want the world to know about us. Truth is, I didn't want to share you with the world. I didn't want its jealousy and resentment to stain you. I didn't want this world to do to you what it'd done to me. But if I keep you to myself, the world is never going to know how wonderful you are."

Emotions jammed my chest. I couldn't separate them. They were a mix of everything and almost felt like too much. I bit my bottom lip to stop it from trembling and palmed his face.

"I'd still date you if you lived in a studio apartment in East Hollywood and played in a local band that had zero chance to get signed."

"If Dante succeeds in forcing me out, I'll definitely be looking for that apartment," he joked.

We were an odd couple. He was a hopeless medical case, and I was a woman in heat on top of him. The absurdity of this situation made me want to laugh. So I did.

"Was my speech funny?" Frank asked, grinning like a fool.

"Not really."

"Okay then." He paused, then the smile lines near the corners of his eyes deepened. "Do you seriously think Isabella and I should record a duet?"

"Yes, I do."

"I'll ask Brooklyn to reach out to Maria tomorrow."

I couldn't explain what exactly I felt at that moment. My heart was big and loud and drummed against my ribs so hard, I thought it was going to burst.

I love you, Frank Wallace, my inner voice said. *I love you and I won't let anyone harm you. Not your so-called best friend, not the world, not your demons.*

Chapter Five

Frank's second surgery went well. The doctors were able to remove the loose fragments and successfully replaced the plate in his right shoulder. He returned home from the hospital the same day and spent the first forty-eight hours in bed under the spell of a morphine-induced sleep. Janet flew in from Arizona to spend Christmas with us. Corey came by a few times. Brooklyn practically lived on the property. She was already on the phone in the office every morning when I woke up and usually stayed until after dinner. Roman slept on the ground floor of the east wing.

Ashton's eighteenth birthday was around the corner and between car shopping, the documentary, and keeping an eye on Frank, I felt as if there weren't enough hours in the day to get everything done.

Christmas wasn't my favorite time of the year, mainly due to the shitty memories of my father, who'd always gone off the rails during the holiday season, and this year, with everything that had happened in the past few weeks, I dreaded the worst. It was a strange recurring feeling of doom somewhere below my chest. Dark and confusing, it crept up on me randomly. During a shower, during breakfast, during conference calls with potential sponsors.

I worked in a spare room down the hall while Frank was slowly coming back to his senses after the surgery. My end-of-the year editorial for *Rewired* felt like a bitter goodbye and I almost teared up while typing it. We hadn't made any official announcements on social media about my stepping down yet, but Shayne's face was all over our YouTube channel and people started to take notice. I even received a few emails from the German fans. They were under the impression I'd left the magazine for good and wanted to know what publication I worked for now.

The biggest event of December, not counting Frank's surgery, was the inception of our film-baby's name.

It was official. We titled the documentary *Dreamcatchers*.

I loved it, and so did Maria and Isabella.

A couple of days after Frank's impromptu appearance at the rehearsals, Levi, Ashton, and I had gotten together for a night of pizza and brainstorming in my Burbank apartment. Of course, my brother's ideas were never good, but it seemed unfair to exclude him from the decision-making process. He'd worked his ass off these past couple of months. Obviously, I credited all his drive to Frank's involvement.

Some people wanted to change the world and some people wanted to meet celebrities while changing the world. My brother was the latter.

Bottom line, I had been ready to do whatever needed to be done to keep him away from the Xbox.

Things were great until several days after Frank's surgery when there came a call that ruined everything.

Levi and I had a meeting at the Guitar Center on Sunset with the Schecter rep about possible *Dreamcatchers* sponsorship. I was running late because Frank had been a pain in the ass all morning. His new meds made him moody and we'd spent a good hour fighting over a toothpaste tube.

"They cannot do this while he's in recovery!" Brooklyn's shriek drifting through the small crack under the office door caught me off-guard.

I was on my way out, but my feet stopped in their tracks on their own accord. My body stiffened.

"That's not what we discussed. He was looking into their offer." There were more words, some very angry and some very rude. Then a slam and a growl. A real fucking growl! The woman was pissed.

I walked over to the office and pushed the door open.

Brooklyn stood in the center of the room, face red, phone on the floor.

Dread seized my bones. "What's going on?"

She blinked at me rapidly. Her jacket seemed too small for her double Ds when she tried to breathe. "KBC is going to fire Frank."

I felt dizzy. "How?" My chest caved. "I thought he was going to move forward with what Dante proposed."

"The label feels he's a liability now. We kept the second surgery under wraps. I don't know how they found out, but they want him out altogether."

"How can they do that? Why now?" I couldn't wrap my head around what I'd just heard. Yes, I agreed with Dante. Frank wasn't fit to tour with Hall Affinity. I'd seen it with my own eyes—the misery he'd been in. But kicking him out while he was down was low, even for KBC. Their methods had been deemed questionable in the past, but this didn't sit well with me.

"They have a strong case." Brooklyn rubbed her temples to relieve pressure. "They're free to let artists go as they please, Cassy. We're not talking about a middle level record label here whose biggest client is bringing in all the money. We're talking about a major company who has all the money and who owns one of the biggest rock bands on the planet."

"Can't Frank's lawyers build a case too?" I sounded desperate. Like a child whose candy was being confiscated.

"For God's sake, Cassy!" Brooklyn whipped out her hands and waved them in the air, her eyes blazing with anger. "He had enough cocaine in his system to kill a damn cow the night of the accident. He clearly doesn't understand what he's doing anymore. One day he'll kill himself trying to somersault on stage per the fans' requests."

She knew! She fucking knew.

I felt as if someone had just punched me in the throat. My breath caught. I didn't know what exactly upset me more—the fact that Frank's personal assistant was privy to his medical records and I wasn't, or the fact that his record label was kicking him to the curb. Either way, things were shit.

Then came a long pause. Brooklyn paced the office, chewing on her bottom lip and cracking her fingers.

"Since when did drugs become a crime in rock 'n' roll?" I muttered.

"Parts of the contract were revised last year before the label went public with the reunion. Because of possible complications, neither KBC nor the insurance company want to be responsible for accidents caused by his mismanagement of his health. That includes narcotics."

"But that's ridiculous."

"It's not." She shot me a blank stare. "Hall Affinity is an investment, and KBC wants to protect that investment. There're plenty of bands that replaced the original singer and did quite well. Journey, Black Sabbath, Stone Temple Pilots. It's business, Cassy, and Frank is a casualty."

Whether I liked it or not, Brooklyn was right and I appreciated her honesty.

"I still need to tell him." She dropped her arms to her sides and strode past me. "Is he awake?"

"Yes. Do you want me to tell him?" I asked as I followed her.

"No, honey." She shook her head. "It's best you take a back seat for this one."

We found Frank on the terrace. I stood in front of the sliding door and watched Brooklyn through the glass. He sat in a chair and gazed at the waves crashing into the rock formations.

I had to remind myself to breathe. My heart thudded against my ribs, and my stomach turned. I couldn't see his expression while

Brooklyn delivered the news. Only his back and the slump of his shoulders. But I imagined the color leaving his face and the anger brewing in his eyes, and the scariest thing was that I could picture all these changes in such vivid detail, my brain almost hurt physically.

Brooklyn's features went sour. She waited for Frank to react, but he continued to stare into the distance as if the answer to all his questions was hidden somewhere on the horizon.

"He needs some space right now," she rattled off, stepping inside, and marched to the office.

My gut told me to stay away, but I went against its wishes and wobbled onto the terrace.

"I'm s-sorry." There was a stagger in my voice.

Frank remained silent. A mask of indifference covered his face.

I walked over to the chair and rested my palm on his shoulder, needing a physical connection with him. His muscles twitched from my touch, but he didn't react otherwise.

"Do you need anything?" I tested the waters.

"No."

"Do you want to lie down?"

"It's fine," he slurred. His stitches were still raw and sensitive and he'd taken a whole lot of pain meds earlier, which probably only worsened his current state of mind.

I could only guess what the news Brooklyn had dumped on him was doing to his head.

"Are you sure? You don't look very good."

"I just got fired from my own band, doll." He looked up at me. "What do you suggest I do? Celebrate?" There was a sudden shift in his tone, from indifferent to cold.

For a second, I'd forgotten about the meeting. My brain was preoccupied with Frank. I expected some sort of tantrum again, and the silence worried me more than ever.

"I want to be alone for a while," he finally said, his gaze trained on the ocean.

I felt rejected. "I can stay...We can talk about it if you want..." I offered meekly.

"I don't want to talk, Cassy. I want to be alone."

And just like that, he slipped away. From the world. From his responsibilities. From me.

The news hit the internet when I was battling the gridlock on the PCH. My phone buzzed nonstop. Emails, texts, and notifications kept coming, and as much as I wanted to shut it off, I needed to call Levi to tell him I was running behind.

I'll be a little late," I explained. My GPS, however, indicated the delay would be more than *a little.*

"KBC just dropped your boyfriend!" he yelled, voice wheezy. "Did you know about this?"

My mind was blank with rage. "Do we have to discuss this right now?" I was pissed at Frank for shutting me out and pissed at the label and the people there who deemed him another throwaway, someone they could use and abuse and then toss aside. Just like Isabella.

"What the actual fuck!" Levi continued to ramble. "Firing the face of the band."

"I really don't know what to tell you."

"Who the hell goes to see Hall Affinity for Johnny Z?"

Levi was right. Johnny was merely a regular guy next door in designer clothes with a bass strapped over his neck. Carter was a hired gun. He didn't have a say. His job was to smile for the cameras and keep those drums going during the shows. But then there was Dante. A guitar god. A virtuoso with the smile of a sinner and the manners of Casanova. He didn't have the gift of the voice, but with the addition of the right singer, his charisma and his solos could probably still sell out an arena. He was everyone's—women, fans, tabloids—favorite.

So, yes, realistically, the band could totally pull off the tour with the proper replacement.

My head pounded and I barely saw the road. It was all just a huge blur of cars. Different sizes and shapes with a wall of red brake lights and a throng of arms stuck out into the salty air.

"You know what? My mom's on the other line," I lied. "See you in a bit."

Unsettled, I killed the call and tossed my phone in my purse.

The Guitar Center was busy and the crowd made me oddly uncomfortable. I didn't know what exactly it was—worry for Frank or worry for our relationship, but halfway through the meeting, I excused myself and rushed to the bathroom to call Janet.

My emotions got the best of me.

I needed to know he was okay.

"I believe he's sleeping," Janet said.

"Will you please call me if there's an emergency?" I had no idea why I'd said that. It was my gut's idea.

"He just needs some time to process, child. He'll come around."

I returned to the floor, but my head wasn't right. Levi did most of the heavy-lifting for the remainder of the meeting, and I utilized the only tool in my arsenal that still semi-worked. My smile. My cheeks soon started to hurt from the constant flexing, but hooray! The rep seemed very interested in the project, specifically in Frankie Blade's involvement. He even joked about Dante needing to switch to Schecter. Poor sap probably hadn't heard about Dante and Frankie getting a divorce.

I felt like I should have mentioned this tidbit, but then again, what kind of a guitar company rep wouldn't know something that big?

When the meeting was over, Levi walked me to my car.

"I'm going to throw something out there," he said, tone serious. "Just don't get all wound up, okay?"

"Sure." I didn't think it was possible for me to get more wound up than I already was. My body ached. It was a strange phantom pain I couldn't explain, but I wondered if that was what Frank was feeling at this moment.

"This may be a good thing." He lowered his voice since we were in a crowded parking lot and every other person here was probably a Hall Affinity fan. "KBC dropping your boyfriend."

I stared at him with my mouth agape.

"Hear me out. If this is the label's final decision, going on record for *Dreamcatchers* can be our big break and his moment of truth."

"Are you suggesting he becomes part of the film? I thought we agreed this was going to be Isabella's story. We can't even begin to compare them. Their careers are light years apart."

"We already have an okay to use their footage from the last studio session. They're dynamite together. If he sticks to his plans and records the song with her, this is going to jump-start her career, along with his solo one."

"He won't do it."

"How do you know if you haven't asked?"

"I know. I'm his fucking girlfriend." Although lately, it hadn't felt that way at all. I felt like Frank's roommate. We'd stopped speaking the same language sometime after his accident. We'd stopped having fun.

"Well, don't jump into it." Levi rolled his eyes. "Feel him out first."

"He's a fucking mess," I hissed, instantly regretting the words. "Getting in front of the camera is the last thing he wants right now... Actually, I don't even know what he wants anymore."

"He's that bad, huh?"

"Yes."

"I'm sorry. I really am." Levi rubbed the back of his neck. "I know dude's going through hell after the surgery, and I'm not saying do it right this moment. But if you think about it, you'll see—this is a good thing for all of us. For me, for you, for Isabella, for him. There comes a moment in every major artist's career when he has to make changes. This is his. *Dreamcatchers* is a perfect way for him to be heard."

Levi's words made sense, but Frank was a wreck, and I couldn't fathom asking him to emotionally commit to my project.

"Why aren't you managing rock stars?" I asked with a smile. "You'd be pretty good at it."

"I already have a baby to grow and nurture. Besides, now that his mom is taking a break, it's double duty for me." He grinned.

"Asshole." I punched his shoulder. "Mom is on vacation. She's coming back."

"She better."

I drove home with the music blasting full volume. My choice of album was almost symbolic. I had an overwhelming urge to live through the pain of my first teenage heartbreak, so naturally, I played *Breathe Crimson*.

The first thing I saw when I pulled up to the house was the Navigator parked in the driveway and its owner smoking on the terrace. Roman stood nearby with his hands locked together. I called it his war pose.

I cut the engine and stared at the picture before me. It made no sense. Dante Martinez hadn't been on this property since the day he and Johnny came over to tell Frank they wanted a new singer. All the communication between the band members was done strictly via lawyers.

"What's going on?" I asked, stepping out of the car.

"Hey, short stuff. How are you doing?" Dante hollered from the chair. His right leg was swung over his left one and he was mouth-torturing a cigarette.

"Do you need a knife?" I gritted my teeth and began my approach.

"A knife?" He quirked his dark brow.

"Last time I checked, cigarettes weren't cutting it if you planned on stabbing someone in the back." I stopped at the bottom of the stairs and matched his hard stare.

He blinked at me a few times, then laughed. His laughter was rough and deep. Smoke puffs floated from his mouth and nose. "You've got some dark humor, darlin'."

He pulled the cigarette from between his lips and brought his body forward. For someone who smoked so much, Dante had awfully perfect teeth. White, shiny, and even. I wondered if they were real. I wondered if anything about him was real.

"Well, what can I say? Life taught me all my jokes." I couldn't read his expression. He was every bit the mess he should have been. Eyes bloodshot, cheeks sunken, hair tousled. Only, he wore his vices proudly. He didn't hide any of his bad habits, be it cigarettes or drug addiction. He didn't look high to me right now, but I couldn't think of any other somewhat logical explanation behind his visit.

"Frankie-boy isn't letting me inside." Dante motioned at Roman. "I want to talk to him. Can you get your man to come out?"

"I wasn't sure if you were on something." I hopped up the stairs and stopped in front of the door. "But I am now."

Dante's gaze followed me. "Come on. I drove all the way from the West Side."

"You should have called first."

"I did. Asshole hasn't picked up his phone since last century." He stared down at the tip of his cigarette and ashed it into the planter near the chair. His manners were nonexistent. Just like his compassion and sense of brotherhood.

"I don't want to be the middleman. If you need to talk to him about something, don't ask me to take messages."

"Come on," he groaned in frustration. "You're already the middleman. You've been one for a while now."

"I don't know what you're talking about," I brushed him off.

"I'm not that stupid, Cassy. I understand you more than you think. You're a young, idealistic, full-of-drive, never-bitten-in-the-ass-by-the-big-guys-before woman who thinks the world is still worth saving. I know he was open to my offer because of you. Because you agreed with me the first time around. Because you're scared for him. Because your judgment isn't clouded by all the love he's been feeding on all these years. He's so fucking terrified of letting all the people who worship him go because he still thinks he needs to keep making them happy in order to validate his existence."

My heart leapt into my throat. I turned to face him and took a step in his direction.

"Guess what?" Dante's gaze roamed my face. "He doesn't. He just doesn't see it. But I do. I have for a while now. You do too."

"And what do you see?"

Dante slipped his cigarette back in his mouth and took a long drag. "The world can't be saved, darlin'. As long as there are people like Lilly, your father, or my parents. The world is going to burn one day. We probably won't be here for the final countdown, but who's to say we need to carry its weight on our shoulders until our dying days. Especially if we systematically contribute to the reduction of our own term here, on this planet. Frankie-boy made history. He'll be fucking forever remembered. Now it's time he takes it easy."

Worry and confusion pulled at my chest. This conversation was more than I'd bargained for. "Why are you here, Dante?"

"I didn't have anything to do with the label's decision to fire Frankie-boy. I stood by my original offer. I want to keep writing music with him. We make good shit together."

"*Made*," I corrected.

"That's only if he wants to play the victim."

"I don't think victim is the right word here."

"It doesn't have to be." A grin flashed at me.

I rolled my eyes. Dante's attitude was a crossbreed of narcissism and arrogance, a whiny illegitimate baby of two really horrible personality traits that could never figure their shit out, but my feet remained fixed.

"If you want to be upfront, let's be upfront." I crossed my arms on my chest and waited.

"I'm a what you see is what you get kinda guy, darlin'." He put out his cigarette against the cement block the planter sat on and left it there. "Frankie-boy should at least get an ashtray." I heard him mutter.

"Whose idea was it?" I asked.

"Don't know what you're talking about, short stuff." Dante gave me a lazy shrug, leaned back in his chair, and switched legs.

"The cocaine," I whispered.

"Oh, I don't know. I think it goes all the way back to South American indigenous people. They didn't have lessons on recreational drugs in my high school. So I can't be too sure."

"Very funny."

"I was just trying to make you laugh. You look tense." The corner of his mouth tipped up.

"I wonder why."

Dante continued practicing his self-serving smirk on me. I continued to wait for his confession. We weren't going anywhere.

"You didn't answer my question. You wanted to be honest, then be honest."

"Which question? You asked a whole lot."

"This is pointless." I shook my head.

"Look, darlin'." Dante got to his feet and moved closer. "Do you really think standing in front of twenty thousand people is a piece of cake for someone who hasn't done it in seven years?"

"No, I don't, and look where it's gotten him. You're supposed to be his friend. You're supposed to watch his back."

"I never wanted things to happen the way they did. You know better than anyone that this is for the best. No matter what he wants others to think, the crash fucked him up. He can't do it. His body can't take the beating anymore. I'd rather have the label fire him so he can live a few extra years than have him continue to self-destroy. Tell me you don't agree."

In a sick way, I did. I agreed with what he said, but I still loathed him for his methods.

"You should have told him that yourself before the four of you made grand plans to tour the world."

"I did." Dante pulled out a cigarette pack and patted his pocket for his lighter. "He didn't listen to me. He didn't listen to his mother. Maybe he'll listen to you."

I watched him walk off and climb into his Navigator with my heart pounding in my throat. Every single thing that came out of Dante's mouth made perfect sense.

"You're still invited to the album release party!" he hollered from the car before closing the door. "Frankie-boy wrote the damn thing."

"Yeah, right." Amused, I rolled my eyes. "Fuck you and your party," I told him before he drove away.

The house was abnormally quiet. Brooklyn and the nurse had already gone for the day and I was expecting to find Frank either sleeping or on the back terrace, but he wasn't in either place. Anxiety gripped my insides. He wasn't well enough to be elsewhere. I checked the studio and the office next, then headed to the gym. Nothing.

Every one of my calls went to his voicemail. Panic rising, I rushed to the garage.

The Ferrari was gone.

"How the hell did you not see him leaving?" I fumed at Roman while Janet was having a breakdown in the living room. She looked every bit of her sixty-three years. Ruffled and on the edge, stress lines lodged deep in her face. Part of me wanted to hug her and tell her things were going to be okay, but I didn't quite believe the notion myself. Frank was upset and full of meds that came from pill bottles with a *may cause dizziness* warning. Oh, and he had one good hand, the same one that hadn't mastered the art of holding a spoon yet.

"Aren't you supposed to be his bodyguard?" I stared at Roman expectantly, waiting for an explanation.

"He must have left when I was taking a lunch break."

"Great." I palmed my head to stop it from spinning. Of course, it didn't help. "There are a dozen people in the house and no one heard him starting a car that sounds like a rocket launcher."

"I can reach out to a buddy of mine at the sheriff's station, Miss

Evans, but that will complicate things. If the man doesn't pick up his phone, he doesn't want to be found."

Janet was hysterical. "He's in no condition to drive a car. He can't even brush his teeth."

"I'm going to call Brooklyn," I muttered, stepping out to the terrace to get some fresh air. Despite the blasting AC, the house felt stuffy.

Brooklyn confirmed what Roman had said. If Frank didn't answer or return my calls, he didn't want to talk to anyone.

He just needs to cool down, she told me in a flat tone. Frank sure had an interesting habit of taking off without warning.

Minutes turned into hours, hours turned into an entire night. I tried to pass my time by alternating between checking TMZ headlines and pacing the terrace, but fear and memories twisted me inside out. Eleven years ago, my father did exactly the same thing. Left without telling anyone. And never came back.

No, Frank would never do something like that, my inner voice tried to cheer me up. *He has responsibilities.*

My father also had responsibilities. Us. Me and Ashton. He walked anyway.

Janet was passed out in the den and I was on my third coffee, checking social media and reading statistics on missing persons, when the cataclysmic rumble of the engine rolled through the front yard at five in the morning.

Phone clutched in my hand, I charged outside. The glimmer of headlights moved through the thick winter fog that hid the mountain ridges and covered the property. Sharp relief settled in my stomach when I saw the Ferrari mingling with the colorful blaze of the Christmas tree. The grind of its tires against the driveway was deafening as it pulled in. My gaze darted around the vehicle nervously, looking for damage or dents, but there were none. The front lights remained on, and they beamed bright, blinding me.

"Where the hell have you been?" I hopped down the stairs and hurried to the driver's side. The ten-hour-long panic attack and too much caffeine caused a quiver in my hands. "Do you know what time it is?" I cried out.

The window was down, but Frank didn't move. His left hand stayed curled around the steering wheel. His wind-tangled hair hung chaotically over his forehead and neck.

"You can't do this! You can't just take off whenever you feel the need." Trembling like a leaf, I pulled the door open and looked him over. "You could have crashed." The air outside was cold and small clouds of condensation left my mouth as I spoke.

"Been there. Done that," Frank gritted out, shutting off the engine. The soft shimmer of the Christmas lights skated across his cheeks.

Anger ripped into me. "Are you serious?" I dipped down, and my hands quickly roamed his chest and stomach. I didn't know what I was searching for. Maybe traces of blood, maybe scars that hadn't been there before he left, maybe my sanity. "We were worried sick." My voice broke as I continued to fumble with his clothes absent-mindedly.

"I needed to get out of this house," he said, sounding defeated, then suddenly grabbed my wrist. It wasn't a tender lover's touch. It was a *stop-it* touch. My desire to know he wasn't harmed annoyed him. I felt it in the vigor of his grip. His eyes closed for a moment, and the expression on his face was a strange mix of confused and morti-fied. Part of me wanted to yell at him and part of me wanted to wrap my arms around his body and cry like a baby. I did neither.

Instead, I freed my hand from his grasp and stood. I waited for him to move or say something. My pulse raced like the losing horse on a track.

"Come on. Let's go inside," I whispered.

No reaction. I got silence in place of a reply.

"Frank?"

His chest rose slowly as he drew in a long, calculated breath through his teeth. "I just lost twenty years of my life's work, Cassy. I'm not a very pleasant person to be around right now."

"I understand that and I'm sorry, but you don't have to do this alone."

Jaw tight, he turned his head to face me, and his eyes gazed up at me. They were dark and impossible to read. "I do. It's better that way."

My head spun in millions of different directions. My heart split right down the middle. At that moment, I understood why he'd experienced a delay during the crash. Shock. He'd never expected it, like I'd never expected him to say the words he'd just blurted out. *After everything we'd been through. After everything I'd given up for him.*

Hurt swirled in my stomach. I didn't need to be told twice. I was a smart cookie, as my mother would say. I got the hint. "Fine. If that's what you want."

Tears filled my eyes and the staccato beat of my heart made it difficult to talk.

Walk away, Cassy, my pride urged while my brain was trying to come up with a plan of retreat.

There was none. There was only a colossal amount of anger and the need to get out of here. Swallowing down my emotions, I rushed inside and started packing my laptop and my gear. My hands shook, but I kept on shoving everything in my bag without looking. I was mad and disappointed. With myself. With Frank. With life.

Watching a man who had the entire world at his feet and millions of dollars at his disposal sulk over the things he had no control over while he missed out on all the things he could actually control had become tiring.

Unshed tears blurred my vision as I hauled my bag down the stairs and to my Honda. Frank was still inside the Ferrari, withdrawn.

"You want to be alone?" I halted with my chin jerked up. "Fine. Be alone."

Silence.

"You've been shutting me out ever since you came back from the hospital," I continued, my voice a pathetic wobble. "I'm not an accessory. I'm here for you whenever you need me, whenever you feel down, whenever you're upset. Please understand, if you're going through shit, I'm going through it with you. I hurt when you hurt. I bleed when you bleed. I suffocate when you suffocate. I feel every single thing you do, yet you don't want to let me in. I'm willing to listen to all your secrets, all your desires, and all your pain and take everything with me to the grave, but you won't talk to me. You keep me at arm's length from your heart while I've willingly given you mine, and it's driving me nuts, Frank."

I heard the ragged pull of his breath, but his face remained an impenetrable mask of indifference.

"Look at me, Frank." My eyes sat on the elegant profile of his face.

He didn't react.

"Okay. Call me when you're done being a spoiled, self-centered, testy asshole," I spat, popping my trunk open.

His silence said it all. Frank Wallace had no idea how to be in a relationship.

Neither did I.

He was my first and probably my last attempt at steady. Fuck men and fuck commitment.

I drove off without saying goodbye to Janet.

A week had passed since my ridiculous fight with Frank. Apparently, my rock star was defective, and as much as I wanted my heart back, I didn't qualify for a refund.

In his defense, he'd been calling and texting like crazy, threatening me with a daytime visit to ensure enough people saw him in my apartment complex. It was the worst kind of blackmail. He'd even sent Brooklyn with a huge teddy bear with a card that said, "I'm sorry." Ashton had been roped into helping her bring that thing up the stairs and now the stuffed animal was taking up half the living room. But I didn't have the heart to throw Teddy away.

First, it was too big for a dumpster. Second, it was too cute to give up.

Frank Wallace had gotten under my skin. He'd owned my mind the entire week we'd been apart. Each time I came out of my room, the oversized animal's grin put a new dent in my pride.

It was the morning of Ashton's eighteenth birthday when Roman showed up at my front door wearing a jersey and a baseball cap. Still in my pajamas and without a lick of caffeine in my system, I gawked at him through the cracked door and wondered why he was here this early and, further, why he was here at all.

"I don't have any more room for flowers and stuffed teddy bears," I blurted out.

"Don't have any on me, Ms. Evans." Roman shook his head and peeked inside. "Didn't you get the message?"

"What message?" I'd pulled an all-nighter working on the email campaign for the potential *Dreamcatchers* sponsors and had gone to sleep close to sunrise. The last thing I'd cared about when the doorbell woke me was checking my phone.

"Boss would like to take Ashton car shopping."

"Come again?" I blinked through the fuzz in my brain and threw an over-the-shoulder glance at my brother, who was scrambling to his feet from the couch.

"Mr. Blade's present for his eighteenth birthday," Roman explained.

"No! He's not getting a car from Mr. Blade!" I snapped, ready to shut the door, but it was too late. My brother, who sported only junk food-themed boxers, pushed his way out onto the deck.

He stared at Roman with wide eyes as he stood there in underwear that was covered with soda and burgers. "Are you for real?"

This wasn't happening!

My mother and I had found a nice 2005 Toyota Corolla in Glendale two days ago and the owner had agreed to hold the car until tomorrow. We planned to tell Ashton about the present tonight during dinner. Frank and his bottomless pit of a wallet were about to ruin our surprise.

Roman's gaze darted between me and my brother. "Mr. Blade is waiting in the car."

My heart sputtered.

"Sick." Ashton grinned. "Give me five minutes, man."

"I'll be downstairs." Roman nodded and glanced at me.

"You're not going anywhere," I told Ashton as he breezed past me.

"Eat me, sis." Ashton shoved his middle finger in my face and slid back inside.

"I won't allow this!" I growled to the empty space in front of me.

"I'm eighteen. You can't tell me shit."

"Fine! Then I need half the rent before the first," I countered.

"That's blackmail!" he screamed from the bathroom. "Besides, I'm already working for free."

"It's called internship, asshole!"

"It's called slavery."

In my peripheral, Roman was cracking up.

"This is unbelievable." I gritted my teeth.

"We'll be in the car, Ms. Evans," he noted before leaving.

"Do I need to bring my social security card?" Ashton yelped from the bathroom as I shut the door and hurried to look for my phone.

"We're not going anywhere," I shouted, dialing Frank's number. My pulse roared and my hands shook.

His voice on the line was sweet and made me ache all over.

"You can't do this," I said. "You can't just show up here unannounced and fuck up my brother's birthday surprise."

"You haven't returned my calls."

"You wanted to be alone."

"Not anymore."

"It doesn't work that way, Frank. You hurt me and then send me cheesy presents, hoping a stuffed animal will earn my forgiveness back."

"You didn't like the teddy?"

"He's too big. There's not enough room for him in my apartment."

"There is in my house."

I took a deep breath to defuse the anger rushing through my blood. "I don't want you to buy Ashton a car."

"I'm sorry for being an ass."

"You're not hearing me, Frank," I pressed, my voice firm but my legs wobbly. "He needs to learn that nice things only come to those who work hard. Getting him a car right now will undo months of effort. It's not how you teach someone to be a responsible adult."

"Please let him have a fun day."

There was a knock on my door. "Are you ready or what?" Ashton bellowed impatiently and I knew then and there that I didn't have a choice. It was either let my brother leave with Frank or tag along to ensure he didn't buy a car he couldn't drive. Or worse—a motorcycle.

"Okay," I said into the phone, my tone flat. "You win. I'll be downstairs in twenty minutes... Actually, make it thirty. I haven't had my coffee yet."

"We can buy coffee on the way," Frank offered.

"I like my home-brewed coffee better."

"Okay," he agreed. "I'll see you in half an hour."

I took my sweet time getting ready, just to piss him off. There were nine hysteric messages from Ashton on my phone when I finally finished with my hair.

Downstairs, the Escalade waited across the street. Roman hurried to open the back door and I slid inside. Butterflies filled my stomach despite all the anger that still ruled my bloodstream.

Frank was seated next to me. "Hi, Cassy," he said, flashing me his signature playboy smile, the one he used for the crowds during his shows.

"Hey." I let my eyes wander over his body. He wore a pair of jeans and a T-shirt. A jacket was thrown over his shoulders, right arm in a sling.

We hardly spoke during the drive. My mind was preoccupied with my mother. I wasn't sure how to tell her about this.

Hey, Mom! The man who may or may not be my boyfriend just bought Ashton a car for his birthday. You can put the money back into your 401k.

Thinking about the range of her possible reactions gave me whiplash.

Ashton enjoyed the spotlight. After assuming DJ duty, he and Frank launched into a lengthy discussion about the lyrical content of Body Count songs.

We eventually arrived at a car dealership in Beverly Hills. The lot stretched over the entire block and looked unapproachable with its glimmering rows of luxury vehicles that my brother had no business dreaming about, let alone driving.

"Frank," I muttered over Ice-T's rapping as we pulled into customer parking. "This is too much."

Ashton killed the music. The door swung open and the hum of the lot poured inside. He jumped out of the car so fast, I didn't even get a chance to blink.

Frank remained in his seat, his hand covering mine. He turned to look at me and I heard deep, anxiety-ridden breaths. "Please come back, Cassy."

The words were a shockwave inside my head. A warm, gooey feeling filled my chest. The man didn't waste time. He went straight in for the kill, bypassing explanations.

"I thought you said this was a relationship?" I glared at him, dumbfounded. My heartbeat thrummed in my temples.

"Yes. It *is*." He stressed the present tense. "And I want you back in my life."

"But that's not how relationships work." A shaky exhale left my lungs. "It's not always about hot sex and midnight drives to Ventura County. It's about being there for each other when people are at their lowest. And you don't let me do that for you when you hit bottom. You shut down and you won't talk to me."

I didn't understand how exactly I knew this since I'd never been in a serious relationship before. My knowledge seemed to have been gathered from my own childhood observations of my parents. Everything my father hadn't been able to give my mother was what I wanted. And I wanted it from Frank. The whole nine yards. I just didn't know whether he was capable of giving me the things I longed for.

The real Frank Wallace, the one most Hall Affinity fans didn't know, was a very complicated man. A man with demons who kept crawling out of their hiding places, and the prospect of meeting them terrified me.

"I wasn't in a good state of mind, doll," he said quietly. "I had to let you go because I didn't want to hurt you."

"But you did hurt me, Frank. I cracked my heart open for you and you didn't even acknowledge it."

"And I'm sorry. I truly am."

"I don't know if that's enough anymore," I confessed. "Is this how it's going to be every time your head isn't in the right place? Are you just going to shut me out until you feel better?"

"It won't happen again."

Ashton's excited voice slipped into the car. He and Roman were talking to a salesman. "Don't you understand what you're doing?"

Confusion flitted across Frank's face.

I motioned toward the door that was still wide open. "He doesn't have a father figure in his life. He looks up to *you* and I don't want you to buy him a car and then disappear from his life. We've already been through this with our father. Do you have any idea how difficult it is for me to keep him straight?"

"I'm not going to disappear. I want this—us—to work."

"Well, it won't work unless both parties are trying, and you haven't been, Frank."

His hand squeezed mine. "What do you want me to do?"

"I want you to get help. Real help." My voice shook. "I know you don't think you have a problem, but you do. You're not thinking straight and you're mixing alcohol with painkillers. That only damages your body more and delays the healing process."

Frank stared at me for a long moment, recognition lining his features. "Okay." He nodded, lacing our fingers together.

"You promise?"

"I promise I'll get help. Just come back." He inched forward and pressed a soft kiss to my cheek. My body reacted instantly. Goosebumps erupted across my skin.

"I have to think about it," I whispered, completely frozen.

"Can I ask about an ETA?" he crooned.

A muddy laugh escaped my throat. "You're worse than a toddler." I pulled my hand out of his heated grasp. "Depends on how upset my mother is when I tell her about this." I motioned at the door and scrambled out of my seat, needing a little distance. He was too hard to resist.

Be still my heart, be still and don't let this man ruin the walls you've built.

Frank stayed in the Escalade while Roman and I monitored Ashton. It took me a good hour to talk him out of buying a Corvette. My voice was shot from all the arguing and my head started to hurt. I was ready to throw myself on the ground in front of that monstrosity of a car if all else failed. Ashton was like a leprechaun chasing a pot of gold, dead set on the baddest, shiniest ride on the lot. For a moment there, I thought of dragging Frank out of the Escalade to assist me with fixing the loose screws in my brother's brain, but the idea of having my name and photo in the tabloids didn't appeal to me.

"How are you going to parallel park this car?" I fumed staring at the bright yellow hood of the Corvette. The color was cheesier than a pizza topping.

"I'll learn." My brother grinned from the driver's seat, stroking the dashboard and the upholstery. He was somewhere between adorable and embarrassing. I wouldn't be surprised if he started to lick the windshield.

"No, buddy. You need to know how to parallel park *before* you buy a car, not after." I turned to the sales associate. "Can you show us something...smaller and less flashy?"

Eventually, we agreed on a Z4. The look on Ashton's face when he got behind the wheel of the BMW was priceless. He beamed brighter than the Christmas tree set up in the reception area. Now I simply had to explain this to my mother, and the mere thought of the upcoming conversation gave me chills.

Once all the paperwork had been handled, I returned to the Escalade. Frank was on the phone but hung up the moment I flung the door open to slide into my seat next to him. Undeniable tension riddled the cool air, but he tried to defuse it with a smile.

"I'm not feeling very comfortable with my brother driving a sixty-thousand-dollar car alone," I said, scouring his features.

"He'll be fine."

A pause.

"I hate you a little bit right now."

"Only a little bit?" Frank laughed softly. "You two owe me a ride, by the way."

"I think we can arrange that. I don't know where we're going to put you, though."

"We'll probably have to go without you."

"Ahh, I don't know about that." I shook my head. "You're a bad influence, Frank Wallace."

"I'm trying not to be." There was no pretense in his voice. He spoke from his heart and he spoke the truth, and as much as I wanted to hate him for putting me through hell this past week, I couldn't. There was something about him—maybe his vulnerability or maybe his efforts—that made me want to hug him and hold him close until the end of forever.

I loved him that much.

"Frank?" I reached for his hand, my gaze aimlessly roaming over the interior of the Escalade. "I think time apart is good for us." I wasn't sure I meant it.

"I think we've been apart enough."

"Things have to change... You understand that, right?"

"Yes. I do. And I promise to work through my issues."

"Thank you."

He looked at me with such intensity, my cheeks started to burn. "I'll call you later." I slipped out of my seat. "I can't let Ashton drive that car alone."

"Okay." Frank nodded.

I didn't like how easily I'd forgiven him, but I didn't like my life without him either.

My mother thought I was on drugs when I told her about the Z4.

"You're joking!" she exclaimed over the phone.

"Mom, I'm not joking."

"Well, who is this man?"

"I'll tell you soon." I had to. I couldn't keep this secret from my own mother much longer, especially since Frank wasn't being careful anymore.

Truth was, in my mind, we were back together. I simply hadn't told him yet. He deserved to suffer just a bit more.

"Why can't you tell me now?" she insisted.

"I'll see you in a couple of hours, Mom."

"Did you have to get a two-seater?" I scolded Ashton as we cruised down Sunset Boulevard with the top down and Post Malone blasting on the radio.

"Sorry," he said in a singsong voice. "I wasn't planning on driving my entire family around in this car."

"Watch the road, Schumacher."

"You need to chill, sis." He laughed and turned up the volume. The shit-eating grin on his face grew wider.

December in Southern California was just as sunny as the summer months. People on the sidewalks sported shorts and tank tops. Palm trees stood tall and green. The ocean breeze was a pleasant cool against my skin as we pushed through the late afternoon traffic in West Hollywood.

Christmas decor along the streets was the only indication of winter.

The dinner went well, considering the fact that Ashton and I arrived at the restaurant in a brand new Z4. It was a tiny Japanese place that was hidden away in one of the older buildings near the busy corner of Crescent Heights and Santa Monica. We ate an obscene amount of sushi and a cotton-soft cake that literally melted on my tongue. At some point, our mother tried to get Ashton to return the car, but obviously, it was a crapshoot.

I was exhausted by the time we finally got back home. Family gatherings always wore me out, no matter how low on drama they were.

A call from Frank came in the middle of the night. I scrambled for my phone, knowing it was him before my eyes registered his name. My room came alive and my heart nearly beat out of my chest at the sound of his whiskey murmur.

"How did it go with your mother?"

"It wasn't as bad as I thought it would be." I sat up. "It's late."

"I know. I'm sorry. I wanted to hear your voice."

"Well, you just did."

His soft laugh warmed my trembling heart. "Will I see you tomorrow?"

I contemplated. "Possibly, but I have more conditions."

"I'm listening."

"I need you to be open with me, Frank. I'm not your enemy. I'm not out to get you and I would never wish you ill. If you really want us to work, you have to talk to me. You have to tell me what's bothering you, because I can't read your mind."

"What do you want to know?"

I shivered as his words rolled through me. My gaze slid across the darkness of the room and froze on the digital clock on my nightstand that read four thirty.

"Right now, I want to know if you're man enough to sing me a song so I can go back to sleep." I flopped on a pillow, anticipation growing inside me.

"Is this a test?"

"Yes, it's a test." I giggled.

"Okay." He paused for a second. "What would you like me to perform?" A playful lilt entered his tone.

"Well, it's almost Christmas, so..."

"Are you in the mood for a Michael Bublé song?"

"This task is obviously meant to embarrass you, but I'm not a sadist. How about something else?"

Silence took over the line. I rolled on my side and readjusted the phone to hear Frank better. My stomach fluttered.

At first, it was just a whisper, a soft mix of sounds, a low hum. The words spun and echoed inside my head, glimmering like little stars, and they were hopeful and beautiful. Eyes closed, I let the familiar melody take over my mind and lull me to sleep.

The song was "Hallelujah" from *Grace*.

"I'm going to sue KBC."

This was the first thing that Frank told me when I stepped inside his Malibu house the next day. Bag in hand, I crossed the room and halted beside the blazing Christmas tree.

"Say something, doll." He neared me, and bittersweet warmth skated along the length of my body.

"What do you want me to say?" With a thundering heart, I glanced up at the star at the top.

"You don't approve." He pressed a chaste kiss to the back of my head.

I felt a rush of closeness as his hand skimmed over my waist. The fabric of the silk dress I'd picked specifically for him felt like armor. A bulletproof vest designed to prevent me from the full effect of his touch.

"I don't think you should." My gaze continued to inspect the decorations hung from the tree in thick bunches of semi-ellipses as I let my bag slip to the floor. "I know you feel like you've been wronged, and yes, you have, but I don't think it's going to bring your health back. What this lawsuit will do is give you an extra headache."

There was a pause, then Frank's hand popped in front of my face. He was holding a small box with a red bow.

My heart skipped a beat. "What's this?"

"Your Christmas present." He pushed my hair aside, and his mouth dropped to the nape of my neck, his lips tracing a ticklish trail over my skin.

Goosebumps puckered my flesh. "Are you trying to distract me?"

"Maybe."

I opened the box. Inside lay a bracelet. It was delicate and exquisite and matched the chain of the diamond solitaire necklace Frank gave me several months ago.

"Nice try, rockstar." I grinned.

"I do value your advice, doll, but can we continue the serious conversation after dinner?" Frank's lips returned to my neck.

"You're taking them to court on principle," I continued, needing to voice everything I had on my mind. "While your band will be gearing up for a tour with a new singer, you'll be wasting time you could be spending writing new music and money you could be using for something useful on a pointless lawsuit that will probably drain you emotionally and end in a typical anticlimactic matter. A settlement in exchange for a promise to never try to bark at the label again."

I was glad a tiny glass Santa Claus that hung from the tree was on the receiving end of my speech. Crumbling from the effect of my words, he tore his mouth from my neck and drew me closer.

"It's not worth your effort," I explained. "You're so much better than this. You and Isabella have incredible musical chemistry. Record the single. Let the world hear you. Fuck everyone else."

He responded with grim silence.

I put the bracelet back in the box and slid it into my pocket. "I know you probably think I'm pushing for your collaboration so hard because she's my artist and I want to jump start her career. I do and you can help her with that, but I wouldn't tell you any of this if you two were shit together. You aren't. You're going to break so many fucking hearts with your music, you have no idea."

He spun me around. We were face to face now, mere inches between our bodies. He looked radiant in his vulnerability. His eyes dazzled in the ever-changing lights of the Christmas tree.

"All I'm hearing is *fucking*, and we haven't done any in weeks." A smirk cut through his cheek. "How about we fix that problem first?"

"I thought you wanted to start with dinner?"

"I changed my mind. You turn me on when you talk business."

"Asshole." I cupped his chin and pulled him to meet my lips. A ghost of a moan left his throat. He sunk his hand in my hair. I'd forgotten how much I loved the feel of his tongue in my mouth, how much I loved the hard press of his chest against my softness, how much I loved his deft hands roaming my curves.

The kiss was a lingering flame. A gentle flutter of a lost butterfly. The final swirl of a fall leaf. Each flick of our tongues and each pull of our lips burned so hard, my lungs struggled to breathe.

Frank smiled lazily against my mouth. And that split second, when he grinned like a kid, felt as if all the rainbow colors burst inside my chest.

"I missed you," I said, pulling away for a second to drink him in.

"I missed you too, doll." He cradled the back of my head. "I hate that we fought."

"That's what couples do."

"Screw other couples." His lips came down on mine fiercely. For a man who'd recently had two surgeries and had only one functioning shoulder, Frank was pretty persistent. He licked every corner of my mouth and inspected every fold of my dress. I didn't mind. On the contrary, I reciprocated. My small hands slid over his hard lines, eager. He'd lost weight and rigor, but his body was still lean, toned, and beautiful. With all its ink and scars. With all its pain and grace.

Our feet fumbled across the room in a slow, delicious dance. We kissed as if we hadn't seen each other in a thousand years.

"I want to be inside you so bad," he mumbled against my cheek deliriously, pulling me to his chest. "Right now."

"What about your parents?"

"They went to Catalina. They won't be back until tomorrow evening."

"What about—?"

His thumb pressed to my swollen lips to shut them up before I finished my question. "I gave everyone the day off." He waggled his brows. "Today the house is all ours."

I leaned back, and my eyes ran along the breadth of his shoulders. He wasn't allowed to take the sling off during waking hours for another four weeks.

"We're going to have to get very creative, baby." I brushed his chin with my index finger. "That couch right behind you looks comfortable."

Eyes hooded, he glanced over his shoulder. The corners of his lips curled up in a subtle smile.

"Why don't you sit down and relax?" I whispered. Anticipatory shivers rolled down my spine. My panties dampened from the lust gathering between my legs.

Frank did as I asked. He lowered himself to the couch and slid a pillow behind his back. Wanton excitement lit up my body. I rushed over to the iPod station and skimmed through his music catalogue, glancing at him mischievously. My lover was about to get an iconic treat à la Kim Basinger. Or, at least, I was going to do my best. And definitely without the hat. Hats weren't allowed in this house anyway. We were boycotting Dante.

Frank shifted and readjusted his cock that was clearly straining against his jeans as I flipped my hair and docked the iPod, a pleasant buzz fogging my head. The Christmas lights swirled across the artwork-studded walls and the sheer-shaded windows of the living room.

My pulse quickened. Desire set my flesh and blood on fire.

I watched Frank's expression change from lax to heated as the jazzy, mid-tempo tune blared from the speakers. He bit his bottom lip and rested his hand on his erection. His eyes shone with a sinister glow.

I moved across the room slowly, swaying my hips to the tempting beat of the song. My dress was a knee-length wrap with a zipper on one side. There wasn't much to work with, but I'd worn a pair of sexy pumps and a lace lingerie set and I wanted to show off. I wanted to strip and I wanted to ride Frank in the most inelegant way.

His breath hitched as my fingers began to play with the skirt, dragging the light fabric up my thighs. He parted his lips to suck in more air through his teeth. A grin of satisfaction spread to his stubbly cheeks. Men truly needed so little to be happy. It was almost too easy.

I stopped front and center to ensure Frank had the best view and whirled on my heels. My heart thrummed along with the music. Potent and tasteful, the melody became my pulse. I felt its erotic beat in my temples and dripping between my thighs. Dizzy with lyrics, my head continued to spin. My hair whipped across my face and I couldn't see anything but the blurred lines of Frank's silhouette splayed over the white upholstery of the couch.

He breathed hard. His lungs couldn't catch up with his want. This craving that filled the empty space between us was a deadly case of passion. Hips rolling, I inched closer and pulled down the zipper of my dress to reveal some more skin. Frank's hooded gaze followed my every move, his hand squeezed his erection. He was a goner.

Satisfied with the results, I wrestled the silk off my shoulders and let it fall to the floor.

He released a strained moan. "I'm going to come in my jeans if you keep this up."

"Is that a challenge?" I laughed, taking a step forward. My hair fell down my back and over my breasts in messy cascades of black.

Frank tore his hand from his bulge and reached out for me. "Come closer, doll."

I obliged. He ran his palm along the curve of my waist and to my bare hip. His thumb slid beneath my lacy panties.

"Patience." I slapped his knuckles lightly and retreated.

He let out a groan, and his eyes grew darker.

The song reached its peak and the ragged rhythm galloped through my body, twisting and bending me like a willow tree. I was raw and undone between my legs and parts of me needed Frank to put out the damn fire he'd lit. Other parts of me were enjoying the torturous look on his face.

My hands moved around my back to unhook my bra. Cupping my breasts, I swayed to the music. The unsteady click of my heels meshed with the leisurely beat of the drums and the rough grit of the vocals.

Frank patted his thigh invitingly and I strutted toward the couch to take the space between his legs. Gliding my hands over my skin, I peeled off my bra and it dropped across my shoes.

Face flushed with delight, Frank snaked his arm around me and palmed my ass. His gaze danced a lustful path up my body.

I could tell he was torn between touching me and touching himself, and part of me felt bad that he only had one good hand, but I was dead set on making him forget about his injuries. I was a girlfriend on a mission. And the mission was to give my man an orgasm.

Dropping to my knees, I reached for his zipper and freed his cock. He was beautiful, hard, and ready for me to suck him. Fingers tangled in my hair, Frank tossed his head back. A ravaged growl lingered on his lips for a few seconds before he released it into the music.

I took him into my mouth slowly, wetting him and relaxing my throat. His hips bucked. His body stiffened. The tip of him slid in deep, salty precum blending with my saliva.

"Fuck, baby." I heard him mutter under his breath as his hand pushed against the back of my head slowly and carefully. My belly squeezed at the guttural sound of his voice. He was the epitome of masculinity—tight, sensual, and writhing under my touch. Every part of me ached for him after seven nights of absolute loneliness in my bed, but I wanted to grant him his pleasure first.

Inhaling deeply through my nose, I slid my mouth around his length, all the way down until there was no room left.

"Oh God. Yes," he murmured, nearly convulsing beneath me. His rasp reverberated inside my head, and my sex clenched with need.

I worked his cock with delicacy and attention. My tongue swirled over each ridge of his thickness in sharp precision. Quick, skillful, moan-inducing movements, until he neared the edge.

Releasing him from my mouth, I gasped for air and stood. He was spent, eyes closed, lashes fluttering, hand gripped around his wet cock. My hips wavered as I slid my panties off and straddled him. My shoes were still on and he grinned at me like a teenager who'd just gotten his first blowjob. Heat flashed where our bodies connected. His thickness pressed to my center, which pulsed as I moved along its length with a sluggish rhythm, teasing him.

Frank was panting with need. His broken breaths grew louder and he grabbed at my waist.

"Shhh, baby." I palmed his cheeks. "Relax. Let me do all the work. You can make it up to me in a couple of months."

He laughed feverishly through his frenzy, and my emotions swelled in my chest. It was almost too much. Too many feelings. My mind spun out of control. I rested my hands atop the back pillow to leverage myself.

"Come on, doll. Put me out of my misery. Fuck me already."

I leaned forward and planted a gentle kiss on his forehead. "As you wish." His skin was slick with sweat and I rubbed my chin against the side of his face. He was every bit the mess a person in his delicate situation should be, but he was my mess. And I wanted to make him feel good.

Our bodies mingled, mine small and lithe and his large and trim. We fit together perfectly. My thighs moved carefully, rocking to the dark, slow beat. The song changed and we were now wrapped into the divine voice of Leonard Cohen's "Thousand Kisses Deep." I froze at the tip of him, soaking in the final moment of the prelude as our flesh brushed one last time. Then he slid into me gently, his hand gripping my leg. I lowered my body onto his, every single inch of his cock buried in me so deep, there was barely enough room to breathe.

A tremor rushed through my limbs from the friction of our skin. My head fell back. I was losing my mind, and euphoria had begun to take over. Nothing existed right now—just the insanity of us. My body welcomed his modest thrusts. Rolling my hips, I pumped him carefully, ripping low, pleasured growls from his chest. He remained still, hand on my thigh, lips invitingly open.

We were caught up in a wild trance of sex, pain, and rock 'n' roll. It was an agonizingly slow ride. I rocked to the music against his lap, my bare breasts bouncing tauntingly in front of his face. Craning his neck, he reached for my left nipple, and I arched to give him better access. He sucked me into his mouth ravenously. The devilish flicks of his tongue were going to be my undoing.

"Does it feel good?" I asked, quickening my pace to match the tempo of the next song.

"Is that a rhetorical question?" He laughed softly.

"I want you to be comfortable, because I'm just getting started," I explained, licking his cheek.

"Oh, I am comfortable, doll." A smirk tugged at the corner of his delicious mouth. "You have no idea."

"Then we're good." I lifted myself up and then sank down.

He responded with a strangled moan against my shoulder. Skin to skin, we were burning up. His bunched up shirt dampened against his chest from the blend of our sweat. It was a filthy dance—the cadence of our movement, the hurricane of our labored groans. Our climax built at a steady, measured pace until our bodies reached the perfect height to fall from. Then we tumbled down together, irrevocably connected. Physically and spiritually. It was the most beautiful descent of my entire life.

Exhausted, I dropped my head into the crook of Frank's neck, my hands remaining on the couch to ensure his shoulder was out of harm's way.

His large palm cupped my head as he tried to catch his breath.

"I know Christmas isn't until the day after tomorrow, but Merry Christmas," I purred. "Now we're even."

"That was the best present I've ever gotten." Still inside me, he continued to stroke my hair in his strange, almost fatherly manner.

"I'm flattered." I giggled.

"You should be, doll. Making a man full of meds orgasm is very difficult."

"Mission accomplished."

He laughed, then I did too. There was something incredibly tender about this absolutely dirty moment. I didn't want it to ever end.

Later, when we finally summoned enough strength to get up from the couch, I ran a bath. We sat in a tub full of bubbles, the remnants of our sexual adventure washed away. The water level was low to ensure Frank's stitches didn't get wet. His skin around the scarring was bruised and discolored and he seemed tense at first—my gaze on his damaged nakedness terrified him. I wasn't sure if it was his cuts and marks that he didn't want me to look at or something else. Something he'd hidden from everyone for so long, he'd forgotten he had it, and I was going to find it first.

"I don't see any scars when I look at you," I said, running a washcloth over his other shoulder. The elegant curve of his muscles made me want to lick him clean.

"What do you see?" He stared at me somberly as I continued to tend to his body.

"Passion. Heart. Music."

The intensity of his gunmetal gaze sent chills down my spine. I felt his fears. They were dark and deep.

"Scars don't take anything away from you, Frank. They give you what you may have not had before them. Strength."

A small smile touched his lips.

"You have this ability to turn shit to gold with words."

"That's what everyone tells me."

He snapped his index finger and sent a splash of soapy water my way.

My washcloth dropped into the tub. "That's totally not fair." I shook my head and rubbed my eyes. "I can't even get you back for another month."

His expression turned serious. "Remember when I told you the night we met that I don't believe in coincidences?"

"Yes. Why do you think we aren't a coincidence?"

He dropped his gaze to the blanket of bubbles and gathered some in his palm. "Meeting people is part of my job. Some days, I meet hundreds, some days, I meet thousands. It's overwhelming. You begin to spread your spirit thin. At first, I tried to remember the names of those who I came across often so that I wouldn't be that dude who doesn't even know the people who support his music and his cause. But after a while, every face started looking the same. They all blurred. One meeting isn't enough for me anymore. So I talk to a person, then I move on. I turn it off. I have to. Because if I don't, I'll go crazy. I'll keep the other person's emotions in me until there's no room left for my own. It's a terrifying feeling when you're so suscep-tive to everything that's going on around you. It weighs on you. The problems of everyone else. You have to have a switch. On, and you're rich and famous. Off, and you shed the world's heaviness and drown in your own. Then that day, fate kept pushing you into my arms over and over again. It was as if she whispered, *Look at this woman. She's going to change your life. Don't be a wuss. Be a man and talk to her, not a fucking tool. Forget the switch.* And by the end of the night, I started wondering why she wanted me and you together so much. Now I know."

Frank paused and gazed up at me. Our eyes met.

I was in awe. His confession moved me yet alarmed me at the same time.

"Don't analyze it, Cassy," he said as if he sensed me trying to paint a different picture of him in my head. A real picture.

I understood him. I understood why he didn't want to talk about it anymore. He was scared. And I was going to let it go and be what he needed me to be. His light.

"And here I thought you liked me for me." My lips were twisted in a pout. "Turns out, some chick named Fate gets all the credit. Was my fun personality not enough?"

"Your fun personality, your yoga, and your striptease skills." He grinned and splashed more water in my face.

"Grrrr," I growled at him, balling my fists. "You'll pay for that in due time, Frank Wallace."

"I don't doubt it. But until then, I'll take a strip show every night before bed."

Chapter Six

"I'm glad you decided to continue with us, Frank," Linda said, smiling politely as she returned to her MacBook to make a few notes.

"It's not your fault my bandmates and the record label want me out." His hand squeezed mine softly. He'd been taking off the sling for a couple of hours every morning per his doctor's request, but temporary loss of motor function didn't allow him to do much with his right arm yet. It was baby steps on the way to a full recovery.

We sat at the table inside the den. Brooklyn stood off to the side with an iPad in her hands. Face screwed in concentration, she looked through the list of the venues that would work for the screening.

Since Frank had finally expressed an interest in possibly doing an interview for *Dreamcatchers,* she wanted to be part of the decision-making process. I didn't press for more yet, because Frank's mind was preoccupied with the upcoming collaboration with Isabella, but my gut told me he was almost ready. I just needed to give him some space. Let him come to us on his own terms. Without pressure.

As we discussed right before Christmas, he'd started talking to a counselor. His mood had improved greatly in the last couple of weeks, and I hadn't seen him touching or looking at alcohol, which was a good sign. The only thing we still disagreed on was the lawsuit.

Frank refused to let it go.

"Half of these are union." Brooklyn's voice drew my attention back to the meeting. "I wouldn't even bother." She shook her head, her gaze jumping between me and Frank.

I willed my mind to concentrate on the present. "This is a nonprofit project, so I don't see why it matters."

"You'll be jumping through hoops for months," she countered in a snappy tone. "I'm just trying to save you some time."

"And I appreciate it." Smiling, I freed my hand from Frank's grasp. I didn't need his protection when people in his entourage opposed me. Levi and I had already been jumping through legal hoops for a while since we'd had to set up a corporation to produce the film. More red tape made no difference anymore. That was one of the reasons why I'd taken a step back from *Rewired*—to ensure we had all the bases covered.

Linda came to the rescue. "When are you looking to record the single?" she questioned Frank, making more notes. Her fingers tippy-tapped against the keyboard of her Mac. Dressed in a suit and with her hair styled to perfection, she was the definition of impeccable. Sometimes I wondered if the woman slept at all. Sometimes I wondered if she was even human. With a mile-long roster of celebrity clients she handled publicity for, Frank was probably the nicest. Despite all the luxury he enjoyed surrounding himself with, he was a simple man. Roman and Hannah loved him. I saw it in the way they spoke about him when he wasn't near. Even slimy douche Corey adored Frank.

And I adored being his girlfriend. He was like sunshine, even in his darkest moments, and everyone clung to him, hoping to get a bit of his warmth.

"In the next month or two," he said. I heard a lick of excitement in Frank's voice. For the first time since the accident, he sounded like himself. "We're trying to get Gary Torino on board."

"Really?" Linda gazed at me, looking for confirmation.

I nodded.

Gary Torino was best of the best, an industry veteran who'd produced over two hundred albums. Three quarters were platinum. Half of them sat at the very top of the Billboard chart.

Frank wanted to go all out with "Afterburn."

"I haven't heard it yet, and I'm already impressed." Linda typed up some more notes.

"It's still pretty rough," Frank explained. He'd only attended one rehearsal, but now that he was finally on the way to recovery, three more sessions were lined up for the next couple of weeks.

"Can you guarantee Billboard?" Brooklyn barked from her spot.

I could almost taste her annoyance. It plagued the air like the smell of rotting leftovers.

Linda flashed a cunning smile and the spark in her eyes told me she was going to make it happen. Despite the fact that there were no guarantees in this business. Never. "We can probably try for a Grammy nomination as well."

"I like that!" Frank beamed. It was a magazine cover-worthy grin. I hadn't seen him this fired up in weeks. He was riding the high of anticipation, and I was hoping it would make him change his mind and give up the idea of the lawsuit.

"Do you have any questions, Frank?" Linda asked.

"I think you answered them all." When he stood, she did too, and they shook hands.

"I'll have my girls start on the proposal today, and we'll send it over to Brooklyn as soon as it's ready." Linda slammed her MacBook shut and slipped it into her bag. "As always, it's a pleasure, Frank."

"Pleasure is mine." He grinned.

"I'll walk you out," I offered and rose from my chair. Brooklyn's unhappy growl behind my back was the last thing I heard as I left the den.

"He looks good," Linda noted as we made our way over to her

SUV parked in the driveway. She pulled the door open and tossed her bag on the passenger seat. "How's his shoulder?"

"Better. He's seeing a doctor in a couple of days. So we'll know more then."

The January sun was perched high in the sky, its rays glittering in the generous falls of the fountain water. The light breeze that danced across my cheeks was soft and cool, typical for a Southern California winter.

"Any news on the replacement singer?" I asked carefully, my voice almost a whisper. Not that anyone could hear us. Frank's yard was the size of my entire apartment complex. "Off the record, of course."

"Management is in talks with a few candidates right now. I'm sure you understand these are some big shoes to fill." Linda narrowed her eyes and inched closer. "Looks like it's going to be either Marshall Burns or Joel Frederick."

"Really? *Frederick?*" I tried to hold the sudden rush of anxiety at bay. "He can't hold a note long enough for the crowd to hear it." *But he's a great showma*n.

"He had vocal cord surgery last summer."

"He did?"

"His team just wanted to keep it under wraps while he was in recovery. I heard he nailed all the *Hollow Heart Dream* songs during his audition."

"Shit."

"Promise me you won't tell anyone. Not even Frank."

"Of course. You have my word."

"It's up to Dante to choose who he wants to play with anyway, and my gut tells me he'll go with Marshall. He's a bit more down to earth and easier to work with."

"Is it bad I want this tour to flop?"

"It's very difficult to stay impartial in your position. I'd probably feel the same way if I were dating Frankie Blade." Linda laughed softly. "You made a smart move by distancing yourself from the magazine. You don't want Levi and the rest of the team to be caught in the crossfire when the press finds out you're dating Frank. Have you reached out to the social media agency I recommended?"

"Not yet."

"You should do it before TMZ takes notice. I would also suggest talking to your mother and brother."

A shiver ran down my spine. The idea of going public was like a flu virus, incubating, waiting to hit me and my family. "I'm scared," I confessed.

"Which is normal," Linda explained. "But as long as you prepare yourself for what's coming and stay away from social media when it hits the tabloids, you'll be fine."

I allowed her words to settle. My job was stressful enough to have taught me how not to let things get to me, and while I liked to think of myself as a thick-skinned gal, with Frank, everything felt different. It was as if he possessed all parts of me—my body, my mind, my heart. He was embedded into my thoughts every second of every day, and it was the most terrifying feeling ever.

"Don't you dare tell him or anyone else about Joel and Marshall," Linda warned me as she got into her SUV. "Not even your imaginary pet."

"My lips are sealed." I ran my fingers along my mouth and turned an invisible key to let her know I'd keep quiet forever.

After our goodbyes were said, I went back inside. The thunder of Brooklyn's voice raged in the den.

"You shouldn't have kept her," she fumed, pacing around.

Frank stood near the window and stared at the ocean, his faced withdrawn.

"Your name will be in circulation with their Hall Affinity press releases. Do you really think it's a good idea to share a publicist with your former bandmates?" Brooklyn continued, ignoring my presence.

"First, I like her and I trust her instincts," Frank responded in a flat tone. "Second, I want my name to be shoved into every inbox that gets Hall Affinity news. It's still my fucking band. I made them. The world should remember that when they hear someone else singing my songs."

I recognized the struggle in his breath, loud and heavy puffs against the muffled rumble of the ocean. He'd seemed fine just a few minutes ago, which made me wonder if Brooklyn had said something to him while I was gone or if he'd led me to believe he was getting better when he wasn't.

"It's not like Linda Schwab is the only good publicist in town," she retorted.

"I'm keeping her. End of story," Frank said and walked out of the den.

There was a shift in the air. A change.

"I can't with him!" Arms flinging, Brooklyn rolled her eyes. Then her gaze jumped over to me. "He's so goddamn stubborn."

"Tell me about it." I shook my head. "I'm out of ideas on how to make him give up the stupid lawsuit obsession."

"Honey." Brooklyn gave me a fake smile. "Nothing's going to stop that man from trying to get back at KBC. He's hurt, embarrassed, and angry. So you can take it down a notch with your daily deep throat treats."

What do you know? The woman had sense of humor after all.

A week after our initial meeting with Linda, Dante's first on-camera post-Frankie Blade interview hit the internet.

It was a cool, foggy Malibu night filled with the distant rustle of palm trees and the croon of the ocean. Wrapped in a blanket, I was sitting on the terrace with my laptop, going over my pitch, when an email notification with Levi's name popped on my screen.

The link in my inbox that I instantly clicked opened a YouTube video. There were very few people in my life I truly hated. My father probably took the top spot, but at that moment, Dante's name dominated my *worst person of the year* list. The headline pissed me off.

"Hall Affinity to Reveal Their New Singer's Name Very Soon: Guitarist Dante Martinez acknowledges the band has been going through a rough patch and fresh blood will definitely breathe life into the ensemble."

A time stamp indicated the video had been uploaded an hour ago. The view count was nearing two hundred thousand and I felt like I was late to the party.

Drawing a loud breath through my teeth, I hit the Play button and started watching the interview. Dante's smug face filled the screen of my laptop. Eyes glazed, smile tipped all the way up, he looked higher than Mount Everest. A thin fringe of dark stubble shadowed his jaw and cheeks. The man was in his element, as always.

My stomach felt queasy as I listened to the string of slurry words pouring from the speakers. A strange sadness washed over me.

Backstabbing jerk, I thought, dragging the slider forward after the two-minute mark. This interview was an insensitive slap in the face. Dante could have done without it, but, of course, the man fed his ego with loads of attention. He had to go in front of the camera and tell the world how the band hadn't been the same ever since Frank's accident.

My phone pinged.

"Bad fucking timing, huh?" Levi muttered, his voice on the line low and full of worry.

"You don't say." I minimized the window.

"What do you think?"

"Considering how many diehard fans Frank has and how much fuss they'll make once the band announces the new name, Isabella will definitely get some of the attention. She's in the center of a major battle. Not that I like it, but if that's how KBC wants to do it, we can play along."

The upcoming mayhem in the press that Isabella would be dragged into right in the middle of recording "Afterburn" with Frank wasn't my main concern. She was a tough cookie who'd been at war with the world ever since the shitty label in San Francisco had dropped her. Frank, on the contrary, wasn't ready to fight. Not yet, anyway. His fragile physical and mental health were the main reasons why I kept on asking him to scrap the lawsuit. Having Dante flaunt the replacement singer news while Frank was trying to get on his feet again felt like a cheap trick.

A thud snapped my attention back to reality. I quieted and listened with my breath caught in my throat. The noise had come from somewhere inside the house.

"Let me call you back," I told Levi, getting to my feet.

More racket. My heart leapt.

I set my phone on the table and stepped into the living room. All sorts of possibilities rushed through my mind.

Were we being robbed?

Roman hadn't been sleeping on the property anymore. Janet and Billy had returned to Arizona after the holidays. It was only the two of us.

The noise was coming from the east wing. Pulse roaring, I ran down the hallway over to the studio. The door was wide open. Frank stood in front of the mixing board that had apparently just taken a beating. Blood was smeared on the knuckles of his left hand.

Awareness of what was happening hit all my senses.

"What the hell?" I rushed over to him and reached for his wrist. "Let me see."

He silently jerked his hand away.

"Come on!" My voice went a pitch higher. "Let me see!"

He stumbled back as if he didn't want to be touched. His eyes darkened.

Heart pounding, I gazed at him and then around the studio, looking for more signs of damage. Some of the picture frames lay on the floor, shattered. Crushed glass and shards of plastic littered the carpet.

"Fucking cunt." I heard his whisper, then a kick. Only after something hit the wall, did I realize it was his phone.

Every single cell in my body told me to leave. Something about the way he was behaving—the unpredictability, in particular—troubled me as much as the scene before me, but I didn't dare move. I froze, dead in my tracks, trying to think of the right words to say or the right questions to ask. There weren't any. My mind was blank with searing panic.

Frank tossed his head back and stared at the ceiling with a steely expression. "Son of a bitch has the fucking nerve to invite me to the party after flushing twenty years down the toilet."

My brain cells clicked. Brooklyn worked hard on filtering all of Frank's correspondence, but she couldn't monitor his personal phone. It must have been the album release event that made him turn his studio into the set of a post-apocalyptic blockbuster.

"Can you imagine, doll? Bitterness laced his voice.

My shock was still raw. "Let me look at your hand," I asked tentatively.

"Does he expect me to just show up and pretend like nothing happened?"

I took a deep breath. "Why are you letting him do this to you? He's moved on. You should too, Frank!"

"That's fucking easy for you to say," he spat, swinging his hand in the air as if he was looking for something else to hit. His words were a jagged razor shoved into my chest.

"Are you serious right now?" I positioned myself between his body and the wall of broken equipment to stop him from wreaking more havoc to what was left.

He inhaled sharply and finally looked down at me. "Yes, I'm dead fucking serious. Do you have any idea how it feels to be rotting in this house while your ex-best friend is whoring your band out?"

We stared at each other heatedly. His storm-filled gaze burned so hot against mine, I felt it in my chest, melting my ribs and my heart along with them. The dim light illuminating the side of his face accentuated his anger. I didn't like what I saw in him.

He was unhinged. Completely lost in his pain and devastation.

"So you destroy your house because of some asshole who's not worth one second of your time?" I was doing my best to keep my raging emotions under control. Someone needed to stay calm, and it looked as if that person had to be me. Frank had been balancing on a slack wire for far too long. Apparently, it had snapped today.

"It's my fucking house. I'll demolish it if I want to," he growled.

"That's not what we agreed on!" I cried out. "We're supposed to talk about things, Frank. Like adults! Instead of driving off without a word or breaking shit." I motioned at the mess on the floor and his hand.

"They're going on a fucking tour while I'm wasting away."

"You're not wasting away. You're about to record a single."

"I can't fucking do anything with one arm."

"Well, you'll never get to use your second one if you keep hurting yourself."

Eyes wide, mouth twisted, he pushed past me and walked out of the studio.

I followed.

When we reached the living room, Frank shifted gears and halted in front of the bar. He pulled out a clean glass and a bottle of liquor and poured himself a shot.

"Don't," I said, my voice wobbly.

"Silently, he brought the drink to his mouth and took a sip.

My heart sobbed in frustration. "Frank." I moved closer and held out my hand in hopes he'd surrender the glass. "Please."

No reaction.

"I'm serious." I took another step. The inches of space between us that was poisoned with ugliness shrunk.

My heartbeats were fast and shallow.

Tossing his head back, Frank swallowed down the rest and gave me the empty glass. "Here."

I glared at him, fury boiling in my chest.

"Take it or leave it, doll." His deep whiskey voice was filled with defiance. It sounded a lot like an ultimatum.

Leave, my pride and my common sense whispered. But instead, I grabbed the glass. My hand shook. A thousand bitter words crammed my throat and threatened to come out, but I willed my tongue to remain quiet. There was no point in talking to him when he was completely out of his mind like this.

His loud footsteps boomed through the hallway and disappeared into the bedroom.

At first, I couldn't move. A wave of unpleasant memories of my father swept me under. They were a dark vortex of fragments of my broken childhood and they made me wonder if my mother had tried hard enough and if I was wrong to think about leaving this house and the man who lived here. They made me wonder if I was a quitter too, if I was a bad girlfriend, ready to desert a person at his worst. The thought was like a hot flash. It hit me the instant Frank touched the drink and now it refused to go away.

Minutes passed before I finally gathered enough courage to move. Every muscle in my body was tight with worry. Confusion and anger brewed in my stomach. My fingers felt clammy and foreign as I went through the bar and emptied every single bottle that had alcohol in it.

Part of me expected to find more wreckage in the bedroom when I went to check on Frank, but there was none. Shoulders slumped, he sat on the edge of the bed and stared at his knuckles. Silent and still. A shimmering streak of moonlight spilled across the floor, slicing the room in half.

The night was almost perfect. Except for the faint smell of broken promises and alcohol in the air.

"I'm going to work for a bit," I said calmly and returned to the den to finish my pitch. Three hours later, when I slid under the blankets, Frank was passed out.

"Didn't he have a therapy session today?" Brooklyn muttered, checking Frank's calendar on her iPad as we surveyed the gruesome results of his outburst inside the studio.

He was still asleep and I didn't dare wake him. As a matter of fact, I wasn't certain if I could face him just yet. Last night's fight only strengthened my belief that Frank was spiraling out of control. He was falling and he was taking me along for the ride, and I wasn't sure I wanted to go.

"Yep." Brooklyn's voice dragged me back to the studio. "Looks like he's missing his 11 a.m."

"Great." I shook my head and stared at the pack of ripped wires sticking out chaotically from one of the output panels. "Do you think I'm a horrible person for wanting to call Janet?"

"Why would you do that?" Brooklyn's brow arched up.

"I didn't know how to handle him yesterday. I'd never seen him that...upset."

"Trust me, Janet is the last person you want to call when Frank is going off the rails. Although he's not her son by blood, they are the worst when they get emotional together. You don't want to worry her for no reason. It's best if you talk to Billy."

"What do you mean for no reason? He hurt himself last night."

Brooklyn tore her gaze from the iPad and looked at me. "He's rich, famous, and talented. Self-destruction is in his blood."

"And you suggest we just watch and don't interfere?"

"No. Therapy usually helps him get back on track. You can't expect him to simply snap out of it overnight, honey. Not after everything he's been through these past seven years."

"I don't want to be passive about his drinking problem. Isn't there anything else we should do?"

"Like what? What do you have in mind that we haven't tried yet? Committing him? I'd like to see you try that."

A shuddered breath left my lungs. I'd already considered talking to him about AA, rehab, and meditation. We'd addressed the problem, but we'd never addressed how exactly he'd keep himself in check.

Brooklyn continued to stare at me. "I've been working for Frank for over ten years," she spoke calmly and reassuringly. "I've seen his ugly side more times than you can imagine. Fame is overwhelming, Cassy. Especially when you need to meet the expectations of the entire planet. Imagine that everything that made you—your face, your body, your voice—is taken away from you in a split second. Imagine getting cut and rebranded countless times just to be able to meet those unrealistic expectations. I've been there through all of that and you haven't. So don't tell me how to do my job. He's been in rehab before. He's talked to dozens of different psychiatrists. Trust me when I tell you, it's best not to push him over the edge and, instead, let him come to a decision gradually. When he's ready. If he truly wanted to hurt himself, he would have done it a long time ago."

I disagreed wholeheartedly, but I didn't want to spread my feelings thin by engaging in a pointless argument. I was saving myself for my conversation with Frank. Promises without some kind of a plan didn't cut it anymore.

I spent the rest of the morning working in the spare bedroom. There was a certain level of avoidance in my relentless chase after the empty inbox. I'd probably typed close to a million words by the time the knock on the door finally broke me out of my email-composing trance.

I dragged my gaze away from the screen and across the room to where Frank stood.

Our eyes met.

"Sorry, I didn't mean to bother you." He'd shaved. His arm was back in the sling, which made me wonder if he'd done way more to himself last night than busting his knuckles.

"It's fine." I closed my laptop. "I was going to talk to you anyway."

He began his approach, but stopped before reaching the desk. His expression conveyed a multitude of emotions, yet I couldn't pin down a single one.

"About yesterday..." There was a slight rasp in his voice as he wavered.

"I can't stay in this house if you drink." My words tumbled out of my mouth and stunned him into shock.

"It won't happen again, doll," he finally whispered, moving toward the desk sitting between us. I lifted my chin and got to my feet, needing to be taller, needing to feel stronger, needing to be in charge. For once. Although everything inside me was plummeting.

"I promise." Frank reached for my hand. "I'm sorry for how I acted yesterday. I was upset and I wasn't thinking clearly." I remained in my spot, my body unmoving, unable to react accordingly.

He circled the desk and cupped my cheek. "Please don't be mad."

"You already said that before." I shook my head.

"I know, but it'll be different this time."

"You need help."

"I know. I know." He nodded. "I overreacted and you're right. I shouldn't waste my time being pissed about something I can't change."

"Okay." He'd admitted the problem, but I needed to hear more. I needed him to give me a solution.

"I promise you it won't happen again, doll. Just stay with me. Please." He snaked his arm around my waist and drew me closer. It was a dizzying embrace. Soft, warm, and painfully familiar. Just the way I liked him. And for a moment there, I wanted to believe him. I wanted to give him the benefit of the doubt. The things that I'd prepared to say—my warnings, terms, and conditions—had been wiped clean from my mind by his touch and his heartbeat. He was dangerous.

"Please reconsider the lawsuit?" I asked, my pulse a wild drum in my ears as I rested my hand on his chest. "For me, please."

Frank was silent for a second. "I'll think about it," he finally said.

The following day Brooklyn received an email from Gary Torino. He was thrilled about "Afterburn" and could spare two full days at the end of the month. So as soon as the dates were locked in and all the arrangements were made, Jay Brodie PR got to work. The first press release went out on Monday, and Isabella's official Facebook page raked up over forty thousand likes in less than twenty-four hours. Her social media platforms exploded. Literally overnight.

I couldn't believe my eyes when I looked at the stats. Levi was on cloud nine.

Frank spent the remainder of the week in his studio creating a scratch track for "Afterburn." Some of the equipment he'd destroyed was replaced fairly quickly, enough for him to get started. We hardly discussed the lawsuit again. He was so wrapped up in the song that I feared I'd kill his music mojo. Instead, I tried my best to keep him away from social media, TV, and the internet in general. Hall Affinity teased to unveil the name of the new singer's name in the upcoming weeks and since the announcement seemed to coincide with the "Afterburn" campaign, it was imperative Frank stayed focused.

Dante publicly wished his former bandmate good luck with his new endeavors. The press release with his official statement hit my inbox six hours after Jay Brodie PR sent out the first "Afterburn" email blast, and I laughed at Dante's speech for a good minute. No matter how the man tried to spin it, he was still a backstabbing jerk.

When Levi finally sent me the *Dreamcatchers* rough cut, Frank was caught up in the voodoo of music and refused to leave the studio. We watched the film on my laptop, surrounded by the monitors and panels of output gear.

Leaned back in his chair and clutching its left arm, Frank was silent while the cut rolled. His expression grew hard each time he saw images of himself. Per Brooklyn's instructions, Levi used only minimal footage of Frank from the rehearsals.

Too nervous to sit down, I stood behind his chair and observed his reactions. We'd spoken about an interview only once after his last meltdown and he'd been thinking about it ever since, but I hoped that seeing the cut would help him decide faster, because we could no longer postpone setting the screening date.

"What do you think?" I asked after we finished watching.

Frank spun in his chair to face me, his features twisted in concentration. "It's very compelling, doll. I love how it's turning out."

The edge in his voice indicated there was more, but he kept it to himself. At least for now.

"Are you still not sure about my offer?" I probed.

He stared at me candidly. His penetrating gaze reached deep into my soul and every fiber in me felt his hesitation. "I don't want to steal Isabella's screen time."

My tongue was tight and heavy inside my mouth. "Trust me, you won't, but if you want my honest opinion, I think that in light of everything that's happened in the last couple of months, this is a way for you to really be heard..." I stammered and blushed like a teenager because it seemed wrong to give him my sales pitch, but he reminded me of a newborn baby that had just come into this world, screaming, kicking, and uncertain of what to do. Uncertain of whether the universe accepted him for what he was without his band and everything he'd accomplished with those three people who didn't care to fight for him.

He just needed a push.

I matched his stare. "Your insight can draw a lot of attention to all the wrongs that are plaguing the industry. Can't you see why I don't want you to move forward with the lawsuit? It'll make you look greedy. Sharing your true experiences will make you look human. People are drawn to vulnerability."

"You know better than anyone that lawsuits in my line of business aren't always about money." His voice was like an acidic peel.

"I know, but people don't see it that way unless you're fighting a collective fight. And that's not the case here. For the label, you're just a disgruntled former employee. For the fans, you're just another money-hungry celebrity to yap about on the forums. This is the way your fans—including myself—will see you if you try to sue a corporation for millions of dollars when you already have enough to feed a country in Central America."

The tension brewing between us reached its peak. Frank's steely glare was like a torch to my face.

"Well"—he tilted his head—"at least you're honest." The grind of his jaw told me I'd hit a sore spot.

"I'll always be honest with you. It's called a relationship."

Frank's expression softened. "You're right, doll. I have more than I need. The difference between me and people born into wealth is that I earned it with my blood, sweat, and broken bones." He dropped his gaze to his arm resting in the sling.

"I'm not insinuating anything, Frank. I'm simply giving you facts. This is how people will perceive you and your actions if you sue KBC. I'm not going to sugarcoat the situation merely because I don't want to hurt your feelings. Otherwise, what's the point of doing all this?" I motioned at my laptop. "If you really want to fight the good fight, I've got one going on. Join me."

Eyes narrowed, he evaluated my words.

"And just so you know, being objective is very difficult for me when it comes to this project. I have to be absolutely transparent with you and with our viewership."

A hint of a smile passed his lips. "No woman ever told me I had too much money."

"I don't care about other women. When will you stop comparing me to everyone else?"

"I'm not comparing. I'm admiring."

Blush crept up my cheeks.

"You know what, Cassy Evans?" He leaned forward. "I've never dated a film producer before."

I replied with a tiny laugh.

"I know we haven't discussed this lately, but I believe it's time we go public. I'm tired of the secrecy."

My heart lurched in my chest. Frank's words took me by surprise. With everything he'd been going through emotionally these past few weeks, I hadn't allowed myself to venture back into that territory. We'd put that conversation on hold.

"If I'm part of your project, we can't keep walking on eggshells, doll. Besides, people will figure it out anyway." He licked his upper lip. "I'm going to burn next to you every time we're out in public and I can't hold your hand or touch you."

Heat pooled at my core. I needed so little to get turned on.

"Okay." I nodded and moved closer. "You can touch me right now to get a head start." My height lingered above his body seated in the chair. He shifted and pulled me to stand between his thighs. I sunk my fingers in his silky hair and brushed it away from his face.

"So we're doing it, right?" He looked at me through his long, dark lashes.

"Yes." A giddy smile stretched my lips. My head spun from the realization that we weren't just a phase. We were going to take a step forward in our relationship—no matter how dysfunctionally codependent it was—and make it official. "Could you give me a couple of days to talk to my family?"

"Of course." Frank drew me closer, filling the space between us with his want, erasing the distance and making us one. His warm breath tickled my skin through the thin fabric of my shirt as he buried his face between my breasts.

I loved him like this, undeniably needy and all hot and bothered.

Emotions of every color began to clog my chest.

"My mother is dying to know who you are," I said, kissing the top of his head. "I haven't told her yet."

"It's probably a good idea for me to meet her before we're all over the internet. I wouldn't want my mother to find out I was seeing someone through the tabloids." He tore his cheek from my breast. "Oh, wait. That's exactly how my mother has found out about all my girlfriends."

"You're impossible." I laughed. My happiness was infinite. "You need to stop talking about your ex-girlfriends and other women. You're taken."

"Consequences of being famous." He grinned up at me, eyes bright and shining.

"I'm surprised we've been able to cover this up for so long," I confessed.

"I'm honestly surprised too." His palm skimmed down my back and cupped my ass. "Doesn't matter now. We're worldwide, baby."

Later that evening, while Frank was holed up in his studio, I took the liberty of stalking my brother's Instagram account. His last photo, posted two days ago, was a selfie of him and Levi sitting in front of a large monitor with a screenshot of Isabella's face in After Effects.

He'd changed his handle from @ftninja2001 to @ashtheman2019.

working on some sic shit with my bro @LeviBernstein, the caption below it read.

There were no photos or videos of Frank anywhere on his feed other than a few snippets of live Hall Affinity footage, which was fine. Half of L.A. had gone to that show.

After I'd ensured Ashton hadn't been posting anything he wasn't supposed to, I dialed his number.

"What up, sis?" he yelled. Loud music boomed in the background.

"Where are you?" I asked suspiciously.

"At Levi's."

Relief washed over me. Thank God, it wasn't some bar or a strip club. Ever since Frank bought Ashton that car, I'd been dreading the call from the police to inform me my brother was arrested for something insanely stupid. Like breaking into Selena Gomez's house. "Don't you have school tomorrow?"

"I'm crashing here."

"Can I talk to Levi, please?"

"Why are you calling my phone then?"

"Because I need to talk to you too," I explained. "After I talk to Levi."

The next thing I heard was Ashton shouting over the noise, followed by the thunder of footsteps and the rattle of a soda can.

"What's going on?" Levi barked. The smack of his lips and the grind of his teeth told me he was eating. "Did Frank see the rough cut?"

"Are you corrupting my brother?"

"Don't you worry. He's on his best behavior." Levi's voice dropped to a conspiratorial whisper. "I told him I'd take him with me to interview Athena Angel."

"Don't feed him lies."

"I'm not lying. Did you see the press release? She's gearing up for a new tour."

"I haven't checked the *Rewired* inbox today," I confessed.

"Okay. I got something for you." I could hear Levi moving to another room so we could continue in silence. "I know you don't want to do any on-camera work right now, but I haven't told Shayne about it yet. I reached out to Bennett's manager last month about an exclusive and he specifically asked for you."

A surge of adrenaline hit my bloodstream. During my first two years working with Levi, I got excited about every single interview we locked in. Eventually, when it became part of the routine, I stopped getting emotional, but once in a while, when we nailed down an artist with a story worth sharing, I felt it again. This rush was a reminder of why I did what I did. We created a connection between artists and their fans. We lifted the veil. We let others see who the people injecting their soul into every song they wrote really were.

"I'd love to meet him, but"—my voice shook—"Frank and I are going public and I don't know if this is the right time for me to be getting back in front of the camera."

Levi was silent for a long moment. "Your name is all over this interview."

"When do you need an answer?"

"We have a couple of weeks to decide. Bennett's not fond of the press in general. The label is super picky about publications he speaks to, so I can stall, but ideally, if you could give me an answer before the first, that would be great."

"I want to do it, but I'll need to think about it. By the way, I showed Frank the cut and he loved it. He's still considering my offer, but I believe it will be a yes. For now, let's just lock in the screening date because I can't pitch without it. How does April sound to you?"

"If he decides to be part of the project and I have to add more footage, that'll be tough."

"Isn't tight deadline your middle name?" I laughed.

"No shit."

"All right, then I'm emailing Maria tomorrow about April. Give me my brother now."

"We're not smoking weed, I swear!" Ashton bellowed over the phone after Levi returned it to him.

"I need to talk to you about something else." My tone was serious.

"Okay. You're not moving to Tibet or anything like that, are you?"

"You wish." I paused. "Frank and I are going public, which means you'll probably get stalked on social media and be approached by reporters. I want you to be aware of this and I want to make sure you understand you can't talk to anyone about me and Frank."

"I got it."

"People will promise you money, Ashton. A lot. For exclusive info and photos. Your only response is no response. Capiche?"

"Okay."

"If you open your mouth, Frank and I will never speak to you again and you'll be off *Dreamcatchers*."

"Geez, why you gotta be so mean?"

"I'm not mean. I'm just trying to make sure you understand the situation."

"I'm not dumb. I get it."

"Okay, great. Let's call Mom tomorrow and see what day is good for a family dinner. Frank wants to meet her."

Saying those words out loud felt strange. If someone had told me six months ago I'd be introducing Frankie Blade to my mother, I would have laughed in their face.

"And hey, Ashton," I added before ending the call. "It's probably a good idea for you to set your Instagram account to private. At least for now."

Chapter Seven

Gary Torino was a fiftysomething no-nonsense guy who worked mostly out of his Sherman Oaks studio. On day one, the band was scheduled to arrive early to track the instrumental parts first. Frank and Isabella weren't needed until after lunch.

It was a hectic morning with an incident of spilled coffee and a fight over the toothpaste tube. Frank had been on edge the entire week. The therapy sessions helped him to stay sane, but despite my attempts to keep all the electronic devices with internet access out of his reach, he still managed to find ways to read the news. I suspected Corey was the one who fueled Frank's anger by purposely feeding him updates. Slimy bastard pushed for a lawsuit even after Frank had expressed his desire to postpone filing the paperwork with the court.

We left Malibu at noon with Roman driving us in the Escalade. Our windows were cracked slightly, just enough to let the salty scent of the ocean inside. It was almost peaceful, not counting Frank's knee jerking to my left.

"I think your mother hates my guts," he said as the car began to slow down in anticipation of the upcoming traffic light.

"No, she doesn't." I shook my head. "I think it went really well actually."

"I'm pretty sure she'll poison my spaghetti next time I show up."

I laughed. "Why would she do that to the only boyfriend I've ever had?"

"Did you tell her not to believe everything she's read about me in the tabloids?"

"She won't hold your divorced status against you for long. Don't worry."

My mother wasn't a woman who cared about celebrities, but after I told her who I was seeing, she read everything she could find about Frank on the internet. Including the rumors about all the women he'd dated and the rundown of his short-lived marriage to Heidi Fox.

"Did I hear that correctly?" Frank leaned closer, and his breath tickled my cheek. "Am I the only boyfriend Cassy Evans has had?"

I nodded. "My bar is extremely high, so most candidates don't make it."

"Is that so?" He nipped at my ear.

I loved him when he was playful and I missed our late-night drives and our secret dinners under the stars. I wanted that magic back. There were glimpses of it here and there—in his occasional smile or in a teasing kiss, but it wasn't enough to make me forget about his slip-ups. The fear of losing him to the alcohol again settled deep in my gut like a soccer ball-sized tumor.

The second we stepped foot into the studio, Frank was thrust into the middle of the creative riot that dominated Gary's sanctuary. Story, Andy, and Kit had already recorded several takes and were on a break. Isabella was in the booth with her headphones on, waiting to get started.

I waved a quick hello to everyone and claimed a small couch in the corner. My mind was racing in millions of different directions. I'd expected going public to cause some sort of a bang in the press, followed by the rabid crowds of paparazzi. We'd agreed that we'd just let it happen, let the story run its course. Without any fuss, without any announcements, without any interviews. The lack of gossip almost scared me, but at the same time, I understood that people couldn't really know we were together unless we made appearances and flaunted our relationship in front of the cameras. We hadn't so far. Frank spent most of his days at home or in therapy while I worked on *Dreamcatchers*. Today was the first time we'd actually gone somewhere together in one car, and contrary to my predictions, no reporters tried to attack us on the way to the studio.

Coming out felt almost anticlimactic and I couldn't tell whether this calmness bothered me or I was happy that my family was off the paparazzi radar. At least for now.

Gary's workspace was a dark jungle of glass walls, framed photos, shelved awards, and tables full of equipment. Invisible energy emanated from every corner of every room. I couldn't believe I was in the center of this rock 'n' roll mecca—a place where some of the biggest rock hits had been created under the supervision of a short, soft-spoken man with a receding hairline.

Isabella did several takes, trying out various things. She looked for the right match with the music. Her guttural voice jumped up and down. I could hear the raw power in her breath as she twisted the notes, dragging them, dropping them, then lifting them up.

Frank settled next to the monitors and watched Isabella until Gary had enough to create additional scratch tracks. I'd brought my laptop and attempted to get through an ever-growing pile of emails, but Levi and Ashton, who couldn't come since filming during day one wasn't allowed, kept text message attacking me with memes and video requests.

Maria had arranged catering and we took a thirty-minute dinner break at around six.

Frank was the last one to step into the booth later that evening. He stood behind the glass, tall and impressive, and his gunmetal blue eyes shone intently. I observed him carefully, devouring every move of his lips and every heave of his chest as if the song were my oxygen. His voice had a way with my heart. The experience felt far more intimate than a live show. I was witnessing the birth of something new, something I happened to help create.

My phone pinged during the second chorus. Not wanting to miss a moment, I finished watching the take, then checked the message.

Levi: It's Marshall Burns!!!

My heart dropped to my stomach.

Is that official or still a rumor?

Levi: Someone posted a video of Dante and Marshall on Reddit thirty minutes ago. It just hit TMZ and BuzzFeed.

Thanks.

Levi: You need to see the video.

A link popped up on my screen next. I set my laptop aside and rose from the couch. Panic pulsed through me when Frank's gaze flicked over to my face. Offering him the best smile I could muster, I then rushed out of the lounge and called Linda.

"I thought they weren't going to announce the name for another week!" I fumed, pacing the small restroom.

"That was the plan," Linda said with a heavy sigh.

"So someone leaked it?" I asked for clarification.

"Yes."

"Why did it have to happen today?"

"I'm sure you know firsthand that this is absolutely normal these days. It's not the nineties anymore."

"Yes." I stopped in my tracks and tried to think. Keeping Frank away from his phone these past couple of days had been difficult. "It's just bad fucking timing is all." A sardonic laugh escaped from my lungs. "Would you keep me updated? Please?"

"I'll do my best, but it's out of my hands now."

Linda ended the call.

I drew my phone away from my ear and pulled up the message exchange with Levi. My panic grew bigger with each second as I watched the Reddit video of Dante and his new sidekick—Marshall Burns. He was a fresh face with the body of Adonis and the voice of Orpheus. A rock 'n' roll version of a Greek god, who nailed all the high notes in a thirty-second-long snippet of "Adrenaline Lane" that had been uploaded by an anonymous user. If anything, Marshall's looks would be distracting enough for the crowd not to realize he was an impostor. His own band's sophomore album peaked in Billboard's top ten last summer. I'd interviewed him a few times. The man could hold his own on and off stage. Obviously, he was no Frankie Blade, but he was younger and possessed enough charisma to fill the shoes of his predecessor.

When there was a soft knock on the door, I called out, "Just a second." Then I slipped my phone in my pocket and took a deep breath. News had never rattled me like this before. Levi and I had lived through a lot of band break-ups, but everything was different with Frank. Too personal.

Putting my plastic smile back on, I marched out of the restroom and returned to the lounge, where I continued to pretend things were great until we finally left the studio at around midnight.

Exhausted, Frank climbed into the back of the Escalade and slumped against the seat. The silence thickened as the car steered onto the freeway. There was a certain level of awareness that hung around us like a rain cloud, but I was too scared to speak first.

"Something I should know about?" Frank finally asked, his voice low and raspy after multiple takes.

Contemplating, I grabbed his hand as if it would stop him from checking his phone. "I think this should wait till tomorrow."

He turned his head to look at me and paused a few seconds before posing the question, "Who is it?" The faint lines in the corner of his left eye deepened.

The silence that filled the space between us was lead heavy.

"Marshall Burns," I replied after a moment.

Frank remained abnormally calm. His gaze swept over my face, lingering on my lips. Suddenly, he was unreadable, surrounded by an impenetrable wall he'd built in a matter of seconds.

I squeezed his hand and brought my mouth to his. "Fuck Marshall Burns. Fuck Dante. Fuck them all."

"You have a way with words, Cassy." A light chuckle met my breath. "Especially the swear ones."

"So I've been told."

I wasn't sure when exactly it happened, in the car or at home, that I sensed the turbulence Frank was experiencing, but it woke me up in the middle of the night—the invisible dread. Restless, I lay on my back and stared at the streaks of lingering moonlight seeping into the bedroom through the cracks between the shades. The pitter-patter of my heart against my ribs filled the deafening silence that reigned in the house.

Stretching my arm, I brushed the sheets on the side of the bed Frank usually occupied. They were uninvitingly cold. Had he slept at all?

I found him in the dining room. Legs spread, head tossed back, he was sprawled in a chair that had been positioned to face the ocean view. His silhouette, framed by the shimmer of the moon-light coming in through the unshaded window, looked dejected. A bottle and a glass sat next to him on a table. His phone lay beside them.

I smelled liquor on his breath from across the room. He was wasted.

"Come to bed," I said, approaching him.

Frank didn't move. His face remained still, eyes dark, as if he hadn't heard me at all.

"Please. You have a really long day tomorrow and you need to be rested." I knew I sounded patronizing and policing, but I had no idea how else to talk to him when he was like this—*like my father*. Some-times I succeeded. Sometimes I failed. There was no rhyme or reason behind his responses to the various approaches I'd tried.

"He's pretty good," Frank rasped out.

I rounded the chair and positioned myself in his line of view. "Why do you do this to yourself?"

"Because it's my fucking band." His icy gaze ran over the length of my body and stopped in the vicinity of my breasts, maybe too tired to go further, maybe too distracted by the sight of my nipples showing from beneath the lace of my slip.

"You need to let it go, Frank. For your own sanity. Please."

"Can't you tell how empty I am, doll?" he slurred. Each word, soft and slushy, felt like a struggle, and as much as I wanted to cuddle him and put him to bed, my common sense told me my kindness wouldn't do him any good. I'd been too kind too long.

Popping my hip, I folded both arms on my chest and asked, "Do you know what else is empty?" My chin jerked up in the direction of the table. "That bottle."

He raised his hand and pointed at his chest. "That'd be me." A cheeky smile touched his lips.

Acid rose at the back of my throat. I had to look away for a moment.

"Don't be mad, baby." The crack in his voice cut so deep, it hurt to breathe.

"You have a chance to do something good, something really meaningful." I paused to get more air in my lungs. My heartbeats were mad and loud. "But you choose to let people who don't give a fuck about you drag you down."

"Do you have any idea how it feels, Cassy?"

"It feels like shit. Doesn't mean you should let it take over your emotions."

He was silent. The moonlight gleamed over the ink and scars on his bare chest.

"It's my own damn fault," Frank said finally, reaching for the glass. "I built something that I couldn't handle. I sold myself to the devil, to the suits, to the fans. Everyone got the piece they paid for. There are no more pieces left. Nothing to create new music from. I'm fucking dried up."

"That's not true," I countered. "You have a lot more music in you."

"Don't be naïve." He chuckled, bringing the drink to his mouth.

"This song you give me so much credit for isn't mine. I'm just riding piggyback."

"You're drunk, Frank. I don't see why we need to discuss this right now. Let's go back to bed."

He ignored me. "Tell me, you seriously think I deserve all the praise I'm getting?"

"You and Isabella are amazing together. Fans will love you both." I stepped closer.

"You promised to be honest." He dropped his gaze to the drink in his hand and scanned the leftovers of the liquor.

"I am being honest. I think what you're doing is very noble."

Frank drained the glass and set it on the table next to the empty bottle. Just like my father, he was a miserable drunk. Talking to him was like talking to a wall and I hated it. He made little sense and refused to compromise. But what I hated more was the horrible feeling of dread that had been clutching my gut all night. I was losing this battle to Frank's demons. Everything we'd built over the past few weeks was crumbling right now like a house of cards.

He said it then, "She's better off on her own."

My heart stopped beating. Tightness pulled at my chest. "You're going to bed." I reached for his hand.

"In a bit." He shook his head.

"Come on." I slid my palm into his to lace our fingers together and made an attempt to get him up, but he was too heavy. "Frank, I'm serious. We have a long day tomorrow."

His other hand rose from the arm of the chair and grabbed at my leg, pulling me closer. I stumbled and lost my balance. My chin landed on top of his left shoulder.

"You smell nice," he slurred against my cheek as I tried to steady myself. His alcohol breath was hot and unpleasant.

"I'm really tired. Please, let's just go to bed."

Frank's hands continued to roam my body aimlessly. "You're the best girlfriend I've ever had, doll."

At that moment, the compliment didn't matter much, because something dark lurked between us. We weren't whole anymore.

I woke up at the crack of dawn. My head pounded and every muscle in my body ached from last night's struggle with Frank. It'd taken me a good hour to get him to calm down.

He slept like a rock while I paced the bedroom and checked my phone. Marshall Burns was all over Facebook and Twitter and judging by the comments, most Hall Affinity fans weren't as upset as I'd thought they'd be. Of course, a few die-hard Frankie Blade followers didn't shy away from posting their opinions, but objectively speaking, Marshall was a good choice.

In the kitchen, Hannah was preparing breakfast. She sensed my anger instantly. The bags under my eyes were probably another reason why she asked me if everything was okay.

I shook my head and tossed my phone on the counter, needing a break from Marshall's face. "He was drinking again yesterday."

"Aye!" Hannah's brows knitted together. She palmed her cheeks and gave me a sympathetic look.

"I don't know what to do," I confessed. My mind roared after my hell of a night and I couldn't imagine pulling another twelve-hour day in the studio. Besides, it'd be double the work with Ashton and Levi there today. But the main question was whether Frank would be able to lay vocals hung over.

"Maybe you should tell Mr. Billy," Hannah whispered, handing me a container with creamer as I fixed myself a cup of coffee.

"Maybe I will."

My phone rattled against the marble countertop. The call was from Ashton, and while I was tempted to let it go to voicemail, my brother calling me this early could only mean one thing—an emergency.

The panic in his voice twisted my stomach. "My car is gone!" he screamed as a wall of noises came from the background.

"What do you mean, gone?"

"I mean it's gone from where I parked it." The din of the street traffic muffled his hysterical sobs. "Someone stole it!"

"Where are you?"

"I'm at Samy's. I went inside to take care of business. Came back out, the car's gone."

I closed my eyes and drew a deep breath through my teeth. Today hadn't even started yet, but it already promised to be a total shitshow. "First of all, why are you at Samy's? Second, where did you park?"

"I told you. Levi asked me to pick up a lens."

Fucking Levi, I growled internally.

"I understand that. Where did you park your car? On the street? In the lot?"

"On the street."

Somehow it didn't surprise me at all. My brother and road signs weren't friends. I should have seen this coming.

"Where on the street?"

"Behind the building."

"Why didn't you valet it?"

"A bunch of assholes blocked the entrance. I didn't have time to wait around."

Smiling apologetically at Hannah who was unwillingly subjected to my brawl with my brother, I took a generous sip of my coffee to get my brain going. "I'm sorry to tell you this, but your car is probably on its way to some impound lot in Venice Beach."

"Well, I have to get it back!"

"It's not going to happen until tomorrow, Ashton."

"I've got gear in the trunk. I need it for today."

Of course, as if my life didn't need more complications. Babysitting two grown men had never been so much fun. "Are you fucking kidding me?" I gritted out.

"You know what?" Ashton huffed. "You're a shitty sister."

"And you're a shitty car owner."

I pulled the phone away from my ear and tried to think. Frank didn't have to be at Sherman Oaks until eleven. Technically, he didn't even need me to go with him, but last night's drinking spree made me doubt his ability to make important decisions today.

"Okay, check the signs and talk to the attendant," I told him on my way to the bathroom. "If the car was towed, please find out what forms of payment they take and if they can take a credit card over the phone."

There was a message with the address of the impound lot waiting for me when I stepped out of the shower.

"Great," I muttered, staring at the text for a good minute. Annoyance brewed in my gut.

First, I called my brother. "Do you have proof of insurance on you?"

"Umm..." He paused.

"Ashton?"

"In my email."

"Can they take my card over the phone?"

"No, they said the credit card holder has to be there to pay in person."

"Okay, I'll get you an Uber and I'll meet you there in an hour."

Then I called Roman. "Could you please come over right now?"

"I thought Frank said ten."

"I have to go get the stupid BMW out of impound. You'll need to drive Frank to Sherman Oaks." I paused to catch my breath. "He was drinking last night, so he's probably hung over...and not in a very good mood. I'm going to go ahead and wake him so that he can get moving, but I need you to be nearby since I won't be here."

Roman cleared his throat. "I understand."

"You have to make sure he's there by eleven. Gary is leaving for New York tomorrow, so vocals must be recorded today."

"I got you, Ms. Evans. I'll be there in thirty minutes."

Frank looked frazzled when I woke him.

"I'm sorry, but you gotta get up." I shook his shoulder lightly, my phone in my hand.

"What?" Hair mussed, face sleepy, he rubbed his eyes and absently stared at me through the shadow of his flitting lashes. His clouded gaze ran over my mouth as if I were speaking Arabic.

"Roman will be here in a bit. I'll meet you at the studio." I pulled the blanket aside and helped him sit up.

"What time is it?"

"It's eight."

Confusion crossed his features. "I thought we didn't have to be there until eleven."

"Don't ever buy anything for my brother again. Asshole got the car towed." Rolling my eyes, I nudged Frank off the bed and ushered him to the bathroom.

Dazed, he stepped into the shower cabin and fumbled with the controls. Water splashed against the glass.

"I'll meet you at the studio, okay?" I said, putting the finishing touches on my makeup.

Frank's hangover was evident. Palms against the tiled side of the cabin, head down, he lingered somewhere on the edge of awareness, and seeing this reminder of his recklessness the night before drove me mad. The last thing I wanted to do was leave him alone, but Ashton was blowing up my phone like crazy.

"Okay." Frank nodded, lifting his face to meet the stream. There was weakness in his every move and breath.

"Hannah made waffles!" I shouted on my way out.

Ashton was already waiting for me when I pulled up to the office of the impound lot that was somewhere on the outskirts of Santa Monica. It was in a crappier part of the city, across from the cemetery. Beat up asphalt and plastic dumpsters greeted me as I maneuvered my Honda between the rows of vehicles. My head hurt from lack of coffee and sleep.

Inside, there was a mile-long line and it took me a minute to find Ashton.

"I thought you were going to ditch me," he said under his breath as I wormed my way into the spot between his shoulder and some woman's oversized Coach bag.

"I'm having an extremely bad day. Let's just get this over with."

"That's why I need my own credit card."

"Oh, really?" I stared up at him with every intention of mentally burning him to the ground. "So you can forget it somewhere too?"

"It wasn't like that."

"Then how was it, huh?" I hissed. "You dragged me all the way across town because you can't read road signs."

My observation was met with a dramatic pout.

We waited for nearly an hour. By the time Ashton finally received his precious car keys back, I had two missed calls from Roman, three texts from Brooklyn, and all signs of a heart attack.

Frank never made it to the studio.

Panic crawled up my throat as we hurried to leave the building and get to our vehicles. I dialed Frank's cell twice but was greeted by the same generic service provider programmed voice message.

"You owe me the Uber fee and the three hundred bucks I just paid for your car," I snapped at Ashton as we walked through the lot.

"You're joking, right?" He gave me the side-eye.

"It's called adulting, buddy."

I knew he'd never have that kind of money unless he started smuggling drugs or got a job as a male stripper, but I couldn't resist the urge to yell at someone, and between Roman, who, according to our phone conversation, had missed Frank earlier this morning, and my brother, it was obviously going to be my brother.

On the way to Sherman Oaks, I called Frank's house phone and asked Hannah to check the garage. Of course, the Ferrari was missing. My anxiety shot through the roof. It clawed at my thundering heart like a predator, tearing it into small pieces. *This wasn't happening. Not today,* I thought as I dialed again and again, only to hear the same recording.

The burst of cool air blasting from the vents pricked my cheeks and I could barely feel my face, but the tremor that took over the rest of my body compensated for that numbness tenfold. The seconds seemed to drag by as if this were a three-day cross-country drive.

When I arrived at the studio, Ashton and Levi were already there, unloading their equipment. Without saying a word to them, I brushed past the cluster of cases and hurried to find Brooklyn.

Inside, a dozen stupefied gazes were shot at me. Isabella was in the booth, doing a take. Her voice felt dangerous, stronger and riskier than yesterday. Hunched over the control board, Gary didn't see me come in.

Maria, however, looked concerned.

"I thought Frankie was supposed to be here by lunch?" she whispered as she pulled me to the side.

"He's coming down with something, but he should be here soon." I felt like shit lying to her, but I had no idea what else to say.

Hey, Maria. No one knows where the man who's supposed to record a duet with your daughter today is. But he did get drunk last night and threw himself one hell of a pity party, so chances are, he'll be gone anywhere from two days to two weeks.

In my peripheral, Brooklyn was waving at me.

"I'm just nervous," Maria confessed. "This is such a big deal for Izzy."

"It'll be fine." I offered her a smile. "These things happen all the time. He hasn't been feeling well for a couple of days."

The song ended and I heard the rattle of the door. Then Ashton was pushing one of the cases down the hallway, and Levi was right behind him with his camera bag in tow. I almost wanted to tell them to hold off on setting up the gear but realized that would only alarm the rest of the team and the band.

Frustration pinched my chest.

"Let me see what his assistant says," I told Maria and followed Brooklyn to the small lounge at the quieter end of the building.

"I thought you two were coming together," she sputtered, shutting the door so we could both have a breakdown in private.

"I had to leave early to get Ashton's car out of impound. Roman was supposed to drive him here."

"I cannot believe this shit." She stilled and squeezed the bridge of her nose.

"Did you call Corey?"

"He hasn't spoken to Frank since last night."

Artists were eccentric, but dropping from the face of the Earth today of all days?

"You said to give him space." I threw my hands in the air, unable to control my emotions. My head spun from the raging pain zapping through it. "Now he's probably somewhere halfway to Vegas, drunk and with a broken shoulder!"

"You need to cool the fuck down." Brooklyn shoved her finger into my chest, her voice taut with anger.

"Don't fucking touch me!" I slapped her hand away. "You can just say it. You don't like me. You've never liked me. But I seem to be the only one who wants him to get better."

Her face twisted. "And you don't tell me how to do my job." She whirled around and marched over to the door.

"Where are you going?"

She gave me a sideways glance. "To look for Frank."

"I'm going with you."

"No, you're not. You're staying here."

It hit me then. Being Frankie Blade's girlfriend wouldn't be easy. I'd be responsible for his every word and every mistake. People would be looking at me the way Isabella looked at me when I returned to the recording room—with bitter disappointment in her eyes.

I promised her she'd be heard. Instead, I'd let her down.

Frank's no-show stunt made me feel like a complete failure of a person. I could only postpone the news for so long. It was nearing dinnertime when the message I'd dreaded all day popped up on my phone.

Brooklyn: He just came back home drunk and tried to fire me. I wouldn't wait up.

What do you want me to do?

Brooklyn: It's your project. Studio time is paid for.

I put my phone away and summoned the leftovers of my self-control to make an announcement. "It doesn't look like Frankie will be able to join us today after all."

A collective gasp filled the room.

"I know this is a big deal for you all." Lying to everyone's faces made me sick to my stomach. "He truly is sorry, but he hasn't been well these past few days."

I stood in the center of everyone and willed my mind to block their accusatory gazes.

"Is he going to be okay?" Story asked, fingering the strings on his guitar.

"Hopefully." I despised myself for this farce. Frank wasn't ill. He was a coward. "I do think we should finish the single." I turned to look at Gary, unsure if he was up for it.

The man gave me a one-shoulder shrug. "I'm good until midnight."

Isabella was silent a long moment. Her eyes hardened. It made no difference whether she was going to record "Afterburn" right now or later. If she chose to finish tracking today, it'd be the only song on the album produced by Gary Torino.

"The studio is paid for," I explained. "It's your song. Your call. Whatever you decide."

"Sure." She nodded. "Let's get this baby done since we're all here." Her smile was like a knife to my chest, a painful twist. I could tell she felt cheated, and sadly, there wasn't a single thing I could do to make it better.

Only Frank had that power.

Isabella returned to the booth for another take. Too wired to watch, I stepped outside to get fresh air and clear my head. The distant hum of Ventura Boulevard replaced the blasts of music. Clouds hung low above the Valley. Shy spurs of first fog licked the hillside. The evening was perfect. Dark, crisp, and full of dreams. Just not mine.

Levi found me a few minutes later. "What's going on, Cass?" Hands in his pockets, he strolled up.

I glanced at my phone, hoping to see a missed call or a message from Frank. "Don't know."

"He's not really sick, is he? He changed his mind. Am I right?"

I disregarded his question because I didn't have an answer. "Let's get whatever we can for now." A shuddered breath left my lungs.

"I guess the interview is out too?"

"I honestly don't know."

Levi didn't press for more.

The light rattle of Isabella's wheelchair cut our conversation short.

"My eyes can't take this cockfest anymore." She steered over to us.

I laughed softly, wondering yet again where this girl found the energy to joke while everything we'd been working toward was falling apart.

Levi rolled his eyes.

"What?" I slapped his chest with the back of my hand. "It's like eight against three in there right now."

"Sure." He snickered and glanced at his phone. "I'm going to check my time-lapse. And you two"—his index finger bounced between Isabella and me—"behave. Don't break any hearts while left unsupervised."

"Can't make any promises!" Isabella hollered. "It's not every day you meet a girl with a bondage-ready chair."

Laughing, I watched Levi disappear inside.

"He seems very tense." She shared her thoughts on my partner.

"It's all the Red Bull he drinks."

"That explains it."

I wasn't sure what else to say or where to even start. I had too many things on my mind right now. But I felt that I was more responsible than anyone for Frank's behavior. Had I tried hard enough with him? Had I done everything I could?

"I'm sorry about today, Isabella."

She gazed up at me with her big, stormy eyes, which were full of defeat. "Why? It's not your fault."

"It is. I told you I'd make this happen for you."

"It's not the end of the world that a two-time Grammy winner doesn't want to collaborate with some chick from the San Jose ghetto. I've been lowballed all my life, so I'll get over it."

"People suck," I offered her my theory.

She took a deep breath and pondered something for a few seconds. "If this is what fame does to people, I don't think I want it." I heard the tremor in her voice. "Look at me." She jerked up her chin. "I'll never get up from this chair. I'll never have another dance. I'll never have another walk on the beach. But I *will* sing because that's what gives me freedom. That's what makes me who I am. Nothing or no one is going to stop me."

I felt her rebellion against her circumstances with every single cell in my body. Tears welled in my eyes, but my gut told me to hold them in, to wait until no one could see me.

"You're a beautiful young woman," I said. "You have your whole life ahead of you. You'll sell millions of records and you'll tour the world. And if Frank isn't part of it, that's okay. His loss."

I had no idea if she was going to sell that many records in the world of streaming, but I needed to tell her that because I truly believed she had something others didn't.

"You shouldn't take the blame for his shortcomings. You can't change a person if a person doesn't welcome the change."

Isabella sounded a lot like my mother, and I wondered how a nineteen-year-old disabled girl had this much wisdom when a thirty-eight-year-old man with everything one could dream of didn't have enough guts to stand up to his weakness.

"I wish it wasn't so complicated, Isabella."

"It doesn't have to be. We tend to create our own demons when we could be doing something else instead of self-pitying."

I let out a ragged sigh. My heart was a fresh wound, and Isabella's words hit me hard. "I wish he could see that."

"It must be difficult." Her eyes remained locked on mine. "Being with someone like him."

I kept silent.

"I'm crippled, not blind." She shook her head. "You really think I can't tell you're an item? Have been for a while now."

For some reason, a smile touched my lips. As much as I hated Frank at the moment, one mention of us stirred me up and warmed my shivering heart. Even at his lowest, he was like an eclipse, shadowing everything else, drawing all attention. And I hated him for that.

"You look at him the way Ayala used to look at me—like I was her whole world." A pensive expression crossed Isabella's face. "Then one night when we were at a party, she got too drunk and I was too soft to stop her. Now I can't walk and she's somewhere in college in Alabama. In a few years, her record will be expunged and I'm still going to be in a wheelchair."

I needed a second to process.

"Sometimes people we care about don't care enough in return." Isabella broke our eye contact and looked up to the dark sky. Her voice was a deep rasp after hours of singing. "Sometimes letting go is the best thing we can do because we're risking everything for that one person when that one person can't be saved. There's no point in dying while trying."

"How do you know when to let go?"

"That's the thing. I don't know. If I did, I wouldn't be in a wheelchair."

It was a profound exploration of human relationships that came from someone who hadn't been an adult long enough to lose so much.

"You know what?" I kneeled and grabbed her hands. "We don't need anyone, Isabella. When Levi and I decided to do this, it was your story and it should stay your story and no one else's."

"You're very kind to me. Most people wouldn't care to do what you and Levi are doing."

"There's enough hate and ignorance. I see so much of it every day online, and I wonder how we're still a civilized society. If we're not kind and if we continue to be selfish, the world may end sooner than we expect."

"It's too bad you're straight, Cassy. Because I would totally ask you out right now." She grinned.

"I might switch camps if Frank and I don't work out. I'm about to give up on men."

"Men are headaches. I'm in a band with three and they drive me nuts. I'd ditch them all if the fuckers weren't so goddamn talented and I didn't love them to death."

"Can't live with them, can't live without them," I agreed.

"You know what they say?" She grinned. "Fight fire with fire. If shit doesn't work out, go find yourself another man...or a woman. Whatever you're into."

"You think that helps?"

"Hell yes, it does. That's the first thing I did after my break-up. Went out on a date."

"Was it fun?"

"Definitely better than sitting home and crying. At the very least, you're getting a free dinner out of it."

"I'll keep that strategy in mind."

"Izzie! Need you in five!" Maria's voice called.

"All right. I gotta go bust out another take, sister," Isabella said, steering her wheelchair toward the door.

I took off for Malibu ten minutes later, leaving Levi in charge.

The French doors on the terrace were slid open when I pulled into the driveway. The garage was closed, and Jeff Buckley's voice drifted at me from the house. I tossed my purse on the couch, then kicked off my shoes and sauntered through the music-filled rooms in search of Frank. My heart raced. I hated altercations, but after having witnessed Isabella's dreams crumple today, I was too pissed off to keep it in check. Raw, unadulterated anger stirred in my blood.

Frank was in his studio. Back against the output panel, he sat on the floor across from the line of newly installed monitors. They were bright and shiny and mounted atop the cherry finish desk, and I wondered how long they'd last. I lingered on the threshold and noted a bottle in his hand.

"How was your day, doll?" Glazed eyes swept up my body and stalled on my lips.

The pungent smell of liquor crawled up my nose. The man was wasted again.

I stepped closer and surveyed the room, looking for traces of more damage. There was none. Today, Frank had resorted to simply drinking himself into oblivion.

"Where were you?" I asked firmly.

"Out and about. Needed to clear my head."

"If you didn't want to be part of this project, why couldn't you just tell me?" I said in a shaky voice. "Why come and do a bunch of scratch tracks and then not show up to record the actual song?"

"I know you hate me right now." He tossed his head back and absently stared at the ceiling. His chest heaved. "I hate myself too. Sometimes I wonder why I didn't die that night on a freeway."

The weight of his words hit me hard. My mind and my heart battled each other. One wanted to slap some sense into this man and one wanted to cuddle him. "Don't say shit like that."

"Why not?" He released a bitter chuckle. "We're all going to die. We should be ready the day we're born. Instead, we keep looking for ways to live longer when, in reality, we're all slowly decaying on the inside." Frank reached for the bottle. "Ask me." His desperate eyes burned through my skin like a torch. "Ask me what it's like, how it feels to rot on the inside little by little, day after day."

I leaned over to take the bottle away, but he shot down my measly attempt by blocking me with his right hand. His shoulder wasn't secured in the sling, and too scared to hurt him, I didn't dare fight.

Instead, I tried to reason, "You promised, Frank. You can't mix alcohol and painkillers."

"Watch me." He grinned and took a swallow. "It's just like the good old days...when Dante and I worked on *Breathe Crimson*. Now he's got a new best friend. Marshall fucking Burns." His Adam's apple wobbled beneath his skin. "You ever tried heroin, Cassy?"

The invisible wall of indifference and pain he'd built grew thicker with each second as he rambled on.

Annoyed and uninterested in hearing his rock 'n' roll stories, I straightened. "You made a fool out of me today. You left us all hanging like we weren't important enough."

"You know you're important to me."

"Oh yeah?" My tone pitched. "How am I important when you don't have the decency to tell me you don't want to be part of my project? You didn't have to agree just to humor me if your heart wasn't in it. I wouldn't have gotten mad or loved you any less. "

"Shhh," he hushed me and pressed his index finger to his lips. "Don't say it. Don't let me hurt you more than I already have."

Fury spread through my chest. "And you also don't have the decency to acknowledge my feelings." My voice broke along with my faith in us. I hated the ugliness we'd become and the game of pretend we'd been playing.

"I don't need you to tell me," Frank murmured, resting his head against the panel. He drew a deep breath, his gaze remaining on my face. "I know."

Emotions swelled in my chest. "Is that all I get? A fucking Han Solo one-liner for splitting myself in half for you?"

He stared up at me with clouded eyes as silent seconds passed between us. "What do you want from me then?" He slurred.

The house felt foreign despite the music. Even the soulful crooning of Jeff Buckley couldn't pacify my rage. "I want you to get help, Frank. Real fucking help!" I cried out. "What happened to you isn't Marshall's fault, and the world hasn't conspired against you. Stop acting like a child and looking for answers in a bottle of whiskey. They're not there."

Jaw slack, he gave me a crooked, shiver-inducing smile. "You know, you're very sexy when you're mad."

My patience had reached its limits. I was unamused and shaking with frustration.

Deep breaths, girlfriend, I said to myself. "Do you even understand what I'm trying to tell you?"

"I'm not that drunk." He shook his head and set the empty bottle aside.

"Yes, you are and you need professional help."

"Fuck professional help."

He pushed himself off the floor and stood. The room suddenly felt small. He wasn't a tall man, but his height was impressive against my five-four. Without a word, he stumbled past me toward the hallway.

I followed.

He halted in front of the wall with the paintings and stared at them for a good minute. "Do you know how much each one of these cost, Cassy?" His gaze whipped to my face, dark and foggy. "Fifty thousand dollars. Can you imagine?"

"Where's Roman?"

"Did you know—" He paused to catch his breath. "The first time I tried chocolate was after Janet and Billy took me in."

My stomach spasmed. I hated that he made me pity him.

"Now I have a piece of paper in my living room that cost more than my birth mother made in a year." Frank continued to stare. "And the funny thing is...I don't know why I even have it."

"Where's Roman?" I repeated my question. I had no idea how disorderly he could get with this much alcohol in his system, but I wanted to be ready for the worst, and my hundred and ten pounds weren't going to cut it against the wall of lean muscle and madness that he was.

"Why?" Frank arched a brow. "You don't like my company?"

"Not when you're drunk," I said firmly.

He turned his back to me and staggered down the hall, every single ounce of his torment weighing on his shoulders, dragging him down to hell. His broken footsteps thudded against the floor like an off-beat rhythm. In the living room, furniture banged and keys jingled.

Heart in my throat, I raced through the house. "Where are you going?" My pulse skyrocketed.

"I'm not in the mood to listen to your pestering. I get enough of this shit from everyone. My parents. My assistant. My manager. I don't need you to police me too."

Ouch. "Excuse me? Me wanting you to get better is pestering?"

Helmet in hand, Frank was on his way to the garage. Skirting around his body to face him, I stood in the doorway and held out my hand. "Give me the keys."

He didn't stop. His shoulder knocked against mine.

"Give me the keys." I twirled around and grabbed his arm.

He jerked away.

My mother was right. Saving someone from himself if he didn't want to be saved was a waste of time.

In the house, Jeff Buckley sang "Hallelujah." The majestic lull of his voice filled the air as Frank rounded the Escalade, his steps unsteady.

"You're not going anywhere!" My shout boomed through the garage as I hurried along the line of cars parked there. All five of them. Including the Ferrari with its muddy wheels.

"Get out of my way, Cassy." He shot me a mean stare and neared the Harley.

Determined, I positioned myself in front of the bike and grabbed the handlebar. My pulse roared.

"Move, Cassy."

"You're not going, Frank!" I screamed, my lungs and my throat tense with panic. "You'll crash!"

The man was so drunk, he'd lost all his marbles. I had no idea how to reason with him.

"Get out of my way, doll."

"I won't. You're going to have to run me over, Frank!"

We yelled at each other full throttle. Angry words spilled and soared through the garage, drowning out the soft sounds of the music. Staining everything good, every nice memory of this house and us with depravity.

Frank was a blur behind the tears forming in my eyes. He grabbed the handlebar and turned the front wheel to twist it out of my hold. I felt it crunch against the cement and grind against my jeans as my foot slid over the floor. Every muscle in me drew tight.

"Please stop it," I pleaded, clutching his wrist. "Please, Frank! I don't want to hurt you."

"I need to ride. Move."

It was a split-second decision. I knew he wouldn't cease trying otherwise. He was teetering on the edge of insane, too stubborn and too drunk to hear me.

I pushed him. I pushed him hard. I didn't want to, but I had no choice. It was either risk his stitches and a couple of bones or let him leave and never come back, because he wouldn't.

Not after this stupid suicide ride he was so hell-bent on attempting.

My heart pounded so hard, my ribcage felt as if it was about to crack in half. The swell of moisture in my eyes made it difficult to see, but I heard a thud. Frank's body had slammed against the Escalade. The helmed dropped to the floor.

"Fuck you!" he cried out in anger and pushed himself off the car. Pain twisted his face. "Fuck you!"

"Well, fuck you too!" I was shaking. "If you want paramedics scraping your insides from the bottom of the ditch, be my guest."

"Who the hell are you to judge me? You don't know anything about me, doll."

"That's right, I don't. Because you won't fucking talk to me. Because you'd rather drink yourself stupid. Guess what? I've already seen one man in my life go down that road. I'm not going to stick around to watch another do the same shit."

My wrath was immense. Apocalyptic proportions. I hated my father. I hated Frank, but most of all, I hated myself for not being enough for either one of them.

Every drop of my blood raged a mad fire. The fury was absolute. Blinded by hurt, I kicked the bike with all the strength left in me. It tipped and fell over, its crash drowning out the sounds of the music and Frank's loud, angry breaths.

Resentment blazed in his eyes. He spun to the Escalade, jerked the door open, and climbed into the driver's seat.

Disbelief choked me. Fists balled, I screamed. It was a spiteful growl. No words. Just noise. My lashes were heavy with tears and I felt them spill down my cheeks one by one, burning my skin. Sick adrenaline ran through my veins.

Frank was out of control. Delusional.

He activated the remote inside the car and I heard the soft scrape of the automatic garage door behind me. Cool air rushed in from the outside. The Escalade's engine rumbled.

Think, Cassy. Think! my inner voice howled.

My gaze scoured the shelves as I searched for something to stop him. My trembling hands sifted through the scattering of useless gadgets. The man didn't have a single tool in his garage that a car owner actually needed.

Grabbing the first thing I deemed strong enough—a wrench, I raced over to the door and wedged it into the chain. A shrill screech pierced the exhaust-filled air as the metal panels came to a halt.

The Escalade was like a beast. It roared, its tires squealing against the cement floor. Cursing, Frank scrambled out of the vehicle and began his approach.

I shook my head. "Please stop." He drilled past me and yanked at the wrench but to no avail. He was too drunk.

Heart thrashing, I charged back into the house to get my phone.

A string of expletives followed by heavy footsteps and the banging of furniture trailed after me while I galloped through the hallway as if the floor were on fire.

"Fix the goddamn door." Frank's voice carried over the noise.

Dialing Roman's number, I ran out onto the terrace. The cold stones bit my feet. The line clicked.

"Ms. Evans?"

"You need to come over right now. Frank is drunk. He just tried to get on his bike." I paused to catch my breath and hopped down the stairs, skipping a step.

"Mr. Blade gave me the rest of the week off," he said carefully.

Behind me, the front door slammed.

"I don't think you understand. He's very drunk and he needs a doctor," I muttered as I walked to my Honda, my keychain clutched in my palm so hard, my skin started to tear. "I really don't want to call in a domestic disturbance, but I don't know how to handle him." My words were turning into sobs.

"I'll be right there."

"Thank you." I breathed out a sigh of relief and fumbled with the key fob to unlock my car. My hand shook.

Frank was closing in on me. "Where the fuck are you going?" His voice was an ugly rasp and didn't sound like his own.

I spun around and matched his stare. He looked dangerous. And not in a good kind of way. His body swayed like a leaf in the wind, ready to drop to the ground.

"And where the fuck are *you* going and where the fuck have you been all day?" I screamed back. "I needed you! Isabella needed you! What the fuck is wrong with you?"

"You broke my fucking door." Fuming, he motioned at the garage door. "Then you tried to fucking assault me in my own house!"

I could see the Escalade's headlights streaming into the foggy yard from under the jammed panel. "Well, why don't you sue me for that, Frank, huh? Since that's your best strategy when things don't go your way."

"And then you tried to fucking kill me."

"Are you serious?" I couldn't believe my ears.

He staggered over.

I rounded the car to stand on the opposite side. I needed to put some distance between us. A barrier.

"You wanted to talk, let's fucking talk." His face was ravaged by pain and anger. "What do you want to know? Do you wanna hear about how it feels when you drive into a fucking wall riding a hundred and twenty an hour?"

"I can't talk to you when you're like this, and I can't be with you when you're like this. You promised me you'd get help!"

"And you're supposed to be my girlfriend, not my fucking therapist."

We went on arguing for endless minutes until the rumble of Roman's car broke us up. He dragged Frank back into the house and called a medic.

I left.

Old, almost forgotten memories of my father flashed in front of me as I steered my Honda down the mountain road. He'd been a sloppy and mute drunk who spent his days glued to the TV with a bottle of whatever he could get his hands on while our mother worked two jobs to support his habit.

But not once during all those fourteen years of living with an alcoholic had I felt the way I felt with Frank tonight. Terrified.

I'd been ignored, but I'd never been yelled at and subjected to the kind of emotional violence he'd put me through.

My hands still shook and my heartbeat was like a damaged vintage tape, pounding, scratching, and getting stuck. I drove without any sense of direction, making random turns and listening to my heavy metal playlist that consisted mainly of classic Slipknot and Avenged Sevenfold. Frank's angry voice still roared in my head and I wanted his screams purged. I wanted today, with all its disappointments and resentment, erased completely.

The bottom of my right foot burned like hell. Roman had been kind enough to snatch a pair of shoes for me before I left. I couldn't bring myself to go back into that house. Not after everything that had happened there.

Hours later, I squeezed my car between two SUVs down the street from my mother's apartment. My mind still raced. I wasn't sure why, out of all people, I came to see her.

We sat in the kitchen surrounded by the soft rattle of the wall heater. The familiarity of the place soothed my aching soul.

"I don't know what to tell you." Still shocked, she shook her head and stared into space as I continued to blow my nose, napkin after napkin. "He needs to want to stop drinking. There's no point in fighting it otherwise. You can threaten, you can plead, you can try the intervention route, but it's not something he can just turn off."

My mother knew all about being in a relationship with an alcoholic. Sadly, she'd never succeeded, which made me wonder whether loving someone was enough.

I left her place very late, exhausted and unsure what to do next. In my apartment in Burbank, Ashton was sprawled on the couch, asleep. An empty pizza box and Red Bull cans sat on the coffee table. The TV was still on. My brother had started to turn into a younger and prettier version of Levi.

I tiptoed into my bedroom, shed my clothes, and crawled under the blankets. After hours of brutal metal and ugly crying, silence felt nice. Comforting even. I dug deep into my brain and tried to fish out happy memories of Frank and me, moments when he made me smile, moments he was sweet and charming, but all I could see was his face vexed with anger and the void he'd become.

I loathed that my worry for him was stronger than my hate and that it pushed me into calling Roman.

"He's asleep, Ms. Evans."

"Is his shoulder okay?"

"Hard to say right now. I'm taking him to get an X-ray tomorrow. Doctor's orders."

"Keep me posted?"

"Sure. Ms. Evans?" He paused. "I'm glad you called."

"The last thing I want is for his name to be dragged through the mud while Marshall Burns is getting all the attention."

"I know you probably won't believe me, but he appreciates it. He'll regret most of what he said tonight when he sleeps it off. Don't take it personally."

"Good night, Roman."

"Good night, Ms. Evans."

It was the doorbell that roused me the next morning. Or afternoon, to be more exact, because the digital clock on the phone read twelve thirty.

Outside my apartment stood a delivery person with flowers. I knew they were from Frank. Phone calls and messages began a couple of hours later, probably when he finally sobered up. I ignored every single one. I wasn't ready to talk to him yet.

I needed space and I needed to rethink my priorities.

Then I had to discuss the duet fiasco with Maria and Linda, which was the hardest conversation I'd had in years. The man had singlehandedly ruined months of collective work, and now we were left to pick up the pieces.

"What the fuck happened to Frank yesterday?" was the first thing Ashton asked when he got home from school.

Leaning against the kitchen counter with my arms crossed on my chest, I was watching the plastic container with a premade entrée revolving inside the microwave. My appetite was absent, but my brain needed something other than coffee. Frank drama aside, *Dreamcatchers* required my undivided attention. Levi and I were in talks with several venues, and now that my boyfriend's involvement was up in the air, things promised to get more complicated.

No one would care about a girl from Northern California if a big name wasn't attached to the project. Linda would have to try really hard to keep us afloat.

"I don't want to talk about him right now," I told Ashton.

He scratched the back of his neck and dipped his head to check what was inside the microwave. "Trouble in paradise, huh?"

"You can have it if you're hungry." I motioned at the container and returned to my room.

The apartment felt too small for the two of us. I couldn't tell whether it was because I was used to the luxury lifestyle of Frank's Malibu mansion or because Ashton had turned my place into a man cave. Everything looked strange. Every detail stuck out. As if my place wasn't mine anymore. Even the gigantic teddy bear no longer made me smile.

I'd never taken Frank for a big texter, but apparently, the man knew exactly how badly he'd fucked up yesterday. He was showering me with messages nonstop. I had to set my phone to silent. By the time evening rolled around, TMZ had gotten wind of what had happened at Gary's studio. According to "a source close to the singer," Frankie Blade decided not to record the duet for reasons that were yet to be explained. I didn't know how this information had become public knowledge.

Still wired from yesterday's fight and all my disappointments, I was sitting in front of my computer and sorting through emails when an unfamiliar number flashed across the screen of my phone. I answered. It was force of habit. It could have been film-related.

"Hello. Is this Cassandra Evans?" the male voice asked.

"Yes." My gut told me that picking up this call was bad judgment on my part.

"This is Brad Finley from *Entertainment Weekly*. Do you have a comment about your relationship with Frankie Blade?"

A rush of anxiety raced through me. I hung up without saying a word and noted a new message from Levi that had just come in.

You're out, it read.

Frazzled, I clicked the link he included.

There they were, the photos of me and Frank from the Ventura gas station. No faces. But then there were other photos of him with Isabella, screenshots from her Instagram with me in the background.

Ready for the worst, I drew a deep breath through my teeth and looked at the headline.

"The rumors are true: Frankie Blade is dating"

"Secret relationship isn't that secret anymore: Former Hall Affinity singer Frankie Blade is seeing music reporter Cassy Evans"

The time stamp indicated the post had gone live thirty minutes ago.

I dialed Levi.

"Is that what it takes to make you return my calls?"

"Sorry, I was on the phone with Linda and I just...needed some alone time."

"We don't have the luxury of alone time, Cass. Margerie Helm just emailed me back. She wants to meet."

"Really?" My heart sputtered in my chest. "You're not kidding me?" The woman had been so hard to pin down, I was about to scratch Melrose Cinema from our venue list.

"No. I'm not. Something tells me you would hate me forever." He paused. "You wanna let me in on what happened to Frank yesterday?"

"You know I can't."

"I assume he's off the project for good?"

"Yeah. I wouldn't count on him. Let's move forward with the editing. I'm not sure he's up for anything at the moment."

"Is there something you're not telling me, Cass?"

"Let's not talk about him, huh?"

"Okay, okay," Levi agreed. "I'm just going to pretend your face isn't all over TMZ next to the face of the man who fucked us over."

I moved my gaze down the screen of my computer. "Hey, at least they got my name right. Already better than Starbucks."

"You should see the numbers. Your interview has been getting tons of hits."

Sometimes Levi's obsession with numbers infuriated me. My soul was torn apart and all he cared about was the magazine's traffic.

"A lot of trolls?" I asked, pulling up *Rewired*'s front page to search for my interview with Frank.

"I suggest you don't look."

I scrolled to the bottom of the post and skimmed through the latest comments while Levi continued to talk.

I wonder if she sucked him before or after.

She should find another job...

I bet she got that interview because she gives good head.

Dante probably watched, bwahaha.

My stomach knotted. I minimized the window and began to pace my room. This was expected, yet the online remarks hurt.

"Are you okay, Cass?" Levi's voice pulled me out of my daze.

"Yes. I am."

I was lying. I was a complete mess for the remainder of the day. I had to shut off my phone because the calls and the messages from the reporters were too much. Deep in my heart, I understood I shouldn't care, but I didn't have enough experience dealing with bullshit. I couldn't just turn my feelings off like Frank could.

But hey, I did give good head. My rock star boyfriend loved it. Or ex-boyfriend. I couldn't really define what he was anymore.

I spent the next day glued to my computer, dealing with the fallout of Frank's studio no-show stunt and dragging countless emails from reporters trying to get an exclusive into my trash folder. The tabloids were hungry for details and kept on blowing up my phone and my Facebook inbox. For the sake of my mental health, I had to change the privacy settings in all my social media platforms, which only made it worse.

In the afternoon, after Ashton got home from school, we set up a small camp in the living room and worked on Isabella's article for *Rewired*. To keep readers up to date with her journey, Levi and I had agreed to post weekly recaps.

I sat on the floor, cross-legged, coffee in hand. My brother was next to me, sipping on his Red Bull and staring at the empty screen. An hour later, we were still only two paragraphs in.

"This article isn't going to write itself," Ashton croaked as I got to my feet and paced. My brain was lagging. This week's piece was supposed to discuss Isabella's experience working with Frank, but since Frank was out of the picture and she recorded the single alone, I had no idea what to put in the goddamned article. The words didn't want to flow.

"Anyone approach you at school today?" I checked.

"You mean like reporters?"

"Yes."

"There was one dude. He was hanging out in the parking lot. I didn't talk to him."

"Good." I gestured at my laptop. "Don't touch anything."

Ashton leaned over the screen and stuck his tongue out."

"You're sleeping in your car if you lick my shit." Laughing, I retreated to my bedroom to make a call.

"He's fine," Brooklyn stated over the phone. "X-ray didn't show any major damages or fractures."

"Is Roman there?"

"Yes. He's staying at the house."

"Thank you."

"You should talk to him, Cassy." Brooklyn's voice softened. "I really am tired of arranging flower deliveries for you," she added sarcastically.

"I'm not sure I'm ready to talk to him at this point. We're in such deep shit with the sponsors and Isabella and her mother."

"Don't worry about money. Jay Brodie's services are paid for. They'll just have to tailor the campaign to suit your needs."

"I'm not worried about the financial part. I'm worried about how this might reflect on Isabella."

"She'll be fine. It's best for everyone that Frank stays off the press's radar for now."

"Is he drinking?"

My question was met with silence.

"Have you considered calling his parents?"

"Billy's here. He flew in today."

A sigh of relief left my lungs.

"You should talk to Frank too. He's not in a very good place mentally and it could help us get him to rehab faster."

Guilt was a horrible feeling. It overshadowed all the other feelings I had in me toward Frank. He was alone and depressed, and no matter how much he'd hurt me by ruining everything I'd been building for Isabella, I still wished him well. I still loved him in a horrible twisted, unhealthy way.

"I'll think about it," I told Brooklyn and ended the call.

I just couldn't get past my pride yet. I needed time.

Frank made it difficult. He showed up at my place later that night, drunk. I was in my room, going over the monstrosity Ashton and I had written earlier. My phone buzzed and Frank's name lit up the screen.

Open the door, the message read.

My heart leapt into my throat. The man wasn't serious, was he?

I peeked into the living room. Ashton was fast asleep on the couch, hugging his laptop. The lights were off.

Please, another text popped up.

A muffled noise drifted at me from behind the door.

I slipped into my knee-length sweater and hurried outside. My pulse quickened, my mind raged. Frank stood off to the side. His right arm was back in the sling and a leather jacket was thrown over his shoulders. He looked every bit the mess a person who'd been drinking for days should look. The dim light illuminating his face accentuated the paleness of his skin and the bags under his eyes. Two-day stubble framed his jaw.

I wasn't sure what exactly I felt at that moment. Pity, sadness, anxiety, or anger. He clung to me like a metal object to a magnet. Even after I'd harmed him. It was perverse.

"I'm sorry, baby," he rasped softly. It rattled in the cool air between us like the fragments of our broken relationship.

I closed the door to make sure we didn't wake Ashton. My head spun. I could feel Frank's despair deep down in my body, but my pride rebelled against his natural charm.

"You're drunk," I said quietly, taking him in. Apart from the sling being in place again and a couple of scabs littering his wrist, he was fine physically. My heart pounded somewhere in my throat and my voice was a measly squeal.

He moved closer so that the space separating us shrunk to a few inches. "I'm sorry."

Still conflicted, I stepped back until my head brushed the cold wall of the building. "Why are you here? And how did you get here?"

"Roman brought me. And I'm here because I wanted to see you. You're not answering my texts."

"I think I have a right to be upset."

"Yes. Yes, you do. And I'm really sorry for flaking. Please come back."

Eyes clouded, Frank leaned forward to snatch a kiss. He wasn't as wasted as before, but I didn't know what to expect from him at this point. After the madness I'd witnessed the other night, I had no clue what he was capable of. The fact that he didn't care someone might see him here with me, drunk, told me he'd completely ignored his sense of self-preservation.

"Don't." I rested my palm on his chest. "You humiliated me."

"I'm lost without you."

"You're not lost without me, Frank. You're just lost. And you don't need me to show you the way. I tried. Look where it got us. You need to figure it out on your own."

"Don't say shit like that, baby. You know you belong with me." He rocked forward and his body lingered against mine. The closeness was intoxicating and I hated everything about it.

"Frank." I grabbed his chin. "How am I going to tell a nineteen-year-old girl you don't want to work with her anymore after you commissioned a fucking PR campaign for a single you were supposed to record together?"

"This has nothing to do with Isabella." He shook his head. "I'm still producing the album. Studio time, marketing, venue. I'll cover all the expenses."

There he was with his wallet, showing off his money.

"This film is important to me. It's not something I'm doing to boost my ego. I believe in Isabella's talent and I believe she, her story, needs to be heard. I love you, but I won't sacrifice my life and my career to be with you unless you have an idea of where you're headed. People come and go. They don't stay. You know it. I know it. And if you can't make up your mind about whether you want to stick around or keep walking, I can't be with you. I can't let you put me on the spot. I can't let you embarrass me in front of people I work with. My credibility and my professionalism are all I have."

His gaze was dark, deep, and full of questions. "I don't want to write music or perform anymore."

"You decided that halfway through recording a song with another artist?"

"Look at me. I can't even button my shirt. Who wants to see someone like me on stage?"

I rolled my eyes. "Self-pity doesn't suit you, Frank. You have a lot more than you think. You can walk."

We stared at each other in silence. His hot, tingly breath licked my cheeks. I wasn't sure he understood what I meant. His eyes seemed distant one second and stormy the next.

"So you're just going to leave me now that I need you the most?" he finally asked, pressing me to the wall.

"I've been there for you, Frank. Through all your drunk nights. I asked you to get help, but you kept pushing me away. You ignored me, then you fucked up my project and put a stain on my name." I paused to get more air. "But you know what the worst part is? The worst part is that I'm in a state of constant terror. For myself and for you. Because you keep challenging death, and my heart can't take it anymore."

Our bodies lined up and I felt the buzz. Even drunk, Frank was still hot like a flame. The gentle graze of his knuckles against my cheek and the hard press of his chest against my breasts made me dizzy.

I missed this, him being so radiant with me. The intimacy we had wasn't just about sex. It was about the stories we exchanged, about the breakfasts we shared, about the evenings we spent staring at the ocean. Our lives were intertwined like the strands of a rope.

"I'm getting help." I heard him whisper, then his lips touched my temple. "I promise it won't happen again. I promise you'll never ever have to be scared again."

"Okay." I inhaled deeply. His scent—sex, money, depression, and expensive cologne—filled my lungs. "What kind of help? What's your plan? I need to know."

"Will you come back?"

"What's your plan, Frank?"

Hungrily, his mouth captured mine. The kiss caught me off guard, and the soft brush of his lips sent shivers down my spine. My brain told me to push the man away. My heart told me to stop listening to my brain. It was a lost battle, and I gave in. Our tongues met. Our breaths lingered. We were spent from the adrenaline racing through us as we continued to indulge in each other.

I couldn't remember the last time Frank had kissed me like this, with this much despair and need. *Or had he ever kissed me like this?*

I almost caved. I almost asked him to come inside so I could put him to sleep in my tiny bed and cuddle against his rock solid body.

Almost.

Then I remembered how ashamed I felt the day he didn't show up at Gary's studio. My reputation was all I had and he jeopardized it by pulling out of "Afterburn" in such a shitty manner.

"Frank," I whispered, breaking the kiss as my chest heaved. "It's best if you leave before someone sees you."

"Who the fuck cares? We're all over the internet, doll. You're my girlfriend. I don't want to leave without you." Stubbly cheek squished to mine, he slid his hand to the back of my neck. "Come home."

My stomach tightened. "I can't be in that house with you when I'm not sure what you might break next. Your furniture or your neck."

"I really am sorry things got out of control. I promise it won't happen again."

"Can you promise you won't ride or get behind the wheel?"

"You fucked up my bike and my garage door and I'm still here, begging you to come back."

He didn't answer my question. "I think distance is a wise choice for us."

He sighed heavily as we stood in silence, cheek to cheek. His hand on my neck and his fingers threaded in my hair felt familiar yet strange.

I cupped his face and looked him in the eye. "Levi and I are about to secure the venue. I have tons of work and you should figure out where you want to go from here."

"I don't want to figure anything out without you."

"I shouldn't be part of the equation. You need to do it for yourself. Not for me. Not for anyone else."

I suspected this conversation was pointless. He didn't get me. He hadn't come here to talk about what had gone wrong between us and why. He'd come here because he wanted me to pat his back and tell him how unfair the world was.

News flash. The world *was* unfair. Just not to him. It was unfair to people like Isabella, people who didn't have the backing of millions of dollars and industry friends, people who couldn't afford expensive surgeries, people who were overlooked because they didn't meet the horrible standards of what society thought was acceptable to be a star.

The world was indeed shit. And the one chance Frank had to make it better, he'd fucked up.

"I can't do this alone, doll." His voice was small, shattered even.

"You're not alone, Frank. You have your parents and I'm still here, but we need to have this conversation when you're sober."

"The house is empty without you. My life is empty without you."

My hands slid down his chest. "Go home." I adored his words. I just couldn't get over the fact he didn't tell me any of this when he wasn't drunk.

Chapter Eight

Frank was quiet for a few days.

The texting and flower deliveries stopped. I wondered whether it was the liquor that was keeping him occupied or Billy. I called Brooklyn twice, only to hear her snobby "you should be here" lines.

Problem was, the damage had already been done. Despite Isabella's overwhelming Spotify and Apple Music streaming stats, Frank's sudden exit from the project cost us several sponsors, which didn't sit well with Maria or Levi, or anyone on our team, for that matter.

The Hall Affinity album release party invite reminder that hit my inbox on Wednesday morning was like another nail in the coffin. I'd been so preoccupied with the duet disaster and my own broken love life that I'd forgotten about the event completely.

Later that night, when I was already in bed, Frank's name flashed across the screen of my phone

Don't pick up, my pride whispered.

As if on cue, stupid butterflies filled my stomach. My need to hear him was bigger than my hate toward everything he'd become. So I answered.

"Hey, doll." His voice on the line seemed abnormally sharp. *Was he sober?*

"Hey." I stared at the empty space in front of me, waiting. My wounded heart hammered.

The silence between us thickened.

"I need to see you before I leave town," he finally said. As always, the man was blunt.

Inside me, I heard something snap, the soft, barely there sound of my self-respect cracking from the weight of his broken-man charm. It was impossible to remain indifferent when a man spoke to a woman the way Frank spoke to me—irreverently. Boldly. Without holding anything back. Without fearing he'd sound weak. "Where are you going?"

"There's a rehabilitation center in Arizona..." The sentence slowly died on his lips.

I felt the air tremble as his words reached my ears and swirled in my head.

"I'm sorry about scaring you," he continued in a hushed tone. "And I'm sorry about showing up at your place the other night. I want to fix this. Us. Our relationship. What we had."

Emotions swelled in my chest. "I'm glad you're doing it, Frank."

"It's a three-month program. I'll probably have limited access to phone or email."

"Phones are evil," I joked. "I'd burn mine if I could."

"I'm sorry for all the shitstorm in the press."

"It is what it is. I knew what I was getting into when I agreed to go public. I only wish the timing had been better."

"I promise things will be different when I come back, doll. Just don't give up on me."

"I'm not giving up on you, Frank. It was *you* who gave up on you. I know you understand why I need time to myself."

"Yes. I do."

"When are you leaving?"

"In a couple of weeks, but I have to see you before then. I miss you."

I was melting like ice cream that's been shoved into a microwave. I didn't like how easily he'd manipulated me into feeling the way I was feeling at that moment—lost.

"I miss you too," I confessed.

"Then why aren't you here with me?"

"You know why."

He quieted for a few moments, then asked, "I disappointed you, didn't I?"

My throat felt tight and my voice grew tiny. "Yes."

"I'm sorry."

"You don't have to keep saying you're sorry, Frank. I know you are. I also don't want you to promise me anything until you get the help you need."

"It's going to be okay, doll. Just give me a little time."

His whisper was like a warm balm, soothing me with reassurance. I heard it in the faint pull of his breath and the subtle change of his tone. *He wanted to get better.*

"You have all the time you need," I said quietly. "I'm not going anywhere."

"You better not. We're worldwide, remember?"

A silly smile stretched my lips. At that moment, my heart believed him.

"Look, Frank, I'd love to chat some more, but Levi and I are meeting with the manager of Melrose Cinema tomorrow morning. I'm hoping to lock in that venue and I don't want to look like a zombie. I should get some sleep."

"Melrose Cinema?" Frank drawled, curious. "Isn't that the red building on the corner of San Vicente?"

"Yes. It is. Have you been inside?" My inner geek came out and I went on to describe the interior. The owner of the place was a retired entrepreneur who'd work for Warner Brothers back in the '80s. His daughter, who managed the theater, was a tough woman to catch.

Apparently, she handled several properties, and I hoped to impress her with our proposal. The venue was perfect. Location, capacity, vibe.

"I don't think I've been inside the building," Frank finally said. "But we used to play in the club across the street. Right after I moved to L.A. They closed the place down in 2006."

"When was the last time you went to the movies?"

"Hmmm, good question. I don't remember."

"Do you want to go?"

"To the movies?"

"Yes."

He paused and I sensed his hesitation. Part of me wanted to rescind the offer. People like Frank didn't go to the movies. Theaters were for regular folks who wouldn't be recognized in public. Besides, the tabloids weren't being kind to him right now.

"You know what?" I shoved the thought to the back of my head. "Don't worry about it. It's a really stupid idea."

"No, no. It's a great idea." He perked up. "How about tomorrow?"

A ragged breath left my lungs. "I have a lot work."

"I have to see you, Cassy. I'll be in the middle of nowhere for three months with no access to phone or internet. I can't go without talking to you. You know we need to. One night. Let's have one night to ourselves. Just me and you and nothing else; so I can take these memories with me instead of the bad ones."

He was too hard to resist. "Okay, but I'll drive. I don't want Roman taking us around town in a limo. Only the two of us."

"Okay. Fair enough. But in my car. We're going in style."

"Deal. I'll see you tomorrow. Let's say five?" I couldn't believe I was agreeing to this after everything that had happened between us, but deep down, I knew Frank needed closure. So did I.

"Do you have a movie in mind that you want to see?" he asked.

"I'm going to consult Google and get back to you on that sometime in the morning."

"It's a date then, baby."

I hadn't been this excited about a movie since the third grade when our mother took us to the Chinese Theater to see Harry Potter. That night, our father had come along and bought us a super-size popcorn pack and a bag of candy. Ashton and I had spent the first half of the movie fighting over the food and missed everything, but those three hours were still the best three hours of my entire childhood. For once, we weren't a crippled version of a family. We were simply a family, and it'd felt incredibly nice, although it hadn't lasted long enough for me to get used to it. Later, at home, our father had gotten so drunk, he'd slept on the couch because he couldn't make it to the bedroom.

When I was a child, life enjoyed teasing me with the things I knew I could never have, but I made sure I did better as an adult. To have all those things I'd missed out on. To do all those things my father had never cared to do with me.

Freshly washed and polished, Frank's Ferrari was sitting outside when I pulled into his driveway. Roman hung back on the terrace. Billy and Hannah were in the kitchen, cooking. Or rather, Hannah was cooking and Billy was monitoring. His diabetes had been acting up lately and he was on a strict diet. I stopped for a second to say hello and made my way to the west wing.

I found Frank in the bedroom. All dressed up, sling in place, he was putting the finishing touches to his hair. Music boomed in the background.

"You're taking this very seriously." Shoulder against the doorframe, I took him in. These past few days that we hadn't seen each other had done wonders. He'd shaved. Light pink colored his cheeks and his eyes shone bright, just like the night we met. I could tell he hadn't touched the bottle. At least, not since our rendezvous outside my place. Everything about his outfit, black shirt that clung to his chest seductively, dark jeans that accentuated his long legs, boots that had probably seen better days, screamed hot, available, and a little dirty.

Frank Wallace was playing for keeps tonight.

"Of course, two hours of Blake Lively." He smirked and circled around. "How do I look?"

"You look like a man who's competent enough to take care of himself in the movie theater if things get too hot on screen," I retorted with a grin.

"Are you jealous of Blake Lively?" Smug smile still on his lips, Frank walked toward me. My body drew tight. Then suddenly, he turned me and pressed my back against the doorframe.

My knees buckled. "You really need to stop fantasizing about other women." I jutted my chin and ogled the fine lines in his face.

"There's only one woman I'm fantasizing about." He leaned in and kissed my cheek. There was an explosion between my legs. Goosebumps ran across my body and my skin burned from the soft touch of his lips. I missed the sober intimacy. I missed the sex and I missed the cuddles and talks after. I missed the showers together. I missed how our crazy schedules didn't line up. I miss the old *gym and healthy lifestyle obsessed* Frank. I missed the old *not a care in the world over-caffeinated* me. I missed us.

"I really am proud of you," I said, resting my hand on his chest. His heartbeat was fast and strong and I liked the feel of its rhythm against my palm. "I know this wasn't an easy decision for you."

He captured my chin and tilted my head up to meet his gaze. "Let's pretend everything is fine, doll. Just for tonight."

I nodded. "Okay."

The theater Frank picked was in the heart of West Hollywood. His hand lay on my thigh as I forged my way through the vehicular hell on La Brea. Our windows were up and the new Black Rain Coming album blared from the speakers. Wrapped in the ferocious pulse of the music, we spoke very little. Words weren't needed. Not right now, anyway.

All this—the alluring neon signs, the crowded sidewalks, the shouting street vendors—reminded me of how much I loved this city. Its electric vibe surged through my veins like the wild drumbeat of an old rock 'n' roll anthem. Warm and familiar, the feeling spread through my chest, taking over the fierce rumble of the engine and the muffled street noise.

Dressed in all dark colors, Frank looked mysterious. Just like the night we met. A smirk danced across his lips when we reached the front of the theater. There was a small crowd near the entrance.

"We can go through the back if you want." He took his hand off my thigh and motioned at the next turn.

"You want us to sneak in." Turning on my blinker, I glanced at the rearview mirror and prepared to change lanes.

"I made a few calls, but we don't have to." He shot me a mischievous smile, and his fingers returned to my skirt. "We're public, remember?"

"So you're totally okay with walking into a theater with me through the front door?"

"Doll, the entire planet knows we're together." He shrugged. "If they want to talk about us behind our backs, we might as well give them something to talk about."

"Are you sure, Frank?"

"Yes. I'm sure. I want us to be a normal couple for one night." His palm slid higher and my blood rushed to my cheeks.

"Do you want me to drive into a pole?" I steered the car into the next lane and hit the brake.

"No." Frank laughed softly and put the fabric on my thigh back in place. "I just can't stop touching you. You're addictive, Cassy Evans. And you look fabulous."

The valet attendant rushed over to meet us. My stomach lurched when the door swung open. For a moment, I expected a barrage of paparazzi to appear from their hiding places, but nothing happened. No one except the security guard was around to escort us into the theater.

Frank grabbed my hand and drew me closer as we mixed with the mass of warm bodies. Being seen with him in public felt both dangerous and exciting. A coat was thrown over his shoulders to conceal the sling, but with his sandy, fashionably disheveled hair and obvious sex appeal, he stood out from the crowd like a sore thumb. Famous people could never blend in. They had something special, something that radiated all around them the same way it radiated from Frank right now, something that turned heads.

The inside smelled like popcorn and hot dogs, and people hurried to their theaters. One of the managers met us in the foyer and showed us to the ticket booth that had just opened up.

Curious glances were sent our way. A few cell phone cameras flashed. It was starting—the madness. In my peripheral, I noted a few people approaching.

"I think you've been spotted," I whispered to Frank as he gave his Amex to the theater employee.

He squeezed my hand. "We're not hiding, remember?"

"No, but something tells me we'll be late for the showing." A rush of anxiety shot through my stomach.

The kid in the booth pulled up the seating chart on a monitor and Frank selected a dozen.

"Why are you buying so many?" I asked in disbelief.

"Trust me, you don't want to sit next to anyone else when you're with me." He grabbed the tickets and the card.

I was regretting my decision to try to be a normal couple for one night. We were surrounded in seconds. Hands with phones shook in the air. Theater security had to step in and ask some of the people to move aside.

"I'm very sorry, guys," Frank said, his voice firm and commanding. "I'm afraid we don't have time for photos." He produced a megawatt smile that was met with a collective gasp.

The crowd quieted to hear him better.

"We don't want to miss the movie, but if anyone was planning on getting popcorn, we're headed that way. I'm buying."

I couldn't believe my ears.

Frank dipped his head and whispered against my cheek, "You want popcorn, right?"

"Sure." I nodded. My face was on fire.

The entire lobby flocked to the concessions area with us. Frank's hand wrapped around my waist was the only barrier between me and the chaos. I could feel the breaths of strangers on my back. I could feel their adoration, their curiosity, their desire. Men and women of all ages stared at us as if we were alien species.

"I'm buying for everyone." Frank handed his Amex to the cashier and motioned at the crowd. "You can hold on to the card. We'll grab it after the show."

Dozens of popcorn bags rustled behind the counter. Once we received ours, the security guard ushered us to the auditorium. We sat at the far back, surrounded by a bunch of empty seats. Another guard hid in the shadows.

"You really outdid yourself with the popcorn," I joked.

"You told me I had too much money. I thought I should start feeding the masses."

"And you decided to start with a movie theater."

"Practice." He shrugged. "Before I leave for a third world country."

"You don't have to do this to impress me, Frank."

"That's not what I'm trying to do here."

"Then why did you buy half the seats?"

"I don't want people to stare when I do this," he explained, capturing my mouth with his. It was so sudden, I didn't have time to react. I gave in to a delicious slow-burn dance of our lips instantly.

On the screen, the trailers played.

"You think you can just kiss me any time you want?" I whispered as our mouths broke apart.

"Oh, I think you want me to." He grinned, plucking a handful of warm popcorn from the bag.

"What gave you that idea?"

"It's the dress, baby," he said against my mouth.

I returned his kiss. A soft, almost chaste brush of our taut lips. And while forgetting the last few weeks of nightmare we'd become wasn't possible, this calmness that he was today felt nice, felt promising, and I allowed it to swallow all my worries. I needed these memories too.

The movie was a blur. I couldn't concentrate on a single scene because my mind kept drifting back to Frank's hand holding mine. By the time the final credits rolled, I was a hot mess between my legs and dying to leave the theater. I hated that he had that effect on me. I hated how much his touch stirred me up.

"It's probably best we wait here for a bit," Frank said after the manager approached us to return the Amex along with the mile long receipt and to let us know about the crowd gathered outside.

"Maybe we can sneak out this time?" I offered.

"Did it freak you out?"

"What?"

"The people?"

I nodded. "A little." In a way, crowds were my specialty too, but today's lobby incident had unsettled me. The experience was equally eye-opening and terrifying.

Frank shifted in his seat and looked down at me, his gaze roaming my face. "I'm glad you agreed to this."

"Did you like the movie?"

"It was"—his features hardened—"intense."

I bit back a smile. Something told me he hadn't been paying any attention. "You had to really think about it, huh? Was Blake Lively not that impressive?"

"Oh, she was *very* impressive." He grinned.

"You and your unhealthy obsession with other women." With a pout, I slapped him across his chest. It was just a light pat, but it triggered something in me and cold panic rushed through my stomach.

Frank didn't move. His eyes were still locked on mine.

"I'm sorry I pushed you," I said quietly, my voice trembling.

"I was wasted and I'm sure I deserved it." He took my hand and rested it against his pec. "I wanted this to be a fun night. Let's try and get out of here, huh?"

"Okay," I agreed.

Frank waved at one of the guards and asked him to have the valet attendant bring the car to the rear of the building. We left the theater a few minutes later and used the back exit.

Outside, the air was fresh. A couple of fans approached Frank to ask for an autograph while I slid behind the wheel of the Ferrari and waited. The kids seemed thoroughly impressed that Frankie Blade took time out to talk to them. He politely refused photos but signed T-shirts and shook hands.

Watching him with other people filled me with warmth. He was kind and attentive, despite the fact that these little uncomfortable moments cut into his everyday life. Or maybe this *was* his everyday life. He'd said so himself. Celebrities were a different breed. They sacrificed their privacy in exchange for immortality. In exchange for their rightful spot in history. Be it politics, science, or music.

Once Frank got to the car, the smile on his face fell. "Let's get out of here." He fastened his seatbelt and rested his hand on my thigh again as if he needed to touch me to keep going. His knee jerked.

"Are you okay?" I asked, shifting gears. The growl of the engine muffled my voice.

Frank turned his head to look at me. His palm on my skirt remained fixed. "I am."

I knew he was lying. My father had also gotten antsy when he didn't get his fix of alcohol. Difference was, my father never acknowledged he had a problem. My lover did.

We merged into the traffic on La Brea and came to a stop at a red light. The Ferrari purred like a wildcat. The tinted windows hid us from the eyes of those who wondered to whom this half-million-dollar car belonged. I wasn't sure my guess at the price tag was correct, but Ashton had once taken the liberty to Google-stalk my boyfriend and that was the alleged amount that had come up online. Although tabloids were never a trusted source of information.

"I had a really nice time," I said, trying to ignore the sudden need in my core when Frank moved his hand up my thigh.

"I'm pretty sure this is the first time I've taken a woman to see a movie." Readjusting his seatbelt, Frank shifted to face me. Then his head neared mine, eyes sparkling, and his hand slipped to the back of my neck to pull me in for a kiss. The assault of his lips was unexpected and raw. He didn't tease or prepare me. He took what he wanted with aggression. I didn't know whether he needed a distraction from what was happening in his head or he wanted me for the same reason I always wanted him—because we were recklessly addicted to each other. Whatever his motive was, though, I welcomed it and I gave in to him.

My foot on the brake shook and my entire body lit up. I clutched the steering wheel harder. Adrenaline filled the air, forcing out oxygen and the remains of our common sense.

We were surrounded by hundreds of hungry-for-gossip eyes.

In my peripheral, the green light flashed. Chest heaving, I broke the kiss unwillingly and hit the gas. The vehicle responded with a rumble and a jerk. It had taken me a while to truly understand the power and the beauty of this car and why Frank loved it so much.

Fingers still tangled in my hair, he rasped against my cheek, "My girl looks very sexy driving a Ferrari."

I liked that he was never afraid to give up the lead, that he didn't have to be in charge all the time. In sex or otherwise. We fit together perfectly.

Frank leaned back in his seat and returned his hand to my skirt. Pleasant chills rushed through me as his apt fingers stroked my skin.

We slowly pushed through the gridlock packing the Hollywood Freeway entrance. I wiggled and parted my legs when the car came to another stop. He caught on quick. His hand slid to my inner thigh and found the lace of my panties. The playful brush felt like almost too much. Even through fabric.

I reminded myself to breathe. My heartbeat was like a Slipknot song, savage and loud.

Frank turned to me and I felt his gaze burn my right cheek. My eyes stayed on the dark road, littered with lights, but my mind was elsewhere. In the land of dirty desires and naughty fantasies.

"Have you ever had an orgasm while driving a Ferrari, doll?" Frank asked, bringing his body closer to mine. His fingers rubbed my clit. My panties remained in place, but I was so wet and sensitive, I felt every movement.

"I don't think I have." Lust filled my voice.

"Looks like it's an evening of firsts for the both of us." He dragged his lips across my cheek and nibbled the tip of my ear. More chills raced down my spine. His skillful tongue caressed my earlobe and his hand continued to work on my sex. This was the most reckless drive of my entire life. My priority shifted. Was it an orgasm or was it getting us back to Malibu safe?

I was teetering on the edge of coming undone when we finally entered the freeway. The tremor of the car only amplified my need as every nerve spasmed.

Frank was panting. With a growl, he pushed my hair aside. His mouth drew a wet path down the hollow of my neck. He had the best lips a man could possibly have. Not too plump and not too thin, not always demanding and not always soft. Just the right amount of everything. A certain touch for each moment and for each feeling I needed to experience.

My every muscle was strained and my arms and legs felt like jelly.

"Frank?" I called, staring at the cars ahead of us.

"Mmm?" He kissed my shoulder as his fingers massaged the sensitive area between my legs.

"I need—"

A light pinch to my clit cut my words off. They stalled somewhere between my throat and lips, a lingering whisper on the tip of my tongue. My hips bucked.

"What do you need?"

"I need to get off the damn road so you can finger fuck me properly," I moaned deliriously. My eyes struggled to stay open. My hands struggled to stay on the wheel. Sexual euphoria swept me under.

"Take the next exit," Frank murmured, slipping his hand under the lace of my panties. The feel of his fingers against the rawness of my sex made me gasp. I was soaked, dripping against his palm. Shaking.

"Do you like when I do this?" He rubbed my clit, then his index finger parted me and nudged its way inside. Just a little bit. Enough to draw another moan from my lungs.

Dizzy from the subtle intrusion, I nodded. "Keep going." My nipples ached for attention. My stomach quivered.

Frank pushed his in finger farther. "How about now?"

Want rolled through me. Heart thundering, I changed lanes. My body shivered from the overload of sensations his lips and hand unleashed.

The car headed for the ramp. We got off the freeway and drove down a dark road that weaved between the hills. I noted sparse properties hiding among the abundance of trees and the lack of lights. This neighborhood looked like the one Frank took me to during our second date, filthy rich and secluded.

Perfect for a quick round of sex.

He kept working me until we pulled into an empty lot at the top of the hill. The shimmer of the night city down below and the curve of the freeway peeked at us from behind the heavy branches. I shut off the lights, dropped the back of my seat, and spread my legs wider to give him access. The engine still hummed and music still played.

Frank lost his seatbelt and spun to face me. Two fingers dipped in. He pumped me fast, his intense gaze locked on mine. I writhed from the waves of pleasure shooting through my limbs. My dress was bunched up around my waist and my bra felt too small for my breasts.

"For someone who claims to be right handed, you're very good," I horsed out. My hips moved, looking to match the rhythm of his fingers. He met me halfway.

"Doll, just wait till I get both my hands back in action." His deep voice meshed with my moans. "You won't be able to walk." A smirk passed his lips.

I laughed raggedly. "Oh, I've already seen what you can do with two hands. I can't wait to see what other tricks you have in store."

We were the definition of indecent. The seat underneath me was damp and sticky. The windows began to fog.

Frank curled his fingers inside me and stroked my clit with his thumb. The combination of pressure was just right. I shook. My climax was close. Waves of pleasure rushed in. *Oh, yes, right there.*

"Let me see you come, doll." He watched me as his hand continued to work.

"I want to see you come too."

"That'll be two rounds for you."

"I can handle two rounds."

Frank twisted his fingers, eliciting my release. I came with a scream. Sweat coated my forehead. He dropped his face to mine, capturing my mouth in a slow, wet tongue-on-tongue kiss. His hand slipped from between my legs and cupped my ass.

I reached for his jeans. He was hard as a rock and begging to be taken care of.

"Let me help with that." I smiled against his mouth and pushed myself up. "Lie back."

"Oh, I love it when my girl is bossy," he murmured, returning to his seat.

I pulled off my panties and crawled over to straddle him. He was beautiful and he felt like my own personal sex machine.

We kissed messily, as if we had a deadline to meet. He bit my tongue. It was just a nip, on the edge of rough but smothered with softness. I reciprocated and drew his lower lip between my teeth. Our mouths battled for control. His hand roamed my breasts.

"Take off your bra, baby," Frank requested and fell back to watch me. "Let me see you."

I did as he asked, pulling the dress off my shoulders and freeing my breasts. Cool air pinched my skin and goosebumps covered every inch of my body. My nipples were hard and achy.

"You're so fucking hot when you're like this." Frank sucked in a loud breath through his teeth, staring at my naked body. "Salacious. On top of me."

His eyes were wild and hooded.

He dropped his hand to my bare thigh and squeezed it. "Fucking perfect. That's what you are, Ms. Evans. And mine." He leaned forward and licked my nipple. Long, rapid flicks. Swept with another wave of arousal, I clamped around his body, grabbed the headrest for support, and tossed my head back to enjoy the flawless work of his tongue.

"Undo me," Frank ordered.

Blood racing in my ears, I unzipped his jeans and palmed his cock. He shifted beneath me to give me more room to work. It was somewhat challenging with his shoulder, but I found my way around. My sex ached against the press of his length. Then I readjusted myself, lining up our bodies so that his tip teased my entrance. This had to be fast and rough. Each time apart from him sent me into a withdrawal worse than the previous one. Tonight, I wanted a little pain.

Frank wrapped his arm around my back and gripped my shoulder, guiding me. Shuddered breaths escaped his chest.

I sunk onto his cock until I couldn't go any farther. Until my legs trembled and my toes curled. My body welcomed the wave of pleasant hurt as it rolled through my limbs.

Frank's features hardened, eyes slammed shut. He enjoyed the actual act of penetration, the act of becoming one, as much as he enjoyed the ride and getting to the finish line.

I took him whole. Every throbbing inch of his length. At this angle, he felt massive inside me. All my sweet spots buzzed as our bodies began to move together. The slick grind of our hips was perfect. My blood thickened, my pulse sprinted. The air inside the car was heavy.

My fingers dove into Frank's hair and skimmed through its thickness. "Slap my ass, baby," I asked between my moans. "I want it a little rough."

He smoothed his hand over my skin and gave it a smack. A gasp left my mouth. I felt the burn spread across my thigh.

"Want me to do it again?" Frank asked, staring at me through the flutter of his lashes.

I nodded.

He knew exactly what I needed. The next smack was a little harder and louder. I cried out and picked up the rhythm. He met the roll of my hips with hard thrusts and another smack. Everything in me, every part, buzzed. His cock had no mercy. He pumped fiercely. His hand slipped to my shoulder to push me down against his length. The leather seats squeaked under the weight of our bodies. We were a mixture of sweat, moans, dirty words, and a sliver of pain. Chasing our orgasms. And the chase was beautiful. For a second, we were truly whole. All his worries filtered through me. All his heartbeats repeated mine.

The release was so intense, I blacked out for a brief moment. My mind soared. My body shook. When I came to, Frank's arm was wrapped around my waist, chin pressed to my shoulder. Mouth open, he was still trying to catch his breath. His broad chest heaved.

My face dropped to his. Cheek to cheek, we rocked slowly, delaying the inevitable. The moment we'd have to separate. The moment we'd have to break this incredible intimacy apart.

"I love you," I whispered, kissing his damp hair. The words didn't check with me first. They simply came out because they wanted to. I was tired of telling him this while we fought. I wanted to tell him when we were sharing a passionate moment. Like right now.

He cradled the back of my head and stayed silent, but I felt the thrum of his pulse spiking beneath my touch.

"Just accept it, Frank."

"It's such a foreign thing for me to say, baby." He was still inside me. Our lust coated our thighs and stained the seat. "Just give me some time to get used to it. The way I feel with you..." His voice wavered, tripped, and faded into the sound of the music. "I can't quite put it into words just yet."

"Says the award-winning songwriter?" I smiled, but something in my chest twitched. I remembered what he'd said to me the other day. He didn't want to make music anymore. Yes, he'd been drunk, but something told me he felt this way when he was sober too. At least, for now.

Being mad at him was impossible. Though twisted, his confession meant a lot.

"That's why it's so difficult. Words are tricky. Wrong ones hurt the most."

"I'm not going to hurt you, Frank." I caught his gaze. "Unless you give me a valid reason to. I'll admit, it's been challenging, but the problem you have is fixable. Everyone feels down. Everyone is miserable at some point in their lives. The main thing is to face it and find the strength to move forward, and as long as you're trying to work through this, I'll be by your side."

It was the strangest thing, talking to a man about recovery while he was buried inside me.

Frank's face softened. "You might be the best thing that ever happened to me. You're smart, beautiful"—a playful glint entered his eyes—"and your blow jobs are amazing."

I laughed and smashed my lips against his. We were a mess, beyond hot. We were smoldering. Nothing else mattered.

A tap on the window was like a bucket of cold water. I saw the jerk of a flashlight. Then there was another tap and a voice.

Panic clutched my chest. "Oh shit. Police." My hands shook as I tried to pull my dress over my breasts. We separated.

Cursing, Frank zipped up his jeans. "Let me get behind the wheel," he hissed.

"No," I protested, sliding back into my seat and lowering the music. "Stay there." I wasn't about to let him crawl across the center console with a busted shoulder. A Ferrari wasn't a very spacious car, after all.

Rolling down the window, I caught only a small glimpse of the uniform and the badge. The flashlight blinded me. Chilly air streamed in, biting the bare skin on my shoulders and knees.

"Ma'am?" I heard a drawl. "Have you been drinking?"

Squinting, I shook my head. My hands were in my lap. My panties were nowhere to be found. My bra was on the floor.

"License and registration?" The officer barked and surveyed the interior of the car. The flashlight jumped over to Frank as he drew the paperwork from the glove compartment.

I scrambled for my purse.

We were silent while the officer scanned our IDs. A few moments later, he dipped his head and asked, "Is this your vehicle, Mr. Bla— I mean, Mr. Wallace?"

Frank nodded. "Yes, sir."

"Is this the V-12 model?"

"That's right."

"How's the shoulder?"

"It's better. Thank you."

The officer handed us the paperwork and the IDs. His eyes darted to me, then back to Frank. "Mr. Wallace, I'm supposed to give you and Ms. Evans a citation for public indecency."

My heart thundered in my chest. I'd been corrupted and compromised by the golden boy of hard rock and his cock.

"I understand." Frank nodded. "Could we leave Ms. Evans out of it and just write one for me?"

Who said chivalry was dead?

The officer cleared his throat. "I suppose I can let you go with a warning." I heard a smile in his voice. "My wife is a big fan. Would you sign an autograph for her?"

The dynamics between us shifted. The officer handed him a blank ticket form.

"What's your wife's name?" Frank asked, fishing out a pen from the glove compartment.

"Sarah."

"Tell Sarah I said thank you for the support." He scribbled a few words on the paper and returned it to the officer. "Apologies for the horrible handwriting. I'm still a bit sore."

"It's all good. She'll be stoked. Will probably frame it. We've got all your records on vinyl."

"Vinyl is the way to go."

"Absolutely. That new guy, Marshall Burns... He's got nothing on you."

"I appreciate it."

"You get better, Mr. Wallace."

"Thank you."

I rolled up the window and watched the officer walk back to his patrol car in the mirror. Grinning, Frank fixed his jeans and shirt.

"Oh my God, that was so close." A sigh of relief escaped from between my lips.

We looked at each other and shared a laugh of amusement.

I spun in my seat and searched for my underwear.

Frank slid his hand over my thigh and whispered, "I have your panties, doll."

"Well, give them back."

"When we get home."

"You want me to drive home like this?" I motioned at my disheveled dress. "What if we get pulled over?" Heat pooled between my legs and I shivered.

"We won't as long as you don't speed." He smirked. "Let's go."

Chapter Nine

Levi and I waited for Margerie Helm, the manager of Melrose Cinema, at the concessions area. Dressed in business casual, we sat on the couch and gawked at the dark, vintage-styled interior. The theater wasn't open to the public yet, and the only people inside were employees tidying up the foyer.

I'd spoken to Margerie on the phone and we'd exchanged a few emails, but she was a thorough woman. She wanted to meet in person before giving us a definite answer.

"Did you two go to the movies?" Levi grunted, handing me his phone.

"Yes." Sore from last night's sex marathon, I was daydreaming. Frank and I had hardly slept. We'd fucked some more after we got home. First in the shower, then in the bedroom. Then in the shower again. Every muscle in my body ached.

"You're on TMZ again," Levi croaked.

I took his phone and scrolled through the gallery of blurred photos of Frank and me inside the theater and the headline.

"Frankie Blade and His Girlfriend Spotted in West Hollywood: The Singer Treats the Entire Theater to Popcorn"

"Was the movie any good?" Levi asked as I returned the phone.

"It was decent."

Smiling, he shook his head and checked the time. We were both quiet for a bit. My mind drifted back to Frank. I wanted us to spend as much time together as possible before he left for rehab. I knew I was playing with fire and breaking my own rules, but I hated my life without him. I hated waking up and going to sleep alone.

"You sure you don't want to come with?" Levi probed. The album release party that Dante organized was tonight.

"I'm sure."

"All right. Suit yourself." He paused for a few seconds, then continued, "Gonna be a lot of interesting people there. You could recruit a few more sponsors while we're knocking out the interviews."

"I'm fine."

"Don't want your boyfriend to get butthurt?" Levi lowered his voice. "Is he scared of being in the same building with Marshall Burns?"

"Considering how he and the band parted ways, I don't think he owes them anything. He's not going. I'm not going either. End of story."

"He wrote the damn album. You're taking his side on this because you two are together, but if you look at it from my perspective, he's a train wreck. He deserted the project he, himself, initiated and he's playing the victim. In reality, he simply isn't fit for touring. Everyone knows it. Instead of scheduling a bunch of dates across the globe, he should have started with one-off shows to see if he was able to keep up with the routine. Now half the planet hates him. It's like seeing a fucking pie you like and buying the whole thing, eating it and then getting food poisoning."

"What is it with men and food metaphors?" I rolled my eyes.

"I sorta hate his ass for stealing you from me," Levi confessed, dropping his gaze to his phone. "You were my girl. I found you first."

"Awe. You're so sweet." I laughed quietly.

"Me and you, Cass... We were the shit. Dream fucking team. I want you by my side when we get our office space."

"I thought you and Shayne were hitting it off."

Levi slipped his phone back into his pocket and moved closer. "She's great in front of the camera. We're rocking it when we're on location, but she's so fucking unorganized... You have no idea. I texted her last night to make sure she remembered to meet me at my place at three and she hasn't even read the message yet."

"She's probably sleeping."

"You should think about getting back to it."

"I *am* thinking about it. I'm already on for Bennett's interview. Just give me some time to rest my brain and figure things out."

In my peripheral, I noted Margerie. She emerged from behind the door with the Employees Only sign and shot us a wide smile. Her fierce gaze matched her no less fierce red hair. My excitement grew as she approached.

"Cassy and Levi, nice to finally meet you."

We shook hands.

Margerie sat on the couch across from us. Her cunning eyes studied me with direct curiosity, and I wondered if she read the tabloids and knew Frank and I were an item. Ever since we'd gone public, I asked myself this exact question every time I spoke with someone.

Levi began. I followed suit. We were so used to working as a pair, our words flowed together as one. He'd been right, after all. Once, we'd been the shit. Best duo on the scene. Industry people loved us. And I was starting to miss those crazy work-filled days.

The release date was still undecided. We were debating between two weekends, and wanted to see what worked best for Margerie.

"I'm sure we can always make room for an event that's aimed to empower creatives. I'd be nowhere without artists." She raised her hands and motioned at the surroundings.

"Isabella is one of a kind. I can't wait for you to meet her," I said proudly. Part of me regretted that Maria hadn't been able to make her daughter's schedule work. Having Isabella here with us today would've been beneficial, but Margerie didn't seem to need more convincing.

"Her voice has one of the widest ranges you'll ever hear." Levi grinned. "Five octaves. Think Mariah Carey, Mercury, Rose. I get goosebumps every time she sings."

The meeting went great. We discussed the details of the event, then chatted about music and movies. Lastly, Margerie said she needed a day or two to run it by her father. Levi and I walked out of the theater wearing big smiles.

"You think it's a go?" he asked on our way to the parking lot.

"Yes. I'm pretty sure it's a yes."

We said our goodbyes and made our way over to our cars.

Halfway to Malibu, my phone rang. Levi was panicking. "Shayne is in the ER. She has food poisoning. You're coming with me tonight."

Shocked, I stared at the line of cars in front of me in disbelief. "No. I am not!"

"We have ten interviews scheduled."

"Ask Ashton to run the camera and do them yourself."

"He's never worked an event like this. You know how these things are."

"I can't."

"It's not like you're going there to screw Marshall Burns. Come on."

Dread settled in my stomach. I squeezed my fingers around the steering wheel harder and tried to rationalize my thoughts. *Rewired* was important to me. Frank was important to me too, but Frank had let me down before and Levi hadn't.

"Okay," I gritted out finally. "Send me the info. I'll meet you there."

Frank was in the gym when I returned to Malibu. Heart pounding, I sauntered inside and positioned myself in front of the treadmill. Even with his arm in a sling, he looked yummy. "There's something I have to tell you," I started. My gaze traced the cuts of his sweaty chest and stomach.

"Sounds serious." He pressed the control button to slow the belt.

I took a deep breath. "Shayne, the girl who's working with Levi, had a medical emergency and he asked me to help him with the interviews tonight at the event *Rewired* is covering."

"Huh?" Frank grabbed the towel from the rail and ran it over his face and neck.

"It's Dante's album release party, the event."

He hit the button again. "That's tonight?" The treadmill stopped. "I thought we decided we weren't going?" He arched a brow.

"I'm not asking you to go if you don't want to. I don't want to go either, but Levi won't find anyone else on such short notice, and he's got a dozen VIPs confirmed. If he cancels, it'll make *Rewired* look really bad."

I wasn't sure why I was even explaining any of this to him. We'd never discussed the events I attended. It went without saying.

Panting, Frank stepped down from the treadmill. "I thought you were taking a break from the magazine?" He got rid of the sling and rolled his shoulder.

The accusing rise of his voice hit me hard.

"I am. And I'm sorry that you feel the way you do, but I'm not going there to party. I'm going to work. I dedicated seven years of my life to that magazine. I owe it to Levi," I spoke calmly, but my blood raced.

"And how do I feel?" His gaze penetrated mine.

I matched his stare. He was unbelievable. I didn't think this would be such a big deal for him. "Like a victim."

"Oh yeah?" His voice jumped. "What do you know about being betrayed by your best friend?"

"This is stupid, Frank!" I cried out. "You wrote the album. You're invited to the party. You have two options. Stay home or make an appearance. Your choice."

Frustrated, I spun on my heels and marched off. My heart thundered. Part of me understood why Frank was so irritable. He struggled with staying sober. Even the smallest things ticked him off. The album release party wasn't a small thing.

Once I was in the bedroom, I surveyed the closet. My camera-friendly jacket and slacks still hung in the corner. My pumps sat on the shelf as if we'd never had any fights or taken any breaks. Levi's message stated that the press check-in was at five, which only gave me a little over an hour to get ready. I grabbed my clothes and my shoes and stepped out of the closet. Frank stood in the center of the room. Visibly distraught, eyes dark.

"I don't understand why you're so upset," I said, depositing my items on the chair.

"Because I don't want you to go to that fucking party if I'm not going."

"This is ridiculous." I shook my head and unbuttoned my shirt to change. "You knew what I did for a living when you asked me out. Levi needs help, so I'm going. To work."

"The magazine means more to you than I do," he whispered.

My jaw fell. I stared at him, dumbfounded, trying to understand if he was drunk or had taken something. "What the fuck is wrong with you, Frank?"

His lips twitched. "Everything."

Here we go with the self-pity again.

Rolling my eyes, I whirled around and headed to the bathroom to fix my hair and makeup. He grabbed my hand in a tight, uncompromising grip and drew me back to him. I felt his heat. Near my heart. In my stomach. Between my legs. Our bodies were close, grinding against each other madly, chest to chest. Frank was hard. Remnants of sweat coated his skin. The rough press of his erection to my center stirred me up. My sex was tender from last night and my knees still had the burns. Oh, yes. Burns were a real thing, especially when you rode a man for countless hours.

He put his left arm around my waist and cradled my head with the other. My chin settled in the hollow of his sweaty neck.

"I'm going to make sure you're full of my cum when you interview Marshall Burns." I heard him whisper in my hair. His deep voice vibrated through me.

My breath hitched. I was soaked in seconds. Frank shuffled us across the room and spun me around. My cheek hit the wall when his chest pushed against my back. Trapped against his tight body, I was lost on this rough, dirty high. Reaching around me, he dragged down my zipper. My hips rolled in anticipation. Something dark and wild brewed at my core. I hated everything about our conversation, yet I loved where it'd taken us.

Frank's fingers found their way into my panties. "So fucking wet." He brushed my clit and a wave of primal need rolled through me. My nerve endings buzzed.

Oh yes, yes. I rubbed my ass against his erection. "Just the way you like it, rock star."

He withdrew his hand from between my thighs and yanked down my jeans. My breasts ached from the lack of attention and the unnecessary confines of my bra. I wanted him everywhere. I wanted every part of my body to be marked by his touch. He was the sickest obsession.

Thrusting my ass backward, I welcomed the intrusion. With a loud groan against my hair and long, deep strokes, he filled me up. In and out. In and out. *Oh God. It hurts so good.* The wall muffled my whimpers. My legs shook and my feet slid across the floor with each thrust and each exhale. Frank was fucking me raw. Like an angry animal. His left hand gripped my waist to steady us, his right one clutched my breast. He was loud and unforgiving. His broken moans rang in my ears.

This was the best kind of undoing. Sensuously savage. Like a sizzling rock 'n' roll beat. Hard, fast, and erotic. A flame around my shuddering core.

My mind drifted and blanked. I slammed both palms against the wall for leverage. My climax was near and I knew Frank's was too. His strokes quickened, then his body began to convulse against mine.

He came with a growl and his hand wrapped around my neck, pinning my cheek to the wall as I thrashed from my own release.

There was a long pause. We were destroyed and struggled for breath.

Frank spoke first. "Now that you have me all over you, baby, you can go." The rough edge of his voice as he growled it into my ear sent shivers down my spine. Thoroughly fucked and newly aroused, I clenched around his length.

"You like when I talk to you like that, don't you?" He pressed a gentle kiss to my temple and pulled out. Slick wetness coated my thighs.

I was wrecked in the best possible way, and my core still thrummed from the orgasm. "You really are a man of many talents."

"Maybe we'll do a movie of our own sometime." A soft chuckle. His recognition returned. He'd returned to his senses.

I spun to face him and traced the curve of his chin with my index finger. "We'll definitely talk about it when I come back."

Twenty minutes later, when I was loading my gear into the Porsche, dressed and ready to leave, Frank rushed outside. Freshly showered, he trapped me against the car and buried his head in the crook of my neck.

"I'll miss you."

A soft laugh escaped my lungs. "I'll be back in a few hours." I brushed his damp hair away from my shirt. "You should get the hot tub going."

"I like that idea." He kissed my cheek. He was like a plush toy, a man child, the absolute opposite of the Frank who'd fucked me as if it were his last day on Earth half an hour ago.

The party was held at a high-end hotel in West Hollywood. I hit the heavy afternoon traffic on the way there and arrived thirty minutes late. A large crowd gathered on the sidewalk. Most sported black T-shirts with the burning butterfly design, the official Hall Affinity 2020 tour merch. Mean-faced security guards chained up the empty step and repeat area. A few telephoto-lensed cameras could be seen among the fans.

I valeted Frank's Porsche and hurried to the back for a check-in.

"What took you so long?" Levi barked, rushing over. Anxiety twisted his face. I suspected he'd had at least five Red Bulls since we'd parted this morning. I could determine his intake by his level of jitteriness. He was definitely on high alert.

"Shut up. You're not the one who drove to Malibu and back twice today." Smiling, I grabbed the press pass from the girl at the Jay Brodie PR table and slapped it against Levi's chest. "Come on. Let's see how bad it is."

We were close, but not to the point where I could possibly tell him about the real reason for my delay—Frank fucking me senseless against his bedroom wall. Blaming everything on traffic in this city was normal. Although those of us who were born and raised in L.A. couldn't use it as a valid excuse. It made us look dumb and, therefore, worked best for the newcomers.

"They have us upstairs on the patio," Levi rambled on as we walked through the long, brightly lit hallway.

The entire pool area and half of the ground floor, including the ballroom, was closed off. The hotel staff that worked the event fussed over the buffet. Anxious chatter and the crackle of walkie-talkies filled the hallway and danced around me. The familiarity of it all hit me like a tidal wave. I missed being a full-time reporter.

A slew of voices drifted from one of the lounges as we passed.

"What time is the red carpet?" I asked Levi, noting familiar faces inside. Johnny. Carter. A couple of girls who looked awfully plastic. Waiters carried trays loaded with exotic hors d'oeuvres. No Dante. No Marshall.

"Six thirty. Did you not go over the itinerary at all?"

No, I was busy chasing an orgasm. "I didn't have time." I turned my head to look at Levi. "I didn't exactly plan on conducting ten interviews today." Then I really looked at him and grimaced at the multiple wrinkles across his shirt. "Is your steamer broken or something?"

He returned my stare with a scoff.

We entered the ballroom and headed for the spiral staircase at the far side, behind the small, performance-ready stage. There, on the wall across from us, hung a massive Hall Affinity poster. The new line-up. With a cocky smirk and tousled blond hair, Marshall Burns was in the center. My stomach drew tight and not in a pleasant way.

At that moment, I felt for Frank. I understood why he was upset.

On the patio, Ashton was guarding Levi's gear. We had a small corner with a stunning view of Sunset Boulevard and the jagged bloodred horizon. The *Rewired* banner stood behind a small leather couch.

"Brother." I scanned his outfit. Black shirt, jeans, sneakers, hair slicked back. He looked decent.

"Sister."

Our gazes collided.

"Behave." I smoothed the sleeve of his shirt and grabbed a small clipboard from Levi to check whom we were interviewing first.

"Relax. I've got this." Ashton grinned and gave me a thumbs-up. This was his first major event, and he looked chipper. I suspected that later on, he'd attempt to get some selfies with the VIPs. His Instagram feed was littered with photos of Isabella and other people he'd met while helping out Levi. I was starting to see a pattern. My brother was a celebrity stalker in disguise. Honestly, half the people who worked in the industry were. As long as the privacy rules didn't get broken, it was okay. Everyone was a fan. Just not everyone became an idol.

The noise of the party clashed with the noise of the street and while our spot was beautiful and free of foot traffic, I'd definitely have to scream through my questions, which I loathed. My throat always took a beating during such annoyingly loud events, and Levi hated tweaking sound in post.

"Do we have to interview Dante?" I muttered under my breath, scanning the list of artists. It wasn't really a question, but more wishful thinking.

"It's his party." Levi grunted. "It's not like we have a choice."

"How about you do it?" I offered.

I was shot down with a joke. "My makeup doesn't look good on camera."

"Okay." I drew a deep breath and tried to concentrate on the task at hand, interviewing rich, possibly drunk and high rock 'n' roll folks. Thinking about hot sex with Frank and other fantasies needed to be put off for later.

Setting the clipboard on the couch, I glanced at the party below. People began to spill into the ballroom. Drinks were served. "I need to use the restroom. I'll be back in a couple of minutes."

"If you see Dean Foster, bring him in."

"Copy." I tossed Levi a smile and hopped down the stairs. The song playing in the background was from the new Hall Affinity album, which was officially releasing next week. Mastered, titled, and properly packaged. If anything, the leak had only raised more interest. A little birdie named Linda had mentioned that preorder numbers were sky high.

Curious gazes swept over me as I made my way across the ballroom. My pulse kicked up, my awareness heightened. After all, I was dating Frankie Blade. Attention was expected. Whether these people liked me or not, we were a couple. Chin up, shoulders straight, I pushed past the loud knots of people and ducked into the dimly lit hallway.

Dante's silhouette swam into my line of vision. Beer bottle in hand, he was attached to a Hannah Montana knock-off who propped up the wall. Her skinny leg was wrapped around his booted ankle, hand shoved in the waistband of his jeans. My stomach rolled. The man clung to his twenties like shit to a shovel. It wasn't cool anymore. This sick obsession with younger, barely legal females made him look desperate and unattractive.

Dante heard the click of my heels and tore his face from the teenager's. His clouded gaze swung my way. The girl's hand remained on his crotch. No surprise there.

"Hey, short stuff." His voice was weak and sluggish. "You're looking gorgeous."

I slowed my pace.

The compliment didn't go unnoticed. Hannah Montana wannabe grabbed his shirt and attempted to pull him back to her. He didn't budge.

I stopped and tried not to laugh at the scene in front of me. "Thank you."

"Is Frankie-boy here?" Dante drew the girl's hand from his jeans and shooed her away. She strode off with a sour expression.

"He's not coming."

"What? Why?" Brows knitted, he moved closer. The unbuttoned top of his black shirt revealed a good portion of his chest. He wasn't as finely cut as Frank, but he had something even better—the dark, bad boy sex appeal that made women crazy.

"Are you seriously asking me this question after you put up a billboard-sized photo of Marshall Burns next to the album artwork Frank created?"

The space between us shrank to a couple of feet. I caught the smell of cigarettes and alcohol on his breath.

"Cassy, darlin'." Dante rested his hand on my shoulder. "I did the best I could. I called. I emailed. I came over. You know what he did? He told me to go to hell. I guess we'll be meeting again there then."

"You do know the age of consent in California is eighteen?"

Confused, he lifted his brow.

"How old is the girl?"

His face relaxed. "She's legal."

"Are you sure?"

"Why are you so worried about me, darlin'? Don't you have a man to be worried about?"

"Because you're drunk and because you need someone to tell you this shit."

Dante slid his palm down my shoulder. "Frankie-boy is a lucky guy. If he hadn't asked you out first, I would have asked you out myself." A lopsided grin touched his lips.

A nervous laugh escaped my throat. "When was the last time you actually asked someone out?"

With a potent expression in his eyes, he took his hand off my elbow and raked it over his dark, messy hair. "Umm, maybe 2009."

"You really are out of practice."

"I don't need to chase women. They usually chase me."

"Spoken like a true douchebag."

"Why do you hate me so much, Cassy?"

"Okay, you're way off here, buddy." I held up my palm. "I don't hate you. Hate is a very strong word, but I don't like what you did to Frank and how you did it."

"You know I had no say in it."

"I know you, Johnny, and Carter didn't fight back when KBC decided to fire Frank. You just stood and watched the label tear him apart."

"You know nothing about our contracts."

"I don't need to know about contracts. You're a coward."

"I'm here to play a fucking guitar, darlin'. I don't want to play with fucking fire and wait for some asshole in a suit to decide my future."

"You won't have a future if you keep burning through your present like you're some immortal god."

"Tell that to Frankie-boy. He was the one who pulled the plug on your charity project. Where is he now that I'm trying to save this fucking sinking ship?"

"You know what, Dante? Fuck you."

My heart hammered and my pulse raced. I brushed past him and hurried to the restroom. He was drunk and there was no point in continuing this conversation. Besides, I hadn't come here to fight Frank's battles. I'd come here to conduct interviews for *Rewired*.

On the way back, I noticed Marshall's perfectly styled blond hair swimming through the crowd near the bar. Shaking off my unease, I marched upstairs and found Levi and Ashton taking goofy selfies against the city backdrop. They'd bonded over the course of the past few months, but seeing them work together was still strange. Once upon a time, Levi had hated my brother. Hell, I'd hated my brother. Now he was everyone's favorite. Even Linda had a soft spot for him.

Of course, nothing went according to plan. Dante was too busy. Dean Foster, bassist of the band who'd frequently toured with Hall Affinity before Frank's accident, was too high to understand my questions. Tommy Bryce from Black Rain Coming politely refused to be interviewed.

We took a break at around eight when the party shifted toward the stage. Armed with a new bottle of beer, possibly his tenth, Dante staggered over to the microphone and rattled off a quick thank you speech, then asked for Marshall to come up. I watched them from the patio. They seemed at ease with each other, like old friends who'd been through thick and thin, and I couldn't help but wonder if the label wanted a singer that had the same features as the original front man so the audience wouldn't feel overly cheated.

Dante finished monopolizing the microphone and let Marshall speak. The man had a nice deep and raspy voice that soared across the ballroom and danced against the walls, and from what I'd heard from Linda, he'd nailed all the Hall Affinity classics during the audition. His range wasn't as wide as Frank's. He lost at least an octave, but the label probably didn't care and most fans wouldn't notice since Frank had hardly employed his higher pitches.

The crowd cheered.

Johnny and Carter jumped on stage and the four of them ripped through the intro of "Adrenaline Lane." Marshall was great. Sexy, confident, young, and sharp. The full package.

I knew despising him wasn't going to make me or Frank feel better, but I couldn't will myself to enjoy what I saw.

That was the moment I understood that everything I'd been working on all these years was no longer valid. My personal life had completely taken over my professional and the notion terrified me because I couldn't be objective anymore. And as a reporter, I needed to be objective.

This performance happening in the ballroom, no matter how messy, was good. Marshall Burns was good. He had the right chemistry with the rest of the band members. Sure, Johnny looked a little fazed, but Dante was having the time of his life, which was important since he essentially called the shots.

Objectively speaking, this was a great jam. Subjectively speaking, I wanted to throw a dozen raw eggs at them for having a good time while Frank spent his evening at home alone, struggling with depression.

The band played two songs and stepped down. The party went on. A couple of minutes later, Linda showed up upstairs with Marshall in tow.

"Look who I've got here." Smiling, she nudged him in my direction.

He extended his hand for a shake. We locked gazes. His eyes were the color of mocha. Wide, bright, and looking for a challenge.

Swallowing down my emotions, I slid my palm into his and said, "Marshall. It's a pleasure to meet you. I'm Cassy with *Rewired*. Congratulations." My voice sounded foreign. Mechanical. I tuned out all my Frank thoughts and tried to think about interview questions and things to discuss.

"Likewise." His grip on my hand was strong. "We've met before, haven't we?"

"Yes. A couple of times. Last summer. During the *Walk the Dark* campaign."

"That's right." The spark in his eyes and the slight tilt of his head told me he remembered me. Did he know I was seeing the man he'd replaced? "Backstage at the Palladium?"

"Yes."

He shook hands with Levi and Ashton and settled on the couch across from me. My brother helped him with the microphone.

"Count me down, boys," I blurted out into the space in front of me and rolled my shoulders to get rid of the building tension.

The noise of the party—drunk laughter, rock music, clanking of glasses—floated up from downstairs and cut into my speech, but I blocked it all out.

"Marshall. It's great to have you here with us. So..." I smiled at him. A wide, professional, camera-friendly smile. "How does it feel to front one of the biggest rock bands in the world?"

My stomach was suddenly queasy.

"Well, in all honesty"—he laughed—"I still can't believe it." His words meshed into one muffled roar. My brain understood everything he was saying, but my heart was too restless to react accordingly.

Halfway through my second question, the chatter downstairs elevated. I heard a sea of footfalls moving up the stairs, but Levi's camera was in my way and the LED light was blocking my view. Noise entered the patio. Marshall turned his head and leaned back to see what was going on.

Then I saw Frank. He was surrounded by a small group of people, most likely some super fans who believed groping a celebrity would give them power and talent. If only that were the case, I'd be on my way to the presidency.

Dressed in an ensemble that slightly resembled one of his *Breathe Crimson* era stage outfits—tight black leather pants, black see-through shirt, and a suit jacket—he looked all kinds of messed up. Though he was now allowed to take off the sling, he'd chosen to wear it, which made me wonder if the dependency was psychological or if he simply came here to play the role of a victim.

And he was drunk.

I heard it in the crack of his voice, I felt it in the pull of his broken breaths, and I saw it in his red-rimmed eyes as he marched over.

Marshall turned back to me. "This is quite unexpected." His smile faltered, but he was a trooper. He quickly mustered it up again. Our eyes locked, and I wanted to smile too. Only, my face froze.

Frank ignored the camera and approached the couch. My heart all but beat out of my chest when he offered his hand for a shake. "Marshall! Congratulations." There was a great deal of sarcasm in his tone. "Great party."

His frame blocked the LED panel and in my peripheral, I could see a mix of horror and amusement on Levi's face. Ashton stood off to the side with his hands in his pockets, expressionless. Probably due to shock.

"Thanks, man." Marshall shook Frank's hand. "I hope your shoulder is getting better."

"I'm sorry to interrupt... I won't stay long. You mind if I steal my girlfriend for a couple of minutes?" His gaze slid over to me.

"Frank, we're in the middle of an interview," I gritted out, trying to keep my cool.

He didn't seem to understand what he was doing. Any trace of recognition or awareness was buried deep under the euphoria of intoxication. Jaw slack, he reached over to me. His hot breath stuttered. Blinded by drunk affection, he dipped and attempted to kiss my cheek.

I leaned back to avoid contact. "Frank, I'm serious. This is not the time." My face burned with shame.

"Why not?" Eyes wild, he straightened up and motioned at Levi. His body swayed. "It's not like you're streaming live."

The crowd on the patio grew. We were surrounded by a wall of whispers.

"I'm sorry," I mouthed at Marshall, getting to my feet. "Could we resume in a bit?"

He nodded apprehensively.

"Why don't we step out for a second?" I hooked my arm through Frank's and led him toward the stairs. Everyone followed.

"You look really nice, baby," he muttered against my hair.

"Why are you here? I thought you didn't want to come?" I whispered through my teeth.

"I missed you."

He tripped as we moved down the steps, and his body careened into mine. I halted and threw his arm over my shoulder.

"Ah, the prodigal son returns!" Dante screamed from the bottom of the stairs. Beer in hand, shirt unbuttoned, he was even more pathetic than Frank. Sometimes I wondered if they subconsciously competed with each other for the train wreck of the year title.

Anxious murmurs rolled through the ballroom. People pulled in toward the staircase from all directions. I felt their gazes on me.

"Nicely done, brother!" Frank bellowed. "Great party. Love the poster." He jerked his chin at the band photo on the wall. "Who's the singer?"

This was war.

"Please stop it," I hissed. "You're drunk. You're making a fool of yourself."

A Guns N' Roses song played in the background.

"Could have been you." Dante raised the bottle and a mean smirk tweaked his lips. "If you weren't so fucking self-centered and actually thought about the band, not about your name."

We reached the bottom of the stairs. Frank slid his arm from my shoulder and stumbled over to the stage. I followed. So did the rest of the party.

"What was that you said to me earlier?" Dante swung the bottle at me. "That someone had to show me the path." His smirk vanished. "Did you check on your boyfriend first? Does he know where he's going?"

"Just don't." I shook my head. Hurt and embarrassment pushed against my chest. Hard.

Frank spun around and shot Dante a hateful look. "You stole my wife!" *Oh God! Not this!* "You stole my band! Now you want to steal my fucking girlfriend!" His hand danced in the air, pointed at Dante.

This wasn't good.

"Please stop it!" I shouted and stepped closer to calm him down, but it was too late. Cameras flashed. Laugher diluted the noise of the ballroom.

"Don't fucking tell me to stop!" His drunken wrath was now directed at me. "You short-changed me for a goddamned magazine."

My heart stopped beating. His words sliced me open. "There are people here, Frank," I said firmly. "You need to calm down."

"Yeah, buddy. You need to calm down!" Dante croaked, moving to stand by my side.

"Are you happy, Cassy?" His gaze swept over the stage, then back at me. "Or are you tired of fucking a guy who can't use both hands?"

The blood drained from my face. "That's enough, Frank."

"Is that why you came here? To find a replacement for me? Someone who can fuck you properly?" His slurred voice was like a slap in my face.

A giggle rang out somewhere in the crowd. My entire body felt like it'd been set on fire. I'd never been subjected to this kind of public humiliation before. My words were stuck in my throat along with my breath. Tears swelled in my eyes.

Frank jumped on stage and twirled around in front of the microphone. A few claps came from behind me. Dizzy with hate, he trotted around the small podium as if he was looking for something he'd lost. Maybe his sanity. His frenzy seized all the air in the room.

I watched him through the gathering mist in my eyes. Part of me knew this wasn't my Frank. This was the alcohol talking, but part of me hated him for bringing us into this stupid squabble with Dante, for making us a spectacle.

It hurt too much.

"Could you please come down?" I asked quietly, nearing the stage.

He ignored me. "You guys want to hear a new song?"

The crowd responded with a cheer.

"Frank." I held out my hand. "Please come down."

"Just wait, baby." He shook his head and pulled out a piece of paper from the side pocket of his jacket. "I wrote some stuff the other day." His fuzzy eyes settled on my face. "While you were mad at me."

"Please come down."

"Johnny! My man! Can you help a brother out?" Frank whipped his hand in an attempt to unfold the paper. "Fucking sucks when you're disabled, right?" A silly grin passed his lips.

Scattered laughter filled the ballroom.

Not able to bear this anymore, I got up on stage. "Everyone is making fun of you. Let's go home."

He gave me a confused look. "I just got here, doll. I'm going to sing the song I wrote."

"Please." I clutched his elbow.

He jerked away. His body swayed backward and slipped from my grip. The rattle of cymbals filled the room as Frank wrecked Carter's drum kit on the way down. I dropped to my knees to help him, but he was too heavy and too drunk.

"What is wrong with you people?" I cried out, glancing at the sea of spectators. "He just had two surgeries! Someone help him!"

Johnny and Dante hopped up. I saw Marshall making his way through the crowd. Cell phones and cameras continued to record. My body shook. I couldn't tell if it was anger or something else. Emotions of all colors surged through me. From the darkest to the brightest, they fought within me as I watched Johnny and Marshall helping Frank up.

"My song," he slurred, looking down.

Someone picked up the paper from under the destroyed kit and handed it to him.

"You gotta hear this, baby." He dragged his gaze to me and a lopsided grin curled his lips.

Dante stepped in. "You're ruining my party, man. Get your ass down."

"I wrote the fucking album! You wouldn't have a party if not for me." Frank tried to shake off Johnny and Marshall, who held him straight.

"Can we please stop this?" I thrust myself between them. "What is it with you rock stars? What are you, in sixth grade?"

"See?" Dante giggled. "Listen to what your girlfriend says."

"Why don't you keep my girlfriend out of it?"

I turned to Frank and rested both palms on his chest. His heartbeat was scary loud. "Stop this. There's press here. You two are going to be all over the tabloids. It's not worth it."

"Yeah, not worth it, Cassy. But you felt the need to be here tonight anyway, even after I asked you not to go." A sad smile twisted his lips. "Is that how you love me?"

"Please don't drag me into this." My voice was low, but I knew that people could still hear us, and if they couldn't, they'd be reading about this on TMZ's front page in two hours.

"Why not?"

Johnny wrapped his arm around Frank and pulled him toward the edge of the stage. Marshall assisted.

The crowd swallowed them as they descended. I waited a second. Carter lingered in my peripheral. He held out a hand and helped me get down. My knees felt like they've been skinned and glued to my slacks.

"Are you okay?"

"I'm definitely better than your drums."

"Ah, it's not a big deal." He shrugged.

The attention of the entire room was on Johnny ushering Frank to the exit. Cameras clicked, and then I heard a collective gasp. I ripped my way through the wall of security with Carter one step behind me.

In the middle of all the chaos, Frank and Dante were engaged in a pathetic fist fight. Or more like a drunk dance. I didn't know how else to describe their swinging and shaking and the slew of profanities there were exchanging. It felt a lot like my high school. Only worse.

"Enough you two!" I grabbed Frank's hand and stared at Dante. "Stop provoking him. He's going to hurt himself."

"Stay out of this, Cassy," Frank growled, swaying backward. The crowd moved along with him to make room.

"I'm not going to stay out of it until you stop this," I hissed.

Dante laughed. "Since you've got one hand. I'll let you hit me first, Frankie-boy."

"No one is hitting anyone."

"Just get out of my way." Frank gritted his teeth.

"I won't!"

"Get out of my way, Cassy!"

"I won't. You're going to have to hit me first if you want to get to him!" Fists balled, I looked him in the eyes. Part of me almost expected a punch, but what came at me instead was worse. It was a kick to my gut, to my heart. A kick to all of me and everything I was.

"Just stop fucking suffocating me with your goodness!"

Cold dread hit my bones.

A murmur swelled in the ballroom.

"Fine. If that's what you want, Frank," I said. My voice trembled and broke. This was the last straw.

Swallowing down my unshed tears, I turned around and walked away.

Ten minutes later, I called Roman's cell from where I was hiding in the hotel restroom. I didn't have to. Not after the horrible words Frank had just thrown at me in front of three hundred people and a dozen reporters, but the sick part of me, the one that loved him stupid —loved him unconditionally—at least wanted to make sure he had someone to take him home.

"Could you please pick him up?" I asked Roman, then gave him the address.

· · ·

Apparently, Frank hadn't told anyone he was going to the party. Billy confirmed when I called home that Frank hadn't taken any cars from the garage. My only guess was that he'd Ubered here from Malibu.

I heard a knock.

"Hey! You there?" Ashton called.

I scanned my reflection in the mirror. The tears had messed up my mascara and my hair looked like a bird's nest.

"Are you okay?" He knocked again. My brother didn't let up.

"Yes. I'm fine."

It was such a lie. I was nowhere near okay. Hell, I wasn't even sure I would ever recover from what Frank had just said or the way he'd said it. At that moment, his eyes had told me he truly believed his own words. I was suffocating him. Me and my goodness. Whatever the fuck that meant.

"Can I come in for a second?"

"Why?"

"I want to make sure you're okay."

"I just said I was okay." My voice ugly-pitched. I was ready to punch the wall to get rid of the frustration and anger that filled me up, but my body ached from too much sex and my ballroom rescue mission. I wasn't Frank. I didn't want any more fractures and bruises. He'd given me enough. They weren't literal, but they felt very real. They were a hole in my heart and a rip in my soul.

"You don't sound okay," my brother pressed.

Head pounding, I crossed the restroom and unlocked the door. Ashton slipped in and his eyes roamed my face and my outfit. For the first time in my life, my brother actually expressed concern about my well-being. It only took a millionaire rock star to humiliate me in front of the rock 'n' roll elite.

"What are you looking at?" I tossed my hands in the air and paced.

"Levi and I can finish the interviews if you want to leave," he muttered, fumbling with the sleeve of his shirt.

I wasn't sure if anyone would want to do interviews after the scene Frank had made, but I didn't care to stay anyway.

"Okay, you two are on your own then." A ragged breath left my lungs. I was still in shock. My mind ran in thousands of different directions. My heart hurt. Physically.

"Do you want anything?" Ashton asked, inching toward the door.

"No." I froze in the center of the restroom. "I just need to drive around a bit and clear my head."

"I guess I'll see you at home?"

"Yes. You'll definitely see me at home." I laughed bitterly and pushed back the new wave of tears that pricked my eyes.

"All right then. Later, sis." Ashton stepped out and the door closed.

I was left one-on-one with the mess in my head. Anger and helplessness zapped me again. I hated that, despite making me cry and ruining my night and possibly my reputation, Frank was like a bad splinter, buried deep beneath my skin. Constantly reminding me about his presence.

I slipped out of the building through the back entrance a few minutes later and rushed over to the valet to pick up the Porsche and be on my way.

There was no plan. No destination.

Reeling, I drove down Sunset with the windows down and the music full blast. A sea of text messages began to assault my phone shortly after I left the hotel. I ignored them all. I knew some, if not most, were from Frank, but my heart was in pieces. Talking to him right now would only make things worse. There would be apologies, and then tomorrow, there would be another drunk fight.

Instead, I turned up the music and continued my drive. I welcomed the stinging of the wind against my tear-stained cheeks and the exhaust fumes crawling into my nostrils. I welcomed anything that didn't smell like a bottle of liquor or a dozen broken promises.

My agony rendered desire for more pain, but a different kind, to offset the affliction that was already there, created by Frank. New ink. A good hour or two of lingering hurt.

That was how I ended up in front of my tattoo shop. The soft scent of burning sage greeted me as I stepped inside. The attendant flashed me a crooked smile.

"Do you have an appointment?" he asked as I neared the counter. My heart hammered in my chest. Being here after blowing off my new tattoo artist felt strange.

"No."

"All right. Let me make sure Jax can take you." The kid skirted over to one of the stations that was out of my line of sight. Muffled whispers carried over from across the room.

This was a bad idea, Cassy, my inner voice said. *You fucked this one up real good.*

Two seconds later, Jax's head with the military cut popped out from behind the oriental-style screen divider. Our eyes locked and he smiled at me. It was a warm, kind, and beguiling smile.

And for a second there, I felt calm and at ease. The feeling only lingered for a fraction of a second, but it gave me hope.

Just like last time, I was seated on the couch and given a cup of tea while Jax was finishing up with his current client. My phone kept buzzing. Text messages. Phone calls. Emails. Facebook. Twitter. Instagram. With everything going on, I totally forgot to reach out to the social media manager Linda had recommended.

"I didn't think I'd see you again," Jax said once his client left. He looked the same. Hot. Fit. Happy.

"Yes. I'm sorry about flaking out on you."

"It's okay. Things happen. I'm sure you have a valid reason."

Yes, I fell in love with Frankie Blade, and now that he turned out to be just another rich jerk, I'm crawling back for more ink and perhaps sympathy. Although I don't deserve the latter.

"I guess you could say so," I muttered, getting to my feet to shake his hand.

Did he read the tabloids? Did he follow Hall Affinity? Did he know I was seeing Frank? All these questions swarmed through my head as we walked over to his station.

"Any idea what you want to get?" Jax asked.

I took a deep breath. My voice was barely there. "Honestly, I'm not having a very good day. What do you recommend for a broken heart?"

He stared at my face for a good minute, studying me. "I would recommend something that doesn't remind you about it?"

"Makes total sense."

"You should get a tattoo that represents you." He spoke as if he knew what had happened. Even if he did, he was kind enough not to ask me any questions.

"I don't even know who I am right now," I confessed.

"You, Cassy Evans, are a Wonder Woman." He smirked and grabbed a brochure with designs from one of the shelves. "And I've got just the thing for you."

Chapter Ten

I woke up to the familiar stinging sensation on my newly inked shoulder blade. The noise in the living room told me Ashton was home. My head hurt. My chest felt cold and hollow. Frank's words were a stigma branded into my brain and they burned. I lay in my bed and stared at the ceiling for what seemed like forever. The dread of facing the slander that had flooded social media overnight made me anxious.

Summoning all my courage, I scrambled for my phone and flipped through my notifications to weed out potential trolls. The last two days had been hectic. Between meetings and sex with Frank, I hadn't been checking my inboxes or my follower count, but seeing three thousand new fans on Twitter shocked me. Online attention was obviously expected, but witnessing it for myself left me stunned and my heart started racing.

Swallowing past the tightness in my throat, I sat up, then logged out of the app and logged back in to make sure it wasn't some kind of glitch.

The numbers remained the same. Obviously, most of these users were following me for one reason only, to spy on Frank.

Too bad for them. I wasn't sure that we were still a thing. I didn't want us to be a thing. Not when he couldn't control himself in public. There was nothing that could possibly erase all the dirt he'd poured on me yesterday at the party.

Shaking off my unease, I returned to my Twitter feed and scrolled through the posts until my eyes caught a grainy shot of Frank and me on stage. It was from last night. I tapped the image to zoom it in. Instead, the picture began to move. It was a GIF. Frank destroying Carter's drum set and me trying to get him up.

Oops!...I did it again! the text under it read.

Acid coated my throat. I exited the app, slid from my bed, and paced the room. The tremor that took over me was from deep in my bones. A mean rattle. I shook, my breath an uneven quiver. We were a fucking GIF now and the entire planet was going to keep making fun of us for the rest of eternity. Unbelievable. It only took us a few days after we'd gone public.

My phone buzzed in my hand. It was Levi.

"Did you check your email yet?" he asked, his tone full of panic.

"No. I think I'm just going to disappear for a couple of years," I joked, walking over to my computer.

There, in my inbox, sat an unread email from Margerie Helm. My gaze skimmed over the text. *What? No!* I rubbed my eyes and read it again. Disappointment pulled at my chest.

Levi was still on the phone with me, quiet. His shallow breaths roared inside my head.

"That can't be!" I muttered and stepped away from the computer. "Did she seem like a stuck-up bitch to you? I mean, she runs a fucking movie theater."

"I'm sorry, Cass. I know you probably don't want to hear it, but it sounds like she's not fond of all this attention you're getting in the tabloids."

"So it's my fault we lost the venue?"

"No. That's not what I'm saying. I'm merely pointing out a potential problem."

"What do you want me to do?"

"Nothing. I'm not asking you to do anything. I didn't think people actually paid attention to this shit. Okay, so a guy got drunk and made a spectacle of himself. Who cares? He's not even part of the project anymore."

My rage was like a flame, burning everything around me. My room, my hope, my heart.

I killed the call and rushed into the living room. Ashton was watching TV and eating, my guess was lunch since it was too late for breakfast. A pile of textbooks sat on the coffee table next to his laptop. His gaze followed me as I torpedoed my way through the apartment, tossing and turning everything that stood in my way.

"What are you looking for?"

I stopped. "Your car keys?"

"They're by the door." He motioned at the line of hooks on the wall and continued to chew on the slice of pizza.

I stomped across the living room and grabbed the set.

Ashton finally caught on. "Wait! What for?" He sprung from the couch and stalked me to my room with pizza in hand. "What do you need my car for?"

"I'm returning it."

"No!"

"I am, Ashton. This is not up for discussion."

"It's my car. Frankie gave it to me!"

I drew a deep breath and lowered my voice. My throat was stiff and itchy from last night. "Get out of my room, please."

"It's my car." Ashton pouted.

"No, it's not. It's a handout from a guy who doesn't know what the fuck to do with his money."

"That's not fair! What does it have to do with my car? Why am I being dragged into your stupid fight?"

"There's no fight." I walked over to my closet and grabbed the first thing I saw, a sweater and a pair of ripped skinny jeans, exactly what my emo alter-ego needed after countless hours of heels, makeup, and designer slacks. "You remember my eleventh birthday?"

He blinked at me with confused eyes and took a bite of his pizza.

"You were too little." I looked at the empty space above me. Forgotten memories passed through my jaded mind. "That morning, Dad gave me a twenty-dollar bill. Maybe he was too lazy to get a present or simply didn't know what I liked, but he put the money into my birthday card and told me to buy whatever I wanted." I had to pause because sifting through images of my father always rattled me. "Then, that night, he came into my room and asked for the money back because he didn't have any for beer."

My brother's face remained expressionless and his jaw stopped moving.

"I don't want you to be disillusioned about people, Ashton," I said calmly. "I know you have this image of Frank in your head, but he's not what you think he is. No one is. And if you're going to keep trusting people with everything you have, you're going to get hurt badly."

"You sound like you're on your period."

"I'm returning the car. You're going to find a part-time job and Mom and I will help you get another one."

"When am I going to work? I've got school. I'm helping you and Levi with *Rewired*."

"Welcome to adulthood, buddy." I slapped his back and shoved him out of my room. "Now get out. I need to get dressed."

Fifteen minutes later, I was leaving the parking garage in the BMW with an empty backpack in the passenger seat. The only pleasant part of this ride was Black Rain Coming blaring from the speakers. My brother's taste had improved greatly since he started helping us with *Rewired*. Metalcore wasn't on my preferred genres to listen to list, but Cameron Koller had an interesting voice. An outcast, the original trailer park kid from the rural Midwest, he was real to the bone. With an interesting story to tell.

Adjusting the volume, I pulled onto the road. Frank's Porsche sat across the way from the complex, shiny and foreign in this neighborhood. I always had to park it on the street because my apartment only came with one garage spot that, up to now, was being occupied by Ashton's car. Correction. Former car.

Fury filled my chest. I steered the BMW into an empty space between an SUV and a Ford, cut the engine and marched over to the Porsche.

Not my car, not my problem. My inner bitch laughed as I drove it down the street to the tow away zone.

Good luck looking for it, asshole.

My mood skyrocketed. Revenge, no matter how immature, felt good. However, it didn't take long for disappointment to replace my high. Its hold on my confidence made me sad. Made me angry. Made me hate Frank for not trying harder.

When I finally got to Malibu, I was a ball of conflicting emotions. I parked the BMW in front of the garage and got out. The house felt different. Shattered. Loud. Uninviting. My Honda still sat in the driveway. The French doors on the terrace were slid open and I heard a slew of muffled voices drifting at me from the inside.

Brooklyn and Corey were hunched over the coffee table in the living room, their faces glued to their laptop screens, gloomy. They were probably working on a reputation repair strategy. I noted Billy's silhouette lingering on the terrace. He was on the phone.

My heart twisted inside my chest. I was no longer sure if I was in any condition to see Frank and stay calm, but I needed to get this over with, grab my things, and be on my way.

Brooklyn tore her gaze from the laptop and looked at me, then at my backpack. Her expression remained sour.

"Is he awake?" My question floated through the room.

"He's in the studio," she explained.

Corey gave me a tight-lipped smile. His hard eyes told me he didn't want me here.

"Great. Hopefully, we won't have to see each other." I strode over to the coffee table and dropped the BMW and Porsche keys into Brooklyn's lap. "Trade ya cars?"

"What?" she asked, confused.

"I'm returning the BMW. Porsche is probably in an impound lot somewhere in the Valley."

"What's it doing there?"

"Resting."

Brooklyn batted her lashes at me, expecting an explanation. For a moment, I felt sorry for her. She was going to be the one looking for that damn Porsche. Not Frank. I would be very surprised if he was able to string two words together right now.

"Sorry." I shrugged and walked down the hall to grab my things from the bedroom.

Blinded with rage and hurt, I plucked everything that belonged to me—dresses, shirts, pajamas—from the drawers and the closet and shoved it all into my backpack, not bothering to fold anything.

"Cassy!" Frank's voice carrying through the house told me coming here was a huge mistake.

He sounded broken and desperate, and his despair shot straight to my heart, clutching it for dear life. My walls made of hate, ice, and anger were melting.

There was no warning. He dropped to his knees and his arms wrapped around my waist like a chokehold. I couldn't move. A gasp was stuck somewhere in my chest. My hands were still in a drawer, plowing through my clothes, separating the ones he'd paid for.

"I'm sorry," he whispered against my sweater, his breath a hot, pulse-jarring caress on my stomach. This heat he carried around was worse than kryptonite. I wanted to fall apart for him right there and then. It took all my willpower not to give in to his deadly charm.

Bracing myself, I spoke, "Frank, please stand up."

"Tell me you forgive me." He tightened his grip.

"I can't."

"Please."

Slamming the drawer shut, I dragged my gaze to his sandy hair splayed over my sweater. "Frank, please let go." My voice was firm and uncompromising. My heartbeat, a thrashing inferno against my sternum, was anything but.

"I'm sorry for what I said last night. I didn't mean it. You're not suffocating me. You never have." He tilted his head back. His eyes, bloodshot and hollow, pleaded for sympathy, but I didn't have any to give.

"Do you even remember any of it? Or did you have to read TMZ to get a refresher?"

He pressed his pale face to my stomach. "Please, baby." I felt it then. His tears soaking my sweater, warm and terrifyingly familiar against my skin. They were little reminders of what he was. They were his fears, his dreams, his vices. They were impossible to ignore.

"Frank, please stop," I said, brushing his hair, despite knowing I shouldn't. Its softness against my fingertips was like a splash of nice memories. Memories I didn't want right now. Anger was my fuel.

His shoulders shook. His entire body shook. I'd never seen a man cry like this before. Only on screen.

"Frank, you know this isn't going to undo what you've done."

"I can fix it. I promise."

"No, you can't fix it." Exhausted, I dropped my hands to my sides. "Please let go before I call for help."

He loosened his grip and his head tilted up. I refused to look. My gaze was trained on the wall. His brokenness was my weakness and I couldn't afford to be weak anymore.

"Say something, doll." He ran his palm over the small of my back.

"What do you want me to say?" I continued to stare at nothing. "You made a fool out of me, yourself, and our relationship. The entire planet is laughing at us."

We were a fucking GIF.

"I'm sorry... I'm sorry... I'm sorry..." His whispers were sharp gasps that cut me deep, cut me into pieces.

"Don't get me wrong..." I paused to take a breath. My throat stung and my lungs were out of oxygen. The room felt stuffy despite the AC and an open window panel. Even the wind was like a lick of a chemical burn. "I knew what I was getting myself into by being with you and by agreeing to go public. I can take online jokes. I can take hate mail. I can take paparazzi ambushes. What I can't take is you ruining everything I've been working for these past five months in a matter of seconds."

Frank clutched my sweater. "Just tell me how I can fix it."

"You can't," I snapped, my tone accusatory. "Levi and I lost the venue. The management doesn't like the kind of publicity your connection to the project is providing."

I grabbed his hands and freed my sweater from his grasp. "Please don't make this harder than it already is." My gaze dropped to his face. Our eyes locked.

"Don't do this to me, doll. You know I need you more than ever right now."

I took a step back, wishing to distance myself from the tempting heat of his body. Desperate, he crawled toward me. It was pathetic and painful to watch and I couldn't bear another second of this spectacle.

"Frank, please stand up. If you keep being careless with your shoulder, it'll never heal."

He froze, still on his knees.

We were broken. We were irreparable. We were over.

"I need peace of mind to finish *Dreamcatchers*. I'm sorry." I choked back the tears. "I can't babysit you anymore. Yes, I know this makes me a shitty girlfriend, but I tried to be there for you. Problem is, I don't think I can anymore. I simply don't have it in me to watch you ruin yourself and what's left of my life and my career."

"So you're going to leave me?" Wounded eyes pierced me like a pair of scissors. One stab, double the hurt. "I thought you said you loved me."

"Sometimes love isn't enough, Frank," I countered, my heart a thousand fragments. "It sure isn't enough to cure your alcoholism." It hadn't been enough to cure my father's either. And between my mom, Ashton and me, we'd had a lot to give. He just hadn't wanted any of it.

"I'll get better." Frank reached out to grab the stretched hem of my sweater. "I promise I will. I swear on my goddamn voice, I'm going to check into rehab tomorrow. Just don't leave me."

"We talked about this. You promise and then you slip. And every time you do, you drag me down with you, and it's terrifying because I never know if we're going to come back from it. Me loving you won't make you want to get help. *You* need to want it, Frank. You need to understand that it's for your own good. Don't do it for me. Do it for yourself."

"I can't do it without you."

"You're going to have to, Frank. I'm sorry, but I don't like who I've become with you. I don't like that my world revolved around you like you're the fucking sun. You know what else I don't like?"

He held on to my sweater and stared at me.

"I don't like that I have to hurt you to stop you from hurting yourself."

And that was it. I grabbed my backpack and left.

At first, Frank called, texted, and sent flowers relentlessly.

I didn't respond to any of the messages and didn't listen to the voicemails. They kept piling up on my phone like mail on the porch of a house where no one lived.

My heart needed time to heal and regroup.

The endless Hall Affinity emails that flooded my inbox daily in light of the upcoming album release were more than enough. New singer or not, one mention of the band stirred up all my memories of Frank that I tried to tuck away to the darker corners of my mind.

On Monday, Jay Brodie PR released an official statement regarding the incident during the album release party. Frankie Blade issued a public apology and a promise to get help. Sadly, thousands of

Oops!...I did it again GIFs and *someone give this guy crutches* memes had already been circulating all over the internet. Twitter. Tumbler. Instagram. Facebook.

Frank's meltdown was the hottest topic of the week. Possibly the month. Possibly even the year. He'd gone from the most admired man on the planet to a pathetic joke in a split second.

And my name was attached to this embarrassing moment like a label to a new pair of jeans. Even if you cut it out, it'd still scratch and irritate you.

On Tuesday, Ashton came home early. Apparently, someone in his school made fun of Frank, and my little brother took matters into his own hands. I'd never pegged him for a fighter. At least not outside his X-box games. Though tall, he was too much of a wimp to throw punches. His aggression, but mainly his need to defend Frank's nonexistent reputation, surprised me.

On Wednesday, *Flutter*, the fifth Hall Affinity album, finally hit streaming devices and shelves. It reached the number one position the following week, three days before the annual Bowl N' Roll event. The same evening, Dante was added to the charity's list of attending guests.

I contemplated asking Levi to take Shayne instead. My heart was too fragile to withstand another assault. But Linda confirmed Dante Martinez wasn't doing any interviews.

I spent the rest of the month searching for a new venue. Unfortunately, all my efforts were to no avail, which only caused more tension between Levi and me. Isabella was booked for a series of shows and charity appearances in Seattle and we couldn't postpone it any longer. The screening had to happen before the second week of April.

In my defense, I continued to grill the managers of the clubs that were still undecided and even reached out to a couple of places who'd rejected the project. Bottom line: I was desperate. I was ready to work with anything. Even the back of a restaurant as long as it could fit a stage and a projector.

Unlike my heart, my new ink healed nicely. Jax had wonderful hands. The needle was his paintbrush. At first, the idea of having a comic book character imprinted onto my skin had seemed crazy, but the moment he showed me the sketch, I knew she was the one.

She was a representation of the new me. A warrior. An independent woman who didn't need a man, even if said man kept sending her flowers every week like clockwork, long after his calls and texts had stopped, long after he'd vanished. From my life. From the public eye.

Gone.

I'd made it clear when we last spoke that I didn't want him to seek me out anymore. His silence could mean many things. Maybe he'd checked into rehab just like he'd promised or maybe he'd gone on another drinking spree. Maybe neither of those things. Whatever he'd chosen, we'd fallen apart. We were an affair that hadn't lasted. A relationship that hadn't withstood the storm.

A fading memory.

Having Heidi Fox tarnish this memory during Bowl N' Roll wasn't something I'd been prepared for. Meeting ex-Mrs. Blade in general wasn't something I'd been prepared for. We didn't run in the same circles. The chances of us ever bumping into each other were very slim. Practically nonexistent.

After Heidi and Frank called it quits, she stopped hanging out with musicians and left the scene. According to her 2013 *Cosmopolitan* interview, they were too unstable. A couple of months later, her name had resurfaced online. She'd been rumored to date some billionaire from Costa Rica. That hadn't lasted long. Up next was a famous tennis player. Then an A-list Hollywood actor. Heidi Fox didn't waste any time. Especially since time hadn't been kind to her. She wasn't a glorified girl-next door with golden skin and perfect blond hair anymore. Just like Frank, she was the victim of a scalpel. She was a nicely packaged product to sell. In her early thirties, the woman was still beautiful—tall, fit, long-legged with perfect facial features and impeccable makeup, but when it came down to it, Heidi

Fox was merely a pretty girlfriend-for-hire. Whatever happened to her aspirations to change the world?

Heidi was making her way through the upper concourse of the bowling alley in the company of Caleb Waters when I saw her from my spot across from the step and repeat area set up in the reception of the bowling center.

Earlier red carpet attendees had already been teamed up and escorted to their lanes. Bets had been made. Drinks and appetizers had been served. The floor buzzed with energy. Starstruck ticket holders chased after celebs. Security chased after starstruck ticket holders. Those who didn't want to be bothered hid in the private rooms upstairs.

The newly arriving guests were lined up for a photo op by the PR girls running the event.

Levi and I had been here since five. We planned to wrap it up after catching the last wave of VIPs who arrived late.

Bowl N' Roll was by far one of the most tiresome charities of the season. A casual snob-fest. Usually, I enjoyed it. But not this year. Reason number one, Dante's presence, although he'd only shown up on the red carpet for a photo session and we hadn't had a chance to talk. Reason number two, the countless stares of other guests and the press. *Darn you, Frank!* Reason number three was walking through the concourse next to the skateboarding sensation right now.

"Hey!" Levi's head emerged from behind the camera. Pulling his phone out to summon Carlos back to the red carpet, he jerked his chin at the group of people moving in our direction.

"I know," I mouthed, trying my best not to roll my eyes as every single reporter gawked at me. Being under a microscope drove me nuts. Sometimes I felt like I couldn't be myself anymore. One wrong move or word and I'd end up on TMZ again. Like I had last week. Someone had taken photos of me leaving my gym, and a few days later, they'd appeared on various Hall Affinity fan sites and had eventually made it to a few tabloids.

At least people who worked the red carpet refrained from calling me names or asking me questions about Frank. My Twitter and Instagram, on the other hand, were flooded with message requests from certified weirdos. People didn't seem to grasp the concept of privacy.

Levi and I shared a concerned look as the couple strode over. Cameras flashed. Voices grew louder. Caleb Waters was obviously the main attraction. The biggest name in skateboarding after Tony Hawk, the man had just signed a ten-million-dollar deal with Nike.

The PR gal leapt over to the center of the step and repeat and held up a sign with Caleb and Heidi's names. A few reporters who had no idea who the two were made notes. Others plunged forward. In my peripheral, I saw Carlos. Both cameras up in the air, he ripped through the crowd and pushed his way to the front of the line.

My palm that was wrapped around the base of the microphone dampened. My cheeks hurt from hours of smiling. The unraveling chaos became too much, and I hated Frank for making me despise something I'd once loved—doing press.

Caleb was battling a barrage of questions while a silent Heidi clung to his arm. They moved along, nearing our side of the red carpet. A microphone was thrust at them right before they met up with Levi's camera. More questions poured from the guy to my right. I stepped back, contemplating whether Caleb Waters was worth the hassle. *Rewired* readers probably didn't care about skateboarding.

"I think I'm skipping this one," I whispered to Levi.

"Are we done then?" He surveyed the reception area to make sure we didn't miss anyone. When I followed his lead, I caught a glimpse of Dante's hat bobbing above the heads of the people crowding lane twenty-two. I heard a long rumble of the ball, followed by the crash as it knocked into the pins. Everyone on the floor cheered and clapped.

"Yes. Let's pack." I nodded, returning my gaze to Levi.

He reached for the LED panel to turn it off. As if on cue, one of the PR girls leapt over. Then she grabbed my elbow and said in a low voice, "I know *Rewired* doesn't feature sports, but Caleb is endorsing

Richie Kingston's next record. He'd appreciate you helping him to get the word out."

"Our readers are mainly rock music fans," I said with a smile. Turning down an interview with a person who had over five million followers on Instagram went against my beliefs, but I had no desire to be anywhere near Frank's ex right now, even if her new beau was in cahoots with a Grammy nominee. "I'm not sure how well the interview would be received by our target audience."

The girl matched my smile. "I understand that." Her face remained calm. "If it makes any difference, Tommy Bryce will appear on a few tracks."

My curiosity was piqued. A metalcore guitarist on a hip hop record? Experiments like this intrigued me. Adrenaline rushed through my veins. Getting first dibs on this exclusive info that, to my knowledge, hadn't been released yet was worth being in close proximity to Heidi Fox for ten minutes.

Levi and I exchanged a quick glance. He powered the LED up again.

"*Rewired* would be happy to chat with Caleb as long as he'll be willing to talk about Richie and Tommy's collaboration," I said quietly, needing verification.

"Absolutely." The girl patted my forearm and stepped back. Her gaze flickered over to the skateboarder, who was about to wrap up his interview with another outlet. They had a brief, covert exchange before he stepped closer.

Deep breaths, Cassy. You can do this!

I tried to ignore the anxiety as we dove into the first question, but Heidi's stare was like a dancing laser beam across my skin. Burning me raw. Her smile didn't reach her eyes. Her perfume, however, reached my nose as if the woman had bathed in it before going out. Distracted by my emotions, my tongue didn't listen to my brain. They were in total disagreement. I stuttered, not once, but twice. It was pathetic because the woman posed no threat to me whatsoever. But the sea of cell phones floating above my head did. People were taking photos of me interviewing the man who was seeing the woman who used to be married to the man I was still allegedly with.

Talk about complicated.

My stomach lurched. Swallowing down the nausea, I went on with my next question. Dark-haired with a rough, freckled face, Caleb was a well-spoken charmer. He and mute Heidi Fox seemed like an unfortunate mismatch.

I was on my fourth question when a bright light entered my line of vision.

"Excuse me for a quick second." Giving Caleb my best smile, I turned toward the string of reporters huddled around Levi and motioned at the phone pointed at my face. "Could we please get that out of the way?"

The light jerked back.

"Thank you. Please keep it there."

Snide whispers swept through the crowd. Great, now I had haters because I didn't want some paparazzi wannabe with a cell phone to blind me and the person I was interviewing.

Shifting my attention back to Caleb, I resumed our chat. Then my heart jolted into a mad sprint when Dante's thin frame emerged on the opposite side of the red carpet. His slow movements and silly grin indicated he was drunk.

There was an obvious shift in the air. Thanks to Frank's confession, the world now knew about Dante's indiscretion with Heidi.

I noted the change in Caleb's voice. Obviously uncomfortable being in front of the cameras in the company of a woman and a man who slept with each other some years back, he rushed through the last question.

Heidi continued to smile.

"Pleasure to meet you, Cassy." Caleb shook my hand. "Thank you for your time."

"No, thank you for *your* time." I hurried to shut off the microphone. "I'm excited to hear what Richie and Tommy came up with."

"Caleb, my friend!" someone called from the crowd.

The obnoxious cell phone light swam closer and darted between me and Heidi while her date tried to get away from the impromptu photo session. The owner of the phone was a kid Ashton's age— skinny, medium build, wearing a black hoodie. It was obvious he was trying to make a quick buck. I knew every face on the scene and his wasn't familiar.

"Do you have credentials?" I asked, scanning his clothes.

The barrage of voices surrounding us grew louder. People began to push as Dante continued his approach. The light jumped over to him, then back to me.

The kid had some nerve.

Pulse pounding, I barreled my way in and reached for his phone. "You can't film without credentials."

"Fuck off, bitch!" He threw his other hand out. At first, I didn't feel the impact of his fist against my chest. My breath caught. The microphone slid from my palm. My body tilted backward and landed against a warm mass. Someone propped me up from behind. People began to scream. It hit me then, both the rage and the ache that spread to my throat and stomach.

My head roared. I didn't know what it was—the insult, the lack of privacy, Heidi's presence, or this pitiful attempt at assault, but I wanted to hurt this kid back. The thought terrified me, especially since I wasn't a violent person.

"Security!" a voice shouted as I scrambled to my feet.

Levi's horror-ridden face came into focus. "Are you okay?" He grabbed my hand and helped me up.

Unable to speak, I nodded. The crowd grew tight. The air felt heavy. I blinked through the haze in my eyes and settled my gaze on Dante's hat. He shoved everyone aside with his elbows and stepped closer. "Are you good, short stuff?"

In the background, people were screaming and running.

A lollipop stick danced in front of me. I palmed my cheeks and tried to calm down. I'd never been hit in my life. Especially not by a stranger and not while I was working.

"Do you need a doctor?" Dante dipped his head to look me in the eye.

A couple of cameras in the back flashed, but the rest stayed idle.

"I'm fine." I sounded like I had a fork stuck in my throat. I sure as hell felt that way.

"Is she hurt?" someone asked.

"She needs to sit down."

"Shit," Levi spat out and spun around. His camera stood off to the side, unattended.

"It's too fucking crowded," Dante slurred, torturing the candy between his teeth. "Let's take her upstairs."

"I can't leave my gear," Levi told him.

"All right, just come find me when you're packed, huh?"

The cameras made an attempt to follow us, but security guards pushed everyone back to the red carpet.

The private room Dante took me to was empty and looked a lot like an Irish pub. Two pool tables sat on the right. The bar was across the way. Bottles of all shapes, sizes, and colors lined the shelves. A huge crystal chandelier that hung from the ceiling offset the deep green upholstery that draped the couches and the chairs. The cool quiet swallowed the noise that ruled over the busy lanes and the rest of the downstairs.

Overwhelmed, I sat on the couch and tried to breathe through my hysteria. The kid must have hit me really hard, because I could feel it everywhere, a dull ache that ran from my head to my toes. Even my teeth hurt. The entire top row.

"You want a drink?" Dante asked, hovering.

I shook my head. Being alone with the man brought back nasty memories.

"Suit yourself." He rounded the bar and grabbed the first bottle his eyes landed on.

My gaze followed his hands as he filled a glass with ice cubes using swift, elegant movements. The man made a great bartender. He looked the part too. The dark, brooding type with his sleeves rolled up and his jewelry-clad forearms bared. Lifting his eyes to meet mine, he cocked a brow. "You sure?"

There was no malice in his tone. No regret either. He seemed overly calm considering how much shit the tabloids had posted about him after everything that happened at the party. Frank wasn't the only one whose reputation took a public beating. Although Dante's reputation was born out of scandal.

In a sick way, I envied his no-fucks-given attitude and his ability to block out and move on. He was a natural-born asshole superstar who didn't care about anything or anyone but his own gain, and I was merely a girl with my heart in shambles. Playing the role of a good Samaritan wasn't like him. Contrary to what he'd once claimed, we weren't friends. Just the opposite. We were foes. Yet here we were. Alone. Maybe it was time for us to dot the i's and cross the t's.

Still reeling, I took him up on his offer and rubbed my chest in an attempt to evict the pain. "Okay, I'll have one, but not too strong." My voice was a hoarse whisper.

Dante poured himself a glass and took a swallow. His features crinkled. "Don't worry about that punk." He grabbed another bottle. "They have security cameras here. They'll catch the fucker."

Drawing a deep, painful breath through my teeth, I watched him finish mixing his drink and move on to making another one. He spun around to face the shelf and scanned its contents, then fumbled through the cabinets and fished out a tiny umbrella.

"Ah!" A silly grin passed his lips. He raised his hand to demonstrate his find. "This has your name written all over it, little lady." A smirk.

I smiled at his goofy remark. Apparently, this was just a pretend pub. Dante continued to work on the drink. Bottles clanked. Ice rattled.

The silence that stretched between us was awkward. I felt like I was behind enemy lines. Witnessing said enemy cooking up the cocktail of death. For me.

My phone buzzed. Levi wanted to know where I was. I sent him a text explaining we were in one of the private rooms upstairs.

Once satisfied with the results, Dante grabbed both glasses and walked over. "It'll make you feel better." He handed me the one with the dangerous-looking blue liquid.

I took the drink and stared at the umbrella. "It seems like it'll make me feel the opposite of better."

"Anyone ever told you that you have a great sense of humor?" He circled the room and deposited his hat on the pool table, then tossed his lollipop into the nearest trash can.

"Yes. Frank did."

We locked eyes. His were dark and impenetrable, and I wondered how much he'd had to drink.

"Look... I'm sorry things got out of control during the party." There was a real apology in his tone.

"I can't even go to the store now. I have to get my groceries delivered to me."

"It's that bad, huh?" Dante stared at the bottom of his drink, confusion evident in his features. "Why do you need to go to the store anyway? Have Hannah do it."

"Frank and I aren't together..." My voice shook. I didn't know why I was telling any of this to Dante. He was partially responsible for the clusterfuck my life had become, but he was the sweet monster. The charming kind you wanted to keep talking to.

His gaze drifted back to me and his eyes wandered across my face. "How come?"

A sarcastic laugh escaped my throat. "Do you really have to ask me that after everything that happened?"

"I don't know what's going on between you two." He shrugged and took a swallow of his drink. "He's not fucking answering my calls."

"Of course he's not. You didn't stand by him when the label decided to fire him. You didn't even have the decency to put up the original promotional poster at your party. Instead, you slapped Marshall's face next to Frank's artwork."

"That doesn't explain why you two aren't together anymore."

My frustration began to choke me. "Because I don't want him to make any more promises he doesn't plan on keeping. I'm okay with him breaking those promises when they're made to me. I can take the heat. I grew up with a man like that. But I'm not okay with him breaking promises he made to a nineteen-year-old girl. Publicly. You just can't do that. You can't give hope to a person and then take it away. It's not right."

I paused. My heart thundered inside my battered chest. I brought the glass to my lips and took a sip of my drink. It wasn't half bad. Sweet and bubbly. Like the old version of me. Pre-Frank. Right now, I was a ball of hurt and bitterness, and I didn't like who I'd become a single bit.

"You can't protect everyone, Cassy. People flake and cheat. It is what it is. A cutthroat business. Not a charity. You don't get a label to invest money in you unless you have what they're looking for and it's not always the talent."

"Exactly. And people like you and Frank who actually pull some weight in this business and have a chance to change things around for younger musicians resort to hiding in the shadows, letting the labels rape the artists emotionally and financially."

Seconds passed as Dante stared at me intensely. His palm that was wrapped around his glass remained still, as if one wrong move was going to interrupt his thinking process.

Then there was a knock.

"Hold that thought, short stuff." He threw his hand in the air and cracked the door open. A wall of noise reigning the lanes drifted into the room. Levi marched in with my bag in hand. He was accompanied by a police officer and one of the guards who'd worked the red carpet. Dante stood back as I answered questions. It was over so soon, it felt like I'd dreamed the entire conversation. The only indication of the officer ever speaking to me was the business card he gave me before he left. I slid it into the side pocket of my bag and returned my attention to Levi.

"Are you sure you're going to be okay?" Levi asked as soon as the three of us were alone. "I can give you a ride home. We'll pick up your car tomorrow."

Another knock came. It was the band's manager, Javier. He gave me an apologetic smile and approached Dante.

"I really am fine," I reassured Levi. It was a lie. The tremor was everywhere. In my hands, in my knees. In my stomach. I was on edge, needing a moment of calm, needing resolve. Facing the crowd milling around the bowling alley terrified me. "I'm just going to chill for a bit."

Levi shot Dante a warning glance. "If you get her into trouble, hot shot, I'll make a blooper reel from all the footage we have of you and send it to TMZ."

"I'd love to see that," Dante came back with a droopy grin. "I'm told I'm funnier when I'm high."

My drink, barely touched, waited for me on the bar. As soon as Levi and Javier exited the room, I rose from the couch and grabbed the glass. My head hurt and an invisible rock sat in my chest.

"Are you sure you don't want someone to check you out?" Dante probed, pulling another lollipop from his pocket.

I blinked at him.

"Geez, get your mind out of the gutter, woman." He leaned against the pool table and fought the wrapper. The top three buttons of his shirt were unbuttoned. "I mean...like a doctor."

"Right." I surveyed my surroundings and took another sip. "Is there a restroom in here?"

Dante motioned at the door behind the bar and shoved the lollipop into the corner of his mouth. "If you change your mind, let me know. The ER is open twenty-four seven."

"Thanks."

When I shed my shirt in the restroom, the huge bruise forming on my chest bone told me the attacker had every intention to hurt me. My anger intensified. Swallowing past the uncomfortable tightness in my throat, I studied my reflection.

You're okay, Cassy, my inner voice said. *Breathe.*

The alcohol had already taken charge of my bloodstream when I returned to the pub area. Back against the edge of the bar, Dante sipped on his drink.

"You don't look well." He turned his head toward me. "You're positive you don't want me to take you to the hospital?"

Shocking revelation, but I noted a lick of concern in his hazy eyes.

"No. It's just a nasty bruise."

Dante skirted around the bar. The fridge door slammed. Cubes of ice clattered onto the counter.

"My parents use to beat the shit out of me," he said matter-of-factly, fully concentrating on his task. "I'm not telling you this because I want you to stop hating me. Hate all you want. I deserve it." His lollipop jumped from one side of his mouth to the other. "I'm telling you this because you're about to try the world famous bruise remedy from casa Martinez."

I couldn't see exactly what Dante was doing behind the bar. I sat on a stool and watched his hands fumble around as the seconds ticked by. Finally, he held up a plastic bag full of ice and a towel. "Voila!" A grin spread across his cheeks. "Put it where it hurts."

"Thanks. That's very thoughtful of you." My shoulders quaked in inaudible laughter.

"Don't make fun of me, short stuff. It was either this or nothing when I was growing up." He shook his head and threw his unfinished candy in the trash. "Aspirin was hard to come by in my neighborhood."

Frost bit at my fingers when I took both offerings. I wrapped the towel around the ice pack and then placed it against my chest. Cold hit my bones instantly, overpowering the pain.

Dante went back to his drink. "Works like a charm, huh?" He motioned at my glass and raised his brows as if to ask if I was ready for a refill.

"I think I'm good. I still have to drive home," I politely refused.

The light buzz I was feeling was more than enough to chase away the distress the downstairs incident caused me. Unlike Dante, I didn't need to get wasted to cope. There was a reason I hardly drank. Socially or otherwise. I feared I'd become like my father. *And Frank.* I feared I'd develop alcohol dependence.

Dante leaned forward and propped his chin on his hand. "You mind if I ask you a personal question?"

"Depends on the question."

"Who ended it? Was it you?"

"Yes."

Dante straightened. "Too bad for Frankie-boy. You're one of the good ones."

"He cost me a venue."

Dante's brows jumped up his forehead. "Do tell." Curiosity laced his voice.

I readjusted the ice pack and took a deep breath. The ache was still there, but it was less severe. "There's nothing to tell. The manager of the theater we really had our sights on pulled out of the project after the footage from the release party went viral."

"Shit. That fucking sucks. Who's the manager?"

"Margerie Helm. Peter Helm's daughter."

"Wasn't he a movie producer back in the '80s or something?"

"Yes."

"And you're sure my party is the reason she changed her mind?"

"Yes. I'm pretty sure. She was all chatty during the meeting and the morning after the party we received a very unwelcome decline. The woman did a complete one-eighty on us. Levi tried calling her, but she never responded. Considering Frank hasn't kept a single promise in over six months, it's safe to say no one in this city except the tabloids probably wants to be associated with him."

"I gotta give it to you, Cassy." Dante swung his drink in my direction. "You're ballsy. I can see why Frankie-boy likes you so much. You've seen his ex. You're a great upgrade after that dummy on a stick."

"You fucked that dummy on a stick."

"Good thing I was high when it happened."

He spoke about all his shortcomings, mistakes, and faults with such ease, it made me wonder if he had any conscience left after two decades of doing coke and bathing in liquor.

"I guess he didn't like me as much as you think if he chose the bottle over me," I said bitterly.

"You should know better than anyone, it's never like that. You don't choose the bottle—the bottle always chooses you."

His words were like a bitch-slap. Unexpected and weak yet irritating.

"Bottle, blow, cigarettes," Dante continued as his cloudy gaze drilled into me. "It's the only way some of us can do it."

"I don't believe it."

"Because you never had to play a fucking guitar in thirty arena shows back-to-back until your fingers bleed. It hurts less when you're numb, darlin'." The cranky twist of his lips told me he was losing his cool.

Acute silence met his statement. I was taken aback by his confession. I didn't quite buy the reasons he'd given me, but they made sense nonetheless. They were his truths.

He downed his drink and slammed the glass against the bar counter. "No one wants to grow up and be a fucking pawn. You think all we dream about is blow jobs and drugs? When you sign up for this gig, you're buying a one-way ticket to hell. You're going to get abused left and right and the only way to stay relevant is to be two steps ahead in this game."

"Does being two steps ahead entail betraying your best friend too?"

"Even after he fucked up your charity thing, you're still taking his side."

"I'm not. I'm stating the obvious."

"*Your* obvious. Not mine. He's just as much of an arrogant asshole as I am. Do you really think I want to go on tour with Marshall Burns?"

263

"You seemed cozy the last time I saw the two of you together."

"Part of the job." Dante grimaced, his fingers dancing against the smooth surface of the bar. He looked ravaged. "Making sure people actually believe we're thrilled to have a new singer who doesn't need an army of medics."

We fell back into silence. The tension building between us was thick with dark, conflicting emotions.

Dante grabbed another bottle and refilled his glass. His hands shook. The man didn't know his limit. How he could stay in control of his thoughts and actions with so much alcohol in his system baffled me.

"Do you ever want to stop?" I asked, drawing the ice pack away from my chest.

"Every day, but then I remember all the horrible shit I've done and realize I won't last long clean and sober."

"Have you tried?"

"I do once in a while—" He paused abruptly, as if the right words had escaped his mind. "Give it a shot, I mean."

"What makes you stop?"

"Why are you grilling me about my bad habits, short stuff? I'm a fucking lost cause. I'm going to be forty in less than two years. It's too late for a change."

"Because you're making it sound like you can't play music without selling your soul to the devil."

"Oh, you can." A cunning smile tilted the corners of his lips. "Just not the kind we write. It's rock 'n' roll, baby." He slipped his hand into the back pocket of his jeans and pulled out a small plastic packet.

My pulse leapt. Ice pack still in my hands, I narrowed my eyes.

"Don't fucking look at me like that." He shook his head. A credit card was wedged between his fingers.

I'd seen drugs. I'd seen people doing drugs. I'd seen what drugs did to people. Everyone in this city needed a pick-me-up to get through the trenches. Be it powder, needle, or liquor. Coke, heroin, and acid were injected or sniffed at almost every single VIP table of every single club in Hollywood, Downtown, or in the Valley. This was the capital of entertainment. The city of dreams. Some realized. Some broken. People either did drugs to stay afloat or to get through the dark. But the fact that Dante had enough nerve to flaunt his stash while we were having a conversation about the very reason why Frank and I weren't together anymore shocked me. Everything about today shocked me. Starting from Margerie Helm's email and ending with Dante Martinez shamelessly snorting a dozen lines in front of my eyes.

"Shouldn't you at least lock the door?" I asked sarcastically, sliding from the stool.

"This is my room. There's a guard outside. No one comes in unless I say so." He dropped his head to get another hit.

I set the ice pack on the bar. "I guess I'll leave you to it." My heart thundered.

Dante tore his face from the powder and shot me a glazed look. "You want me to walk you to your car?"

"I'm fine. You know, you really should try again."

"I don't have anyone to try for." He rubbed his nose.

"You don't need anyone. Do it for yourself."

"Is that what you told Frank before you dumped his ass?"

"Why are you bringing him into this?"

"Because he's always here." Dante's index finger ping-ponged between our bodies, which were separated by the bar. "He's always with me and with you. Once he gets under your skin...it's for good. You can't get him out. Tell me it's not true."

I couldn't. Frank was in every part of me. In every inhale. In every exhale. In every thrum of my pulse. Even after countless weeks of silence, he occupied my thoughts. He sneaked into my dreams. A small fraction of me still hoped I'd get a random 4 a.m. call. And he'd be sober. He'd be the man I met last September. Warm, funny, charming.

"See what I'm talking about?" Dante threw his hands in the air, eyes wild, voice rough. "You can't. Because I'm right. I'm always fucking right, darlin'." He dipped his head and drew another line.

Frozen, I stared at the glittering row of bottles on the opposite side of the bar. The loud thumps of my heart pounded in my ears.

Go home, Cassy, my inner voice whispered. *This man doesn't care about your goodness either and he won't give you the answers you want.*

Truth was, I didn't know what answers I was looking for or what exactly I was trying to do. Save the world? Sadly, the world didn't want to be saved. People were happy and high. No one wanted to be miserable and sober.

"Good night, Dante," I said. "Thank you for the ice pack."

He jerked his face up, his hair flipped and fell across his shoulders in a dark, messy cascade. Then our eyes locked.

A ragged exhale left his mouth. "Fuck me." Swaying, he tilted his head back and stared up at the ceiling. His body went limp and disappeared behind the counter.

It wasn't until I heard the thud that my brain turned on.

"Dante?" I called, rounding the bar. My pulse was a furious chase in my veins.

He lay on the floor, lips blue, arms spread, eyes bugged out. Spasms twisted his long body.

All the oxygen in the room was gone. "Oh my fucking God!" Mind blank with panic, I dropped to my knees and slapped his cheek. "Dante?!" He continued to jerk beneath me. Foam spilled from the corner of his mouth.

Oh my fucking God, oh my fucking God! Heart, stomach and legs quivering, I sprung to my feet and rushed for the door. The sounds—the clatter of pins, the rumbling of balls, and the drunken screams of guests—crashed into me like a ton of bricks. The security guard was standing right outside.

Gasping for air, I clutched his suit jacket-clad shoulder and shouted, "Call a medic! Dante Martinez just OD'd!"

Chapter Eleven

The West Hollywood café where we were meeting Maria and Isabella for lunch was like a beehive without a queen. Loud. Unorganized. With price tags that didn't measure up to the quality of food. A long line of bodies snaked through the dining room. In the booth next to ours, a toddler was crying a river. Ignoring the demon child's assault on my ears, I spun my laptop toward Isabella and said, "I think The Spot will be great. I know you prefer ground floor, but they do have an elevator. We're just waiting for confirmation that their restrooms are ADA compliant."

Isabella studied the images that carouselled on the screen. Her sandwich and soda remained untouched. Maria sat by her side. Levi was sprawled on the bench, sipping his six-dollar latte.

"What about that lounge on Cahuenga? The one we looked at last week? Was that Swan Café?" Isabella looked up from my laptop to her mother, seeking a reaction.

"We liked it." Maria nodded. She seemed exhausted with stress. Thanks to Jay Brodie PR, her daughter's schedule was brutal. There were appearances to make and interviews to give. There was sudden interest from several local radio stations and an inquiry from a TV show.

"If we don't hear from The Spot's management by the end of the week, we'll reach out to Swan Café," I said, mustering up a smile. My phone lay on the table next to my coffee. Its screen was littered with email notifications. "As a matter of fact, they jumped at the offer. What we have to keep in mind is that with their floor layout, setting up a projector could be very tricky. Also, their maximum capacity is only two hundred and fifteen people, and we think using a small venue might be doing you a disservice now that there's so much interest."

"Don't forget about sponsors and special guests. We'll need room for stand-up banners and merch tables." Levi set his latte aside and rested both elbows on the tabletop. His gaze darted between Maria and Isabella. "Cassy is in talks with three larger venues that we both think are a much better fit than Swan Café. I believe at least one will come through. I say let's sit tight for a few more days and not rush into it."

Maria returned my smile. Hers was just as unenthusiastic and dull as mine. Obviously for entirely different reasons. She wasn't the one who'd witnessed Hall Affinity's guitarist's brush with death five days ago. But that didn't make her problems any less important. As a matter of fact, her problems were my problems. We lost Melrose Cinema because of my then-boyfriend's drunken hysteria, and I was determined to find a new venue. Unfortunately, we were running out of time. Linda insisted we make a decision by the end of this week. She couldn't push back the screening announcement any longer.

My phone blinked at me with another email notification. Though Shayne had taken over most of my duties at *Rewired*, I still checked my inbox religiously day and night. It was a stupid habit, to stay in the know. Even after I'd promised myself to dedicate the next month and a half solely to *Dreamcatchers* and Isabella's band.

But then, what if Margerie Helm had changed her mind? What if

Frank had come out of hiding? What if Ashton had gotten into a fight again?

Only, it was Dante's name that lit up my screen.

Our last encounter concluded with him spitting foam on the floor of the bowling alley in Calabasas. Shock had blurred some of my memories, but I recalled the thick panic that'd taken over the building as paramedics rushed Dante into the ambulance. He'd been taken to the nearest hospital, and I'd spent a good hour sitting behind the wheel of my Honda in the parking lot, willing myself to start the car. The following morning, his name had been in every single headline. By afternoon, Jay Brodie PR had released an official statement. Dante Martinez had pulled through. Alive, though not well, but on his way to recovery.

It'd been a minute since the update. Naturally, the preview of the email that'd just hit my inbox caught my attention.

Flicking my gaze to the screen, I skimmed over the text.

Jay Brodie PR PRESS RELEASE: Dante Martinez Exits Hall Affinity in Light of Health Crisis

Disbelief tightened my chest. I blinked, hoping this was my sight playing tricks on my brain, but the words were still there. Clear as a Southern California Sunday morning. The background noise muffled. Demon child's screams faded. Isabella's voice was a thousand miles away.

"Could you please excuse me?" I stood with my phone in my pocket and forced myself to smile. "I'll be right back."

In the restroom, I read the press release twice.

It's with heavy hearts that we announce Dante's departure from the band due to health issues that require immediate medical attention.

My head spun. I didn't understand why the news affected me so much. Strange worry settled in my stomach. Worry for Frank, worry for Dante. Worry for people like me who'd been going through life clinging to every song and every emotion the songs evoked.

Dark puzzling worry for everyone and no one in particular.

Was it the end of the road for the band or was it the beginning of something new, perhaps something different?

The tornado of questions that swirled in my head made me dizzy.

The news about Dante's exit from Hall Affinity spread like wildfire. By the time I returned home, it was everywhere. Twitter, Facebook, his official Instagram account. Shayne had already published a quick post on *Rewired*, but of course, Levi pushed for a proper editorial. With all the man's accolades, a list of his best solos, and a gallery of his hottest red carpet outfits. A farewell worthy of the subject.

Do you want to do it? his late-night text read.

Torn between hate and respect for the man in question, I contemplated. Dante and I had quite the history. I knew everything there was to know about his music. Almost two decades of rock 'n' roll debauchery. The man had written some of the most iconic guitar riffs of the twenty-first century. I could knock out a banging article. The piece had my name written all over it, but my gut told me to take a step back and let Shayne finish what she'd already started. And my gut had never lied to me yet.

I simply couldn't be impartial anymore. Not after the conversation Dante and I'd had right before he OD'd. This wasn't my editorial to write. This was someone else's.

I knew it and Levi knew it. He didn't try to change my mind when I refused.

The call came after midnight when I was already in bed. My stomach flipped. The number had been programmed into my phone by Dante himself years ago. And I was realizing it only now.

He sounded different. There were occasional long pauses between the words as if he needed to make sure what he was about to say was exactly what he wanted me to hear.

"How did you get my number?" I asked, slightly stunned. I didn't remember giving it to him. I'd been the one on the receiving end.

"I've got powerful friends."

"Such as?"

"Geez." There it was again. A stop. "It's public record."

"Is everything okay?" I probed.

"Yeah."

"I saw the press release."

"It was never my band. It was always Frank's... We were all just tagging along."

"Says the man who tried to kick the other man out."

"It wasn't like that." His speech slurred. He paused again. "I've had a moment of clarity."

"What's going on with you, Dante?"

"I'll live."

I didn't know how to react. There was clearly something wrong with him health wise. He sounded lost and tired, but each question I posed was dodged.

I wasn't sure why he was calling, and the fact that he was actually calling rendered me speechless. The silence between us deepened with each passing second.

Dante broke it first. "I wanted to thank you personally for not leaving my ass to die."

A laugh escaped from my chest. "I mean, I do hate you for what you did to Frank, but I'm not going to stand and watch you choke on your vomit just because you're a selfish asshole."

"Was it really that bad?"

"No, but you scared the hell out of me."

Dante's voice crumbled with lingering anguish. "I think you're a very kind person, Cassy. I'm glad you were there."

"You're welcome."

We fell back into another long moment of silence. Talking to Dante on the phone was strange. Almost too intimate.

"Did you ever report that punk who pushed you?" he questioned.

"I decided not to. He's in high school and his parents begged me to reconsider. He erased the footage."

"Are you sure?"

"Yes, he erased it in front of me."

"Trust me, people say a lot of shit and then two years later, your homemade porno movie is all over the internet."

"Honestly, I don't have it in me to deal with a legal hurdle right now. We need to lock down the venue for the screening, and it's been a stressful week."

"You still haven't found anything? How hard can it be if Frank's name is attached to the project?"

"We're not publicizing that he's financing the album production. The documentary is nonprofit. His contributions are registered as donations. Besides, his stunt at your party was a big turnoff for people. We lost several sponsors because their reps felt very strongly about the footage of Frank circulating online. A lot of Isabella's fans are teenagers who are still in high school. We can't have a drunk lunatic as the face of the campaign."

"Drunk lunatic, huh? So you're not going to give him another chance."

"I'm not a genie bottle full of chances. He had plenty."

"I really did root for you two."

"You were also the one who accused me of stealing demos and then came on to me."

"Oh, darlin', I did a lot of bad shit. I do apologize for accidentally coming on to you. I was probably high. Doesn't mean I don't want other people to be happy."

"I'm not sure you have the slightest idea what you're talking about."

"You don't give me enough credit."

"I haven't seen you doing anything to deserve my credit. Music doesn't count."

I heard a groan of frustration. "You're a very difficult woman, Cassy."

"So I've been told."

"Now I see why no one wants to work with you." He laughed.

"People do want to work with us, but it's not that easy. If you haven't noticed, Isabella isn't your typical nineteen-year old. We need to make sure the facility meets ADA requirements. Not all do. Many places that were willing to donate their premises are located inside older buildings. Some are simply too small. I'm trying to find something similar to Melrose Cinema in size and layout, but most theaters aren't willing to shut down for a nonprofit event on a Saturday night during the new James Bond movie release week."

"What can I do to help?"

His question was unexpected, an eerie whisper inside my head. "I'm not asking you for help, Dante."

"I'm not implying you are, but if there's anything I can do, you can tell me."

"I think maybe you should concentrate on getting better instead of making promises you might not be able to keep."

He was quiet. The stillness that stretched between us on the line was like rubber. The words that followed next almost hurt.

"Listen to me, Cassy," Dante spoke, tone soft and serious. "I know you're mad at him for all the shit he did, but you should call him. I'm not saying forgive him...just call him."

"Why?"

"Because life is fucking short, Cassy. Because you're here one minute and gone the next."

He ended the call before I had a chance to respond. There was one part of me that wanted to dial his number and demand an explanation. But instead, I dialed Frank's. My heart palpitated inside my chest. My ears rang. Anxiety swirled through my stomach. The room suddenly felt like a box. A trap. A prison. And the only way out was the voice on the other side. The voice that never answered.

And then, three days later, I received an email from an anonymous sender with photos of Frank and another woman. Grainy, zoomed-in, cell phone quality images that didn't tell me where and how he was, that didn't tell me anything except the obvious. He had someone to console him. He didn't need me.

Fine. I didn't need him either.

There were other hot, willing, and less complicated men.

Like Jax.

"Let me take a look again." My mother held out her hand, tone demanding.

"There's nothing to see there, Mom," I countered in a low whisper. "He's somewhere in Hawaii or Aspen, trying to seduce an elderly woman."

As always, I was exaggerating. The woman in the photos didn't look *that* old, but she wasn't my age either. She was just an odd choice for someone like Frank. Baggy pants, boyish haircut. There wasn't enough for me to work with. The photos weren't great. I'd been waiting for them to surface online or flood the tabloids ever since they'd hit my inbox two days ago, but nothing happened. Frankie Blade was still off the grid. Even the flowers stopped coming.

My mother's palm jerked in front of my face impatiently. With a groan, I gave up my phone.

We waited for Ashton on the oversized couches next to the magazine stand in the lobby. He was in one of the glass cubicles with a bank representative, opening his checking account.

"I really don't understand why you dragged me out here." I sighed loudly and surveyed the lines snaking along the teller windows, wondering if anyone here read the tabloids. Being the trending topic on TMZ for a couple of days had its drawbacks. This was the city where everyone needed to stay up-to-date with the celebrity gossip. Naturally, right after Frank's meltdown, random people approached me in public. Not so much now, weeks later, but the anxiety of being watched and judged was constantly there. Like a tumor. I could feel it squeezing my guts every time I stepped outside my apartment.

The AC was working full blast and the cool air pleasantly danced against my skin.

"I haven't seen you in forever," my mother croaked, bringing my phone to her face to zoom in on the photos.

"I was just there the other night, Mom."

"You had one cookie and left twenty minutes later."

"That's because I'm busy. You know the screening is in five weeks. There's too much to do. I promise we'll have a real dinner after Levi and I finish this project."

We fell into a short moment of silence.

"Honey, I don't think this woman is someone he'd date," my mother concluded after careful inspection of the images that were clearly a very poor attempt at paparazzi.

"But he's somewhere and he's with someone." I didn't know why it bugged me so much. I was the one who'd walked out. I was the one who'd ignored his calls and texts for weeks before he'd finally given up. Now that he clearly had a companion, my jealousy was getting the best of me. The day after I received the photos, I decided to follow Isabella's advice. I'd texted Jax and asked him if he wanted to grab something to eat.

There was no way in hell I was going to cry myself to sleep for years to come while Frank was moving on with his life. Never.

"Did you try to call him again?" My mother didn't let up.

"No."

"I think you should, honey."

"Why are you taking his side?"

"I'm not taking his side, but the man has clearly gotten under your skin. Both of you need closure."

"Mom." I turned to face her and tried to use my nicest voice. "Did you like getting eighty phone calls a day?"

Shoulders slumped, she returned my phone. "I don't like you right now, Cassy."

"It's because I had my heart ripped out of my chest and tossed into the trash," I hissed through my teeth. "Can we not talk about this anymore?"

Telling my mother about my break-up with Frank and about the photos was a mistake. I'd never expected her to try and understand him, especially since she'd lived with an alcoholic for over fifteen years and because she'd seen the footage from the release party, but she kept bringing it up, and it drove me nuts.

It made me nervous.

It made me doubt my decision to agree to a date with Jax.

It almost felt like I was cheating.

He was picking me up at six and I spent a good hour styling my hair and changing outfits while a cloud of guilt hung over me. My overactive mind kept going back to my very last conversation with Frank, looking for something to hold on to, looking for the words I'd missed then, looking for a way out of this date. But then I remembered what he'd said to me at the party, how my goodness was suffocating him. And my anger returned tenfold.

At five fifty-five, my phone buzzed. Jax was downstairs. After I tossed my ID and credit cards in my Michael Kors purse, I slid into the matching dress booties and hurried to leave the apartment before Ashton showered me with more questions.

The sun sat low on the horizon and opulent shades of orange and red streaked across the darkening sky, propped up by the tall palm trees lining my street. The sidewalk was littered with dog-walkers and runners, and I felt naked in front of all these people. The wild thrum of my pulse in my temples made my head hurt.

Jax's convertible was parked across the street. He stepped out of the vehicle and skirted around to open the passenger door. Skittish, my heart jolted into a sprint. It wasn't the same beat that pumped through my veins when I was with Frank. This was a broken rhythm. A poor imitation. A rough demo.

"Hi." I halted, unsure of what was appropriate, a hug or a handshake or maybe a kiss on the cheek. My stomach turned over when Jax closed the distance between us.

"Hi." He gave me a megawatt smile and opened his perfect muscular arms. They begged to be admired and they probably were, just not by me. "You look beautiful."

What the hell am I doing? "Thank you." A nervous laugh escaped from between my lips. I remained still.

He leaned forward and our chests collided in an awkward embrace. His smell, aftershave and expensive cologne, crawled up my nostrils. His body was hard and warm and his T-shirt felt nice to the touch. There were so many insignificant things that my brain registered and evaluated while we stood glued to each other next to his car that it almost felt too clinical. As if I was comparing him to Frank.

Actually, I *was* comparing him to Frank. Weight, height, skin tone, eye color. They were nothing alike, which was exactly what my battered heart needed. A change. A distraction. A different man.

We drove with the top down, Nirvana blaring from the speakers, a cool evening breeze dancing across our skin. Pushing back my nervousness, I did my best to enjoy the ride and the company.

By the time we arrived at the restaurant, a small Brazilian place in the heart of Hollywood, both my mind and my hair had turned into a hot mess. Thick accents and the mouth-watering scent of exotic barbeque welcomed us as we made our way to the door.

"I'm sorry I forgot to ask you, but do you eat meat?" Jax checked as we joined the end of the line. "They do have vegan options."

"I'm fine. Thank you." I inched forward as the group in front of us moved. His palm rested carefully on the small of my back, a gesture too intimate and unexpected.

Inside was dim, loud, and busy. Almost chaotic. The kitchen staff spoke Portuguese and the patrons looked drunk and happy. A hostess escorted us to a small table in the center of the dining room.

My eyes darted left and right as we settled.

Jax sensed my unease. "We can go somewhere else if you're not comfortable here." His inked hand slid across the table to meet mine, but I didn't have the heart to reciprocate.

"No, this is fine." I shook my head and swallowed down my apprehension. The fear of crowds that I'd developed after the release party fiasco was all Frank's fault. Fear of dating was his fault too. Fear of being alone. Fear of failing. Fear of not meeting expectations. *Fear of never being enough for anyone.*

We started off with appetizers and drinks. The buzz hit me almost instantly. My tortured mind didn't fight it. On the contrary, I embraced the dangerous daze, and for the first time since my break-up with Frank, it didn't feel like the sky was falling. Deep down, I knew this calm was just an illusion. A fake. A cloud of magic dust that was going to evaporate the moment the alcohol's hold on my consciousness weakened, but I was enjoying the ride while it lasted and I understood why Frank was so drawn to the numbness liquor provided.

Intoxication made all the bad go away, made all the pain, confusion, and the feeling of hopelessness disappear.

The realization terrified me.

"Have you been here before?" I asked Jax, trying to keep our conversation going. My tongue felt thick and heavy inside my mouth. I was on my second drink. On the way here, we'd resorted to discussing music and now, it felt like the right time to talk about other things. Or just talk. Because time seemed like it had stopped. Every second turned into a minute and every minute turned into an hour.

"A couple of times." Jax nodded.

The food looked and smelled delicious, but my stomach continued to riot. I didn't know what exactly it was, but the barbeque tasted like paper, the air was too hot, and rivers of sweat streamed down the nape of my neck.

"How did you find it?" I shot him another question, tossing the pieces of meat around on my plate with my fork.

"A friend recommended it."

"I'm so sorry to bother you," an unfamiliar voice spoke off to the side. I felt it, the presence of a foreign body. Someone invading my personal space. A stalker? Paparazzi? One of Frank's fans? Heart in my throat, I tilted my head up to see who it was. A thirtysomething bearded man hunched over our table. Acid bubbled up the back of my throat when he gave me a grin, then followed up with a curt nod. I waited, but nothing came.

His gaze swept over to Jax.

"I know I'm probably way out of line here, man"—he tossed his large, heavily inked hands in the air—"but me and my wife are huge fans. We loved you on *Mad Ink*. Just came out here for a weekend from Minnesota."

Relief instantly replaced my agitation. Always expecting people to approach me in public by default, I'd forgotten about Jax's TV show appearance.

Smiling, he dropped his utensils on the table and held out a hand for a shake. "Thank you, brother. I appreciate it."

A large woman with dark curly hair and thick makeup, most likely the beard's wife, was barreling her way through the cluster of tables.

"Any word on the second season?" The man asked.

"No second season."

"Bummer."

"I know, but it is what it is, brother." Jax fished out his business card from the front pocket of his jacket and handed it to the beard. "Hey, if you want to get some ink, come see me."

"I'd love to, but we're leaving tomorrow."

"Whenever you're in town again."

The wife finally made it to our table. More handshaking and fangirling took place. I watched them through a curtain of hazy blur. My head, my mouth, my limbs were like cotton.

"I'm so sorry again, but do you mind taking a photo with us?" The beard whipped out his cell phone. "Please."

Jax stood. "Sure. Absolutely."

A cell phone was thrust at me. I took it and scrambled to my feet.

The Minnesotans sandwiched my date and grimaced for the camera. People inside the restaurant stared at us as I clicked the button. Moments later the couple was gone. Their squeals still rang in my ears when we settled back down.

"I'm sorry about that," Jax said with an apologetic smile on his lips.

"It's okay. I..." I paused mid-sentence, unsure whether he needed to hear about my regular run-ins with the paparazzi and creepy fans of my ex.

The silence that swelled at the table felt heavy. Like my head.

Jax cleared his throat. "Just so you know, I'm not a stalker or anything, but I heard about you and Frankie Blade."

My pulse jumped. "Oh." I bit my bottom lip and continued to stare.

"It's none of my business," Jax said, then went on, "You don't have to tell me anything or explain anything. I'm just really glad you texted."

"It's over," I said quietly.

He tilted his head in question.

"Between me and him," I explained. I had no idea why I was telling that to my tattoo artist. Except that I needed to vocalize it to someone other than my mirror reflection, to manifest my break-up as something real. Frank and I weren't anything anymore. We parted ways over a month ago. Because I was suffocating him with my good-ness, because he couldn't keep his promises, because he was like everyone else—a rich ass who didn't see how lucky he was, a selfish child who was wasting the second chance he'd been given.

"I like you, Cassy," Jax said quietly. "I really do. You're funny. You're smart. You know what you want."

"Except when I need a new tat." I stifled a giggle.

"Well, for that, you have me." He smirked.

"True. Sometimes I get tired of making all the major decisions."

"I know you're probably not in a good place right now, but I really want this to work."

My throat was tight with sudden panic. I wanted it to work too. I'd never had a boyfriend before Frank. Men came and went. Kind of like tampons. Or seasons. Now that I'd gotten a taste of a real rela-tionship, I wanted someone to cuddle with, someone as uncomplicated as Jax. Someone with a job, someone who liked rock music, and someone who wouldn't scream, drunk-drool, and embarrass me in front of hundreds of people.

Was that too much to ask?

"Why don't we pretend we just met," I said, reaching for my glass to finish my drink.

"We can do that," Jax agreed. "Whatever pace you want this to move at."

"You're very..." I stopped to look for the right word, but my brain was a spinning inferno. "...nice."

His features remained calm, but his eyes changed. There was a shift in the air. I felt it with every numb cell in my body. I didn't know what it was. Apprehension. Malevolence. My drunk mind couldn't process his signals correctly.

We talked some more and ordered dessert. Our conversation revolved around Jax's work on the TV show and my larger than life documentary project that was failing miserably. We left late. I was inelegantly drunk and my mouth refused to stay shut. The streets were filled with people. Nightlife was at its peak. We drove along the busy stretch of Sunset Boulevard, top down and radio up.

"Thank you for tonight," I said when the car came to a stop at a red light.

"Thank you for coming." Jax turned his head to look at me. His face was a pleasant blur. I felt his palm slide over mine. He laced our fingers together ever so carefully. My body drew tight with aware-ness, but there were no sparks and electricity like with Frank, and I wondered if the *fuck like a rock star* expression implied that regular people didn't click with each other the way rich, famous, and shame-lessly hot did. Although I had to admit, Jax was insanely handsome. He'd caught my attention the moment I met him, but then again, we'd met before Frank came along.

A commercial replaced a Five Finger Death Punch song on the radio.

"Have you ever been to a car show?" Jax asked, his voice meshing with the hum of the traffic.

"A long time ago."

"Would you like to go with me sometime next month?"

"It depends on when. If it's after the screening, I'd love to," I yelled over the noise that swirled in the intersection.

The first beats of the next song poured at us from the speakers. It took me a few moments to recognize the melody. My spine stiffened when Dante's guitar pierced the air. I wanted to pull my hand out of Jax's grip, but my body was so numb from all the drinks I'd had earlier at the restaurant that I just sat there like a statue, holding my breath, until the light turned green and the car moved.

The song was from the new album. Hearing Dante and Frank together felt strange. They didn't even speak anymore, yet millions of people were probably eating, kissing, or making love to their music right now. It was a moody ballad. A little dark and dramatic, but with a touch of tender light. The notes filtered through me, healing and hurting. Eventually, the music and memories became too much.

"Do you like Slipknot?" I asked Jax after I lowered the volume. My voice and my hands shook.

We were on the freeway. The wind swept my hair against my cheeks and stung my bare shoulders.

"As a matter of fact, I do." He nodded and flashed me a grin.

I docked my phone and opened my heavy metal playlist. A wall of angry sounds hit us a moment later.

"You're my kind of girl, Cassy." Jax laughed.

I smiled and let the song carry me into dark bliss. The ragged rhythm of my shattered heart matched the drums, and the hum of my pulse followed the bass thrum. When all else failed, music always came to my rescue. Music was my one true love, my driving force, my best friend, my pillow to cry on, my punching bag. Unlike people, music was always there when I needed it most.

My recognition returned by the time the convertible rolled

through my neighborhood. The dog walkers and the runners were hidden in their condos, and the street was empty and quiet.

Jax pulled up to the curb. I noted him putting the gear in Neutral, which could only mean one thing, he didn't plan on letting me leave too soon. A disturbing knot twisted my stomach. I disconnected my phone and the music stopped. The silence between us thickened with each passing second.

"I had a great time," Jax said, shifting toward me. His eyes roamed my face.

"Me too." It was a partial lie. This date had given me whiplash. I'd gone from the lowest low of self-doubt to the highest high of drunk overconfidence at least a dozen times since he'd picked me up from this very spot four hours ago.

Then it happened. He leaned forward and his face neared mine. I knew what was coming, but my body failed to respond to the pleas of my brain. I couldn't explain the reason behind my stupor. Was it alcohol? Was it jealousy?

There were no fireworks when our lips collided. He had a nice mouth. Soft, warm, and positively unmemorable. It was like any other man that had kissed me before Frank.

"I'm sorry," I squealed, pulling back. My heart banged against my ribs so hard, I could barely breathe. "I can't do this, Jax. I really do enjoy your company, but I don't like you the way you like me." My voice leaked torment.

He stared at me with lost eyes, resolve and disappointment crossing his face. His breath, hot and minty from the gum, fanned against my cheeks.

I snapped out of my half-drunken stupor and hurried to unfasten my seatbelt. "I'm sorry I led you on." My trembling whisper filled the cold stillness surrounding us. "You're a very nice guy. I just don't think I'm ready."

All the blood in my veins rushed to my head. My entire face, including the tips of my ears, burned with embarrassment.

Jax slid back into his seat and rested both hands on the steering wheel. "I guess it's true what they say." His throat bobbed as he spoke. "Nice guys finish last."

I wasn't sure he wanted to hear encouraging words from me.

"I'm sorry." I pushed the door open and climbed out of the car. "Thank you for dinner." Our gazes locked one last time.

"Good night, Cassy," he said with a sad smile.

"Good night."

I stumbled through the empty courtyard, fighting the sudden tears. Ashton was still awake, watching TV, and for a second, I envied the simplicity of his life. His biggest problem was getting into a community college. He hadn't had his soul crushed by the idol from his adolescent dreams. He didn't have a huge nonprofit project that was failing to meet all possible deadlines. He didn't have people trolling his social media or strangers emailing him even stranger photos.

"Was the date that bad?" he bellowed from the couch as I trudged past him into my room.

"Don't talk to me for a week, will ya?" I slammed the door shut and tossed my purse on the chair. My head was full of cotton. My lips, still numb from the failed kiss, quivered. Flames of anger danced inside my stomach.

Kicking off my booties, I scrambled for my phone and hid in the bathroom. The ache swirling deep in my chest pushed and pulled, threatening to crack my ribs open. My pulse roared. Back against the cold tiled wall, I dialed Frank's number and waited.

Your call has been forwarded to an automated voice message system recording...

The line beeped.

"You know what, Frank?" I began, my voice slurring and stuttering. "I hate you. I hate you for all the broken promises. I really thought you were different. I thought you understood what I was and what this project meant for me and for all the people involved when you agreed to be part of it, but you're just like everyone else. Just another ignorant and selfish asshole who hides behind his money, who'd rather crawl back into his hole and watch the world and people in it go down in flames." My throat was tight with worry. Tears swelled in my eyes. "I hate you because you won't let me move on. You let me down and I'm all alone sorting through your shit. I wish I'd never met you. I wish I'd never known you, because I can't fucking unlove you. I can't fucking get you out of my head and it's driving me nuts. It's suffocating me. But I suppose you know a thing or two about that since my goodness is too much for you. Since you'd rather wallow in self-pity and let the alcohol numb the pain. I wish you'd seen it through. I wish you'd understood you'd been given a second chance for a reason. I wish you'd let go of the past and let music take you on a new journey. I wish you'd accepted your failures and moved on."

Tears spilled down my cheeks. My sobs muffled my speech. "I wish you'd let me be there for you instead of pushing me away. I wish you'd kept your promises. I wish you'd loved me back at least a little bit. At least for a second... I gave you my heart. I gave up everything I had for you—my career, my sleep, my sanity, my reputation, my privacy. And you know what you gave me? Memories that hurt and bruises to my soul. I don't know how to stop thinking of you, how to stop worrying about you, and how to stop loving you. And I hate you for that. For making me love you so much." My lungs were out of air. I pulled the phone away from my ear and stared at the blurred screen. There were more words, but they felt like an afterthought. Everything that I wanted and needed to say had been said.

So I hung up.

I woke up late with a mean hangover and it took me a good minute to will my eyes to open. Ashton had gone to school and the apartment felt abnormally silent. I slid from the bed and wandered around in search of my phone. Vague memories of the overly emotional voicemail I left for Frank after the unsuccessful date with my tattoo artist swarmed in my head.

Melodramatic seemed like a good word to describe yesterday's verbal diarrhea. One more reason to stay away from drinks. They made me absolutely irrational.

My phone was still in the bathroom. It sat on the counter, battery low, screen full of notifications. Deep down, I knew I wasn't going to find any messages from Frank. We were past the point of no return. It'd been over a month since he'd disappeared. Yet I still looked. I skimmed through all my texts and all my inboxes. I even listened to all my voicemails. Most were from reporters wanting to talk about Frank. A couple wanted to speak about Dante. His exit from the band was still the hottest topic in music. And then there was one from a person I didn't expect.

Hi, Cassy. This is Margerie Helm. I'm writing to see if you're still looking for a venue. I understand you might be hesitant to reach out to me since my initial reaction to certain events that were publicized online was very strong and I decided not to move forward with our arrangement; however, I've had a conversation with a friend of yours who wishes to stay anonymous at this time and some things that were brought to my attention during our chat made me reconsider my decision. So I'd like to meet Isabella. I'll be at the theater all day tomorrow and Thursday. Give me a call back when you can.

Chapter Twelve

I adored April. Mornings were fresh. Evenings were crisp. It was the perfect month and we had the perfect venue, the beautiful Melrose Cinema that sat on the corner of Doheny and San Vicente, at the far end of the infamous half-mile-long stretch known as the Sunset Strip.

Matters of my ruptured heart had to be put on hold.

Margerie Helm had never revealed the name of the person who'd reached out to her, but all signs pointed to Frank.

Almost three months later, he was still off the grid. Silent and invisible like a drop in the ocean while his million-dollar empire was being torn apart, trashed, and tarnished.

The worst comeback of all time. That was how the newly postponed Hall Affinity World Tour was dubbed by the press. The label's attempt to replace Dante after his sudden exit was met with a huge backlash from disgruntled fans. Nobody wanted to see Marshall Burns and a random guitarist doing karaoke.

Without the Toxic Twins 2.0, Hall Affinity was just another nostalgia band. A piece of history. A bundle of memories. Memories I had to let go of to make more room for the new ones. Without Frank.

Maybe it was my psychotic voicemail that had kicked his conscience into gear or maybe it was his desire to simply correct some of his mistakes before moving on to a new chapter of his life. All that mattered in the end was that we had everything we needed to make a big splash in the industry with *Dreamcatchers*. Even without Frank's name on the banners, we were everywhere. On every website and in every inbox. An unstoppable force.

Sleep wasn't my friend the night before the screening. My head spun in dozens of different directions, like a broken carousel at a deserted amusement park. My brain obsessed over every little detail. After endless hours of tossing, turning, and staring at the ceiling, I gave up. The first rays of light had already sneaked into my room through the opening between the curtains. Trying to chase a sliver of sleep while the rest of the city was waking up seemed pointless.

In the living room, Ashton was snoring up a storm as I tiptoed to the kitchen to make coffee. Nothing bothered my brother, not even the close proximity of technology. He slept with his laptop near and his phone clutched in his hand. It was equally disturbing and endearing.

I spent the first half of the morning consuming caffeine while responding to urgent emails and working on *Dreamcatcher's* social media posts. My personal accounts were still set to private, but the number of weird messages and follow requests from people I didn't know had been declining steadily.

My short-lived affair with Frank was becoming a thing of the past. *Finally!*

At nine thirty, I marched back into the living room to wake up Ashton.

"Rise and shine, brother!" The teddy bear in the corner was grinning as always. "Big day today. Gotta go save the world."

"Already?" I heard a groan and saw his chips and guacamole socks hanging off the end of the couch, which made me question us being related again. I didn't understand how a person this long could have come out of someone as small as my mother.

"Yep. We're leaving in an hour. I'm taking a shower first."

"You always take a shower first."

"When your hair is longer than mine, we'll discuss it," I said, heading for the bathroom.

"Screw you, sis!"

Yep, little asshole was definitely my brother.

On the way to West Hollywood, we blasted Killswitch Engage and sipped home-brewed coffee from Metallica travel mugs, courtesy of my partner in crime, Levi Bernstein.

"How about we check out some cars next weekend?" I offered as my Honda merged with the morning traffic on Franklin.

"Sure." My brother's answer seemed very unenthusiastic, considering the fact he'd been constantly giving me grief about having to take the bus to school. Not as much lately, but it had seemed like almost every five minutes right after I returned the BMW. With *Dreamcatchers* monopolizing pretty much all my time, I couldn't find any to shop for a new car for Ashton, but it was next on my agenda.

I lowered the volume. "Are you still mad at me? I thought we were over this."

"My heart is in pain."

"It's just a car, Ashton. I said we'll get you another one and we will."

"It's not just a fucking car. It's a goddamn Z4." He tossed his hands in the air. "Do you know how many people drive a Z4 in my school?"

"How many?"

"None, dude! None! Cuz I was the only one until you robbed me of it. My pride and joy." He followed up with a pout.

I shook my head and turned up the music. "What would I do without you, Ashton?"

"You wouldn't have anyone to yell at, and your couch would smell nicer." He turned to me and grinned, all teeth on display.

"Uhh, about the couch. You'll have to buy me a new one when you move out, buddy."

"You took my car, and now you want me to buy you a couch. What am I? A winning lottery ticket?"

"No, you're a responsible adult. Well, you will be because I'm going to make one out of you."

A middle finger flashed in front of my face.

"I take it back." I laughed at him. "I think you're going to stay a man-child forever."

"I like being a man-child. I'm gonna find myself a sugar mama."

"Jesus, where do you get these ideas?"

"From my sister."

"Asshole." I shot him a sideways glance.

"Runs in the family."

I bit back my smile and concentrated on the road. Having someone around, even if that someone was a total dud like my brother, was nice. His antics made me think of Frank a little less.

A small group of people were hanging out on the sidewalk when we reached the theater forty minutes later. Hall Affinity tees and limited edition *Dreamcatchers* merch lingered in the crowd while security guards lined the barricaded front entrance. The sun was perched high in the sky and the promotional poster above the marquee was bathed in its bright morning light.

Ashton snapped cell photos as I drove around the building and parked in the back near the trucks. Levi was already inside, talking to the sound engineer. He wore his favorite Doc Martens, and a poorly ironed dress shirt peeked from under his black hoodie. The dark shadows beneath his eyes told me he'd slept just as much as I had in the past twenty-four hours. Theater employees and event staff hurried to get their tasks done. People were everywhere—upstairs on the private deck, downstairs on the main floor, inside the auditorium. Their agitated voices mixed with the rattle of the rolling equipment cases and the buzz of the background music.

In the lobby, Carlos was taking photos of sponsor stands and humming along to the new Green Day tune.

"What are you doing here so early?" I questioned.

He dropped his camera from his face and flashed me a smile. "Documenting."

I glanced at my phone. "We still have six more hours to go until the doors open."

"You're here." He shrugged. "Levi's here. Ash-man's here."

"Is that what my brother wants to be called now?" I rolled my eyes.

"Everyone needs a cool name." Carlos shook his head and continued to snap photos.

I pulled up the planner app on my phone and verified all the tables. My heart raced. *It was happening!* After months of driving myself and everyone around me, including my mother, crazy, our hard work was finally paying off. Today felt like a dream. I just wasn't sure whether it was a dream come true or a nightmare.

Were people going to like the film? Were critics going to slam us?

Tucking my phone into the front pocket of my fitted dress slacks, I crossed the lobby and walked outside. Carlos followed.

We made our way over to the sidewalk and stood for a silent moment staring at the massive film poster above the marquee, a black and white image of Isabella in her chair shot from behind against a shimmering, smoky background. An old dynamic microphone was erect on the opposite side of the frame. It'd taken Carlos almost five hours to get the angle and the lighting right. Haunting and exquisite, the photo made a statement. Hanging high above the affluent and trendy area of Sunset Boulevard, it challenged the entire industry. It challenged the minds and the eyes of people in luxurious cars taking this road every day.

"My best fucking work," Carlos said quietly, knocking my shoulder.

"It is," I agreed. "A picture is worth a thousand words, right?"

"This one is, Cassy." He spun around and stepped back into the barricaded area. His camera flashed.

I raised my hand to block my face, but it was too late.

"Come on, you can't take photos of me without permission," I teased.

"Don't worry. You look awesome." He winked and hurried inside.

All the caffeine I'd consumed earlier made me jittery and I imagined others could probably tell by the tremor in my hands and the shake in my voice, but my brain was as sharp as ever.

Gazing back up at the poster, I soaked in the invisible power of the artistic rebellion it represented. The memories of our last week's rehearsal flashed through my mind. At nineteen, Isabella had everything thousands of other artists spent years perfecting—stage presence, amazing voice, dark charisma. She was destined for greatness and I wasn't going to let anyone take that greatness away from her.

Emotions tightened my throat. Certain stories had that effect on me. Stories about people who dared to keep going. Even when the odds weren't in their favor. Isabella's was the one that had to be heard. Raw, honest, real. A journey that deserved every ounce of attention it was getting and more.

Lately, I'd been wondering if Frank and Isabella had come into my life at the same time for a reason, if these two choices were given to me to help me decide which road to take and how to spend the rest of my life. With a man who'd given up or surrounded by people who didn't accept failure as an option. It was a tie between love or an opportunity to make a difference, and the inability to have both hurt too much. In the end, I knew I'd made the right call. I'd chosen wisely. I'd stapled the holes in my broken heart and had picked a person who needed me more, a person I strived to become.

The wall of approaching whispers snapped me out of my daze. In my peripheral, I noted a group of teens. Eyes starstruck, phones flung in the air, they looked harmless, but my gut told me to run. So I did. I charged for the door and hid away from the wannabe paparazzi in the lobby.

Isabella and her team arrived later in the afternoon. She had two back-to-back interviews at two and three fifteen, a soundcheck at four thirty, then makeup and hair. The doors were scheduled to open at six, the screening itself was set for seven. After that, a thirty-minute live set and a Q&A session with the producers and artists would take place. I was part of the panel and the idea of other people, specifically the press, asking questions unsettled me.

By five, the crowd outside the theater had grown to apocalyptic proportions. The Jay Brodie PR team was going for a kill with this campaign, but I never would've imagined that this many would actually show up.

I watched bits and pieces of the soundcheck from the lobby while trying to verify last-minute additions to the guest list with Linda.

"You need to take a break," she whispered, her palm covering the screen of my iPad. "Did you have lunch?"

"Yes." I reached for the clipboard she was holding. *An iced coffee and a handful of almonds isn't going to cut it, girlfriend,* my stomach bellowed. When she gripped it tight, I asked, "Can I see that again?"

Linda didn't budge. "I know this film is your baby and you want to make sure tonight is perfect, but you need to relax." She jerked the clipboard away. "Please go upstairs and take a break. We have a long night ahead of us. My girls will handle the red carpet attendees and all the press check-ins. It's not your job. You're the producer. Your job is done. Now you get to sit back and watch."

Producer. The word hung in the air between us, exotic and glamorous.

"If someone had told me eight months ago that I was going to give birth to a nonprofit documentary, I would've laughed in that person's face."

"Oh, dear." A cunning smile touched Linda's lips. "Life tends to throw us all sorts of opportunities. I danced ballet for six years until one day, a new door opened. I took a leap of faith and never looked back. There's nothing else I'd rather do than what I'm doing right now." She motioned at the people behind the glass doors.

Linda's confession shocked me. She was wearing a knee-length pencil skirt and a suit jacket, not exactly artsy attire.

"Ballet? Really?" I tried to imagine L.A.'s biggest PR shark in a tutu, doing pliés and pirouettes. The image was downright disturbing. "You never told me."

"I prefer to keep that part of my life to myself." She laughed.

The music stopped. Sparse claps rang out from the auditorium. The soundcheck was over, and anxious voices along with some of the newly arrived VIPs moved to the lobby.

Then my heart stuttered and began a slow descent to the floor. Across the way, I spotted Janet's silver hair among the cluster of bodies. Craning my neck in the direction of the group to make sure my sight wasn't playing tricks on me, I reached for the clipboard Linda was holding. "Let me see that?"

"Cassy, I told you that you should take a little break," she protested.

I skimmed through the names of the guests, unsure of whom I was actually searching for. "How come you didn't tell me Frank's parents were going to be here?"

"It was a last minute thing." Linda gave me a tight-lipped smile.

I turned around and noted Billy's bright colored ruffle shirt. He looked like a watered-down version of Alice Cooper. The only thing missing was the cane and a top hat. The man was obviously a great showmanship role model.

Isabella was in the center of the gathering. A few phone cameras flashed, then everyone started to slowly disperse. I saw her then— the woman from the photo that someone who wished to remain anonymous had emailed me a few weeks ago. She stood next to Janet. Baggy pants and short hair. It couldn't have been a coincidence.

A blend of panic and disappointment rammed up my throat. I swallowed past the tightness and took a deep breath. As if on cue, Janet separated from the crowd and ushered the woman over to me.

I was a ball of nerves when they approached us.

"Such a wonderful theater," Janet started in a sweet, breathy voice, her gaze bouncing between me, Linda, and the coffered ceiling.

"Thank you. I didn't know you were coming."

She dodged my statement. "I don't think you've met Alisha."

"No." I willed myself to smile at the woman. Up close she looked much older than in the photo. Although the quality of the image wasn't the best. I couldn't even tell where it'd been taken. The two were sitting somewhere. On a bench? A couch maybe? "I don't believe so."

A hand was extended to me. "Very nice to meet you. I've heard a lot of great things about you," the woman spoke, her tone soft.

"Really? You have?" Taken aback, I slid my palm against hers and shook it. My mother raised me to be a polite person, even during questionable moments. Like the one right now.

The madness unfolding both outside and inside the theater was unfathomable. The noise, the cameras, the staff running around, the fans pushing against the barricade. I couldn't wrap my head around the chaos or around the fact that a woman who'd apparently been spending time with my ex-boyfriend was here. The question of *why* danced on the tip of my tongue, but I didn't get a chance to ask it because the screams were suddenly amplified by thousands.

A storm of flashes illuminated the red carpet and the press plunged toward the limo that rolled up to the front.

Heart in my throat, I stepped closer to the doors and stared at the warzone the sidewalk had just become. My fingers felt clammy. My pulse rushed. I'd forgotten about Janet and Alisha.

While our VIP guest list consisted of a few very influential people in the music industry, those weren't the names that caused people to lose their minds. Outsiders didn't know or care for Gary Torino.

Roman's bald head lingering behind the string of security came into my line of sight first. Then Frank emerged from the crowd moments later. He was all light. His presence stole the attention of the entire block. Dressed in black pants, a fitted shirt that highlighted the fine contours of his body, and a plain leather jacket, he looked sophisticated. There was no excessive jewelry or boots with metal studs. Almost as if he wanted to strip himself of all the attributes of his past persona.

I stood in my spot by the door and stared at him through the thick tinted glass with my restless heart pounding so hard, its furious beats didn't allow the oxygen to reach my lungs. The air around me grew tight. I could feel its weight on my shoulders and against my chest. Frank stopped in front of the barricade and went through the throng of hands that were thrust at him, shaking them one by one. Linda followed him like a hawk, occasionally whispering something in his ear as if they were conspiring to do something outrageous. I was so distracted that I hadn't even noticed her leaving my side.

He didn't walk the red carpet nor did he pause for a photo op. Roman led him past the reporters and straight into the theater. The noise sneaked inside at the quick swing of the door. Screams, thuds, and clicks drowned out the wild thunder within my chest for a brief moment.

I had to remind myself to breathe when Frank entered the lobby. Anxiety swirled in my stomach. Then his sharp gaze wandered over to me.

Avoidance and fear clutched my gut. I wasn't prepared to face him like this after three months of silence, with rabid fans right outside and event staff breathing down my neck. My mind tripped and blanked with panic.

Our eyes met. His were disarming, sober, and full of determination. Chin hitched, I accepted the challenge. Crowds were his specialty, but he was also a great teacher.

He started his approach and the closer he got, the blurrier everything else became. I was in a bubble. His bubble, where the sound of our surroundings didn't exist and the space between our bodies was filled with tenacious heat and wanton memories.

"Cassy," his voice said as he neared. "Hi." Then came a smile.

Gentle, intimate, sexy. The kind that made my ovaries melt and my brain short circuit.

Here it was again. The full Frankie Blade effect. The electricity, the fireworks, the zippity-zap that tumbled down my spine. My knees shook and my high-heeled shoes felt like two bricks encasing my feet. The entire world fell away, leaving me one-on-one with the man I thought I'd managed to forget.

The rapid thrum of my pulse told me I was wrong.

Totally useless inside my mouth, my tongue finally moved. "Hello, Frank."

A slew of voices drifted at me from across the room. Isabella's was the loudest. Then suddenly, we were encompassed by a group of raging teenagers. Andy wore a Texas-sized grin. Ashton's goofy smile peeked out from behind Kit's dark mop of hair. Slightly intimidated by Frank's presence and the madhouse on the opposite side of the glass, Story stood back. Their conspiring gazes didn't escape me.

This felt a lot like treason. Hands were shaken. Embraces were exchanged. Janet was hovering.

"What's going on?" I cast a threatening glance at everyone. My heart bounced against my ribcage like a tennis ball.

"I'm sorry. I planned on telling you earlier, but things got crazy." Isabella looked at me innocently through her lashes, then gave me a subtle shrug. "He wasn't supposed to arrive until after six." She half-laughed, half-grimaced at Frank.

Something passed between them. Understanding? Familiarity? I didn't quite catch it, but it was there. In the air. Invisible yet tangible.

"I didn't want to be late." He winked at her and returned his attention to me. "Traffic."

His features remained lax, but his eyes gave away the turbulence of his thoughts.

"Traffic, huh?" I shot him a dubious look and pulled out my phone. "How come he's not on my list?" My question wasn't addressed at anyone in particular. First, I didn't understand why Frank was here. Second, I didn't understand why no one had informed me about his arrival. Third, I didn't understand why others knew and I didn't.

But then we were interrupted.

"The doors are about to open!" Linda hurried us away from the entrance. "Let's get you somewhere quiet." She patted Frank's shoulder and smiled at me.

I needed answers, but there was no time for explanations. The lobby came alive as Roman steered us into the hallway, away from the general admission ticket holders. Frank and I marched shoulder to shoulder, our bodies almost touching. I felt his heat. I caught his scent. I heard his breath. It was the strangest thing, to be able to separate him from everyone and everything else in this ruckus.

We meshed with another group of people. More handshaking, more smiling, more *I'll catch you later*s. Everyone wanted a piece of Frankie Blade. No one cared he'd wreaked drunk havoc at Dante's party three months ago. He was wanted, adored, and forgiven. Just not by me. I still hurt from all the ugly words he'd said at that party.

I heard Maria and noted Ashton steering Isabella into one of the dressing rooms. A roll of thunder came from the lobby. Soft at first, the footfalls grew stronger and louder, overtaking the crackling walkie-talkies and the background music.

In a blink, Frank was swept away by security and I was escorted to one of the lounges, where Levi was entertaining some of the sponsors and potential donors.

Over-caffeinated and confused, I breezed through the crowd on autopilot, willing myself to concentrate on the present and not the past, but all my mind could think about was Frank. The thought of seeing him again churned my stomach.

Gut up, girlfriend, my inner voice said. *You're the shit. You're the shit! Screw this rich asshole trying to ruin your night.*

Shaking off my unease, I smiled as the people in front of me shook hands. Contrary to Frank's belief, the world didn't revolve around him and I wasn't going to let him steal all the limelight.

"Don't you own an iron?" I mouthed at Levi as we crossed paths while bouncing between the guests.

"I was in a hurry." He gritted his teeth and moved on to the next person.

A beat later, we met at the bar. "There's probably a steamer some-where upstairs," I said, shaking my head. "You can't do Q&A looking like the guy who lives under the bridge on Ninth and 110."

He lifted his left foot to show off his prized Doc Martens. "Make it Beverly and 101." Amusement came into his eyes.

"Okay, so you want to be a hipster bum." I snorted out a quiet laugh. Never a dull moment with my partner in crime.

Levi waggled his thick brows and nodded. "Uh-huh."

"Says a Jewish dude from Santa Monica."

"That's how I roll, baby." He spread his arms and clicked his tongue.

"Let's go fix this horror show." I pointed at his chest. "I know you're going for a Kurt Cobain feel, but my OCD can't take this."

All the staff had migrated downstairs and no one except for two guards were on the deck when we went up. My phone squawked as I entered the office.

"I can't find parking!" my mother shouted on the line.

"Where are you?"

"I'm next to a big blue truck."

"At the rear of the building?"

"Yes."

"Okay, hang on." I killed the call and dialed Ashton's number. "Mom just got here. Can you please go out and meet her? Grab a parking pass from Linda."

"Okay," he said in a singsong voice.

"And hurry!"

I slid the phone back into my pocket and absently stared at the items sitting on the shelf in the corner. There, among pencils, note-books, and old tapes lay a small portable steamer.

I spun around and shot my question at Levi. "Did you know Frank was coming?"

He'd already taken off his hoodie and was working his way down the buttons on the front placket of his wrinkled shirt. "Yes. I knew."

"Why didn't you tell me?" I plugged the steamer into the nearest outlet and flipped the switch.

"I'm not at liberty to say." He shrugged.

"Are you serious?" Fury filled my chest. "We work our asses off for eight months and he comes and steals all the thunder?"

The fact that Frank had ambushed me outweighed the fact that he was possibly behind Margerie's sudden change of heart. I was upset, to say the least.

Without a word, Levi pulled off his shirt. We stared at each other intensely, but he didn't grant me an explanation.

"Fine," I grumbled under my breath and motioned at his shirt. "Hold it up."

"It was supposed to be a surprise." Frank's voice came from the doorway.

My heart dropped to my stomach. I tore my gaze from the steamer and glanced at him over Levi's naked shoulder.

The deep quiet that fell over the three of us pushed against my chest. My hands continued to work on Levi's shirt, but my brain stalled. I didn't know what to say or where to begin exactly.

"Do you mind?" Frank took a tentative step forward, entering the office and swallowing up all the air inside.

When Levi shifted, I ordered, "Don't move!" Then I returned my attention to the shirt. He froze at my command like a kid who'd done something wrong. "Let me finish it." I needed a human shield. Another body to protect me from Frank while I gathered all my defenses together.

The thick clouds of steam dancing in front of my face obscured the lines of his silhouette. Hands in his pockets, he stood in the center of the room and patiently waited for me to finish tidying up Levi's shirt. Minutes passed. None of us spoke. Long, awkward silence stretched, testing everyone's limits.

The fabric was as straight as a framed piece of paper. Another second, and it was going to combust.

"I think it's good, Cass," Levi finally said. "Thanks."

Mute, he moved to the side to put on his clothes. I shut off the steamer and set it on the desk. My gaze avoided Frank's. Talking to him was inevitable, but my denial waged a war with my common sense. They fought ruthlessly inside my head as I watched Levi exit the office. In a rush, he left the door slightly ajar and the distant hum of the crowd downstairs reminded me that I couldn't be gone long. This wasn't the time or the place to discuss our romantic relationship.

"I'm sorry I didn't tell you," Frank spoke, voice deep and steady.

"Why are you here?" Summoning all my courage, I looked into his eyes. They were just the way I remembered them—bright, gunmetal blue, and hauntingly beautiful. My pulse spiked. My tongue stuck to the top of my mouth.

Again, he didn't give me any warning. Closing the distance between us with two wide strides, he palmed my cheeks and said, "Baby, listen to me." His thumbs brushed my temples. "I need to tell you this before you see the final cut, okay?"

Panic raced through my blood. I'd seen the final cut. Two weeks ago at Levi's place. All ninety minutes. Everything we'd recorded and collected over the past eight months.

"I can't do this right now," I squealed, my face hot from his touch. My fingers curled around his wrists with every intent to free myself from his grip, but I didn't. Instead, I let his warmth fill me from head to toe.

"I know you're mad at me," Frank continued. "I know I don't deserve your forgiveness, but I needed to go away for a bit. I needed to clear my mind and figure out what to do with the rest of my life."

"I'm glad you took the time to work on your issues."

"I'm sorry I didn't call back. I didn't want to make more promises I wasn't sure I could keep."

"Good." I nodded and pulled his palms down, away from my face.

"I missed you like crazy."

"Well, hate to disappoint you, but I was too busy sorting through the pile of shit you left us with to miss you."

"I know it probably doesn't mean much, but I am sorry."

"Why are you here, Frank? To capitalize on our work? You had the opportunity to be part of this project... Do you expect me to welcome you with open arms?"

"No. I want another chance. I've been sober for over two months."

"So you checked yourself out of rehab? Come on! You know better than that."

"It's not like that, doll. I'm only here for the event and my sponsor is here with me. Alisha. You just met her. We're flying back to Arizona tomorrow." He paused to take a breath.

I felt stupid for being jealous, but my wounded pride didn't want to give up yet. "How do I know you won't slip again?"

"You don't. And I don't either because I can only take it one day at a time, but I can promise that I'll do my best. I'll work as hard as I can."

"We've been through this before, Frank. You've said that same thing to me but failed to keep your word."

"It's different this time, doll. Please just give me a chance."

His chest heaved. So did mine. Then something between us shifted.

Memories began to flood my brain. He was so easy to forgive, and it terrified me. My emotional dependency on him terrified me. "Do you have any idea how difficult it was for me to leave you?" Inhaling sharply, I refused to let the tears spill. "It was the hardest choice I've had to make in my entire life, but I'm content with it. I'm happy with where I am and who I am. Even if it's without you."

He stared at me intently. "I know, and I'm sorry I put you in a position where you had to choose. I'm sorry I humiliated you. I'm sorry I said those words instead of the ones you deserved, and I'll work hard for the rest of my days to make it up to you." Fortitude settled into his features. "I love you and I want you back in my life."

I felt it then. A warm balm wrapping around my heart and healing its countless cuts and gashes that I'd endured while being with this man.

"Frank..." My lower lip trembled as I tried to think of a reason to say no and put an end to it, but nothing seemed good enough. "There are hundreds of people waiting for me downstairs."

"I know, and that's why we're not going to talk about the things we need to discuss until later, but I need you to know at least this much before you watch the film. I need you to know that I love you more than anything."

Our faces were so close, I could almost taste him on my lips, taste his fear and taste his hope. My head spun and my knees shook. My entire body was under some kind of magical spell. There was a certain level of alarming awareness that pricked my skin when he spoke about the film and I feared the worst, but we didn't have enough time to get into details.

A light knock dragged me out of my stupor. Then a throat cleared and a head popped in from behind the cracked door. "I'm sorry to interrupt," one of The Jay Brodie PR girls said, her eyes ogling Frank. "But Linda needs you two for a photo."

"Okay. Tell her we'll be right there," I replied with a smile. My face was burning and my heart was whamming against my ribcage, restless.

Once she was gone. Frank whispered, "Please. Just give me a chance, doll."

I lay my palm on his chest and stared at the outline of his shoulder. He'd been down and broken so long that seeing him without a sling and with color in his face was strange. "Let's talk about it later, okay?"

Downstairs was crazy. Frank and I were separated the instant we entered the lounge after a quick photo op and didn't get to see each other again until the showing. My mother showered me with a dozen questions about him, but I had no answers. Confusing thoughts that ran through my head only made me hate myself more for wanting to forgive the man. He slid into the seat next to mine moments after Levi had finished his speech. The lights dimmed and a wave of antici- patory whispers rolled through the auditorium. The last three rows, reserved for the VIPs, were sectioned off and crammed full. Security guarded both sides in case someone tried to sneak up for an auto- graph during the showing. We sat at the very back, surrounded by darkness. Up front, the screen flickered and came alive.

I could see my mother's French bun on the first row. Beside her, Janet and Billy seemed to be rekindling their younger years with his arm thrown over her shoulder. Looking around, I noted Brooklyn. Levi's parents. Some of his college friends. The excitement was palpable. I sensed it with every cell in my body, the electrical charge in the air, the lilt in everyone's voices as they exchanged murmurs.

I couldn't describe the feeling that engulfed me when I saw our names on the screen.

Bernstein/Evans

Sweat coated my palms. *Dreamcatchers* wasn't just an attempt to bring attention to all the unfairness. This film was a labor of love, sleepless nights, and too much Red Bull and coffee. It was our child.

The credits on the screen flashed. Soft, soulful music filled the auditorium. This was an all original soundtrack, written by Isabella, Kit, Story, and Andy. We'd also used some of the songs from the bands who'd come forward and donated their time and material to the cause. What I didn't expect was Frank's name.

I knew this wasn't the cut I'd seen at Levi's place when a short clip of his first rehearsal visit popped up on the screen. After he was a no-show for the recording of "Afterburn," Levi and I agreed on deleting all the footage of him from the film. The final cut I'd watched didn't have any.

It wasn't quite clear to me why the theatrical version had the material that had been trashed.

Mouth agape, I drank in the images running in front of my eyes.

Next to me, Frank didn't move or make an attempt to hold my hand. The film was rolling and Isabella's face appeared on the screen first. Her laughter, bright, loud, and bubbly, poured across the dark rows. It was a pulse-jarring sound of happiness that melted my heart. The interview parts alternated between backstage and concert footage, and Levi had done a great job piecing all the material we'd collected together.

My heartbeat began to accelerate when Frank's features entered the frame. He sat in a chair with a lav microphone clipped to his shirt. I could tell this was shot recently by the length of his hair and the sharp, well-defined lines of his cheekbones.

And then he spoke and it was the most honest thing I'd heard from him since we'd met.

I have to confess, my relationship with this project is very complicated. I'm not sure how to describe it. Love/hate maybe. I'm the hated one.

I think the main reason I'm here is because the people who put this film together showed me things I could no longer see myself after being tied to one of the biggest enterprises in the business, and I wanted to share the real story behind who Frankie Blade is and give back.

When you do something for a long time, it becomes part of you, it takes you over and it tricks you into believing that's all you can ever be. This was exactly how I felt after my accident. I couldn't fathom the idea of doing something else. I had the band, I had the name, I had the collection of hits, and I wanted to get back out there and do it again. The same thing I'd been doing for over a decade before the accident tore my body apart. So I spent seven years putting myself back together, just to discover that I couldn't do it anymore.

Meeting Isabella was eye-opening. She managed to do what I failed—without the backing of a major label, without the backing of a huge fan base, without an impressive bank account—write music and perform.

I didn't really see it until after I slipped into a bad depression. It took me a while to come to terms with myself, with my physical condition, with all the changes in my body. I fought it relentlessly at first, and alcohol seemed like the best way to silence all the dark thoughts that constantly filled my head. That pointless fight against time, aging, and health issues cost me friendships and also cost me the woman I love. One can only take so much while living with an alcoholic.

There was always a certain level of awareness, somewhere deep down, but I ignored all the signs for the longest time. When Isabella and I decided to record "Afterburn" together, I let my insecurities take over. I think being fired from my own band drove me to the point where I couldn't function at all.

I have permanent loss of strength in my right shoulder and arm, injuries that were self-inflicted while I was under the influence of alcohol, and blood pressure issues due to my head trauma. All of these health problems prevent me from going back out and doing a two-hour set three times a week, but what I do have is my voice. And that's the only thing that truly matters.

I think we all secretly want to see a fit, model-perfect person on stage, because that's the industry standard, but I believe it's time we rethink this standard. It's time we let music be our guide. It's time we close our eyes and hear a voice. Let that voice make you feel, let it evoke the strongest emotions, let it mend your wounds, and let it love you for who you are. Love your body, love your thoughts, love your skin color, love your accent, love the people around you. Just love.

Because that's what music does. It erases borders, it erases differences. It unites people.

Now that I see all this, I feel reborn. I'm ready to write new music and I'm ready to move forward.

Sure, there are regrets. Tons. If I could go back and do it all over again, I would be smarter about my choices. And I think I may not be giving enough credit to the amazing woman who pushed me in the *right direction and introduced me to Isabella. She doesn't know I'm recording this right now, but I just wanted to say this... Cassy, thank you for showing me that the world isn't shit and that it's full of passionate people. Thank you for everything that you've done and endured for me. I'm sorry we're now forever slated into the archives of history in the form of an internet meme.*

He laughed then and the sound of it was magical. A balm to my aching heart. A whisper of reassurance.

There was so much footage of him and Isabella together I'd never seen. Rehearsing, performing, talking, recording. Endless minutes of musical bliss.

My shock was deep and I didn't dare move. I kept watching until the film passed the midpoint, sifting through my mind, looking for signs, trying to understand how he'd managed to pull it off without me knowing. And how had Levi managed to pull it off? Had my brother been part of this too?

It happened during another clip when Frank's face filled the screen as he spoke. I could see every tiny line and every shadow. Little stamps of time on his skin, barely visible but there. Just another reminder that he belonged to another generation and that somehow we still managed to mesh. Somehow we still managed to make it work.

Heart pounding, I turned my head to face him. His eyes were transfixed on the footage. The flickering images danced across his cheeks, illuminating his skin. That's when I saw it, the wet trail of his tears.

He was laid completely bare, unveiled, and free.

I reached over and grabbed his hand. Our gazes met. Then there was a click, and something light, soft, and new passed between us.

It was the strangest thing, seeing the man I'd had a crush on as a teen for who he really was years later. Seeing all his strengths, his flaws, and his potential behind the blanket of darkness. Feeling him in every breath and every beat of my heart.

My senses were shattered when the film came to an end. I was lost and disoriented and my heart was too full.

The front rows buzzed. There was handshaking, hugging, and even some tears. My mother gave us a shy wave. A few eager fans lingered in my peripheral. Their eyes settled on our seats, wide, bright, and curious.

We waited until the guests began to leave.

"I think I should probably talk to some of these people." Frank braved a smile and rose to his feet. Soft yellow overhead light illuminated his features. Our hands were linked, fingers threaded together, gazes connected. The moment was charged with the gravity of what we were. Whole.

I stood and followed him along the line of empty chairs.

The second we reached the general admission section, we were separated again.

Surrounded by a group of fans, Frank made his way through the auditorium to join Isabella. There was half an hour to go until the performance and everyone poured back into the lobby for another photo op, snacks, and drinks.

Linda met up with me and took me to the VIP lounge, where Levi was accepting congratulations. My memories of his father weren't particularly pleasant. Old-school, business-minded Adam Bernstein never missed a chance to remind his only son that real estate was a far better career choice than a rock 'n' roll magazine. But right now, the man's face sparkled like a ten-carat diamond. I could swear this was the first time I'd seen Adam smile since I met him seven years ago when Levi took me over to his parents' garage, which served as the original *Rewired* office.

Caught up in the chaos, we circled the lounge until there were no more hands to shake. I stared at the door, waiting for Frank. My feelings were bigger than everyone and everything. They swelled in my chest and filled me with an anxious tremor. I needed a minute alone with him. To ask questions and to share how I felt about what I'd just seen. I needed to get all these things out of me before he got on that stage. To make room for more.

"So what's it like, partner?" Levi chuckled. "Being a producer?" He hooked his arm through mine and maneuvered me to a quiet corner, away from the crowd. Although I didn't think we were going to stay unnoticed long.

"Your dad looks chipper," I said, surveying the crowd.

"He thinks I'm about to make millions, ha!"

"Maybe he's not wrong. Did you check the stats?"

"I've been glancing at them, but we'll have to take a better look tomorrow."

He squeezed his eyes shut and took a deep breath. "I fucking love how it turned out, Cass."

I gave him a light punch on the shoulder. "I'm still a little mad. Why the hell didn't you tell me Frank was going to be part of it?"

"He asked me not to."

"When did you record all this?"

"Why do you think I'm going to sleep for a week starting tomorrow?"

My mind raced. I needed to hear everything. I needed details.

"Look." Levi grabbed my arm and shook me out of my daze. "It doesn't matter now, okay? It's done. He didn't want you to know, because you wouldn't have agreed to this after what happened with 'Afterburn.' Just enjoy. The biggest rock star on the planet has professed his love for you in front of millions of people. And I'm not kidding when I say millions. This film is going to be seen by millions. It's the kind of film that *needs* to be seen by millions. It's the best fucking thing we've created together in all the seven years we've been doing this."

Emotions clogged my throat. I swallowed past the developing lump and nodded. In my peripheral vision, I caught Frank's silhouette across the room. People clung to him as he started his approach. His presence was the epicenter of everything, the epicenter that moved in my direction like a comet, burning all its obstructions.

Enthralled, I stood in my spot and tried to breathe through my panic. We were being seen together in public for the first time since the meltdown and it was both real yet unreal. The closeness of our bodies made me nervous when Frank moved to stand by my side.

"Impressive work." He gave Levi a pat on the back.

"I had a great cast."

They exchanged glances and shared a covert smile.

The chatter inside the lounge intensified. I recognized Isabella's voice as Ashton steered her toward our group, the crowd around them thickening and clamping on to us. It was in the air, the invisible power she had.

Frank's hand lay on the small of my back, his other one was in his pocket.

I heard a jingle.

"Ash?" He turned to my brother and held out his palm.

A gasp of surprise left my lungs. "No, you didn't?" My gaze darted from Ashton to Frank and back. Apparently, this conspiracy was bigger than I had initially thought.

"He totally did," Levi croaked. "Your own brother sold you out for a car."

A low rumble of laughter erupted. Face smug, Ashton grabbed the keys and shoved them in his pocket.

"Was there anyone who didn't know about this?" I cried out.

"Not really." Frank shook his head. Others joined in.

"Did you bribe everyone with a car?"

"It was technically already my car!" Ashton countered. "You kidnapped it."

More laughter.

The lounge was too hot. Clusters of people grew together into one huge human mass. It was almost impossible to breathe or speak and I felt like the world had started to close in on me. Frank's hand on my back slid to my side, his fingers wrapping around my waist with a tight grip. A touch of distress. It hit me then. This was an open bar. He was surrounded by hundreds of drinks and waiters floating around with trays.

"Excuse us for a second?" I snaked my arm through his and maneuvered him toward the emergency exit.

Other than a couple of event staffers and a security guard, the back hallway was empty and quiet. Just what we needed. The massive door separated us from the rattle inside the lounge. As always, Frank bypassed the warnings. He spun me to the wall and dipped his head for a kiss. His lips neared my cheek and brushed the corner of my mouth.

I placed my palms on his chest in an attempt to keep him at bay, but the truth was, my heart and my head didn't agree. "You can't just show up here and kiss all the mental distress you've put me through goodbye," I said firmly.

"That's not what I'm trying to do."

"So...Alisha is your sponsor?"

He nodded, circling his hands around my neck and skimming his fingers through my hair. "Are you jealous?" A frown creased his forehead.

"A few weeks ago, someone sent me photos of you and her."

I noted a smirk of amusement in his eyes.

"It's not fucking funny." I shook my head and blinked back the tears that had been slowly building in me ever since I saw Frank's name on the screen.

"You should know it by now." His face neared mine. "You're the only woman in my life."

My emotions were raging. Drowning in his words completely, I continued to stare and waited for more. Suddenly, all my doubts were replaced by guilt and a treacherous tear fell down my cheek.

"What's wrong?" His thumb brushed the wet trail on my skin.

"So there's no other woman?" My voice shook. I believed him the first time, but for some reason, I needed to hear him say it.

"No, there's no other woman, silly." He pulled me closer. "Why are you crying?" Our bodies aligned and clicked like two magnets.

"I thought there was someone else... I went on a date with another man and I kissed him."

"As long as you didn't like it," he mumbled against my hair.

"That's the thing. I wanted to like it, Frank. So I could forget you."

He was silent. My confession didn't render any reaction or questions. Having his arms wrapped around me felt nice and familiar.

"You're not mad? Not even a little bit?" I asked, swallowing down my tears.

"Why would I be mad?" He cradled the back of my neck and pressed his lips to the top of my head.

"That I kissed someone else?"

"I don't think I have a right to be mad at you. At least, not for the things you were doing while I was gone. I pushed you away. I'm here now to correct all my fuckups. You'll give me a chance, right?"

"You know what?" I slipped my hands underneath his jacket and hugged his body. My chin pressed to his chest. "Yes. I think you deserve it. I'm proud of you for fixing the mess you created. It means a lot to me. The support you've given Isabella and the effort you've put into making it right. I love how the film turned out and I love this theater. Thank you for talking to Margerie."

Frank's palm cradling my head froze. "Cassy." A shuddered breath escaped his mouth. "When I reached out to Levi, the venue had already been secured."

Pulling my face from his chest, I gazed up at him. "You didn't ask her to reconsider?"

"No." He shook his head. "It wasn't me."

Shocked, I stared at him unblinkingly. This fact absolutely didn't diminish the importance of his heartbreaking confessions about his journey that nearly six hundred people had just witnessed on screen, but my mind scrambled. "Then who was it?"

"I don't know, doll."

The door swung open and Brooklyn's head popped in. "Jesus, you two! This is not a high school reunion." Rolling her eyes, she hurried over. One of the guards trailed behind. "You need to get ready, Frank. They're about to start."

Flushed, we were straightening our clothes when the distant noise of agitated voices and footsteps came from the other end of the hallway.

My head snapped toward the commotion. I noted Roman's bald head and a loud cluster of people near the employee entrance.

I saw him then, behind the line of security. He looked different. Pale. No flashy clothes. No hat. No women attached to each arm.

Frank didn't move. He stared down the empty stretch of space between him and Dante and I couldn't read his eyes.

Brooklyn was first to react. "What the hell is he doing here?" She walked down the hall, heels clacking against the cement floor.

The air thickened. Something was happening. I didn't know what exactly, but the tension was there, deep, ugly, and undeniable. Atoms were shifting. Voices were clashing.

"You need to leave, Dante," Brooklyn's shriek drifted from afar. She stopped in her tracks, hands on hips. "If he doesn't pick up his goddamn phone, that means he doesn't want to talk to you. I *will* file a restraining order if you keep doing this."

"Stay out of it, huh?" He skirted around her and began his approach. Roman positioned his body at the midpoint between Dante and Frank. He stood tall and menacing. A wall separating the two men.

"Frank," I whispered. "Maybe you should talk to him."

"We don't have anything to talk about."

"You don't need to give him your forgiveness." My mouth neared his ear. "He's not well. Just hear him out."

"It's his own damn fault."

I took a step back and pressed against the coolness of the wall. My voice was a soft, tremulous murmur. "Don't be a hypocrite, Frank. You wanted me to give you another chance after you publicly humiliated me, but you won't give him two minutes of your time? All he wants is to be heard."

I had no idea why I was siding with Dante. Our phone conversation had gotten under my skin. We were all part of a broken circle, quietly hating each other for the things we'd done to ourselves and the people surrounding us, and it had become tiresome, harboring grudges and animosity.

"Please," I mouthed.

Frank's eyes blazed with pain. The tic of his jaw told me he was struggling.

"I'm not here to rain on your parade, Frankie-boy, but I didn't have a choice," Dante shouted, his words soft around the edges. "Because you won't fucking return my calls." He paused. "I'm not asking for your friendship back. I just want to talk. Face to face."

"There's nothing to talk about." Frank turned to look at him. Roman shifted to the side, but the urgency of his movements told me he was combat-ready.

"There's a whole lot and you know it. Twenty years."

"You threw twenty years away when you decided to find a replacement for me."

"You know what?" Dante chuckled. "You haven't changed a bit. I thought time off may have done you some good, but you're still a stupid stubborn fuck who thinks he's invincible. You don't get it, do you?" A crooked, unfamiliar smile twisted his lips. "You don't get to drive yourself into a fucking freeway divider and leave everyone to sort the shit you created for seven years and then come back and do the same thing you did in your twenties when you had all your bones. It doesn't fucking work like that, Frank. You don't get to start where you left off just to kill yourself for it."

Frank whipped around and walked down the hallway. A few feet of space separated them.

"There's no time for this," Brooklyn tried to intervene. "You need to get ready for the performance."

"Well, you don't get to fuck my ex-wife, me, and my band and then pretend it never happened."

A collective gasp filled the hallway.

"Let's not make another scene," I pleaded, rushing over to Frank. "Not today."

Dante's gaze swept over to me. "You look very nice, Cassy."

"You look good too." I nodded, eyeing his features and searching for something to validate my statement. The slight slant of his left eye told me he wasn't well. The health issues triggered by his overdose weren't publicized, but one look at him was enough to see he was a mess.

The door to the lounge flung open, letting the noise of the party spill into the hallway. "We're about to get started!" a voice shouted. "Izzy's looking for you, Frank."

"Okay, I guess if that's how you want this to end," Dante mumbled. A small smile tipped up the corners of his lips. "I'm sorry I fucked Heidi. I'm sorry I was a shitty friend. I hope you enjoy the rest of your night. Say hi to Margerie for me." His words were a confused string of whispers, rolling and tripping.

Frank didn't move, but I felt the wild thrum of his pulse when I grabbed his wrist.

My mind was a warren of questions and ideas. I couldn't imagine Dante doing anything remotely nice, except maybe talking about nice. Something as big as persuading the woman who didn't want to work with us because of everything he represented took guts.

"We really need to get going," Brooklyn whispered.

"So it was you who talked to Margerie?" I returned my gaze to Dante.

"She's a tough one, by the way." He offered a smiled that faded before I could register the full extent of the damage that the overdose had done to his body. "I was seriously considering asking the owners of the Chinese Theater instead, hoping they'd be easier to convince."

"And you think this gives you a free pass now?" Frank asked, but the bitterness in his voice was gone. Sadness was what I heard. "You think one noble act is going to erase twenty years of wrongs?"

"No, I don't." Dante shook his head. His eyes shone under the bright stream of the overhead light. "I think I'm a shitty person and I'm sorry for everything I've done. I'm not going to explain why I did it or what motivated me, because it's fucking obvious. I don't know and I don't fucking remember doing half of this shit." He stopped to catch a breath. There were tears in his eyes. "It doesn't hurt as much when you're high, Frankie-boy, but I'm sure you know that. You felt it, didn't you? When it sweeps you under and when it lies to you and tells you everything is going to be okay, but when you wake up sober, you're fucking devastated. So you go looking for it again. You go looking for that feel-good that gets you through the day, that keeps you conscious and all your demons at bay."

He paused again. His labored breaths roared inside my head.

"Dante, why don't we talk after the panel?" I offered.

He continued to stare at Frank, tears rolling down his cheeks full force now.

"You have what you always wanted, Frankie-boy. Freedom. Don't let your ego take it away from you."

"Preaching doesn't suit you," Frank said quietly.

"It doesn't suit you either. Let's be honest. We both fucked up. We both did things we're not proud of. I'm not looking for some kind of redemption. I'm just facing the consequences of the shitty choices I made. I never wanted you out of the band. I love you like a brother, but we both knew when you decided to come back it wasn't going to work out. The only difference was that I saw it and you refused to accept it. Yes, I stood by and watched the label kick you out, but it wasn't your battle to fight. Not anymore. This, right here"—Dante threw his hands in the air, motioning at the cement walls—"is your battle. This is where you belong. I just wanted you to understand that everything I did was for your own good, even if I did it backwards. That's all I wanted to tell you. That I love you and I'm sorry. That

I'm proud of you and that I want to part ways peacefully. I don't want to leave any bad blood behind."

Frank remained mute. My hand still held on to his, but all the signals were mixed. The silence swelled. Even Brooklyn stayed quiet. Behind the door, in the lounge, people screamed and music played.

I felt the uncertainty and the ache. It swirled around us like a cloud of dust above a dirt road that had just been touched by a set of tires.

Tense seconds ticked by as Dante wiped his left cheek with the back of his palm. "It's good that you're getting yourself sorted out. The bottle is a bitch. Once she has her claws in you, she's never going to let go." The words were slowly dying on his lips. "I know it. I've been trying to shake her off for almost two decades. Now I can't even play a chord I wrote. A lost fucking cause."

His helplessness crept through the air between the three of us.

I didn't have the right to speak. This was their fight. Instead, I squeezed Frank's hand. A reminder that today, he'd been given the benefit of the doubt and now it was his turn to give.

He cleared his throat and stared at Dante. "You want to try? It's an acoustic set."

"I thought you'd flaked out on us again!" Isabella shouted as guards ushered us into the dressing room. "We're ten minutes behind." She stared at Dante with frazzled eyes.

"¿Cómo estas, mija?" Dante jerked his chin and gave everyone in the room a once-over.

Andy and Kit looked mildly shocked. Story kept blinking.

"Thank God!" Maria cried out.

"You up for doing a Hall Affinity cover, Izzy?" Frank wrestled off his jacket.

"I thought we weren't doing any covers?" Her gaze flicked over to Dante. "Didn't you just quit the band, dude?"

"I did." He nodded.

"So is this like a mini-reunion?" Andy perked up.

"I guess you could say that." Frank grinned.

"We don't have time for this, guys!" Brooklyn flung her hands in the air and pointed at him. "You need to follow me." She turned to Dante. "I don't know what to do with you, so talk to Cassy."

My brain went into high gear. I pulled out my phone and shot out a quick group text to Ashton and Levi. *Livestream.* This was an unexpected turn of events. Six hours ago, I had no idea Frank would be here tonight to perform with Isabella. Now Dante was here too and the three of them were going to improvise.

I took a spot at the side of the stage, trying to stay out of the way and let the crew get everyone ready. Levi seemed to enjoy the spotlight. He stretched his neck and rehearsed his speech. Frank stood next to the small opening between the curtains and peeked at the audience. The entire theater, quiet and at a standstill, was waiting.

I heard a swarm of whispers when the lights finally dimmed. Isabella spun her chair to face me and I gave her a thumbs-up.

She patted her knees and grinned. "Heard that break-a-leg saying?"

I bit back my smile.

"They better make me into a fucking meme after we hit Billboard's top hundred."

Levi squeezed his way onto the stage and marched over to the microphone. Noise rolled through the crowd.

"You're good for him," Dante's voice said near my ear.

I turned my head to look at him. Up close, he appeared worn out. "Are you okay?" I asked, studying the faint traces of damage that lined his face.

"I'm good."

"Are you getting help?"

He nodded.

"You'll tell me if you need anything, right?" I didn't know why I said that, but I needed to make sure I let it out into the universe. In a sick way, I was worried about him.

"You can't keep trying to save everyone, darlin'," he said with a smile. "Just save the ones who matter." His gaze jumped over to Frank.

Thunderous applause wiped out the questions that swelled in my head. Isabella and the band took the stage next. When she reached the microphone, the auditorium went still. It was the strangest kind of silence. The calm that usually came before the storm, and the name of that storm was Frankie Blade. At least to those who'd gathered here tonight for an evening of music. To me, he was Frank Wallace. The man I loved.

The rumble of clapping hands and whistles swallowed me and my thoughts entirely when he finally walked out on stage. Story ran through a chord, and I recognized one of the original songs.

"I think you've probably noticed we had a little change of plans tonight," Frank said, adjusting the microphone.

The audience laughed.

"We wanted to surprise everyone," he continued. "Guess what? I've got a friend of mine hiding backstage right now. He plays a guitar, so we thought..."

I couldn't make out the rest of the words. The noise inside the auditorium was hell on earth as Dante strode across the stage, waving at the crowd and smiling. A guitar was placed over his neck. Watching the three of them together was something out of this world. In a way, they were all beaten and broken by whatever life had thrown at them, but the music they made was just the opposite— healing and powerful, and I could feel each note, each pitch, and each harmony in my bones as the melody saturated the cool air with its rebellious bliss.

Stunned, I held my breath for what seemed like an eternity. It was only hours later when we were finally ready to leave that I could finally let the cool air settle into my lungs.

Frank and I were standing outside, near the idling truck that the crew was loading with gear, when he asked, "Do you want to go for a ride?"

"Sure."

I didn't know where the limo was taking us, nor did I care. The streets we passed were peaceful and void of nightlife, just what I needed after endless minutes of shaking hands, smiling, and occasional mini-panic attacks in the restroom.

Remnants of adrenaline still rushed through my blood, but the high of the accomplishment had dissipated. I was crashing. And I was crashing hard. My emotions were like apples, pears, and celery sticks tossed into a blender. A juice cocktail the taste of which one wasn't able to tell anymore. Too many ingredients.

Frank stayed quiet. A light touch of exhaustion clouded his eyes. I could almost see it taking shape in the slack of his jaw, the flutter of his lashes, and the slow rise and fall of his chest beneath his layers of clothes. Tonight wasn't easy for him. He hid his fears well, better than most, but I felt them. I recognized them in his every word and his every move.

Spent and wrapped in the purr of the engine, we sat next to each other. Thigh to thigh. Dangerously close yet not close enough. The invisible line of unuttered questions that separated us grew thinner. Our hands lay on my lap, locked together. The privacy screen was up and no music played.

I broke the silence first, needing to express some of the things that raced through my mind. "You did the right thing." My eyes swept over the elegant shape of his face, admiring. "For Dante."

"Everyone deserves a second chance." Frank chuckled softly. "Or a hundred and second in his case."

"I really do think he means well. He just doesn't know the right way to do it."

"You did notice"—Frank dropped his voice to a whisper as if he was about to say a blasphemous thing—"he fucked up an acoustic solo."

"The crowd didn't care." I pulled out my phone and checked the livestream stats Levi had messaged me a while ago. "We hit over a hundred thousand views."

Frank took a deep, controlled breath and stared at the empty space in front of him. "He won't be able to keep this a secret unless he doesn't plan on picking up a guitar at all."

"You're worried about him." Biting back a smile, I spun to see him better and studied his expression.

"In all of the twenty years I've known Dante, he's never actually apologized for anything. Not even for..." His words faltered and remained unsaid. He shifted and rolled his shoulder. "Actually, I don't think it matters anymore." His gaze returned to me. "I think maybe he did me a solid by fucking my ex-wife."

"Is that so?" An inaudible laugh escaped my lungs.

"Yes." Frank's hand reached for my cheek to cup it. "I met you, doll."

Blood surged to my cheeks. But I wasn't blushing. I was burning. The entire world felt like it'd been lit on fire. "You were amazing today. It takes courage to do what you did for Isabella and for Dante."

"You never cease to amaze me, Cassy Evans." A tired smile lifted the corners of his mouth. "You want to know what I like about you the most?"

"Enlighten me." I slipped my hand in his hair and raked my fingers through its thickness.

"Your goodness," he whispered, his lips near my ear. "Wanting to make this shitty world we live in a better place without asking for anything in return."

My heart pounded. "Not quite accurate." I brought my face to meet his. Our soft breaths mingled between our mouths and the gap separating us was suddenly filled with invisible energy. Supercharged. "I do want something in return."

His brow arched in silent question.

"You," I said. "And some sleep."

"You have me, doll. I'm here." He paused. A twinkle lit his eyes. "I can't guarantee any sleep just yet."

"What can you guarantee, Frank?" I brushed my lips against his.

"I can guarantee an orgasm," he teased back.

"You think the promise of an orgasm is going to get you in my good graces?"

"I hope so."

He was smiling. My eyes were closed and I didn't see it, but I felt it in the slight lilt of his voice. His hands slipped down the curves of my body, slowly and carefully. A deft touch. A prelude. I shifted and pressed my body to his.

"You're still on probation, Frank Wallace," I murmured.

"As long as I have to report to you."

We drove in silence for a while longer, until the limo began a slow climb through a dark Hollywood Hills neighborhood.

"Where are we going?" I asked, staring out at the sparsely spaced houses we passed on the way up.

"Just wanted to show you something."

"Didn't you take me here once before?"

"Yes, I did." He nodded.

A few minutes later, the limo came to a stop in front of a vaguely familiar property sitting near the cliff overlooking the city.

"This was our second dinner date spot," I gasped, stepping outside. The house had been finished and gated.

"Yes." Frank slid from the car, grabbed my hand, and drew me toward the property. "It's where I kissed you for the first time."

"Are you sure it's okay we're here? I don't want to be arrested for trespassing."

"It's totally fine." Laughing, he punched in a code and the gate lock clicked open. "The place is mine."

Shocked, I tripped over my own feet, but Frank grabbed me before I fell.

"I bought the property a few months ago."

"What for?"

He shrugged. "Sentimental value. This was the site of our first kiss."

"You're crazy."

"Come on." He pushed the gate open and led me inside.

We walked down the stone path to the opposite side of the house. The bench was still there and the city still shone bright.

"What are we really doing here, Frank?" I looked up at him, my heart thundering.

"I want to start over, Cassy," he said, moving closer. His voice was sweet and low with a lick of fear. Was he afraid of rejection? "Clean slate?"

"I don't know if clean slate is possible. You're aware we're a GIF?"

"So I've heard."

"You hurt me."

"And I'm sorry."

"Multiple times."

"I did."

"You broke your promises. Multiple times too."

"Guilty." He pulled me into his arms. "But I've had some time to reflect on things, and I know where I'm going now and I want you to go with me."

Everything about him at that moment, the impressive breadth of his chest, the silky touch of his hair, the faint scent of his cologne, felt right. Felt wonderful.

My heart squeezed. I pulled back and gazed up at him through a curtain of tears. "We can give it a shot, but I'm not moving in with you tomorrow."

"No, not tomorrow." He smiled. "Maybe next week?"

"You really like to rush into things, don't you?" I bit my lip and trailed the line of his jaw with my index finger.

"I can't help it. I don't want you going around and kissing random guys." A playful glint in his eyes told me he didn't plan on holding a grudge against me for my unsuccessful attempt to move on.

I grinned and ran my palms down his chest, needing to touch him, needing to feel his heartbeat, needing to know he was okay. "Hi. I'm Cassy. I interview rock stars and produce documentaries. What's your superpower?"

"Hi, Cassy. I'm Frank. I write music and set off metal detectors in airports."

There were no words, no warnings, and no explanations. There was only me and him and the raw cadence of our lips. The velocity of our gasps. The gentle flicks of our tongues. A covert, slightly indecent kiss with no hands and no hugs. Just our mouths and our pulses connected, driven by a maddening rhythm.

"Now you have enough for an anthology, doll," he whispered as we pulled apart to catch our breath.

Epilogue

Dreamcatchers (film)

Dreamcatchers is a 2019 American documentary film directed and produced by Levi Bernstein and co-produced by Cassandra Evans. The film follows the story of a nineteen-year-old singer from Northern California, Isabella Solana, whose debut record contract was terminated by the label after a car **accident** that resulted in a spinal cord injury left her **paralyzed** from the waist down.

Dreamcatchers offers an unfiltered look at the state of the modern music business and features a number of notable guest speakers, including ex-front man of the two-time Grammy winner band Hall Affinity, Frankie Blade.

Background

The idea of doing a documentary came to Bernstein after seeing Solana perform with her band in a nightclub in Hollywood. Both Bernstein and Evans, who co-own Los Angeles-based music magazine *Rewired*, were impressed with Solana's voice and approached her mother/manager about a possible collaboration.

The film was produced on a limited budget through a number of donations. Bernstein, who graduated from UCLA with a Bachelor of Arts in Film and Television, shot and edited the film himself and with the help of several college friends and Evans' younger brother. More than 300 hours of raw footage featuring rehearsals, studio recordings, interviews, and live performances was captured. Originally designed as an attempt to attract the attention of other labels and potential sponsors to help Solana finance and record her debut album, the film changed its direction upon the involvement of Frankie Blade. Blade's initial interest in the project was originally credited to his assistant, who came across Solana's cover of a Hall Affinity song via Twitter, but later, the singer himself confirmed that it was Evans' idea. Sources close to the rock singer confirmed that he and Evans had been in a secret relationship long before Blade decided to collaborate with Solana and it was her idea.

In January 2020, Blade's publicist issued an announcement that Blade and Solana were recording a duet and industry veteran Gary Torino was producing and mixing the single. Burdened by legal issues, health problems, and the depression that his recent stage incident and firing from the band had caused, Blade unexpectedly exited the project.

Solana recorded "Afterburn" without Blade and all footage of Blade was scrapped from the film. Several weeks later, Blade appeared intoxicated at his band's latest album release party. His outburst, filmed by a number of attendees and press present at the event, was leaked online and was harshly criticized by fans and other artists.

The following day, Blade's PR representative issued a statement with an apology. Blade checked himself into a rehabilitation center and several weeks later reached out to Bernstein and Solana to record new footage.

Release

Dreamcatchers was screened on April 25, 2020 at Melrose Cinema in Los Angeles. It had a limited theatrical run and is scheduled to be released digitally and on DVD in October 2020.

Reception

The film received favorable reviews from critics and audiences. Adam McGraw from *The Washington Post* commended Bernstein and Evans for their creativity and their attempt to tackle a difficult subject most would shy away from.

Libby Thornton from *BlackBook* called *Dreamcatcher* "an honest and probably one of the most important documentaries about the music business that has been made in the past twenty years."

Charles Corbin, who writes for *Film Nation*, described *Dreamcatchers* as a "fascinating work of art that gives an outsider a frank yet not always pretty look at what's going on behind closed doors." He particularly praised Blade for his courage to come forward and closely examine substance and alcohol abuse among touring artists and the reasons behind it.

Isabella Solana released her debut album *South, Wait for Me* on August 3, 2020. It charted at number 27 on the Billboard 200 and sold over 20,000 copies in its first week of release. Solana is Spotify's most streamed artist of 2020.

In September 2020, a source close to Solana confirmed that she and Frankie Blade are working on a new project.

THE END...OR NOT QUITE.

If you want to get a little glance into Cassy and Frank's future from Frank's point of view, you can snag a bonus scene here:
https://BookHip.com/QWBZCP

Thank you so so much for reading. If you have a spare minute, please consider leaving an honest review. It would mean a lot to me.

XOXO

About the Author

N. N. Britt is a Los Angeles-based music journalist and photographer whose photos have graced CD covers, promotional posters, t-shirts, and billboards. When she is not writing or drinking coffee, she is probably reading or attending a heavy metal show.

www.nnbrittauthor.com

Also by N. N. Britt

RAPTURE

She is a grieving mother. He is a spoiled rock idol. The only thing they have in common is a flashy tabloid headline. Or so they think.

Running away from her tragedies and the demise of her marriage, Hazel Alexander retreats to a friend's Lake Tahoe cabin with big plans to drown her memories in bottles of wine. Being dragged into someone else's messy, high-profile divorce is not what she needs.

Especially if that someone else is Justice Cross, the frontman of the popular rock band The Deviant.

Born into a family of rock royalty, Justice lives his life fast and easy. When he comes across Hazel while at a local bar, his gallant attempt to get her home safely takes a complicated turn.

A PR nightmare forcing Justice and Hazel to spend time together triggers unexpected and intense feelings between the two.

With the constant attention of fans, haters, and press, now it's up to Hazel and Justice whether they want to fight for their relationship or end it once and for all.

Made in the USA
Monee, IL
03 March 2021